# The Greensward
# Pitch & Sickle
# Book Four

## THE DIABOLUS CHRONICLES

D K GIRL

# CHAPTER 1

The view from Silas's attic room was especially pleasing for the way it took in the graveyard. From where he lay, he only had to roll his head and he could count the headstones in their neat rows. The village of Castle Combe, in the heart of the Cotswolds, was a balm for the senses. A pity they would have to move on today. Silas yawned and stretched, not keen at all to leave the warmth, no matter how much his legs ached from being curled up due to the shortness of the bed. Early December was bringing with it the sharper edge of winter.

The bandalore was in no mood to allow him a sleep-in this morning. The scythe had woken him with a subtle hum, a gentle melody that made for pleasant, though far too early, waking. The predawn sky was a silvery grey with not a cloud in sight, and a kiss of pink tugged at the lowest points on the horizon. Silas slid out of bed and shivered at once. The glass in the window was thin, the draughts many, and winter was creeping ever closer. There was no fireplace in his tiny room, a fact he'd discovered only after Pitch had claimed for himself the larger room downstairs, with a bed fit for at least three sleepers and long enough to have allowed Silas to stretch out fully without his feet hanging off the edge.

'But you can see your dead from up in the attic, Sickle dear,' Pitch had declared the day before, lashes batting a fetching rhythm. 'I thought you'd much prefer it.'

Late yesterday afternoon Pitch had rushed back to the pub where Silas waited, seated warm and comfortable by the fire, thawing out his toes

1

with a pint of cider in hand. 'I've found us the perfect place to stay tonight.'

Silas had nodded, distracted by how resplendent Pitch was, despite a long day's ride. He'd worn a rich black corset vest embroidered with pink roses, and a coat of sea green that tried very hard to rival his eyes, but of course failed miserably.

The daemon did not pay any attention to the looks other patrons sent his way, the sort of looks he usually tended to enjoy bathing in. 'Come, you must see it. Your room is splendid, and you will adore it.'

He'd grinned like a cat who'd found a bowl of cream, and it had made Silas uneasy.

'I'm not sure if I believe you. Is my room infested with mice perhaps? Or is there a nest of sparrows above the bed?'

'Fool. Come along and see.'

They had ridden out of Harvington Hall several days ago, and the daemon had let Silas do all the organising along the way: the finding of lodgings and meals, stabling of horses, and sourcing of sweet treats. It was bloody irritating, not to mention exhausting. And they had not even come close to the teratism Lalassu was leading them towards.

Silas regretted ever buying Pitch a single treat from Mustow Green-'s bakery. The daemon seemed to have taken the thoughtful, regular gestures during their two-week respite at the hall to mean that from now until forever, Silas would provide for them both.

On arrival at Castle Combe, with night descending and his arse aching, Silas had stopped Lalassu in front of the first public house they encountered along the main street and handed an indignant Pitch the pale horse's reins.

'Do go and sort out the stables, won't you?' Silas had said. 'And then find us some lodgings, if you don't mind.' He'd had to work hard not to laugh out loud at the stupefied look on the daemon's face. Silas had hurried into the pub and closed the door with a firm thud.

When he followed Pitch later on to the supposedly perfect lodgings, Silas had been filled with trepidation, certain there would be retribution for daring to order Pitch about. But the daemon caught him unawares yet again. The rooms were indeed very much to Silas's liking.

'Look,' Pitch had exclaimed, gesturing to what was obvious. 'There is a graveyard, and a dull old church.' The daemon's delight as he led Silas to the cottage was, astonishingly, genuine. 'Is it not exactly the sort of place you adore, Sickle? All the death and despair you could want for. And the priest says that the room in the attic affords a wonderful view of the dead, all lined up in their rows. You shall have that one, of course. I'll be downstairs. Are you pleased?'

Silas had mused a moment before he answered.

Was he pleased that Pitch seemed to be going out of his way the past few days to ensure they did not share sleeping quarters again?

Not really, no. Though he'd never say so, not even if he were strung out on the rack.

There had been no repeat of their encounter in that sordid room at the hall. There had not even been another kiss after they left the graveyard that first day. Silas had simply been a means to an end, it seemed. What he'd thought to be an altering moment, a shift in their closeness, was nothing more than a convenient meal for Pitch.

Silas was grateful, of course, that the daemon was strong again and ready to carry on, but the sense of being used cut Silas sharply and left him alone in a place he did not wish to be. Perhaps that was why, when he'd first seen the size of the bed in the room Pitch had sequestered, Silas had found himself making an untoward suggestion.

'We could save some coin,' he had stuttered, 'couldn't we...if we took just one room?'

It was outrageously bold. He wished he could take back the words the moment they were spoken.

'We have plenty of coin.' Pitch had been quick in his reply. 'And besides, I would keep you up all night.' Silas had to steady himself. 'With my nonsense, of course.' The daemon's sly gaze said he knew very well how teasing his words had been. 'You have complained well enough that I'm a restless sleeper and prone to snoring. I think it best you have a good night's sleep before we run into this next monster of yours.'

Silas sighed now at the new day, rubbing his eyes and clearing his head of embarrassing conversations – and too many pints of ale.

Last night they had dined at the Castle Inn, where Pitch had found his taste for attention once more and had wrapped the patrons about his slender fingers. The daemon was a surprisingly enthralling storyteller. Silas had laughed along with the rest, flushing a little as Pitch's eye often caught his.

Pitch had remained in the pub long into the small hours, long after Silas had called it a night and made his way back to his meagre bed. He'd slept well enough, that was true, though that was mostly due to a heavy meal of potatoes and ham hocks and generous frothy lagers.

Silas threw off the covers, wincing at the freshness of the air. He splashed his face with bracing water from the basin and dressed, throwing on his coat at the last with the bandalore nestled in a pocket. He sent a quick hand through his increasingly wayward hair and headed downstairs, doing his best to avoid the creak of steps that would betray his departure. He intended to walk straight past Pitch's door, without a glance in to see if the daemon had returned...or returned alone. He paused on the landing outside Pitch's room. The door was closed, and no sound came from within.

The bandalore filled the silence with a gentle but urging tune. The scythe wished to lead him somewhere, that much was clear, but it did not seem a place of great concern. Silas's understanding of the notes seemed to grow with each passing day, as though the knowledge was rising up from where it had been long buried.

'Best be on, then,' he whispered to the quiet house.

He pressed his ear against Pitch's door, straining to make out any sound beyond. To his horror, the door edged open.

'Shit,' he whispered, grabbing at the brass handle to halt the door's progress.

Silas should have moved on, but he could not resist peering through the narrow gap. Pitch was in his bed, his discarded clothes strewn all about the floor. The sheet was tangled around his hips, one foot poking out from beneath a heavier blanket that draped his legs. His top half was bare, the tattoo evident and stark against pale skin. Silas stared at the markings a long while. Both Bess and the wraith he'd encountered in Harvington Hall had told him the same thing. Some wounds would never heal...not truly. Bess had assured him that the daemon had been made as comfortable as was possible, but his words were not so reassuring as may have been intended.

Comfort was not cure.

And what if the next encounter with a teratism tore at Pitch the same way the Verderer and the Forest of Dean had?

Silas dug his fingers into the door handle. He wondered what Pitch would think of the small parcel that sat at the bottom of Silas's saddlebag: a vial of inky black liquid and a needle with a silver cradle to rest it in. Bess had given Silas a very cursory lesson in how to administer something he called amuletum, should there be an emergency call for it. It was this substance that had mingled with all the other stains on that dreadful bed in the room where Pitch had lain chained.

'I'm not sure this is my most sensible idea,' Bess had declared, worryingly. 'He is not easy to handle when the pain becomes too much, so I would expect you to keep your distance if that is the case. But perhaps...he'll put up less of a fight with you. Even better, he might have no need of the amuletum at all. Mr Ahari's cane should be of some use. But still...I think you should take it. Just in case. Don't worry, you'll not need to have any great skill with the needle. I've set a rune on it, instructions if you will. So all you need to do is set it up and then let it guide your hand.'

Silas had accepted the parcel of course, but with great consternation. He worried about a great many things, not least of all that he might prove a terrible artist; but mostly that if he needed to use the amuletum, it meant Pitch was once again in that dark and painful place where Silas had found him.

He shook himself, coming back to the here and now, where all was very well. Pitch snored lightly. His head was turned away from the doorway, his summer-straw hair a lush mess of curls splayed out against the dark grey of the mattress. The daemon was sleeping peacefully. And alone. Damn if that didn't cause Silas's breath to hitch a little. Pitch stirred, uttering a low groan and moving as though to roll over. Silas turned the handle and pulled the door shut as delicately as possible.

He hurried down to the front door, where the wood betrayed him with a groan of hinges he cursed at. Silas moved quickly through the grounds, the bandalore in his pocket, the scythe's subtle melody leading him onward. Silas moved with haste but no urgency, for he knew that this particular tune did not foretell of any dreadful danger. He understood the notes better today than he had done yesterday, and much better than he had a week ago. Whatever stirred the bandalore was no teratism. He strode out happily on his own, leaving Pitch to sleep off the rotten hangover that was doubtless in store.

He made his way through the churchyard, the tug of the pleasant little cemetery playing at him. Hands clasped behind his back, taking a deep, chilled breath, he made his way through the hodgepodge rows of plinths and headstones. He'd considered sleeping here last night instead of a bed that was as small as the coffin he had woken in. The churchyard had whispered to him, and the graves were turned silvery white by the moonlight at that hour. He had meandered a long while among the rows, tracing his fingers upon the epitaphs he could not read and breathing in that scent he relished so, the grit and loam and coldness that warmed him like no other, despite the iciness of the evening.

Silas rubbed at his shoulder, working out a knot that had burrowed there. The ground was soft beneath his feet, hinting at recent rain, but they'd been lucky on the ride so far. There had been no rain to speak of since Lalassu led them from Harvington Hall. It was as though the moment they were beyond the boundaries of the Sanctuary, nature had regained her composure.

'Good morning to you.' Silas nodded at the cat curled up on the back steps of the church.

The church grim, a feline with a patchwork coat of white and black, meowed him a morning greeting. It opened its mouth in a wide yawn, revealing a vast array of pointed teeth, too many and too large for the mouth but somehow managing to find a place when the animal's lips were shut. Quite horrifying, he supposed, but Silas had seen far worse now.

The melody led him out to the village square and sent him north, away, thankfully, from the brook that skirted the southern end of the main road, which was aptly name The Street. He was working hard not to baulk and tremble whenever Lalassu took him over a bridge or along a riverbank, but his reaction was instinctual, happening before he realised it. Silas shoved his hands into his deep pockets, fingering the bandalore where it lay. The wood was warm, warmer than it would be with his body heat alone. Ready for what awaited. A quiver of nerves took him, but there was the low ebb of eagerness there too. He was purposeful in his stride, set on a course. He had no doubt that this was where he should be in this moment. For all the unknowns, what with Azazel's maleficium, the revenants with their scrying eyes, the painful past of his daemonic guardian, and the Blight itself, the bandalore was a blessed surety.

It called him to his task. And he followed. Simple. Gloriously simple.

The village was quiet, its residents tucked up in their beds. The first of the morning bird calls had begun, accompanying the stranger tune of the scythe as he walked between the row of sandstone homes. His footsteps rang out, overly loud in the silence of early morn, marking his way along the well-maintained road. He passed the last of the terraced houses, with their stout chimneys and low-set doorways, and thought for a moment that the bandalore was about to take him into the fields when he felt a tug of certainty that he must stop. Right here.

He peered at his destination.

A wooden cottage was near hidden beneath the skeletal embrace of honeysuckle and magnolia. An evergreen hugged one corner of the small abode, covering it right up to the eaves where it had loosened some of the slate tiles. The residence seemed unique, in that it was detached rather than leaning against a neighbour as all the other homes did, as though it were set slightly apart from the rest of the village. The fact that it was wood rather than stone spoke of a mismatch as well. The garden might have been quite pretty at one point. There was evidence of structure to it, with cowslip and primroses set among the barren stalks of woody roses, all of which would be a wonder to look upon in the spring when the flowers bloomed. For now, with winter racing in, the beds were drab and colourless save for some winter box that added tiny dashes of white to the landscape, and the hopeful green stalks of snowdrops waiting on the new year. Silas made his way up the stone path, enjoying the peacefulness the garden brought. Though this place had an air of abandonment about it, it was a no less delightful locale.

The front door squealed, swinging wide on its hinges, revealing a settled darkness within.

Shit. Silas froze, fingers curling about the stiff leaves of a winter box. He'd been so busy following the bandalore that he'd not stopped to consider that there might be someone living amongst the dead. 'Hello?'

No greeting was returned. A breeze swept through the garden, touching at his back. Silas moved forward. 'Is anyone there?'

If they were, there was every chance they had opened their door and been startled into silence at the sight of him. They'd not have been expecting a sizable man upon their doorstep at this hour. Christ, what was he supposed to say if that were the case? *Good morning, might I come inside and speak with your ghostly inhabitants?* His surety was dissolving rapidly.

*Come in, ankou. We are not afraid.*

The voice came not to his ears but rather to the inside of his skull, just as it had for all the other lost souls he'd encountered. Black Annis and the besieged Verderer among them. He hesitated. It was tempting, so very tempting to remain outside. But the melody of the scythe was peaceable and calm, the sound sinking lower till it was all but lost and only a far distant hum remained.

This was where Silas was supposed to be. He gathered himself and stepped out of the waking day and into the gloom. He winced as the top of his head glanced against the doorframe. If he'd rushed in, he might have knocked himself senseless.

'Calm down, man,' he muttered to himself.

Bloody hell, if this foray of his went wrong, he'd never hear the end of it from Pitch.

Straightening, shoulders back, Silas blinked as his eyes adjusted to the lack of light. The heavy covering of nature had blacked out all but a small portion of the two windows, and the light that did filter its way in was broken apart by the drifting dust in the air. Silas coughed, feeling it tickle at the back of his throat. The corner of the room shifted. At least, that was how it appeared as the light seemed to gather there and rise up in a plume, the dust rising like a snow shower in reverse.

Silas slid his hand into his pocket, taking hold of the bandalore. The loop in the string slipped over his finger, settling easily, no rush, no bother. He pulled it free, and waited.

# CHAPTER 2

He was no longer alone in the cottage, if he ever had been at all. On the far side of a crooked-legged dining table with a forlorn single chair stood three lost souls. An unenviable sight, considering the state of each of them. One most certainly had died of a broken neck, a young woman whose features were so faded Silas could only make out the hint of where her eyes and mouth lay. The second might well have just been someone standing with a sheet draped over them. For all the distinguishing features that were apparent, they were little more than a haze of dirty white. The third was all too clear, and if Silas had eaten breakfast already, it would have been making a quick appearance now. The spirit was a male, middle-aged, whose belly was slashed wide open, spilling entrails down his front like horrid braces of blackened gore.

*Terrible idea this, he's quite terrifying.*

Though his grey-green lips did not move, the chap was muttering just the same, inside Silas's head.

*Large, isn't he? Why must he be so large?* This came from the haze, he was quite sure. *None of the others were so large.*

*You came. The ankou-of-the-pale-horse heeded our call.* The young woman's voice inside his head was filled with fervour as though she was astonished to see him. Even if she did see him from a sideways angle, as her broken neck dictated.

'I did,' Silas said, glancing down at the bandalore which warmed his palm. He'd not understood the delicate tones of the melody entirely before then, but now he saw it. A summons had awoken him. Not for a teratism, but for a trio of restless souls. 'What is it you want from me?'

*Goodness, what do you think?* the haze sniped. *Your blade, of course.*

*Hush, Martin! Are you mad?* The middle-aged man shook with his horror, and so too did his innards. *Manners, for god's sake, man.*

*I'm terribly nervous...forgive me, ankou...take no notice of me.*

'Of course not, it is quite fine.' Silas cleared his throat. 'Forgive *me* for my confusion. It's just that I've not been called by souls in such a way before.'

*I am a ghost, dear sir,* said the figure who was not much more than a sheet of white, a ghost if ever there was one. *And far too many years old to count, so I'd thank you to address me in the way that I prefer. If you don't mind...oh, blast. My apologies again, sir. You really are quite imposing, and it's normally I who is doing the frightening.*

The portly, gutted man nodded a head that was thankfully intact. *But you are right though, Martin. We do prefer to be called ghosts here.*

The woman with the broken neck sniffed, causing her head to jerk in a most unpleasant way. *Not for me. A peddler once declared I was a most beguiling spectre, a vision of chilling beauty. Have you ever heard such a wondrous announcement?*

Her fellow souls muttered, the white haze seeming to shimmer. Silas said nothing, for what did one say to such a thing?

*I'd like to be addressed as 'spectre' when you send me on my way...if I may be so bold as to ask such a thing of you, ankou.*

He coughed, wondering if perhaps he'd not really awoken at all, for this was fast beginning to feel like a strange dream.

'Well, certainly, I will address you as you wish.'

That seemed to please them all. There was a general shuffling of presence, a sway of light and shadow, a contentment that he could *feel* as readily as see.

*Good chap. Good chap,* murmured the sheen of white. *Seems word of you is right indeed.*

'And what have you have heard of me, might I ask?'

*We keep each other informed, as best we can, of the ankou that are about,* the rotund gentleman declared, and Silas wished he would stay still so his length of innards did not sway so. *So as we know how best to avoid them, if you pardon my rudeness. We are not usually partial to an ankou's blade, you see. And yours is said to be like no other. I'd have let you ride on by and waited for another. But, well, Delilah said we ought not to be so lily-livered, and just because you seemed so frightful on your big horse and all, what was happening was more frightening by half and that it may well be too late, should we delay. We were best to end things while the chance was there.*

That was two of them now who'd spoken of ending things. And it was very apparent now what was actually happening here. It was a surrender of sorts. Silas found himself thinking of the child who had been the first to feel the strike of his blade. The lost soul in the baron's home, where Silas had stumbled his way through a seance. *Release me,* she had pleaded. And he had done so, eventually, after Pitch had thrown a drunken tantrum at the table and frightened all the guests with his temper. That reliable temper could rise again this morning if the daemon woke to find Silas gone. Pitch accused Silas, constantly, of too much fussing. But since setting out from Harvington Hall, it was he who had become more ardent about keeping in each other's sights. Everywhere but the bedroom, apparently.

'So,' Silas said. 'I am to understand that you are ready for the blade, then?'

*I'm not sure anyone is ever ready, not after so long running from it.* The young woman sighed, though it fell to more of a shudder. *But I suppose it's been long enough. One hundred and six years, give or take a month or two, since I was hung for theft out the back of the manor house.* She shifted her shoulders in a way that made her head roll back so violently that for an awful instant Silas feared it would end up hanging down between her shoulder blades. *I didn't steal a bloody thing, I tell you that and swear upon any god who will listen...which is to say I'm swearing to thin air.*

*I'm certain that is not the case,* said the man with his insides spilling out. *We will meet our maker soon enough, and you'll see he's just as I told you so. Magnificent, and most likely with a long white beard. Isn't that right, ankou?*

While Silas considered his answer, wondering if it was right to be honest at such a time and say that he had no idea what awaited those he moved on. All he knew for sure was that death was inevitable and the fate of all. Even the likes of him.

The woman sighed.

The blackness where her eyes might be disappeared for a moment, as though she'd closed them in exasperation. *I don't much care if there is a giant snake with rubies for eyes awaiting us. So long as they will listen to me, when no one here has ever done. I'll tell you too, ankou, for perhaps you can be my confessor and tell your master. I stole nothing, nothing at all. I am not bad, I never was. But Master Biggins...he took so much from me. I hope he's been in hell with a pike up his arse for the past eighty years. I told him, in no terms a lady should utter, to piss off when he tried to drag me into his bed. He didn't like the kick in the balls I gave him and told everyone who would listen I'd taken all his silver and poisoned his cow. A right bastard he was, and not a soul stood up for me. No one uttered a single bloody word to save me, though they all knew what he was about. They just watched me hang. And I cannot tell you how much I despise them.*

She had worked herself into a fervour again, the sound in Silas's head growing ever louder until he was finding it difficult not to wince. Now she gathered herself, smoothing her hands down the front of a dress that might, if he squinted, be seen to be made of light pink cotton. *But, though I've enjoyed every moment I've had to make the lives of the folk in this village a living nightmare, especially those with his stinking blood in their veins, I'm not so keen on it anymore.*

The wraith in Harvington Hall had laid it out. Those spirits that remained did so thanks to the tethers of fury, grief, and disappointment. Being unjustly accused, and hung for it, would certainly make a person angry enough to cling to the land of the living and refuse to let go, Silas imagined. It was just that neither the wraith nor Lady Satine had also mentioned that the lost souls might summon him like he were a hansom cab on the streets of London.

'I am sorry for what happened to you.' And he was, never more aware of how human the ghostly truly were. How human *he* must have been, until some terrible misery made him fit for service to the goddess. 'I can certainly assist you in moving on.'

*Yes. Send us on our way, ankou, for we are done here.* This came from the blur of white. *I've lost count of the years I've clung to this life. Can't even damned remember now why I stuck to it to begin with. Haven't got the foggiest inkling of what or who I was...it's all been fading...which was fine by me. I would have been happy to vanish entirely when the time was right. I ain't no monster...not bothering no one...too much...aside from frightening a folk or two who deign to see me. But now...well, it's different, ain't it? There are strange happenings all about. The gloaming's much too close, and I don't like it. Don't like it at all. It's got ahold of her, they say. What if she comes our way? She's riding out further and further every night, they say.*

The bandalore's string tightened about Silas's finger. 'She? Whom do you speak of?'

*Why, the Lady Howard, of course. Thought that would be who you were headed off to find,* the gentleman with the wide girth and spilling entrails declared. *Two hundred years, she's been riding about in that carriage, keeping herself to self. But that's changed now, so they say. She's taking a turn. A terrible one at that.*

At the back of Silas's neck, beneath the ever-growing length of his unruly hair, gooseflesh rose. He stared at the soul...ghost, rather. 'A carriage, you say?'

Lalassu had woven just such a picture in her mane at Harvington Hall.

The portly chap with all his guts on display drifted through the table, coming closer. It took some effort for Silas not to step away. *That's right. A fearsome carriage and four, so I'm told. Though don't ask me who said so...some things fall away from me, quick as you like.*

*Might have been Screaming Martha down Bath way?* the woman offered.

In the distance a cockerel cried to the rise of the sun.

*Oh, that could be it, yes. She makes a dreadful din, but she's useful when it comes to spreading gossip.*

'Never mind all that.' Silas said it more harshly than necessary, but he was impatient. 'What else do you know of this carriage?'

The blurs of black that denoted each of the woman's eyes expanded. *Oh sweet mercy, you are here for her, then. It must be true that the gloaming has her.*

'The gloaming?' he asked, though he thought he knew of what they spoke.

*Yes, yes. The living folk call it the Blight, so I'm told.* He was told rather a lot. Gossip was rife in the ethereal world it seemed. But here was Silas's first opportunity to learn how the Blight felt for the lost souls it hounded.

'And what do the souls...the ghosts, say of the gloaming?' Silas asked.

*Spectre, if you don't mind.* The young lady was testing Silas's patience now.

'Tell me what you know.'

*It rolls in sure as a fog, whispering promises. Sending you right mad with a craving for them,* the haze affirmed, not without some exasperation. *You know of it, for it is what took the Verderer. They speak far and wide of your efforts to save that forest, ankou.*

'That is how you see it, then? This gloaming you speak of is like a fog?'

*Something like it, so we've heard. We've not seen it at all, and may the good lord protect us so we never need do.* The rotund man actually made the sign of the cross, brushing his fingers through hanging flesh. Of all the odd things before him, Silas found this oddest of all. A ghost in prayer to entirely the wrong god.

*No one who's felt the gloaming brush them has ever gone on to tell the tale.* The smear of white in the air said this. *They're too far gone in the madness for that. We've never had much cause to fear it around these parts though. Not till now. Lady Howard rides out of Tavistock every night at the eleventh hour. Or is it \the ninth? I've no mind for details anymore.*

*The eleventh hour.* The young woman nodded, and Silas wished she would not do such a thing, for this time he heard the grind of her bones. *She travels every night to Okehampton Castle, without fail. Has done for a long while without issue. But now there is talk that many a spectre down her way has suddenly gone missing. And I don't mean fading away – that takes time, it ain't sudden – and if there's an ankou down there, they aren't making themselves known. Most are saying that it's Lady Howard stealing those spectres, forcing them into her carriage. Latest we heard was she's even causing the living to be run off the road. Getting her souls as fresh as can be, locking them in her carriage and doing away with them. Is it true then, ankou? That the Lady Howard has grown monstrous?*

'Well, I cannot say,' Silas said slowly. 'I have not yet laid eyes upon the situation.' But he would bet the coat on his back that he was on the right path to do so. 'But if she has indeed become as you say...monstrous...then it may well be her that I am being sent forth to meet.'

*You don't know these things for sure?* The full-cheeked ghost frowned, a movement which appeared to crush all his features together.

'Not entirely.' Silas shifted, uncomfortable with how he had to answer. 'Not to begin with at least. But it is a carriage that I seek, and to hear your tales now, I can't imagine it a mere coincidence that Lady Howard is known for hers.'

From the moment the unfortunate chap with the guts on display had spoken of a carriage, Silas had known he'd come across the first inkling of their destination.

When Lalassu had woven an image of Goodrich Castle in her mane, he'd not known where it lay or even really what it signified. Simply that it was important. That he would find its meaning.

The second image she presented to him was no less vague than the first.

Their last day at Harvington Hall, Silas had been with Lalassu in the stables, grooming her, which always soothed him, almost as much as the graveyard. Barely had he glanced the dandy brush against her shimmering coat and her mane had risen up from her neck. It swayed and twisted as though caught by a breeze in the airless stables, lifting and knotting and weaving into a discernible shape.

What was revealed was not a location but a carriage.

A marvellous landau carriage, with huge spoked wheels, lanterns upon the front corners, and a delicate ironwork running around the roof like the icing upon an elaborate cake. There was a marking upon the doors, a family crest perhaps, but the intricacy was too much even for Lalassu's talents.

*Perhaps she can yet be rescued.* The woman sounded hopeful. *Lady Howard has haunted Devon for near on two hundred years, and she's kept herself to herself. She does not deserve what has become of her. None of us do. She has been wronged.*

*The gloaming is the scourge, not us.* The utterance from the drifting veil of white was sharp. *We are afraid, ankou. I don't mind saying it. Strange things are afoot. Getting odder still, since all that business in the Forest of Dean.*

'I wasn't aware that word of that had travelled so far,' Silas said. Or that it had travelled at all. There was so little he knew about the souls he was tasked with finding and sending on their way. 'But clearly you know of the Verderer.'

The white haze shifted, and Silas thought it might have nodded. *The natural folk spread word of it. There was a spriggan here, not long ago, talking about two riders in the forest who brought the Verderer back to rights.* There was a long pause, and it seemed no more might come. *At a great cost, though. An entire mine of fae was lost, and at the hands of that daemon you ride with.*

Silas's head jerked up from where he'd been frowning down at the bandalore. 'He's not to be blamed for that. You spread the word right back to those who are saying it, that Mr Astaroth's hand was forced. The fae were not in their right minds, and he gave himself up so that I might escape from their enchantments. What came after...was not his fault.'

An uncomfortable silence prevailed. The morning sunrise was forcing its way in through the thick slumbering remains of honeysuckle and magnolia. Silas thought he heard the distant voice of a farmer calling out to his herd.

*As you say, ankou,* the woman said softly, drifting over to where an old oven sat dark and bulky, unused for untold years. *No harm was meant. We are just saying he's...well, he's disconcerting, is all.*

The man's guts swayed as he edged himself up onto the dining table. Silas's own belly roiled. *It's not that...not entirely...I mean he's damned frightening, no doubt. But that's not entirely it. Saw him arrive yesterday with you...and I couldn't get far enough away, I'll be honest. There's something odd about him. He's not quite right, if you know what I mean.* He frowned, searching for the word. *He's haunted in his own way.*

Silas's gaze flitted over his audience, suddenly irritated. They hardly seemed qualified to speak of not being right. 'Mr Astaroth serves the Order as I do. He is my guardian, and he saved my...life...in the Forest of Dean more than once. Whatever you may think of him, I am very grateful to have him at my side.' The words spilled from him quickly and with far more earnestness than he'd intended. But so be it. He'd only spoken the truth. Pitch was frightening, the gutted man was not wrong in that, but they should not be blinded to all else he was out of fear.

The woman fluttered her hands, sweeping from the far side of the tiny room towards him. *Then we are grateful for him too. Please, do not take offence at our words, that was not our intent. We are simply so very tired of being afraid, you see. Things feel so unsteady, with too many of us being afflicted by the gloaming and in ways no one's ever heard of before. I mean, a woman of the cloth consuming children? And a man of the forest destroying the very thing he loves? Now Lady Howard...I always believed I'd know when the right time came to move on. And I believe it is now. You will send us on our way, won't you, ankou?*

The trio waited on him, their anxiety darkening the room and pushing back his temper.

'Of course,' Silas said. 'I will send you on your way.'

*Will it hurt, do you think?* The haze of white was at the centre of the knotted wooden dining table, half within and half without. *Do the ghosts normally scream when you strike them?*

Christ, now there was a question.

A low, sweet note began to play.

Silas pretended he was busy adjusting the string about his finger. Black Annis had not gone willingly. There had been plenty of screaming there, but then, she was a teratism, far more lost than these souls. The child in the baron's house had smiled at him, and the chap with the slit throat at Knighton House had been theatrical about it, desiring to make his exit on his knees with his arms outstretched. But he'd not uttered a sound as the blade found him.

'Ah...I don't believe so. No.'

*But you don't know that for sure, either?* The portly man's face did that unseemly crinkling again, and his innards swung like the pendulum of a grandfather clock between his spread knees.

*Bloody hell, can we just do this, then? I'm losing my nerve.* The haze of white moved closer to the fellow sitting on the edge of the table, appearing like a bride's veil behind him. The woman shifted to their side. She tried to take the portly man's offered hand, but their fingers brushed straight through one another. The woman made a small sound, and the man consoled her gently. The bandalore's melody was slowly rising, and what a lullaby it was. So delicate and lilting. Like a cradle song. He glanced up at the group. Though her face was mostly a blur, the young woman's fear was not so undistinguished. Silas thought it such a great pity that at both times her life had ended she could not even hold another's hand as she went.

The portly man was trying his level best to reassure her, even though it was a gruesome display. As he leaned towards her, the largest of his entrails caught about his dangling foot, and blood showered down upon the floorboards. Though the blood did not stain the wood, it was still stomach-churning to witness.

*It will soon be done now. There, there.* The man looked to Silas, his face clear of anything but expectancy. *As you will, please, sir. No more dallying about. Done that far too long already.* He glanced down at his belly. *And in the end, I suppose what's done is done, whether I rage about it, or not. I've wanted folks to remember me for long enough. Think it's about time now that I myself forgot.*

He nodded at Silas, who drew back his arm. He wished he had some grand and final words to say to them, an assurance that all would be well. But he did not know that for certain himself, and he'd not lie, here at the end. Silas did something else instead. He pursed his lips, hoping that he was not so dreadful at a whistle as Pitch was at song, and blew out the charming melody of death's blade. It surprised him to hear a near-perfect mimicry of the endearing song that filled his head, and it warmed him to see the consternation upon the woman's face settle into something more contented.

Silas released the bandalore. He wished for no blade here, nothing to concern his trembling flock, and the scythe heeded his wishes. The spinning discs of wood raced out, tracing an arc through the air and carving their way through the ghosts who huddled so closely together that they appeared as one. He watched their faces, each of them, as the bandalore traced its path. If he had feared he might see something terrible there, he was mistaken. There was concern, though not quite fear; there was sadness, thick as winter's snow; but there, at the very last, was release.

What was done was done. How very right the emptied-out man had been.

Silas stood a moment in the empty room, listening to the dance of birds upon the roof, the scuttling of something tiny in the corner. He had a catch in the back of his throat, and an odd sensation settled on him. If he named it, he would say it was the pinch of sorrow. As though he mourned a little for these souls whose own mourners had long since gone from this world. Craving the openness and light of the outdoors, Silas left the cottage and stepped out into a brightness that made him blink and shade his eyes.

Someone stood, facing away from him, in the overgrown garden, up to their knees in wild grass that had taken hold of that section. They swung a cane before them, knocking at some clinging winter-box flowers that had fought their way skyward. Silas did not need the white spots to clear from his vision to know who it was, for he had run his fingers along that waist and followed the curve of that neck with his lips.

'Pitch? What are you doing here?'

The daemon turned with feline grace to face him. The sun was nudging through the cracks of the world behind him, creeping over the slated roofs and through the pear tree across the road, wrapping itself around the bare branches and spilling around Pitch's silhouette like a light on the main actor of a stage. His hair was tangled, the waves about his face the most mussed of all, as though when he'd pulled his head from his pillow, he'd risen quickly and not bothered to even glance at himself in a mirror.

'I should ask you the same question,' he said. 'I went to your room to find your bed cold and empty. Granted, I hardly expected to find you in the midst of a threesome, but I at least thought you would be there, dribbling and twitching your lip as you do when you are sleeping.'

He wore no coat and had his shirtsleeves rolled up, leaving fair arms bare. His corseted waistcoat, gifted to him by Bess, was a subtle lemon-yellow silk. Low down, where it would draw the eye to his absurdly narrow waist, there was bold needlework of two figures standing in a garden of green and pink, a man and a woman decked out in the garb of years long passed, gazing at one another across the line of buttons that separated them. Pitch had neglected to button the top of his waistcoat, the shirt beneath allowing more hint of his chest than was proper. Pitch had either dressed in a hurry or was still so inebriated from his evening that he thought himself to be. Either way, uncouth and rumpled, he was rather too much to look at. And all Silas could think on was why the daemon had gone to his room at such an hour to begin with.

'I didn't wish to wake you. There was no need of it anyway.' Silas gestured absently over his shoulder at the empty cottage. 'There were some souls needing tending...nothing I could not handle on my own.'

Did Pitch flinch at that? No, surely it was more to do with the butterfly that danced about him. A white specimen with two orbs of black marking its wings. It made Silas think suddenly of the revenants with their empty gazes. But this flimsy little creature was far prettier and clearly more resilient, for it was unusual at such a time of year. The butterfly was very intent on landing in Pitch's hair.

He swiped at the fluttering creature, and it danced away. 'Perhaps I'll return to London, then.' Pitch stabbed the end of the cane at a hapless dried leaf. 'If you are quite all right on your own.'

So he had seen the daemon flinch after all.

'That is not what I meant at all.' The thought of the daemon leaving struck him with unease, and Silas found himself being frightfully honest. 'I don't wish you to leave. I've no desire to be on my own.'

Pitch glanced up at him, as he did so often and so well, from beneath long lashes. 'No? I'll stay then, I suppose, if you are going to get so fretful about it. But I'll do so with one condition – that you promise me you will not whistle again.'

Silas lifted a brow. 'That seems unkind. I could ask you not to sing anymore, in that case.'

'You adore my serenades.'

'Terribly sorry, but you seem to have gotten quite the wrong idea about that.'

Their banter was unaffected, light and carefree. Such chats were becoming far more commonplace between them. Pitch seemed less intent on being appalling and lewd and more interested in striking up amiable conversation.

'I don't intend to stop, I'm afraid,' Pitch declared.

'Nor do I, now I've discovered that I have quite the talent for whistling.' Silas fought the smile that tried to rise, enjoying the fact that Pitch was doing much the same. 'It would seem that we are at an impasse.'

'So we are.' The daemon laughed, and the butterfly settled on the top of his head, perched among the waves that took hold of the sunrise and glistened. 'It is so easy to forget you are amusing sometimes, my dear Sickle.'

Silas inclined his head at the backhanded compliment, his face warming at the silly pet name the daemon insisted on. 'Is that how you found me, then? The whistling?'

'No.' Pitch handled the walking cane with a single fingertip placed between the fox's silver ears. He observed it a moment more before continuing. 'I seem to be able to find you quite well these days. I've been here a while. Listening to you talk to your shadows.' He gave Silas a long look, those brilliant eyes of his every bit as glorious as the morning that framed him. 'I heard you attempt to extol my virtues to your disbelieving crowd.'

Silas held his gaze, a task not so intimidating as it had been in the past. Though it often took an effort to ensure his cheeks did not redden under the daemon's ever-searching eyes. 'It was right that they know what truly happened. I only spoke the truth.'

'You made me sound far too heroic.' Pitch ran a finger over one of the emeralds that made up the fox's eyes on the cane.

'You stopped a castle from crushing us...and you gave yourself over to the fae queen so I might escape. I myself thought it damned brave of you. I don't think I've thanked you properly for it either.'

Perhaps lack of sleep made Silas more forthright, or maybe it was that as they stood here amongst a garden bowing down to the encroaching winter, it felt right to lay things bare.

For the first time that Silas could recall, Pitch was the first to look away.

'I was merely doing as I've been instructed.' He shrugged. 'Nothing more. Satty would have had my hide if I reported back to say that you had been flattened...or turned into a mindless lump of rather fetching meat. Now, enough of all that. Clearly you are fine, so I must return to my bed. There is someone there who needs tending and was not happy at all that I had to run off after a wandering dead man.'

'But you were alone –' Silas pressed his lips thin.

Pitch tensed. 'Gods, are you spying on me through holes in the wall again?'

'Of course not. The door was open when I passed.'

'It was closed when I got up.' Pitch regarded him intently. And not without some annoyance, Silas noted.

'I didn't spy on you.'

'And I was not alone. Perhaps they had gone to the privy when you turned Peeping Tom again. I have the damp drawers to prove my night was most full of company.'

That was definitely a lie. Pitch didn't wear drawers. What the bloody hell was this all about?

'God, just stop.' Silas threw up his arms and spun around. 'I don't care if you had the entire village in there. Go. Tend to your conquest, but don't dally about it. I want to leave here as soon as we are able. I learned more of the teratism we face from the lost souls, and there is some urgency.'

'Very well. Calm down.'

'I am calm.' Christ, how did the bastard manage to make the simplest utterances regrettable? 'I'd like to leave no later than midmorning. Try to be done by then if you can.' Silas was quite proud of how snide he sounded. Of how he spoke through the pressure at his chest.

'I'll do my utmost.' The daemon was strangely unreadable. Pitch turned about in a move not so fluid as it should be. His hip bothered him, but he claimed each time Silas enquired that there was no great pain, and that if the ankou asked one more time, he'd find himself short of a few fingers. 'But you will do me a favour in return, Silas.'

'What is that?'

'You will not head out without letting me know again.'

'There really was no need for concern –'

Pitch whipped a glance over his shoulder. 'I am your guardian, ridiculous as it is. You do not get to determine what concerns me. I don't enjoy wasting my energy on such an irritating thing as worry. You should have been in your bed, and you were not.'

Silas swallowed. The reprimand seemed authentic, as though it actually was worry and not inconvenience that bothered the daemon.

'I'm sorry,' he said.

'I don't want your apology,' Pitch replied curtly. 'I want your word that you'll never set off half-cocked without telling me again.'

'You have my word.' Silas wanted to say more. He wanted to ask why Pitch had gone up to his room to begin with. The privy was outside, not upstairs. There was nothing but Silas's paltry bed up in the attic room. He kept quiet, conscious of how close to the surface Pitch's ire stirred.

'Good. Very well.'

The daemon made his way down the short garden path and onto the road, stepping the cane ahead of him with polished delicacy. Silas watched until Pitch reached the square and turned towards the church, vanishing from view.

# CHAPTER 3

Their pace was best reserved for lunatics. To any who watched, it must have appeared that the horses' hooves never touched the ground, so swiftly did Sanu and Lalassu move. The landscape did not warrant such speed. In fact it declared itself wholly unsuitable for such things, laden with deceptive patches of sodden ground and hollows concealing fetlock-shattering rabbit holes.

Or hare holes.

Who the blazes knew which they were? And Silas was not about to make the mistake of misnaming them again. His inability to discern between the two irked the daemon no end.

Silas glanced over at his competitor, who lay like a streak of golden sunshine upon his red mare's back. Pitch's hair was pressed near smooth against his head by the speed of the gallop, and that damned mouth of his was wide with a smile that far outshone the winter sun that met its midday mark low in the sky. It was a clear and crisp day, not a cloud to mar the sky. The first such day since they had departed Harvington Hall. All the rest succumbed to varying degrees of drizzle and cloud.

Silas had become accustomed to the tempestuous weather that cloaked the hall. In fact, he'd almost come to relish it: that sense of being enclosed, surrounded...protected. But Pitch had not shared his enjoyment, he knew. The daemon had been keen to depart, to move beyond the glassy moat and endless corridors, but at least this time Pitch-'s restlessness was not borne of distress and discomfort. Once he was free of his sickbed, it had been difficult to imagine him ever needing it. The wretched melancholy that had consumed him had entirely vanished.

'Is that the best your nag can do, Sickle?' Pitch's laughter was light as dandelion seeds.

He spurred his mount on, his white coat snapping out behind him, its lavish gold thread embroidery dancing against the sunlight. A white coat was the most insensible choice Pitch could have made for riding wear. How it was not already covered with mud stains, Silas had no idea, but Christ it looked fine upon him: a high-collared, wide-sleeved affair chosen from Bess's considerable wardrobe, yet fitting Pitch's finer form as though it had been woven for him. The lemon-yellow corset with its elaborate embroidery was fixed beneath. It was a wonder he removed it to sleep, he seemed to enjoy a tight cinch so much. Pitch was prone to sulking if he was without the whalebone and laces. But Silas did not tease him for it. If the corset brought the slightest relief from his pains, then it was a welcome thing.

Pitch asked, 'Do you tire already?'

'Do I tire? Not bloody likely.' Silas laughed, his warm breath puffing white against the temperate day. 'I'm not some old man who cannot handle a bracing run.'

His amusement faltered. Now there was a new thought to plague him. The wraith he'd encountered in Harvington Hall, the one who had led him to where Pitch languished, had asked a question that still bothered Silas.

*When did you die?*

Odd how such a question could vex him, considering all else that was going on. Revenants heralding the return of maleficium, and fae hounds that regurgitated walking canes, among all else. But vex him the wraith's question did. And frighten him. He may very well be entirely more alone than he could imagine. If Silas were not fresh from his grave, and a great length of time had passed since his death, then those who may have known him...may have loved him...would all be in the ground too. To imagine that no one existed in the world who could remember *him* brought terrible anguish in the pensive, quiet hours of night. Silas might be dead, but to be forgotten was something else entirely.

'You do appear young and supple, I'll allow.' Pitch sat lopsided in his saddle, casting his words over his shoulder. 'But the same cannot be said for your steed. She is lagging most noticeably.'

Silas stroked Lalassu's mane. 'Ignore him, won't you?'

It was an indication of how absorbed into his new life he was that he spoke to his horse and expected she understood. Silas walked among the living and mourned what he had lost, but he *felt* his difference now. Since the encounters with the revenants, the strangeness, the oddness of being an ankou, had all begun to peel away the day he'd cut the head off a corpse. The strike of the blade had severed not just the unfortunate man's spinal cord but the bind that tied Silas to the hollow remains of his life as a purebred. A man.

By the time he lay entwined with Pitch, dragging the lifeless daemon back from the darkness, Silas's own fear of the darkness was thinning. He accepted his lot. Hell, he'd admit he was already coming to resent the short life on offer to an ankou. This life, this strange second chance, gave him the strength to protect innocents, like Charlie. And he relished it. He was not entirely happy that Charlie would be staying on at Harvington Hall after all, but he'd not see the lad out on the roads again. That would certainly not do.

Silas shifted in his seat, adjusting the reins needlessly. He flicked away a strand of hair that played in his eyes, obscuring his view of the rider ahead. And what a fine view it was. Lalassu tossed her head, and her mane rose like a wisp of cloud. She longed to stretch her stride and overtake Sanu. She could do so easily, Silas knew it, but she heeded his wordless request to temper herself and allow the red horse to draw further ahead.

'I think you may have this one, Pitch,' Silas called. He patted at Lalassu's shoulder in thanks and muttered, 'All the apples you can handle, my friend, I promise you. He is not good with losing. You've seen it yourself.'

The pale horse snorted through blown nostrils. Pitch was a terrible, terrible loser. At mealtimes Bess's footmen had learned it was best not to serve him last at the dinner table. And Silas had truly feared for Charlie's safety when he whipped the daemon at several games of whist.

Silas watched Pitch move further ahead. The daemon whooped like he'd won at the races, arms outstretched at his sides. He enjoyed the saddle much more these days, for his hip did not bother him when he straddled the horse. The cane that the skriker had so inelegantly delivered was squirrelled away in one of the saddlebags. Silas had placed it there when Pitch refused to do so, declaring he would leave it behind, for it was not needed and too cumbersome to carry. Bess had rolled his eyes and pressed a hidden button beneath the fox's chin. The cane had retracted to a mere shadow of its former size, and Silas had no trouble packing it into the saddlebag.

Silas smiled, as much from the daemon's evident happiness as his own. This was a careless journey so far, but he knew it would not last. So he'd enjoy it while he could. Pitch positively glowed. Not figuratively, not in this instance anyway, but brilliant nonetheless. Gone was the irritation and jagged restlessness of their departure from Ottelie's cottage. He was well, so very well. Which was wonderful. Enough so that Silas could pretend he was not bothered that Pitch had simply used him to restore himself to vigour. That the daemon had been so desperate in that dark and dank room that he'd accepted Silas's clumsy offering. The experience had been...pleasant...certainly...but there was no need for it to be repeated. In fact, it was far better that it was not.

Pitch glanced again over his shoulder, his tousled locks wrapping around the sheer cut of his jaw. Silas swallowed hard. Definitely far better that it was not repeated.

'Perhaps you enjoyed that bakery too much, dear Sickle,' Pitch called out. 'Lalassu seems to be struggling beneath you.'

Silas sighed. He'd not done so in at least a minute or two; it was time for it. 'You think yourself awfully amusing,' he shouted back. 'Don't you?'

If anyone had enjoyed the bakery too much, it was Pitch. For two weeks they'd lingered at Harvington Hall, and he had joined Silas on a daily afternoon stroll to the graveyard, leaning upon his cane heavily, and making it loudly known that if he had to endure such a boring pastime, the least Silas could do was provide eclairs and tarts. The truth was that Silas had never invited Pitch to join him, thinking such an invitation would have been laughed at. The daemon's company was a surprise and, to begin with, had Silas in a complete fluster. He'd worried that Pitch would want more of him. He'd worried that he would not. And which did Silas truly desire? His head was a muddle every time Pitch was too close. As though there were not far more important things to worry over.

Now, on their journey, the situation had hardly improved. Pitch kept up his crass innuendo, but he also kept his distance. Silas was appalled at how long he would lie awake in his bed, listening for the uneven tempo of Pitch's footsteps in the hall, a gentle tap at the door to follow. The sounds never came.

The distraction of the daemon was dangerous in a world that was even more so.

But the morning ride was doing much to clear Silas's head. Upon Lalassu's back, everything seemed much damned simpler.

'I do not *think* I am amusing – I know it.' Pitch bent low against his mare's neck, his arse high in the air, his focus on the field ahead. 'Why else have you been smiling like a fool these past few minutes?'

Silas started, briefly losing his rhythm. He swore the infernal bastard had eyes in the back of his head.

Up ahead the woodlands teased at the edges of a wide expanse of green grass that appeared to have been tended, cut low and precise. Beyond, the peaks of a rather grand roof were evident, their tips skyward. A mansion skulked up against the treeline.

'I'm smiling because it is a beautiful day,' Silas retorted. 'And I enjoy a gallop as well as you do.'

Pitch twisted about so he could peer over his shoulder. 'I can attest to that.' Those lips, full and pink and always damp, taunted with their upturned edges.

'You would do well to watch where you are going.' Silas nudged his thighs against the leather, and Lalassu loosened herself, stretching, gaining on the red mare. He'd had quite enough of the spectacular view, for now.

'What's the matter, my dear?' Pitch said. 'Am I wrong to suggest you enjoy a thorough gallop, a firm heat between your legs?'

'Oh, for Christ's sake. Turn about, Pitch. You're approaching a jump. You need to pay some attention to the fact you are on a horse.'

The jump was not formidable, simply the remains of a hedge that had once barricaded a field. Sanu could surmount it with barely a lift of hooves.

'I'm always aware of who or what I'm riding, Sickle. Fear not.'

Silas was *not* bothered at all, damn it. 'I hardly fear such a thing. But I'll be much vexed if you fall from your mount and delay our journey.'

'Gods man, I've ridden a cockatrice while it was on heat,' Pitch told the air with much loftiness. 'I'm hardly about to fall from this bag of bones.'

Sanu raised her front quarters, soaring up and over the squat obstacle of coarse branch and ragged foliage. Pitch's coat flared like a magnificent flag. A heartbeat later his pretty mouth fouled up the quiet morning air.

'Fuck!'

And without further ado, the daemon toppled from his mount in a flourish of gleaming gold and white.

# CHAPTER 4

'Pitch!'

Silas moved to urge Lalassu on, but the mare had already quickened her stride, devouring the short gap that existed between them and the fallen daemon. She cleared a much higher section of the hedgerow, but Silas barely noticed, keeping his seat easily. He leapt out of the saddle before the horse had come to a halt. He planted his feet in the soil, steady as though he'd alighted from a stationery carriage and not a massive horse in motion. Silas had become rather adept at riding, if he did say so himself.

'Pitch? Are you all right?'

The ankou spared no thought for the dirt, dropping to his knees alongside the crouched figure of snow-white and gilded material. Pitch was on all fours, freeing one hand to press it to his temple. Silas grabbed his shoulder, trying to see beneath summer-brown waves. '-Pitch? Answer me, can you hear me?'

'Of course I can bloody hear you. Deafness does not come with a fall.' The daemon slapped away his attentions. And Silas saw it then, the bright spoil of blood on Pitch's fingertips.

'Oh Christ.' Silas gripped a slender, twisting wrist. 'You're bleeding. Did you strike your head?'

'Stop fussing, you old maid.'

Pitch fought Silas's hold upon his wrist but without much conviction. Which only deepened Silas's concern. He knew full well the daemon could send him flying if he so desired.

'Then let me look at you.' Silas touched his fingers beneath Pitch's jaw, tilting a sharp chin upwards. 'Show me. Stop being so peevish.'

'Then stop peeving me,' Pitch snapped but did not push off Silas's hold. He moved with it, shifting onto his knees.

Silas brushed aside strands of hair that sought to conceal the damage done. The source of the blood was very clear. A cut at the daemon's right brow, a trickle of crimson that slid its way along his cheek. Silas gathered his own cuff and pressed the morning-sky blue of his coat against the alabaster of Pitch's jaw, stopping the flow of red that had already sent a few drips onto that ludicrously nonsensible white coat.

'You did strike your head.' He met the emerald stare levelled at him.

'No, I did not, damn it.' The warmth of the daemon's breath played at the underneath of Silas's chin. He was at least a head higher than Pitch, even on his knees. 'Will you stop that.'

'What?' Silas frowned.

'That.' Pitch fluttered his hand, close to Silas's face. 'This...what you are doing...with your face.'

'How badly did you hit your head? You are making no sense.'

'Gods! I didn't hit my damn head. Something hit me.' This time Pitch easily tore himself from Silas's hold. 'Leave me be. It is a scratch, nothing more. You are quite ridiculous, with all your wrinkled concern and false niceties.'

Silas sat back on his heels, taking a moment to consider a reply. The daemon's flare of temper had come quite out of the blue. Perhaps it was borne of embarrassment at leaving the saddle so soon after Silas had warned him.

'My concern is not false at all. You had a fall, and I am worried for you.'

'Then stop it, immediately.' Pitch pushed himself to his feet. He seemed steady enough but much displeased at the state of his trousers, swiping at the dirt on his knees as though he wished to punish the material. 'I can't abide your coddling. You do not need to race to my aid every time I get a splinter or chip a nail. Just because you took advantage of me once does not mean you get to place your hands all over me every time I have so much as a graze.'

Silas's eyes widened.

'You are intolerable, Mr Mercer. Do you know that?' Pitch was shouting by the end.

'Took *advantage* of you? How can you say that...I have no idea...' Silas rose back up to where he could not be made to feel so tiny, his anger rising with him. A gentle wind rustled at the few leaves that still clung to patches of the hedge. It sounded ever so like whispering. 'Fine. Come along, then. Seeing as you are quite all right, get on your horse. Let us go. I was going to suggest we stop in at the residence up ahead, but forget it. You have no need of anyone's aid...anyone at all. Bleed away all over that stupid damned coat, and see if I care.'

He was being just as peevish as the daemon, more so, but Silas didn't give a damn. Pitch's spewed vitriol had barbs. Did that blasted, insufferable fool truly believe that Silas had seen him as a target, an injured, vulnerable creature ripe for plundering? Was this why Pitch had gone out of his way to keep at arm's length since they had lain together?

It was utterly outrageous.

Silas stalked towards where Lalassu and Sanu had wandered further up along the rise of the land, towards where the squatting, imposing mansion was now more apparent. Impressive as it was with its peaks and generous spread of windows, he had no time for it.

'Lalassu, come now,' Silas said, as crossly as he'd ever spoken to the mare. 'Mr Astaroth is fine, apparently. Let us go.'

The horse's reply came with a flick of lustrous mane, like a sudden snow shower touching down. Both horses had their muzzles stuck deep into the bare curls and knots of branches of the hedgerow. From within the winter-waning foliage came a rustling, like wings shuffled by hidden sparrows. Lalassu snorted, that indignant way she had mastered, and the whispering of the breeze Silas thought he'd heard earlier was evidently clearer now. It was no breeze.

'Who is there?' Silas stepped in closer.

A squeal, the tiniest sound he'd ever heard, rang out.

'You've done it now.' The voice was akin to tin cups clinking. 'You've angered them, now we'll be eaten for sure. Why did you throw that stone?'

'To get their attention.'

'Well, you have it now.'

'He's as big as a damn bear.'

'And you made the daemon bleed, fool you are. You've got us killed for sure.'

'Shhhh.'

'I shan't.'

Silas edged in between Sanu and Lalassu, who stood with heads lowered, peering at one place in particular. 'I said who is there?'

'What are you on about, man?' Pitch called out.

'I can hear someone speaking...in the hedge...' Silas crouched down, hands planted on his knees. One of the branches to the right was shaking, hard. 'Is somebody there?'

The pebble came from nowhere, but its aim was precise. With a thunk it struck Silas right between the eyes.

'Blast!' He stumbled back, clutching at his forehead.

'Oh dear, what's the matter?' Pitch said, dry as a drained moat. 'Did a bee sting you?'

'It's too bloody cold for bees. Christ almighty.' Silas rubbed at the lump forming on his head. 'I swear something was just thrown at me.'

That held Pitch's attention. He moved as quickly as his limp would allow, shoving past Silas to edge in towards the hedge. Squeals erupted like tiny silver bells chiming.

'Get back, daemon. Get back.'

More projectiles launched from the foliage, specks of stone that peppered Pitch's chest.

'Enoch's balls, it is fucking spriggans.' Pitch lifted a hand, and his palm illuminated.

'How dare you, sir.' Outrage lifted the squeaky voice to new heights. 'We are piskie, not bloody spriggan.'

Pitch sniffed derisively. 'Whatever you are, you've caused me to stain my coat. I like my coat, and I do not like you.' He stepped closer, and fresh squeaks and puny cries rang out.

'Pitch, hang on.' Silas dared not touch him. 'What do you intend to do?'

'To burn the hedge down, what does it look like?'

It was exactly what it looked like. The daemon's palm glowed, and pinpoints of flame sneaked from the creases of his skin.

'Stop. You know you must be careful with using your flame.' Oh Christ. Silas heard it himself then. He was indeed fussing like an old maid, and it was not becoming. The daemon glared, like only he could, and his mouth opened with a no doubt vile protest. 'I'm sorry, I'm sorry. That was utterly unnecessary coddling, I see it plainly. But look about.' Silas gestured at the horses. 'They have no concerns. We are under no threat here.'

'These pissants threw rocks at me.'

'And me, but I'm not about to burn the field down because of it.'

'Because you are so very dull.'

Silas took a steadying breath. 'And you are too impetuous.'

'Undoubtedly. But that does not negate the fact that my coat is stained. These spriggans should be taught a lesson at the very least.'

'Piskie, damn you.' For such a weeny voice, it managed indignation well.

'Go on with you, Silas.' Pitch raised his hand, and the flames slithered higher. 'Were you not in the midst of leaving me anyway?'

'That is wishful thinking on your part.' Silas grabbed Pitch's arm. The flames snaked towards him, close enough that he blinked against their heat. He may have flinched, though he tried his best not too.

'Damn it, Silas.' Sea green flashed, and Pitch snatched his hand away, the flames sinking back into his skin. 'Have I not told you to keep your distance?' As though to punctuate the point, he pressed his other hand to the middle of Silas's chest, warding him back. 'Listen to me, you damned fool.'

There was that shadow again. The same one Pitch had worn in the graveyard at Mustow Green, when Silas had come too close to a daemon-'s fury. There, Pitch had collapsed in on himself, curling up like a street urchin on a winter's night, muttering at a past Silas could not see. Despite all assurances that he had not come to any harm, it had taken long minutes of coaxing to draw Pitch back into the here and now. To chase the shadows of the Hellfield away.

'You told me not to get in your way, Pitch,' Silas said gently. 'And I did not do so now. There is no harm done. And I do not believe you wish to harm these creatures either. Not truly.'

'You have no idea of the things I wish for.' Though he kept Silas back with the press of his hand, it was Pitch who leaned his weight forward, steadying himself against the ankou's chest.

'That is true enough, I suppose.' Silas placed his hands over Pitch's slender fingers. The daemon's skin was warm, and the ankou's touch seemed to surprise him, for he jumped as their skin met. 'But I dare say I am safe in assuming a permanent stain upon your coat is not amongst those wishes. We should ride on before the marks dry too well and seek out the nearest town. I'm sure there will be a laundress there to tend to your coat. We can take a meal while we wait. We shall start to lose the light before long anyway.'

With the arrival of December the days were shortening and growing ever more chilled. They would not reach their destination this day anyway. Silas knew this with the certainty that had become more prevalent as the weeks passed.

Pitch shook his head, his gaze upon Silas's chest, the ribbon of blood framing the side of his face. 'I don't think your nag will much like an earlier stop.' His fingers shifted beneath Silas's hand, but the tense hold of his jaw relaxed.

'She won't deny us a stop to eat, I'm sure. Let's go.' That was the moment when he should have released his hand, set Pitch's free so they could both move away. He did no such thing.

'You ain't going anywhere just yet,' a high, ringing voice declared. 'You'll be staying right there, thank you very much.'

A tiny figure spilled from the hedge, flitting over to where Lalassu now grazed upon the thin spread of grass. The most diminutive creature Silas had ever laid eyes upon settled on the pale horse's saddle. *His* saddle.

'Good day to you, ankou.' The tiny critter resembled a short, crooked stick, with a slash in the bark to take the place of a mouth, two glistening dewdrops for eyes, and three peach-coloured petals linked together to make up each arm and both legs. 'It's said you aren't half as fearful as you appear. And we see it now, don't we, Ped?'

'Maybe, but I'm not coming out, Tar, not with the fire daemon still about,' came the haughty reply. 'Did you not just hear him say he'll roast us?'

The creature on the saddle, Tar evidently, folded its petal arms. 'And did you not just see how well the ankou brought him to heel?'

Pitch stiffened, and Silas placed himself between the very much not-at-heel daemon and the audacious stick creature.

'Now, now. That's enough of all that.' Silas cleared his throat and took the few steps needed to stand alongside Lalassu, who grazed on without a worry. 'Would you care to explain why you assaulted us both with your pebbles?'

'To get your attention, clearly,' a much indignant Ped declared, still ensconced in the shelter of the hedge. 'You wouldn't notice an ant on the ground any more than you would the likes of us.'

'Don't mind my sibling. I'm Tar, and we are piskie, not spriggan. That was quite rude of the daemon to say, to be honest. But we are very much pleased to meet you.' Quite astonishingly the tiny specimen of bark and nature held out one of its petalled arms as though offering a hand to shake. It had neither hands nor sense. Silas stared down at the fragile material on offer, delicate as a butterfly's wing.

'Ah, well...it is very nice to meet you, Tar. I am Silas.' He touched the tip of one finger to the petal's extremity, holding his breath as he did so, fearful that even an exhale might send the creature hurtling. 'And my travel companion is Tobias.' Something awfully like a dark chuckle came from the hedge. Silas raised his brow. 'Is something the matter?'

'Travel companion, you say?' Ped the piskie scoffed, mimicking Silas in a very unbecoming way from where it hid. 'He's a portion more than that, I'd wager.'

'I beg your pardon?' Now it was Silas's turn to bristle, but the critter that was perched upon Lalassu's saddle lifted peach petals, waving them about.

'Take no notice of him. Ped and your daemon share a quick temper.'

Bloody hell, was there no escaping it? Pitch was not *his* daemon.

'Pay no mind to him and listen up. We're much glad to be seeing the likes of you down this way. There's need of a decent ankou in these parts, that is for sure, and you seem a grand fine one at that.'

The flattering was pleasing, but Silas was vexed by something else entirely. 'How do you know?'

'The dead are mighty restless down this way, It figures that –'

'No, no, not that. How do you know I am an ankou, and that Pitch is a daemon?' It was one of many small questions he had and had been forced to put to one side in the face of much larger concerns. 'How is it that you can tell us apart so readily?'

'How can you tell a chicken from a cow, you silly man?' Ped's reply from within the foliage was gruff.

'Hush, you. He's ankou. They can't see so well as us. His eyes are meant for lost souls, but all else stays as human as it was. He wasn't born a natural, and he'll never truly be one, not even in death.' The piskie somehow managed to sit down, the wooden length of its body not so stiff as it appeared, bending where hips might be. 'You can see we have no shadows...that's right, isn't it?' Silas nodded. 'I've not had a chinwag with many ankou. They tend to be in a bit of a hurry and not happy to stop and chat, what with only a year to do their mistress's bidding and all.' Mention of his acutely short life...no, *death* span, sent an unpleasant tickle beneath Silas's skin. 'But we naturals can see each other readily enough, if the both of us wish it to be so.' Silas noted the glance of dewdrop eyes sent Pitch's way. 'We can conceal ourselves too though, and quite well if you are talented enough in such things.'

'Or not so well, like your daemon friend there.' Ped, still hidden, threw in its two-pence worth. 'Colours around him are all...wrong...messed up and tangled. Daemon hues sure enough...but it's like parts of him got caught in a downpour and the shades are running thin. Smell strange too...like he stepped in something he shouldn't have.'

The boggart too had mentioned Pitch's scent.

Perhaps the tattoo did more than ease his pains and was in fact altering the daemon so as not to betray him as a deserter. Had the Berserker Prince perhaps been so powerful that his legion were marked in some way? Branded in such a fashion that he would be recognised for who he was, if drastic steps were not taken to conceal the truth?

But if that were the case, the efforts being made to conceal him seemed to be drawing a lot of attention. Completely defeating their purpose.

'Oh piss off,' Pitch returned. 'You can hardly talk about a stench. You are quite vile.'

'At least I can walk straight.' Ped levelled the cruel jibe from the safety of its leafy sanctuary. 'You don't see me wobbling about like I've got one foot in my grave already. There's something...wrong about you. More than just that leg, I'd say.'

The flames formed upon Pitch's palm, clear, distinct licks of furious orange. 'You little ugly bastard.'

'That's quite enough.' Silas was sharp. 'Both of you. Stop. There is no need for any of this.' He kept a wary eye on the daemon, who had not stepped back. His jaw was set, and his eyes flooded with anger. Just when Silas thought all was well, now he feared the piskies' shelter was in danger, again, of being razed to the ground. Pitch seemed to be spoiling for a fight. One-sided as it would be.

Silas turned his back on the pesky creature with its sharpened tongue in the hedge. He raised his hands, but he was not so foolish as to touch the daemon. 'Pitch, don't bother yourself with the damned creature. It is not worth your time.' That had Pitch's cheek twitching, though his eyes were still locked at a point beyond Silas's right side. 'Pitch...please. Look at me.' The daemon did not do so straightaway. The flames danced orange light against his face, shimmering against the wetness of blood. His gaze slid to Silas. 'It was a foolish jibe. It is talking nonsense –'

'Are you so sure about that?' The growl slunk low, stung through with a desolate note that Silas did not like.

Silas steadied himself. 'I am.' He dared a step forward. The daemon's eyes found him, pinning him into place. They were close enough that Silas felt the heat coming from the flames, fledgling as they were. It was like being in that darkened room all over again, where Silas's body had led him before his mind had a chance to think it through. At the hall he had leapt into the daemon's bed. Here, though, the move was much simpler. Silas raised his hand and cupped it beneath Pitch's upturned hand, where the flames shuddered and slunk on his palm like tiny burning ghosts.

The daemon drew in a breath. 'Silas, you idiot.'

'What? Do you trust yourself so little, you think you would harm me, here and now? You are the idiot, if that is the case.'

Pitch's eyes widened, and his plump lips wriggled between frown and smile. The flames vanished into pale skin, taking with them a daemon's painful angst. 'Gods man, you have grown bold. What has gotten into you?'

A fair question, and the answer was not clear. But he'd crashed through walls to reach Pitch once; a simple touch did not seem so bold.

'I just wanted to ensure you heard me when I told you that I do not think there is anything wrong with you at all. And it is quite a splendid thing, to have one foot in the grave.'

A foolish jest but it drew a roll of the eyes, and the hint of a smile, from the daemon.

A harrumph came from the depths of the unscathed hedge. 'Travelling companions my moss-covered pri –'

'Right! There we are, then,' the piskie on the saddle declared brightly. 'All is well. And my sibling will shut their lichen-infested lips if they know what's good for them.'

Pitch pulled his hand free quickly and turned away. Silas curled his fingers into fists, trying not to think too hard on how his skin tingled.

'Come, let's go, Sickle,' Pitch called. 'If I cannot roast us some spriggans –'

'By all the tits of Mother Jann herself,' Ped spat, 'we are piskies, you blasted great cockhead.'

'You are lucky to be alive,' was Pitch's haughty reply. 'For which you may thank the jelly-hearted ankou and his dreary words of placation. I'd never have heard the end of his dribble if I turned you into a cinder.'

Pitch stomped over to where Sanu had grazed out further into the expanse of the field.

'Please, do not leave us just yet.' Tar brushed a petalled limb at the wood beneath its dewdrop eyes, as though stroking a beard. 'We didn't stop you just to draw your ire. There is something we feel you must see.'

'*You* feel they must see.' Ped, at last, showed itself.

The minute figure shot from the embrace of the hedge like a startled wren, darting to join its kin upon Lalassu's saddle. The horse was no more interested in the second piskie than the first, her mouth brimming with snatches of green.

'Oh my,' Silas said, quiet as could be, for he'd had enough of bad tempers for today.

Ped was a creature of wood also, but where Tar's body consisted of just one stick, Ped's was a tiny branch with twigs sprouting every which way, like an oddly deformed and upright hedgehog. Their petal limbs were the bronze of autumn, and five dewdrop eyes sparkled upon their crinkled bark. All five were fixed on Silas.

'What's your problem, then?' the impudent creature harped. 'Never seen a piskie this fine, huh?'

'That's it.' Silas fought the urge to peer closer at the strange creature. He suspected he'd feel one of those twigs right in his eye if he dared. 'Very fine indeed.'

If one liked bristling things.

'I do hope that the jelly-hearted ankou might indulge us.' Tar was using its finest diplomatic skills. 'I know you fellows have places more important to be, but...well, come and see for yourselves. I dare say you will see things you do not much like.'

# CHAPTER 5

Pitch followed behind Silas, the walking cane in hand, glaring at the ankou's back. He did not have to work hard to be irritated by Silas Mercer. He creased his brow too often with damned *concern*. He was patient as a fucking saint, until Pitch pushed him to a point long past where one of those saints would have lost their mind. And that coat of his...why must it float about him in such a way? Making Silas appear as though he were impassable, strong as a mountain. A resolute wall to shelter behind, if one were inclined to seek shelter.

Which Pitch was certainly not.

It was the fussing that was killing the daemon. By Gabriel's foetid arse, Silas really must stop with the coddling. He had no idea whom he was fussing over to begin with. Pitch had once led a legion of hundreds of daemons. He was a prince and a monster who was more than capable of picking Silas apart like he were a roasted chicken on a pauper's dinner table. If he knew the truth of his guardian, Silas would not be hurrying to find the bakery in every village they passed through, asking after their prowess with a tart. He'd be running ahead screaming for everyone to run for their fucking lives.

Pitch had been a tad unkind, perhaps, in accusing Silas of taking advantage of his wretched state in that windowless room at the hall, but he'd say it again, and worse, if it meant the ankou would stop looking at him so. Gods, Silas could at least *try* to disguise his worry. It would be nice if, just for one day, he hid trace of his fear that the guardian he'd been lumbered with was about to collapse into a slobbering heap of uselessness.

Silas walked ahead, Lalassu at his side, the two piskies upon her saddle, twittering away in the ankou's ear. Pitch thought he heard them say something of an owl being in some strife, but he had no care for their conversation. There was clearly no teratism here. Lalassu's calm demeanour was sign enough. As was the fact that Silas was not blustering about madly in his pockets, searching for the bandalore which always seemed to evade him till the last.

Pitch shook his head. It was truly best for all concerned that he should have stayed in his chains, wallowing in his deserved misery at Harvington Hall, but it was plain the ankou wouldn't have lasted a day out on his own. Even after all Silas had witnessed in the Forest of Dean, here he was, toddling along into an unknown and too-quiet mansion, simply because a couple of fucking piskies had insisted that he do so to rescue some menial creature with a broken wing.

How had the dolt *survived* before they'd been partnered together?

Pitch sniffed, realising the irony of the answer. He'd survived thanks to a daemon who was desperate for some distraction from his troubles. Barely had Silas set foot back in the land of the living in London, and he'd very nearly been shepherded out of it, thanks to the attentions of several deranged harpies. The very first time Pitch had relaxed the ceaseless grip he held on himself, on his power, and had allowed the restless beast at his core to unfurl, even just a smidge, it had been to deliver Silas from where he huddled, shrieking and white with fear, in an open grave with harpies intent on tearing him limb from limb.

The relief that came with letting go had been fucking glorious, to begin with. Pitch had relished snatching at flailing wings and tearing them asunder. He'd delighted in ripping heads free and hurling them every which way, covered in the stickiness of savagery and the slickness of domination. It had been fucking glorious.

Until it wasn't.

Somewhere between the spray of torn flesh and agonised cries, Pitch had been flooded with visions that had for months left him alone in waking hours. They had arrived with a vengeance and thrown him back upon that cursed clifftop, with the Lethe river forging its molten path hundreds of feet below. The unbidden memories had cast him back to where he had stood with his gaze blurred by the lusts of the battlefield, readying to strike out at the spectacular golden glare that flew at him. Seraphiel had been screaming, his cry shattering rocks and making the sky boil.

But Pitch had not listened. Had not *wanted* to listen.

He had allowed the roar within to deafen him. He had not fought hard enough to rid himself of the bloodlust that had consumed him. Seraphiel called on him, over and over, begging him to stop, but Pitch-'s mind...Vassago's mind...had been a firestorm, churning him into a calamity of rage like he'd never known.

Those memories had locked him in their grasp, making him near-mad with horror, until the graveyard tiptoed its way back in.

And a new voice pleaded with him.

'Stop, Pitch.'

Silas. Red-faced and desperate, with a daemon's hands about his neck. Pitch had released his grasp upon the ankou at the same moment Silas's arm lifted and a sharp blow to the head had sent an enraged daemon flying.

Pitch touched his fingers to the place that had been bruised by the bandalore, as he stomped through the field, following after a pair of fucking spriggans and the oaf. Silas turned as though he knew somehow of Pitch's troublesome thoughts.

'Is everything all right?' he asked.

'Aside from being bored beyond all reason?' Pitch spoke smoothly through a thudding heart. 'Yes. I'm quite fine.'

'Are you still bleeding?'

'No.' He was. But that hardly mattered.

'If you'd prefer to wait outside, I'll understand.' Did the man ever bother to run a comb through his hair? By the Celestials, it was unruly. And long. The perfect length to grasp hold of. 'I'm sure this won't take a moment.'

'Gods man, is it your intent of late to just wander off whenever you please, so you might see me scamper after you like some witless pup?'

The less unattractive of the two piskies planted his petal over the other's mouth hole, stifling the words it was about to utter.

43

'No, that's not it at all. I was the one who agreed to listen to them. I did not expect you to have to do the same.'

There Silas went, so careful with word and deed. It was enough to make a stomach turn. And a breath shudder. But it would not do to become too reliant on the gentleness. It was not a gentle world.

'So I'm to wait with the horses like a common stable boy instead? I think not.'

Silas pressed his lips tight, and it was clear he was clenching his teeth. He turned back to Lalassu's passengers. 'Best you show us quickly, so we can be on our way.' He bent his arm; an elbow pressed to the leathers. The piskies scampered onto him, running up his arm to settle on his shoulder like two odd shrunken monkeys.

Pitch wrinkled his nose. Gods, the oaf was growing far too foolhardy for his own good. Though it was, admittedly, pleasing enough to see that Silas no longer jumped at the sound of his voice. That level of fearfulness had been hard to witness. Still, it would not serve for him to grow too brave. Pitch was not about to be set running about, delivering the ankou's grand arse from trouble every moment of the day. That would be tedious. He curled his fingers about the fox head, biting at his lip. And there was a good chance he would find himself not up to the task.

He followed the odd trio into the imposing building.

From the outside it appeared a grand construct of sandstone and gothic struts and points. A delight of eves that all arrowed their way skyward, and iron-latticed windows that hinted at grandeur within. The mansion was hugged at its back by a rich forest that had shed great swathes of its greenery for the fine honey-yellow and fiery oranges of the autumn and close winter. But Pitch spared the forest little time, for he'd had more than enough of such places. It was greatly pleasing that, so far on their travels, Lalassu had not forced them to spend a night on the ground.

Pitch scowled down at his feet as his stiff hip made the crossing of the threshold cumbersome.

Proper accommodations had also meant he was spared the indignity of being seen trying to get to his feet each morning. His hip was always the worst on waking and made him move in a way that was just as the piskie had accused him, like a fucking old prick near to dying. Pitch was appalled at the state Silas had found him in when the oaf had somehow made it to that cursed room at the hall. There had been piss on the floor, blood on the sheets, and Pitch had begged, fucking begged, to be held. It was some small recompense that Pitch could grunt and groan his way out of bed in the mornings without Silas looking on. Trying to bloody help. Trying to rescue him again.

Pitch's cane marked out his path, rapping nicely against the bare stone floor of a wide hallway. He glanced about absently, taking in the rooms he passed by. All were completely empty. The interior of the place was far from complete. There was a room where only half the timber had been laid, another where the stones were absent and dust and dirt were king. He was not alarmed, just wary, and quietly hoping that the piskies would give him some reason to set them alight. Silas strode on ahead down a corridor that grew dim and shadowy further along, where the light could not penetrate deep enough to guide them. His passengers were chattering some nonsense about glass bottles that Pitch paid little mind to. Silas glanced back. With his dark hair and the receding light behind him, he appeared to be part of the shadows themselves.

'They say it is not much further now, in the kitchens towards the back. There are some cages and large pots with cooking that smells awful, they say.'

Pitch waved a careless hand. 'If we get pelted with rocks again by a waiting horde of piskies, I shall beat you soundly. All the while telling you that I told you so.'

The ankou tried hard not to smile, but as was so often the case with things that Pitch said, Silas could not seem to help himself. His smile had a fetching way of buckling his cheeks and narrowing his eyes. 'Fair enough, then. Are you all right to keep on?'

Pitch glared. 'Ask me again, and see if you survive it.'

Silas opened his mouth to say something, another of his endless apologies no doubt.

'Just get on,' Pitch snapped.

For fuck's sake, all he had was a slight limp, he wasn't missing a damn limb. He was quite capable of making his way. Pitch returned to glaring at Silas's back as they continued on.

'Up ahead, to the left, and then the first door on your right. But set us down if you will,' the piskie that was but a mere stick said. 'We don't want to see it again. It's not good for the eyes.'

The corridor was far narrower here, as they tended to be when made for the house staff, and it turned sharply off to the left.

'If you are sending us into a trap or even just a room where I might wind up with spiderwebs in my hair, I'll not be pleased,' Pitch said, allowing his voice to dip low and menacing. He was rewarded with the sight of dewdrop eyes quivering, as though about to slide from their wooden posts entirely. Piskies were the ants of the supernatural world, bothersome but not particularly dangerous, and they did enjoy a good prank. It was highly likely he and Silas would end up in a room bulging with toads, or snakes, or something of the kind. Actually, it could be quite fun to watch Silas flap about if that were the case.

'There might be spiderwebs,' said Ped, a piskie that was most like Pitch himself, that was to say surly and snide. 'We can't be held to task for that. It's stood empty a long while. Which I suppose is why it's so convenient now for these bastards and their foul work.'

'I thought you said there was no one here just now.' Silas touched his fingers to the wide, sloping ledge of the nearest window, and the piskies toddled along his arm and onto the stone. 'Should we be prepared for an encounter?'

'No, no. They don't like the day much. They come here at night to do their mixing and meddling.'

'Night? Not dhampir, are they?' Pitch studied his fingernails, which needed some tending, soiled black beneath from the reins and too much time on the road. 'They are utterly tiresome.'

'Dhampir?' Silas asked.

'An unfriendly bunch, not overly fond of the daylight, and have rather the appetite for blood. Amusing to play with though. I was once given the most astounding blow job by a vampire with buck teeth. I tell you I had puncture marks in the most remarkable places. There's a scar still I think, right on the very tip.' He tugged at his waistband. 'Would you like to see it?'

'No!' The cry came from the piskies. Silas seemed to have lost his tongue.

'Why are daemons so quick to shed their clothes?' huffed the prickly piskie.

'Because they are pretty, and they know it, especially this one,' Tar, the more congenial of the miniscule twigs declared.

'He's also a liar,' Silas said, somewhat roughly. He did not look Pitch in the eye. 'I will assume there are no such thing as dhampir, as there is certainly no scar.'

If Pitch had been sipping a wine, he would have choked on it then and there. He sputtered his laugh as it was. 'Mr Mercer, I am positively blushing.'

It was hardly the right moment to tell him that dhampir were certainly the inspiration for the vampires that filled the pages of many a penny dreadful and far more real than their fictional counterparts.

'You are not blushing at all.' Silas couldn't seem to decide if he wished to smile or scowl, so he shifted between the two with an amusing result. It was the ankou who was blushing, quite profusely, at his own bawdiness, and it was decidedly adorable. Great gods, the oaf was one of the most confounding men Pitch had met. And he'd met a lot of men in his long lifetime.

'Argh, enough.' Ped raised its petals and pressed them beneath the crux of a couple of its many branches, as though covering its ears. 'I don't want to hear any more about daemon pricks. Get on with it, so I can get back to my business.'

Silas was either in shock at his own forthrightness, or he was terrified Pitch might actually strip off his clothes here in the hallway. Whatever the reason, the ankou didn't move. Pitch, tiring of the foray into the looming mansion, took the opportunity to move ahead. The confines of the corridor made it impossible not to brush against the ankou as he went. Gods, Silas was well built, there was no denying it. Hard as the stone this place was made of. With a clearing of his throat, Pitch carried on. He heard Silas follow, the man's presence at his back like a walking shield of royal blue.

The spread of Pitch's coat, a white as stark as new-fallen snow, pushed the air ahead of him, rustling the debris along the way. A silvery-grey feather lifted and wove through the air, joined by a piece of paper, yellow and crinkled, which danced along merrily. Pitch followed the piskie's direction, wrinkling his nose at the dust that lifted. He found the first door on the right. It was opened just a crack. Pitch leaned close so he might see through.

A forlorn sound like the howl of a dog came from within the room, though somehow smaller, more rounded. Pitch's breath snagged all at once as he felt a pinch in his chest.

'Is it safe, do you think?' Silas whispered from behind.

Without answering, Pitch pushed at the door. It swung wide easily.

A burst of fluttering feathers greeted them. The movement came from many places around the room. A variety of birds fluttered, all imprisoned in cages, none of which were adequate for their size. There had to have been a dozen cages or more, he suspected. The soulful noise pushed through the general squawk and titter of the frantic animals, and he spied its source. A magnificent tawny owl who had to hunch its head down low so as not to strike the cage which hemmed it in.

'What the fuck is being done here?' Pitch stepped into the room, and Silas came with him. The ankou inhaled, and a curse left his lips.

It was the household kitchen, as the piskies had said, and differed from all the other rooms they'd seen in that it actually held furniture, utensils, and clear signs of occupation. Too much so. It was ramshackle and overcrowded. Three thick oak tables took up much of the space, their surfaces cluttered with an array of glass bottles of all shapes and sizes, some coloured and quite elaborate, others as simple as a milk jug. The bench which ran along beneath two narrow windows was packed with vegetation of some kind. Pitch recognised rosemary, its scent hinting on the air. In the farthest corner, there was a pile of rags and hessian sacks, flattened at its centre as though it were attempting to mimic a nest and taunt the trapped birds. Pitch sucked a breath through his teeth, eyes narrowed with the ebb of an irritation that caught him off-guard. This room, with its feathered prisoners, raised his ire. But since when did he give a damn about finches?

Silas moved past a cage that was barely as big as his broad hand. It held four tiny finches. They crashed into one another in their attempts to flee from the giant passing them by, but there was nowhere for them to go. Feathers fluttered from between the bars, torn free by their agitation.

'Careful, Mercer,' Pitch snapped. He pressed a hand to his belly, where a wave of nausea plagued him. Actually, he felt quite unwell. His pulse had quickened, and he was unreasonably warm.

'What is going on here?' Silas reached the fireplace, where a rough and blackened pot hung from a tripod over a pile of ashes in the hearth. He leaned down, lifting the lid, and immediately recoiled. 'Good lord, that's horrendous.'

Pitch was assaulted by the odour a moment later. And it was, indeed, worse than a basilisk's bile, and he'd not thought anything could be worse than that. He dry-wretched as the birds held captive in the room went wild with discontent. They squawked and slammed themselves against their bars. All but the tawny owl, whose burnt-sugar eyes stayed fixed on Pitch. He felt the animal's stare bore into him as he threw up a little of his lunch. The creature's wings sagged against its sides, as though it were too exhausted, or too resigned, to lift them.

Silas slammed down the lid as quickly as he'd lifted it, pressing his sleeve against his face.

'That must have gone rotten.' His words were muffled by his coat's heavy fabric. 'What an abysmal place. It's making my skin crawl to be here.' He shivered for good measure.

Pitch felt no chill though; for him it was the opposite. He was heated through, and there was slickness beneath his shirt. The bloody owl would not stop looking at him, and his pulse would not stop thudding. He swallowed down something sour and vile.

'I don't like it here.' The words slipped from him. He'd not intended to set them free.

Silas peered at him through the glass bottle he held. There were sprigs of herbs inside and other things Pitch could not make out. 'Nor do I. What do you suppose all this is for?'

'I don't know,' Pitch muttered. Fuck, what was wrong with him? It was as though part of his insides were shifting about. He walked over to the table nearest to the pile of rags, and the restlessness within knocked more frantically at the back of his throat. Pitch stared down at what lay on the table, his fingers so tight about the fox-head handle of his cane that they ached.

Lying on top of a piece of fabric stained with dark dry blood was the hacked and ruined remains of another tawny owl. Its head was still intact, but its beak had been torn free, along with both its clawed feet, leaving only the stumps of its legs behind. Ants played in the congealing, blackening blood. The bird's rounded chest had been split wide open, its gullet emptied of its gizzards. One wing was spread wide and nailed to the table, while the other had been cut clean off and stripped of its feathers. Those had been collected in a red clay bowl and drizzled with a viscous liquid that reminded Pitch of the sap from a Socotra dragon tree, thick as honey but red as the skriker's eye. Pitch pressed a curled fist to his mouth, certain his roiling stomach was about to eject its contents once more. Sweat ran in tickling beads down the valley of his chest. The scene was abhorrent, certainly, but his overwhelming reaction surprised him. He'd seen far greater cruelty. Seen more dismembered bodies than he could count. But still, his palms itched to draw on the flame and scorch the room to ash. It *pained* him to see this incarceration of stupid, inconsequential birds.

'Let them out,' he hissed. 'Let them all out. Now.' He pushed away from the table and went at once to the owl, who watched his every limping step. 'Silas? Did you hear me?'

The ankou was slow to answer. He was studying the bottles, one in each hand, peering closely at the contents.

'These are bird bones,' he mumbled. 'Herbs too...and...other things I'd like not to think on too much.'

'Did you not hear me?' Pitch's growl came from deep down where the wild things lay. 'I said we must let them out, now.'

He let go of the cane, and it slid from where he'd leaned it against the table absently, falling to the ground with a clatter. The ankou's head jerked up, and that infernal worrisome frown returned.

'Of course, yes, at once.' He hurried about like a frantic valet abiding his master's wishes. A pity Pitch's actual valet, Forneus, was not so impressive a sight as he moved about. He winced. Thoughts of his Arcadian life could not have come at a more inopportune time. Pitch was unsettled enough as it was.

A flurry of freedom worked around him. Birds, crazy with release, darted about the room as Silas set them free, chirping and chittering like they were punch-drunk. Pitch fingered the multitude of latches around the upper dome of the owl's cage. There was the faintest tremble in his fingers. He bit his tongue with frustration, annoyed at how unsteady this room made him, and how cumbersome.

'Fuck.' The latches needed finesse, the slip of a fingernail beneath a catch, and a twist of the wrist to disengage the lock. The movement required a delicacy of which he seemed wholly incapable. The scattering of wings, the mad press of flight on the air, erupted. Silas had released the finches, and they were panicked in their dash to freedom, flitting crazily about the room. But the sight of them, freed of their confines, loosened the tightness at Pitch's chest, placated the strange stirring in his gut. He turned back to the owl's cage. The creature still fixed wide unblinking eyes upon him. Pitch returned his attention to the first of many latches, but his haste made him clumsy. 'Shit, damn it.' His fingernail caught, the metal stabbing into the soft flesh hidden beneath.

'Here, steady now.' Silas had moved to his side quietly and laid his solid, steady hands over Pitch's own. 'Let me help you. We shall manage one each.'

The ankou's grasp was sure and gentle, and Pitch did not resist as Silas eased his hand away from the latch. The ankou stood so close that Pitch felt as though he too were wrapped up in the sturdy warmth of the royal-blue coat Silas wore so well. Again there came the sense of sturdiness at his back, of having a wall between him and whatever it was that haunted him about this room. Pitch's maddened pulse did one last leap and caught its rhythm. Silas still had his hand on him, and Pitch found he couldn't gather the impetus to pull away. Gods, the ankou was a meaty lump really, his fingers much too thick, their skin coarse as though he knew hard work too well, but the weight of his hands was like a reassuring armour, keeping the panic at bay.

Panic. That was it, Pitch thought. That was the sense that rattled him. Entirely odd and strange.

'We will have him free in a moment.'

Silas's voice rumbled against him, his breath shifting the hairs on Pitch's head. And as the daemon did not trust his voice not to waver, he simply nodded. Silas remained where he was, far too close, considering they needed to work around the rim of the cage to loosen all the latches.

They should have taken a side each, but they stepped together, Silas never moving too far from him, shifting their place around the table as they worked. They could have turned the cage itself, but that would only disturb the owl more, so instead Pitch moved with Silas, and the ankou did not question their odd dance. The creature's head swivelled on its neck to follow them, watching each latch come undone.

The last came free with a snap, and the dome of the cage could be lifted away. Somehow they managed to finish with an arm each entwined, Pitch's hands still beneath Silas's broad palm.

Had the room always been this pristinely quiet? All the birds were settled, perched upon the ledges and shitting on the room that had tried to swallow them whole.

'There, it is done.' Silas's whisper joined the stillness. 'We should open a window perhaps?'

Of course they should. It should have been done before any of the cages had been opened. What point an escape if the birds knocked themselves stupid against the glass? But neither Pitch nor the owl moved an inch. The finches had lined up upon a windowsill, side by side, the freedom of the outdoors behind them through a dirty pane of glass, but they showed no desperation to reach it. Pitch stood there, feeling something of a fool, for he did not move either. He stood with his arm still linked through Silas's, his other hand upon the cage lid. It was the perfect moment for the ankou to accuse him of acting strangely.

But Silas waited, patient and even. He'd even managed to smooth out his lines of concern.

Pitch winced as the shuddering at his core bothered him.

He'd always named it battle lust, the surge that gave a Berserker prince his name. The sense of wishing to crawl out of one's own skin. But its presence here, where there was no Watcher army in sight, no Nephilim silhouetted in grand scale upon a blazing horizon, was a concern. Pitch had felt it stir at Goodrich Castle, it had niggled in Highgate Cemetery too, but there had been reason for it. What reason was there here, with his audience of finches and sparrows and disembowelled owls?

Silas waited. Every creature in the room waited, on him. It was not unknown to Pitch, this pause. His legion had moved on his commands; they had lived and died by their prince's word; they could not pick their arses without his say so. But the legion had not waited like this. Those under his command had never been patient.

And after a time, a few still moments, Silas traced his thumb ever so softly along the side of Pitch's hand. The daemon's lips parted, and the very last of the trembling left him. He looked up at the ankou and found himself watched. A small, questioning smile was upon Silas's lips. His hair hung forward as he tilted his head, and Pitch was struck with a longing to run his hands through tangled strands and disappear into their darkness.

'Are you going to open a window?' Pitch said roughly.

'Yes. Of course.'

But Silas kept his place. He did not move away. Just kept on with that bloody rub of his thumb over Pitch's skin. Why would he not go away, damn it? Pitch stamped down the little voice that said *he* could pull away if he so desired to.

Of *course* he desired to.

It would do no good to strike up a need for the ankou's careful hands and stupid, pretty whispers. Plenty of others had brought Pitch pleasure before the oaf blundered along with his ludicrous gentleness. Plenty of others were willing to fuck him senseless and not caress him and soothe him out of pity, as Silas had done. Pitch had seen the horror in the ankou's eyes when Silas discovered him in that baleful room. He'd seen how aghast he was at discovering the daemon was made up of deep cracks and ugly fractures. The irony was that Silas, with all his righteousness, *would* have approved of the torment if he knew the truth. Pitch had done, and would continue to do, terrible things. The stirring within assured him of that. But the ankou did not know. And instead Silas had tried his pathetic best to patch a daemon back together again.

He was still trying.

Idiot. Absolute fool.

Pitch thrust himself at Silas before he could think better of it. Their lips collided with unexpected force, as though the man had leaned in when Pitch thought he would jerk away. The ankou moved swiftly, but not to end things. His free hand wrapped around the back of Pitch's head, his fingers sliding into a wind-ridden tangle of strands. A muscle twinged in Pitch's neck, and he wobbled as he went onto tiptoes to meet Silas's greater height. For some insensible reason Pitch did not let go of the owl's cage, and with their arms entangled, their embrace now had him twisting in a way that tugged at his troubled hip most uncomfortably.

Gods, could they not once kiss without needing the skills of a circus contortionist?

They had lain at odd angles in the hall too, but Pitch had been no more inclined to pull away there than he was here. He didn't wish to risk the ankou coming to his senses and abandoning him altogether. He needed what Silas could give him.

Pitch needed to be steady again.

He pressed his good side into Silas's solid warmth. The ankou sighed into his mouth. Their tongues were coy against one another, teasing, tentative, their lips slick with each other's wetness. Pitch released the cage top, and it fell to the table with a resolute thud. The owl still did not move, at least so far as he knew. He could not be certain, buried as he was in the heat of Silas's mouth. Now with the cage dispatched, he could edge himself into a better position, swivelling around and finding his way into the folds of Silas's coat. His slid his arms beneath, embracing the rock-solid form, feeling every rise and fall of taut muscle. Silas's torso was not all that was rigid about him. The stiffness between his legs mimicked Pitch's own.

They did not break from one another as Pitch aligned himself; Silas would not allow it. He slipped his freed hand down to the small of Pitch-'s back. His touch was light, of course it bloody was, and a subtle moan escaped Pitch despite his best intentions. Silas caught him by surprise just then. The formidable man took a firmer hold of Pitch's body, the hand at the back of his head sliding down to wrap about his shoulders, and in one smooth movement, he lifted the daemon from his feet and sat him upon the table. Pitch spread his legs, biting the inside of his cheek at the tug of unwilling muscle in his hip. Silas slid into the space created without hesitation. The table was not so high that they were face to face, and Silas still had to stoop to keep in touch. The ankou's hands framed Pitch's face, and he grew more urgent in his working of the daemon's mouth. His tongue moved deeper, searching, for what, Pitch couldn't say, but he'd not protest. He opened wider, taking the ankou in, relishing the lustful heat that was rising up to consume all else, eating away at the writhing force the daemon held at bay inside.

They made wet sounds against one another, silly whimpers and coarse suckings that rang too loud in the quiet. Pitch had thought, after their dalliance at the hall, that the roar of pleasure he'd felt might have been borne of starvation. He'd been so fucking hungry when the ankou found him. Perhaps it was desperation that had made the man's fingers such a delight and brought on such utter blissful release. Yet here they were again, Silas dragging him back to the surface, helping him remember how to breathe again. And it was every bit as sweet.

Every bit as dangerous.

Need was a weakness he could not afford.

But Pitch would worry on that later when Silas's prick was not stabbing at his belly, and the ankou wasn't leaning into him as though he meant to lie Pitch on the table and fuck him there and then.

Pitch groaned and wrapped his legs about Silas's thighs, his boots catching in the blue coat. They were tangled up yet again. Silas stopped the kiss, opening a hair's breadth between them, breathing hard into the dampness they'd created. His eyes were shut, but his lids fluttered.

His hand slid to the front of Pitch's trousers, brushing at a button there. Gods. He *was* going to fuck him on this table. Here in this dire and bloodied room.

The move was so unexpected, and welcomed, that the daemon nearly bucked his arse off the table. Of course, the ever-noble dolt took this as sign he had overstepped.

'I'm sorry.'

Silas, the ridiculous man, attempted to shift away, his sudden boldness extinguished. Pitch clenched his legs harder about the ankou's thighs, cutting off any chance of withdrawal. His incubus blood churned with desire, and its flow rang so loud that his ears buzzed and his vision was patched with white. He ran his hand down to where Silas's fingers hovered over the buttons. Daemon and ankou both panted like Azazel himself had chased them here. But there was no angel's halo to flee. The only race they ran was one that would free Pitch of his trousers and allow Silas to do with him whatever it was he craved.

Pitch caught movement in the corner of his eye, but he had no need to turn from Silas to work out its source. The owl had lifted itself up to the rim of its now-open cage and ruffled its feathers as it settled there, puffing itself larger. The bastard was still watching him, he could feel it. Wide eyes framed by a circular ruff of brown-and-white feathers pinned Pitch to the table, every bit as much as Silas was.

But Pitch was not averse to an audience, and he had far better things to do right now than see off a voyeur.

He worked his fingers around the first button, irritated by the knowledge that there were so many more to follow. Fall-front trousers were wonderful but at times an intolerable barrier. Silas's eyes opened and he pulled back just enough that they could look at one another without eyes crossing. His gaze traced every inch of Pitch's face as though he'd not seen it a hundred times by now, and that look he gave the daemon...fucking gods, why must the ankou regard him that way? There was nothing to be admired here. Very little to be wondrous of. And yet, here Silas was, peering at him with a softness that came freely, with no help of an enchantment.

The ankou lay his fingers against the back of Pitch's hand. He moved as Pitch moved, as though the daemon's hand were a glass on a Ouija board and a message was being spelt out. Pitch thought the message very clear. Silas wanted the trousers undone every bit as much as he did. The idea of it made Pitch's balls clench and his pulse dance madly.

Gods almighty.

He struggled to recall when last he'd nearly spilled his load simply while seeking to undress. There was a strange peace to the moment, with Silas present yet unobtrusive. Not tearing and seeking and demanding of him, as so many others were when their lusts took hold. Pitch nipped at the ankou's lip, feeling more unsettled than before, but in a much more pleasant way. His prick was so swollen that it was a wonder the buttons didn't pop of their own accord. At last, one side of the fall-front was undone, and he caught at Silas's fingers, so he could lead the ankou deeper in under the loosened material. Silas didn't protest. He said nothing at all save for a sharp intake of breath, and he went willingly where Pitch led.

The daemon rarely bothered with drawers. There was nothing between him and his trousers. Silas found him quickly, and the heat of the ankou's skin met his hardened flesh. Silas gasped and pressed his forehead against Pitch's brow, whispering something that was not clear.

His fingers curled about Pitch's cock, finding their rightful place. The daemon shuddered, and he tilted his head, searching for the ankou's lips once more. Silas was there to meet him, while down low his hand worked up and down Pitch's length, finding a pace that suited them. The ankou groaned. Pitch arched into his hold.

'Enough, you two!' The squeaky shout had them both leaping like thieves caught in a bank vault. 'Stop it. He's coming!'

And the fragile moment exploded in a flurry of feathers and curses.

# CHAPTER 6

The owl shot into the air in a great bluster of wings, sending dried herbs and whatever else it was upon the tables swirling about. Silas leapt away, springing like a startled deer, his foot catching on Pitch's discarded cane. The rounded piece of wood slid beneath his boot, the metal head screeching out a grind against the floorboards, and he was going down before he could help himself. Of course he landed against a scattering of empty birdcages. He could not have made a more dramatic, or calamitous, landing if he had tried.

'Bloody hell!' he cried as wire pinched at his butt cheek.

One of the piskies landed upon his shoulder, shouting into his ear as he hauled himself back to his feet. 'What the blazes were you two doing?'

'I'd have thought that fairly obvious,' Pitch hissed, grasping at his opened trousers and glaring at the creature so fiercely that Silas wondered if he were reconsidering his threat to turn the tiny thing to cinders. The timing of the piskie's arrival had been horrendous, that much was certainly true. Good god, he'd let himself get terribly carried away, going to appalling lengths to try to wipe that mournful look from Pitch's face. But the daemon had looked so awfully lost for a moment. The room had disturbed him in a way that Silas could not fathom.

He adjusted his coat so that there was at least no visible evidence of how carried away he still was.

Silas cleared his throat and ventured to regather his dignity. 'Pitch has lost a button on his trousers...and I was just seeing if perhaps...I could...repair the damage.' Silas began strongly, but by the end of his delivery, he was every bit as pathetic as his words.

Christ almighty. Maybe whoever was approaching could just stab him and be done with it. If he were dead again, at least he'd not have a chance to open his mouth and utterly humiliate himself.

The piskie jumped from his shoulder and balanced itself upon the rim of the owl's former cage. It was Ped, the creature with an array of twigs jutting from its main stalk, the one with five dewdrops for eyes. And all five were fixed upon Silas now, glistening, he suspected, with utter astonishment.

'Oh by the gods...Sickle...that was just...awful,' Pitch said, trying very hard not to lose himself to laughter as he fixed himself back into his trousers.

Silas nodded, his cheeks aflame. 'I'll not deny it.'

'Well you can play seamstress, if that's what you are calling it, another time,' clucked Tar, the less irritating of the two tiny creatures. It was over at one of the windows, where the finches danced about, quite mad in their efforts to tap through the glass now. 'Will one of you help me with this bloody window instead of gaping? These critters are going to make their beaks bleed for want of avoiding him.'

Just the very mention of *his* approach caused all the birds to bluster anew. The owl shuddered through every feather on its body, fluffing itself up larger, while around it the finches and doves startled into panicked, senseless flight.

'By Enoch's arse,' Pitch said, sliding off the table. 'Who is bloody coming?'

Silas noted the slight wobble that came when the daemon's feet touched the ground. He scanned about for the cane and hurried to fetch it from where it had slid beneath another table. Silas did not expect a thanks as he handed it to Pitch. He knew the daemon resented its existence at all. It was a permanent reminder that he was not so infallible as he liked to pretend. Sure enough, Pitch snatched it from him with a scowl. But coming with that, very softly, was a terse thank-you.

'Don't know the fellow's name. Not like we were going to stop him to ask,' sniffed Ped from where it perched on the rim of the owl's cage. 'But he's here to do his witch bottles early today – usually comes at night. We've just seen him riding up the road. Won't be long before he's on us.'

'Witch bottles?' Pitch said, for once asking the questions and saving Silas from having to show his ignorance yet again.

'Window...please...rather urgent,' Tar squeaked, dancing upon the metal lever that would release the window. A pointless dance, as the creature was stomping on it rather than lifting it as required.

Silas hurried to the window, sending all but the owl into a fresh tizzy of darting, startled flight. That creature sat with all its marvellous feathers bunched, its wide eyes fixed on Pitch, as they had been for some time. Even while Silas had him bared and gasping on the table.

'Careful,' Pitch called. 'You'll have them knocking themselves out if you storm about like that.'

'I'm not storming anywhere,' Silas grumbled.

At least the daemon's curt and unnecessary remonstration helped to subdue the rigid beast still demanding attention in Silas's trousers.

The piskie scuttled onto his arm, and Silas took hold of the latch and lifted it. He needed to give it a decent nudge to have the hinges loose enough, but at last the window swung wide open and the finches took off into the pale light of an early winter's midday. Silas stepped back, so that the array of remaining birds might find their escape. They chittered and squawked their way past him in a blur of dull colour. Pitch had made his way to a window further along and opened it too. The doves wasted no time in taking advantage of the freedom offered. They didn't even wait for Pitch to step away, moving beneath his outstretched arm, not in the least concerned at his presence. In fact, he fancied that he saw one of the birds pause and coo at the daemon before continuing on.

Silas tilted his head to speak to the piskie, keeping his voice low. '- They are using these birds...for these witch bottles...' The piskie nodded, though it had not been framed as a question, for the result was plain to see. Far too many of the bottles lying about contained the tiny, fragile bones of birds. 'For what purpose?' Silas swallowed. 'Is he a witch, this man who approaches?'

Were they about to face another bearer of maleficium so soon? Silas was not sure he was ready.

Piskies it seemed, had wonderful hearing. 'A witch?' Ped retorted from across the room. 'Of course he isn't. Can't tell you the last time we saw a real one of those. No, these bottles are meant to keep witches *away*. Like a bloody owl's kidney could do such a thing. Fools, and the damage they do when they are frightened, huh? The humans have gone and got themselves all spooked about things of late, and these animals are suffering for it. They can blame you two for some of it.'

'Excuse me?' Silas frowned.

'The Forest of Dean ain't that terrible far from here. And the purebreds were fearful of that place long before it seemed to die overnight and then grow back to rights just a few days later. The humans do love their stories, and you can bet there are all sorts about at the moment, getting larger and more terrifying by the day. Specially with *her* riding the roads ragged further to the west.'

Silas set his attention on the piskie across the way. 'Her?'

'The lady in the carriage with its marking of bones.'

'Lady Howard?' Pitch said. 'That's your monster, is it not, Sickle?'

'It is.' Silas had filled the daemon in on the morning ride, though really he'd seemed barely interested.

The piskie leapt off Silas's arm to find a place on the counter. 'Told you, didn't I, Ped? That's why the ankou are here. She needs more than one to deal with her.'

Ped grumbled something that might have been a reply, clambering its way down the bars of the cage.

'I'm not an ankou.' Pitch sounded deeply offended, as though he were refuting having the pox. Pouting did scandalous things to his Cupid's bow lips. It was monumentally distracting.

Silas shook himself, focusing on less pretty things.

'Weren't talking about you, and your funny whiff,' Ped declared tartly. 'There's another ankou down this way.'

'Really?' Silas forgot all else at once. 'You have seen another ankou recently?'

'Oh gods, settle yourself down, Sickle. You know you aren't the only one,' Pitch said, trying to shepherd the owl towards the open window. The grand bird was having none of it, simply puffing its chest further and spreading its wings an inch as though readying to launch an attack.

'Yes, thank you, Pitch, I do know that.' Silas was crisp. 'But I've not yet met one, as *you* know.'

'Gods damn you, bird.' The daemon raised his cane in frustration, bandying it about near the owl, who did nothing at all to shift from the bench. 'Go on with you, you stupid, fucking, moronic, lice-infested, rat-eating fiend. Do you not want your freedom now it's offered?'

He was shouting. Which accounted for how someone could open a door and suddenly step into the room with no one the wiser.

'What the darn hells is all this about, then?' a voice fairly roared, bouncing against the walls and causing the owl to bob its head low, sinking into the ruffle of feathers at its throat. The piskies squealed and fled, moving as quickly as the feathers that swirled with the touch of the incoming breeze.

Silas spun about to face the back of the room. The new arrival had thrown open the door they had paid scant attention too, a door that led in directly from the outdoors. Silas had barely even noticed it before now. So much for paying attention to his surrounds. The man stood glaring at them from the doorway as though not sure it was wise to enter. So, he was not an imbecile, then. He was dressed in the clothes of a fieldworker, his smock a yellowed material blotched with stains. He was gaunt, his cheeks hollow, his head nearly bald with wisps of dark hair clinging in patches. A wide-brimmed hat was being mangled in his clenched hands.

'Well?' he snapped. 'What are you two doing poking about in my business?'

Downtrodden as he may appear, he was not without some balls, barely flinching as he took in Silas's weighty form.

'Poking about in your *business*?' Pitch spoke the way a snake slithered.

Silas eyed him warily, feeling the rise of temper as surely as rain upon the air.

'That's what I said, you bloody fop. Get out of here.'

Pitch swung the cane before him like a pendulum and leaned against the bench. 'And if I do not? What do you intend, sir?' He ground up that last word, setting it afire with disdain.

The man had the good sense to shift uneasily on his feet, but he did not withdraw, much to Silas's disappointment. 'This is all my property in here. You've got no rights to it.' He pulled something from beneath his smock. A substantial knife that looked best suited for a butcher trying to dismember a cow carcass. Bloody hell, the man was either drunk or out of his mind to pick a fight here. 'Go back to your soirees, lads, and all your frills and laces. Leave me to make my coin. You've got plenty of your own by the looks of you.'

Pitch pointed the cane towards the owl, who still perched on the bench within a hop of freedom, the window wide open. Its attention had at last swivelled from Pitch and was now burrowing into the skittish man in the doorway. 'This bird is your property, you say?'

'I caught it fair.' His dull brown eyes darted about the kitchen. '- Fuck...where are all the rest, then? You bastards, they were mine. I caught them –'

'And you stuffed them into cages barely fit for one, with nary a drop of water to be seen.' Pitch pushed away from the bench and walked towards the man. He did not seem to limp at all. 'The owl could barely turn its head without hitting the bars, and you see, that irritates me. As I'm not fond of cages myself.' He stopped just a few feet from where the foolish man still stood, holding up his knife with shaking hands. 'Shall we speak of how you butchered its mate right in front of it? What a sissy I must be indeed, to find that so vulgar.'

'Pretty clear what you are.' The man spat, actually spat, towards Pitch. 'A fucking Mary. I'd wager all the coin I've taken for these bottles on it.'

Silas drew himself up and made his quiet way towards the door. He saw too clearly where this would head if he did not step in. Something about the confinement of these animals had set Pitch off from the moment they had arrived. It must have done, to have him cling to Silas the way he had. His kisses had been as desirous as Silas recalled – they still tingled on his lips even now – but the urgency with which Pitch had bestowed them was worrisome. Silas had shoved his concerns aside in favour of losing himself entirely in the press of the daemon's mouth, but the concerns resurfaced now. He was not fond of cages, Pitch had said. Silas wondered what foul treatment had been dealt him to make him so rattled and ill at the sight of so many here. Had the birds sensed it? For they had been uncommonly relaxed around him.

Silas stopped alongside Pitch and touched his fingers low on the daemon's back, where he hoped no pain lingered. Pitch stiffened at his touch, but only for a heartbeat. He relaxed into Silas as the ankou leaned to speak with him.

'You are right in all you say, but he's a hungry man, and desperate,' Silas murmured, close to the daemon's ear. 'We should move on to where we are best needed.' His next move was madly presumptive and likely would get him punched, but Silas drifted his hand up and down the sway of Pitch's lower back. A gentle rub, and only a couple of times, hoping he might break the hawklike fix the daemon had on the man. As his fingers brushed the silk coat and the svelte body beneath, he felt the relaxing of muscle and saw the slump of shoulders, though Pitch kept his eyes fixed ahead.

Silas withdrew his hand but remained close. 'What are these bottles for?' he demanded of the man.

Dull brown eyes darted between Pitch and Silas. 'They are wards for witchcraft, of course. Potions and the like that will keep a man or woman safe from evil doings.' The man's grin was leery. 'You probably don't hear anything about it in your palaces and mansions.' He brandished a hand at Pitch. 'Where you get gold sewn into your coats like it were nothing.'

'It's not gold, you imbecile.' Pitch sighed, all trace of the serpent gone from his voice.

The man glowered. 'Don't matter rightly what it is. Ain't anything I can afford I'm sure.'

'Very true.'

Silas attempted to re-divert the conversation. 'How long have you plied this trade?'

'Long as people been scared of their own shadows. Night-time is awful dark out these ways. People are willing to part with their coin if they think it will keep them safe from harm.'

'And do they?' Silas asked, nodding at an empty bottle on the floor. 'Keep them safe, I mean?' He wasn't sure what he'd do with the answer. He didn't know the slightest thing about magick. But something told him, it was not present here.

The man barked a laugh. 'The witch bottles? Bloody doubt it. It's a load of dead birds and twigs, but they believe it enough, and that's all I need. Especially down Tavistock way, where there is all sorts of fear-mongering goin' on about haunted roads, a carriage and four that's trying to run folks off the damned road. Now how's about you take your little mandrake there and piss off, while I deal with the only bloody thing you left for me to salvage.' He raised his thick blade and jabbed it toward the owl. The man took a step into the room.

Silas felt Pitch shift beside him, and he decided against waiting to see what the daemon intended. Silas slipped a hand into his pocket, found the bandalore, and pulled it free as the string wound about his finger. He flicked his wrist and sent the hard wooden discs flashing through the air. They curved, rounding to meet the man's temple. The whack was audible, and he dropped like the proverbial sack of potatoes.

It had all happened so quickly that Pitch had not taken a single step nor raised a hand. But now he looked up, his lips parted in what Silas was very pleased to note was astonishment.

'Well, aren't you just a surprise today?'

'What? Weren't you as bored as I with his prattle?' Silas said, shoulders pulled back and chest puffed out a tad more than was really required. 'I think we've seen enough here. It's high time we continued on.'

He was rewarded with the slow rise of a smile. 'Indeed.'

Silas gestured for Pitch to take the lead and head outside, but the daemon shook his head, setting off the gold flecks in his hair. 'You first, brave soldier. And if you'd rather your gobby friend there isn't roasted, I suggest you drag him a little further from the house.'

'Pardon?' Silas blinked. 'What do you intend to do?' But it was a mute question, for he knew full well. Even if Pitch's hand had not begun to gleam. 'Really, is that –'

'By Lucifer's sack, if you ask me if it is wise, I'll burn that silly mop of hair off your head. I shall not fall apart because I set a room on fire.' Much quieter, he said, 'I promise you.'

Damn it. Silas had not intended to remind Pitch of his dark time. 'Of course you won't.'

He glanced over Pitch's shoulder to where the remains of the tawny owl upon the chopping board still stretched, blood thick and blotted, eyes whitening with death. Its mate sat upon the window ledge as though finally considering the benefits of a departure, its head swivelled around so it could keep its eyes upon them, though its claws were faced towards the freedom beyond the cracked and dirty panes. Silas agreed it would not be so bad for this place to be wiped clean.

'I'll wait for you outside...with my friend.' He gave the daemon a crooked smile. 'Oh wait, should we warn the piskies?'

'We aren't half-stupid, you know.'

The voice came from the owl. For a bizarre moment Silas thought the creature had spoken. Then he spotted the twig poking from the feathery layers on the owl's back. Ped looked as though it were cloaked in a marvellous tawny coat.

'Go on then, lads, and our thanks to you.' Tar was visible for just a moment as the owl gave its wings a tentative stretch, preparing to leave the awful room behind. 'Carry on now to where they need you most.'

And with that, the owl flew out and into the clouded remains of the day. Silas gathered up the man he'd knocked unconscious and draped him over one shoulder. He was appallingly light, and the ankou decided he'd leave some portions of the cheese and bread Bess had stocked them with. Some coin as well. Silas left Pitch alone with the empty cages and shattered corpse of the owl.

He was well clear of the mansion when the first crack of flame reached him. He sat upon Lalassu for some time, the horse steady beneath, watching the blaze drive its way through the property, leaping from windows like the tentacles of a vibrant sea creature, setting the air aglow with a stunning merger of autumn reds and oranges. When the daemon at last returned to take up his reins, his lips set in a grim line, he said not a word, and Silas asked nothing of him.

# CHAPTER 7

They rode hard and fast for the remainder of the day and into some of the evening. Night was falling earlier and earlier. Silas supposed there were not so many weeks until Christmas and the new year – the date he had evidently met his demise. He wondered what such a festive time might look like for the Order of the Golden Dawn and whether he'd feel differently when the clock struck midnight of the new year. Pitch said little as they travelled, but he was in a light enough mood that Silas decided he'd not worry. If the daemon was of a mind to keep his thoughts to himself, so be it. Pitch was certainly keen to push Sanu to her limits though, and they broke into a gallop at every opportunity, overtaking coaches and some startled riders with such drama that there would be small chance they would go unnoticed. Silas cautioned Pitch when he once again hungered for a breakneck ride and the road was little more than a smear of shadow.

'We should try to be clandestine, don't you think?'

The daemon had scoffed at the idea. 'What? With you so dark and brooding and the size of two men combined, and me...well, me so delightfully noticeable, you think they are not already talking of us through half of England, perhaps Wales too? Those ghosts in Castle Combe knew of our exploits already. The spriggans stopped us precisely because they knew who we were.'

'Piskies,' Silas said absently, noting the derisive grunt that came from the daemon. 'But they are naturals...' The term the Order used to refer to the supernatural creatures of the world. 'I was thinking more of the humans we have encountered.' For it is they who are the ones who might wield maleficium. Azazel's magick infected the purebreds alone.

'But where is the fun in avoiding them?' Pitch's grin turned wicked. 'Do you have any idea how many fine gentleman and ladies you can bed simply by alluding to the fact you are from the Order? I suppose you do not. You prefer homeless wanderers who dress in rags.'

Silas slid Pitch a sideways glance. He wondered if the daemon was fishing for a denial. Was he perhaps trying to lure the ankou into saying what it was he truly desired? Had it not been obvious enough in the mansion? 'I've asked you not to speak of Charlie with such derision,' Silas said curtly.

He thought of the lad often, not least of all about their parting words. Charlie had grinned churlishly when he'd spoken of Tyvain's plans to keep him busy, and Silas had embarrassed himself with a gasp. The lad assured him there was nothing untoward involved. The soothsayer preferred very short and preferably hairy men, Charlie declared. He was quite safe, and the task was far more exciting than a tryst. When Silas had pushed him on the details, Charlie had twisted his fingers at his lips as though sealing them and grinned through his silence.

'You are such a bore sometimes,' Pitch said now.

'Just sometimes?' Silas raised his eyebrows. 'My, my, I've improved from *always* a bore. Well done me.' Perhaps his promotion came from having his hands down Pitch's fall-fronts. He could imagine so.

The daemon's laughter was as sharp as the temperature. 'You fool.'

'But not *always* a boring fool at least,' Silas returned.

Pitch glanced away but not quickly enough that Silas did not see his lips rise in a smile. 'Certainly not.'

He was coming to know the tiny twitches of the daemon's mood well. The sudden lurches of bad temper were not quite so frequent as they'd been when first they'd met. Silas was actually quite proud of his growing talent for averting the daemon's sullenness, recognising its approach and casting out a flippant remark that would shift the man from his inner weightiness.

That's what Silas had come to see it as: a weight, a heaviness, that was always present. Usually the daemon did well in disallowing it to consume him. There were many, many ghosts that haunted Tobias Astaroth, Silas was sure. Pitch was not cantankerous simply for the pleasure of it.

Though the daemon insisted he was not in any great pain, Silas knew full well he was in *some* pain, all the time. It made enduring the ever-changing currents of his mood far easier to know that it was suffering and not just a bad constitution that barbed his tongue.

The hour was late by the time they arrived at the small town of Crewkerne. They took rooms at The Crooked Swan, a plain but comfortable coaching inn that had fine stables and a decent ale, according to a local upon the street. The Swan had no trouble accommodating them.

'You've caught us on a quiet night,' declared the brisk landlady. 'Plenty of rooms.'

Silas caught himself before he released a disappointed sigh. On the ride he'd thought far too little about the teratism he was to face and far too much of how it had felt to take Pitch in hand, to feel that firm length beneath his fingers and the whispers of need at his ear.

'Thank you kindly.' He nodded, taking his key. 'Can we still get a meal at this late hour?'

'Of course. I'll make sure of it, gentlemen.' The woman was efficient, like her spick-and-span hairstyle, and friendly, but Silas noted that she was having a little difficulty at looking either of them in the eye.

'She called you a gentleman, Silas.' Pitch was snide. 'If only she knew.'

The remark elicited far more laughter from the landlady than it deserved, and she was most definitely holding on to the key too long after she'd set it on Pitch's open palm. But the daemon seemed in no mood for flirtations and took his leave without a backwards glance.

After a quick splash of cold water to the face and having shrugged off his damp and dust-ridden coat, setting it in front of the paltry fire in his room, Silas joined Pitch for a late meal downstairs. The daemon arrived without his cane but seemed to manage well enough. The use of his flame at the abandoned mansion had left him none the worse for wear, which was pleasing. He was without his coat too, having handed it over to the laundress so she might tend to the smattering of blood upon the collar. His wound had long since healed. They took a table by the fire, chasing away the last of the chill that had sunk into their bones on the ride. Pitch rolled up his shirtsleeves, as was his preference, and adjusted his vest as he settled. The corset was cinched tight again, having been loosened to ride. The narrowness of his waist had never been more evident. Fetching as it was, it would not serve him well to lose any weight. He hovered too closely to gaunt as it was.

'What are you frowning about now?' Pitch slid his slender form into the chair like he was warm wax.

Silas gathered himself. 'Nothing at all...I'm just hoping there is enough of the stew left for both of us. I'm famished.'

'Hmm,' Pitch replied. 'A pint will do me. I'm not terribly hungry.'

Silas looked up from where he leaned forward to warm his hands by the fire. Green eyes fixed on him, the reflection of the flames weaving golds and oranges through the emerald. It was plain he thought Silas about to coddle. Pitch dared him to say more at his peril.

'Fair enough,' Silas said and returned to warming his hands.

He shrugged against the glances being sent their way. He'd noted the looks they garnered as they took their horses to the stables and as they made their way to their rooms upstairs. But at least at this late hour the inn was not overly busy. Only three of the other numerous tables were occupied.

A serving girl came to take their order for two pints and one serving of stew.

'You've got the last of it, sir. It will be a nice big serving for you.' A plump and open-faced girl with wide hips and a perfectly lovely smile, if one ignored the missing tooth upon the bottom row, her manner was relaxed and welcoming, and Silas eyed Pitch nervously, quite ready to step in if the daemon chose to play.

Pitch batted his lashes and curved his lips into a beguiling smile, the one that shone from him as though he had not a care in the world. The look that made it very difficult to take one's eyes from him. But that was all he did. There were no lascivious comments, no laying of hands upon the girl's arm and stroking her. The cheerful server did not stutter or stumble; she was not made clumsy by a sudden urge to hand herself over fully to a hungry incubus. She was unenchanted. And much as it should have relieved Silas that she was spared, he felt a tendril of the concern Pitch despised so much.

The server took her leave, moving off quickly to tend to their order. Silas watched her a moment, and as he turned back to the table, he caught the eye of another patron upon him. He nodded, and the man, a bearded fellow with round glasses and near to bald but for a few strands of auburn hair upon his crown, nodded back at him with a small smile.

'Where are you gentlemen headed, then?' the balding man called.

The other pair at his table stopped their conversation to wait on an answer. Men of the office, Silas would wager, with all three sporting spectacles, one with a moustache that was well-waxed and spectacular in its looping shape, the other with trimmed hair along the jawline. They had full pints and glowing cheeks that suggested this was far from their first glass. Scraped plates with a tear of bread and a potato remaining sat pushed to one side, ready for clearing away.

Silas hesitated, uncertain if he should disclose their direction.

'Wherever our horses take us,' Pitch declared, stretching his legs to point his boots towards the fire. The leather creaked as he moved.

'Men of leisure, then.' The moustached one laughed, not unkindly. 'I envy you. The freedom of the open road.'

Pitch huffed a short laugh. 'Yes. Such freedom. So very enviable.'

The man's congenial smile faltered as he caught the roughness in the reply.

'We've had a long day of it,' Silas said quickly. 'And you, gentlemen? Are you from these parts or passing through?'

'Passing through,' said the bearded chap, whose gaze liked to find its way to Pitch. 'Will be glad to get back to London, I must say, after the trip we've had this past day. Those bloody back roads were a nightmare. Told you we shouldn't have listened to a word of that gossip and should have taken the main route as we planned. We've been down Exeter way, doing some stocktaking for our employer, but I can't get back to my bed in Hyde Park quick enough, I tell you. The bedbugs were atrocious in that last place. Don't stay at the Duke of York Inn if you are headed that way.'

The near-bald man nodded and rubbed at his elbow like he were polishing a billiard ball. 'Make sure you stay on the main roads, would be my advice. Strange things seem to happen on those back roads.'

That caught Silas's attention, but Pitch beat him to a reply.

'Gods, I miss London.' He sighed. 'And I miss my wardrobe.'

'Yes, I imagine you would,' Mr Beard declared, with rather a lot of vigour. 'You would cut a fine figure upon the dance floor, my dear chap. A very fine figure indeed. I'm not sure I've seen such a pretty fellow in all my days.'

His companions choked on their ales. The chap who had first addressed Silas laughed unsteadily. 'Easy on there, Harold.' He glanced over at Pitch. 'Ignore him, will you? He's had too much tonight I'm afraid, doesn't know what he's on about.' He eyed the room with evident nervousness, checking if his friend had been heard. Luck was with them, for at the closest table, at least a half-dozen paces away, no one paused in their robust conversation about a game of rugby to pay them any mind.

Silas looked to Pitch. He had cocked his head to regard the men. 'What's wrong in him saying I am pretty? It is true, after all. And if you'd like to share my company in London, I'd be happy to oblige you, sir, in any manner you'd prefer.'

More ale was choked upon. The moustached man would need to order another soon. 'Right, well, that's very kind. Harold, ah...enjoys a dance and a good party, don't you, Harold? How about we get you back to your room now? No more ale for you this night. You're liable to get yourself in trouble.'

Foolishly, it had taken Silas a moment to realise why the conversation felt so leaden and curled with tension. But such flirtations were a dangerous pastime in a world that held no tolerance for the desire of one man for another. Silas pressed his fingertips to the tabletop. He must have dabbled in such dangerous pursuits himself once, for there was no denying where his preferences lay. But Pitch, with no fear of the rules and regulations of humankind, flaunted his charms, stirring the poor man up. He ran his tongue along pillowy lips, turning poor Harold into a veritable jelly who shook off the attempts of his friends to get him on his feet.

'What's the problem?' he slurred. 'I won't touch him...I mean, I'll try not to touch him...I'll just look...honest...'

'I swear to god he's going to get himself arrested before we make it back,' Mr Near-Bald hissed to Mr Moustache, who was grim with worry.

'Pitch, leave the man be, for god's sake,' Silas pleaded. 'You put him at great risk.'

'I didn't start it. He did.'

'Good lord, are you a child suddenly?' Silas growled.

The daemon considered that, one eyebrow lifted. 'If we had such things as childhood where I come from, then I'd be considered a child, I'm sure. Four hundred years is barely life spent living.'

'Four hundred years?' Silas gaped, stifling his words to a whisper. 'You are that old, truly?'

Pitch narrowed gleaming eyes of fire-struck jade. 'How rude of you to say so in such a tone. I'm terribly insulted.'

'I doubt that very much.'

'You have me there.'

'Can we please just eat our meal without causing a fuss?'

'If we must.'

Thankfully, or less so depending on how things went, the serving girl returned with two ales balanced on a tray in one hand and a deep bowl of steaming stew in another. She set them all down upon the small rounded table, while behind her the three gentlemen continued to attempt to take their leave. Harold was being supported by Mr Moustache and led firmly from the room.

'Good night, sweet one,' he called out, waving his arm about in what was presumably a goodbye aimed at Pitch.

'Good night, Mr London,' Pitch returned. 'Sweet dreams to you.'

Silas shook his head but was too distracted by the arrival of his supper to admonish the daemon. The man who had initiated the conversation paused by their table. He waited until the waitress had set down her wares, wished them a good meal, and walked away before he spoke again.

'I do hope,' he began, with a clear trace of nerves, 'that you can excuse Harold. He's rather drunk...and doesn't know what he's on about.'

Pitch crossed his legs. 'I'm sure he doesn't.'

Silas waved off the gentleman's apology with more forthrightness, keeping one eye on the stew, which brimmed with thick chunks of meat and smelled like heaven. 'There is nothing to excuse, I assure you.' He was about to bid the man good night when he recalled something said earlier. 'But tell me, your friend spoke of taking the back roads because of some gossip you'd heard. What was that, I wonder?'

'Well, I'm sure it's all just the nonsense that comes when the days get shorter and nights longer.' The gentleman clasped his hands behind his back, making his rounded belly more so. 'Some are fearing to travel on the main road between Tavistock and Okehampton. There's a castle ruin there at Okehampton, and it's always had its tales...I'm not one for such fanciful things –'

'Silly you,' Pitch said over the rim of his glass.

'Pardon?'

'Never mind him,' Silas said. 'Do go on.'

'Right, well, it's said that the road to the castle is being haunted...quite thoroughly. A phantom coach scaring the living daylights out of travellers who are foolish enough to be out in the small hours. Seems there's been sightings for a long time before this, but things have changed of late. Depending on who you speak to and how much wine they've had, it's either a mad witch in a coach of bone running them off the road or a highwayman with a skull's head demanding their silver. Sometimes it's just a single horseman carrying his own head. All the legends seem to blur into one when people are frightened.' He laughed, but it was brisk and short-lived. He polished his elbow once again. 'But it is safe to say I'd not recommend being on any of those roads at night. We had a terribly rough go of it. Our carriage broke a spoke when my companion, Mr Stone, persuaded us to keep to the back roads. He'd listened to far too many of the stories about ghosts spooking horses and had become terrified we'd never make it back in one piece unless we stayed well away from that castle. We were jolted about so badly I thought I'd broken my arm at first.' He shuddered, touching at his elbow. 'I think I would have preferred to be chased by a ghost.'

'How dreadful,' Silas said. 'Is there truth in any of the stories, do you think?'

Mr Near-Bald shrugged. 'Perhaps? Seems something is bothering a lot of horses in those parts, no denying that. Just before we left Exeter, we heard tell of a wagon rolling about a mile out of Tavistock. Killed the driver and his passenger. I've heard it said they were on a straight stretch of good road on a clear night. Their horses panicked. At what, who can say? But it cost that fellow his life. Terrible affair. Goodness, I'm keeping you from your hot meal with my morbid tales. I best be getting on, then. Good evening to you, gentlemen.'

Only one gentleman replied. 'Evening,' Silas said.

Pitch was too busy stealing Silas's spoon. He dipped it into the stew, stealing a laden portion before the ankou could utter a protest.

'What?' he said through the mouthful. 'It smells delicious. Gods, it's not half-bad.'

'I'll take your word for it, shall I?' Silas glowered. 'I'll have the server bring another.' He was grumbling, but really he was pleased to see Pitch with an appetite.

'She said it was the last bowl, remember. You don't mind sharing with me, do you?'

Silas didn't answer, taking up his ale instead while his stomach growled.

'So, it sounds like your teratism is causing quite the fuss and bother,' Pitch said after another mouthful. He handed the spoon back to Silas, who took it from him with less elegance than he'd intended. Christ, he really was famished. He scooped up a generous serving and tried not to go cross-eyed with delight when the rich, lumpy gravy touched his tongue.

'It would seem so.' Silas chewed slowly, savouring the blend of herbs and the delight of a decently cooked carrot. 'There's no talk of witchcraft at least. Did you know of its origins...Azazel teaching magick to humankind, I mean?'

Pitch sipped his ale, a fleck of froth sticking to his lip. Silas gripped the spoon, squashing the urge to wipe it away. 'Something of it, I suppose. I didn't pay all that talk much mind. It was long ago and not my concern. When I visited this world, it was for pleasure and not for witch hunting, I assure you. That's the Order's bother, not mine.'

'So you've been coming here for four hundred years?' It was too astounding to contemplate.

Pitch snorted. 'Bloody hell, no. I didn't have permission for a long while, though I asked for it long enough. But Lucifer was not to be reckoned with. My place was in Arcadia, it was made plain, and I'd not yet developed a taste for defying their rules.'

Silas wondered if he'd ever get used to hearing Lucifer's name bandied about so easily. 'I thought the Dominion prince was your master?'

'What?' Pitch's gaze fled down to the table. 'Yes, yes of course.' He flicked his hands, warding off the question. 'He was my master, but requests to leave Arcadia had to be approved by Lucifer. They were rare in being granted. He's never been overly fond of this place.'

'Why not?'

'Who can say?' Pitch used Silas's distraction to swipe the spoon from his hand once more. 'He always carried on as though my taste for humanity, their dangly bits and sweet holes, was abhorrent, but it's usually those who protest too much who have something to hide.'

Silas leaned across the table. 'So Lucifer has walked the Earth?'

'He'd never walk it. A carriage is far more his style. The grandest he could find. He's a pompous arsehole that way, does like to swan about. All three of the kings of daemonkind are guilty of vainglory. Asmodeus and Belial do love to preen like peacocks, but dear old Lucifer, well, he outshines them both.'

Slumping back in his chair, Silas took a deep gulp of his ale. It was more bitter than he liked, but its dulling touch was most welcome when it came to talk of daemon kings. 'Lucifer...you know him well, then?'

The spoon stilled halfway to Pitch's mouth. 'More than I would like, and yet barely at all.' He licked at his lips, a frown creasing his brow.

'Is everything all right?' It would be terrible timing if the daemon were to lose his tongue just when his appetite had returned. Not to mention how foul it would make him. 'Are you having trouble speaking?'

That seemed to bring Pitch back from wherever it was he'd drifted to. 'No. I am not. As is so often the case with you, I find myself able to ramble on. But let's talk of more interesting things, shall we?' He offered Silas the spoon, and their fingers brushed at the exchange. Pitch tensed, pulling away first. 'You told me that you'd share the sordid details of your tryst with Charlie.'

Scowling, Silas shook his head. 'I did no such thing. And will *do* no such thing.'

Pitch's grin twisted. 'Very well, shall we speak about *our* trysts, then? For now they are plural, after you manhandled me onto that table. Gracious, you were so very needy then.'

The cruel version of the daemon had made a sudden appearance.

'And you were so very needy before that,' Silas spluttered. 'But I do not mock you for it, nor did it even cross my mind to do so. I am fully aware that you put no weight upon such frivolous things. You satisfy your carnal appetites with no more regard than you show this bloody stew. But there is no need to be a cruel bastard about it. I'd just as soon have ridden out on my own if I'd known so little had changed.' Silas snapped his mouth closed, not sure where that fiery tirade had just come from, but blast it felt good to release it. Even if the part about riding alone was untrue.

The daemon went very still, lashes lowering. Perhaps Silas had been too harsh, but he could not find it in himself to offer an apology. Pitch *was* being cruel. He wasn't blind, he must *surely* know that it had taken some doing for Silas to offer himself and that his shows of concern for the daemon's well-being were not just a simpering act meant to irritate.

Pitch may like to pretend he felt nothing at all, for anybody in particular, but Silas could not live his new life that way. He had awoken to emptiness, a slate cleared of any memory of substance. He had woken alone, without friend or foe. Now he knew he had the latter but he needed much more of the former, and, god help him, he'd thought he might just find it with Pitch.

'I have told Satine on countless occasions that you are better off riding alone.' Pitch was dangerous with anger. 'But in this as well as so many other matters, my opinion counts for nothing. Fear not though, Mr Mercer, I shan't again bother you with my appalling *neediness*. Your services will not be required again, you'll be pleased to know.' It was as though for every inch they drew closer, Pitch used his barbed tongue to leap a mile away.

'I did not ever call it appalling, nor a bother.' He wanted to grab the daemon by the collar. *Your services will not be required again.* Christ, Pitch was a prick when he so desired.

'You did call *me* a bastard though.' The daemon was haughty.

'Because you certainly know how to act like one. You are quite the thespian.'

'There is no acting involved.'

'I am not entirely the fool you take me for.'

Pitch caressed his glass, eyes still downturned. The silence between them stretched until it was unbearable. The clack of billiard balls rang out from an adjoining room, and the players laughed among themselves.

Clearing his throat, Pitch was first to breach the quiet. 'It *was* appalling...what you saw. It seems that I am making a habit of being pathetic in front of you. And I will tell you that it does not sit well with me.' He stumbled there, taking a moment to compose himself. 'You should not have seen me as you did, so reduced by my...my weaknesses...at Harvington Hall, nor should I have been so insipid today, with the birds. I have not always been so reprehensibly inadequate...' He paused. 'That is not true actually. I've been rather a mess for some time. But I regret very much that you have seen it so openly.'

Silas curled his fists so he would not reach across the table there and then and take Pitch's hand. The daemon's unexpected confession had laid him bare, and he looked so very miserable for it.

'Pitch, the only thing that appals me is that you see yourself so wretchedly.' Silas swallowed. 'You were not pathetic to my eyes, not in the least. I would never think such a thing of a man who has saved my life now on several occasions.' And made his pulse shudder and race on so many others. 'And inadequate?' He gave a short crack of laughter. 'Christ, if we are talking of inadequacies and weaknesses, then I should be waltzing about with a sign stuck to my back, warning everyone to stay clear, for I am the most inadequately suited person for this job there ever was.' He was encouraged on by the twitch of Pitch's lips. 'I'm blithering my way along, in case you have not noticed. Why I was chosen...' He shook his head. 'The gods must have been drunk. It's a wonder Lalassu hasn't trampled me back to death and demanded a new rider.'

Pitch's laughter sprang from him, rich and high and delightful. 'You idiot.'

'My point exactly.' Christ, would it be so terrible to just reach across the table and take his hand? The only other occupied table held a couple who were far too busy gazing into one another's eyes to notice any others who might wish to do the same. 'Shall we both just agree that we have seen each other at our worst and that it matters not a whit?'

He slid his hand forward, making a breathless decision to be bold, and touched the daemon's pale hand. Pitch's gaze flicked from the table and up to Silas. He was infuriatingly unreadable. And he took far too long to say anything.

Pitch leaned back, putting a definable distance between them. 'I think I may be more agreeable to that if we were more evenly matched in terrible displays.' He re-crossed his legs, picking at a thread on his trousers. 'Charlie said you are awful at billiards.'

Silas clasped his hand about his ale glass, rejection warming his cheeks. 'Awful seems harsh.'

'Come, along. The table is free now, a game before you retire to your bed and I to mine?'

In that single casual line, the evening's end was made very clear. And Silas could not decide between being hugely insulted, mildly relieved, or utterly confused. So he held on to a little of each of the three. 'If that is what you would like.'

'I do think it would be best for us,' he said, though rather flatly, as though he weren't too sure he thought that at all.

Bloody hell. What were they actually speaking about here? Silas was willing to bet it was not billiards. And if he were to take Pitch's point plainly, then he'd found the answer to his question. Silas *had* been a convenient means to an end. Twice now.

'It probably is best,' Silas said, withdrawing his outstretched hand. 'You're quite right. Shall we play?'

They remained at the billiard table until long after the last patron had left. The landlady stepped in at around two in the morning, asking them to make sure the fire was out when they retired before heading off to her room. They kept to their opposite sides of the table and never came within a foot of one another throughout the various games that were played, and lost by Silas of course. They talked, just talked, and it was oddly pleasant. Pitch regaled him with tales of London parties and dances, of places he thought Silas should visit when next able, like Hampton Court Palace and Gretna Green.

'I don't think I'm much of a dancer, I'm afraid,' Silas said at one point.

'A lesson or two will set you right, I'm certain. I'm rather a fine dancer myself. Perhaps I could...' Pitch bit down on whatever else he intended to say and worried at his lip while Silas made a woeful attempt to line up his shot with unsteady hands. 'Never mind all that. Come on, take your shot. I'll grow a grey hair waiting for you.'

They spoke of everything, but nothing about the Order's business and teratisms and Blight and rotten magick, and not a mention was made of heated, fumbling kisses. Neither was in any great hurry to retire. The fire had burned itself out by the time they headed to their rooms. Beyond the windowpanes, the greyness of approaching morning smeared the horizon. Silas's cheeks ached a little from smiling, but his head was clear, their last drink long since passed. Silas reached his room first, with Pitch's further down the hall. He could not be certain but he thought perhaps the daemon was about to say something. Right at that moment, one of the sleeping gentlemen must have risen to use the chamber pot, for there was a thump from across the hall and the sound of bare feet padding. Pitch turned away, continuing to his room. His limp was more pronounced, but he was no less a fine sight for it. He disappeared into his room without a backward glance.

# CHAPTER 8

A fter rising late, they set off rather bleary-eyed towards the city of Exeter. Several hours' ride, under a bleak and grey December sky, took them to the outskirts of the city. Lalassu guided them south around that busy place, avoiding the bustle entirely. Pitch was much displeased. But then, he'd been so since the laundress had returned his coat that morning with the bloodstain a faint patch of pink still upon his collar.

'Gods, when once we might reach a place that would be mildly interesting, your nag disappoints me once again. If I never live to see another village, it will be too soon.'

If he was four hundred years old and considered young in Arcadia, then Pitch had a long while to go avoiding villages.

'Do daemons celebrate birthdays?' Silas asked him along the way.

'Fuck, no. Do ankou celebrate death days?' had come the reply.

'Seeing as we have but a year to do our work, I very much doubt it.' Silas had grown sullen for a while after that, reminded not only that he knew so little, but that what he *did* know was not pleasing. One year and he'd be done with this life, moved on to wherever it was he was sending all these souls himself.

'Well then,' Pitch had declared. 'I don't see why you can't be the first. Jane would go mad with delight at arranging a party for you. That elemental is uncommonly fond of a soiree. She'd put on quite the farewell for you, once all is said and done and your mistress is ready to pop you back in your grave. That gives us until, what? Summer of next year?' It hardly seemed possible that it had been barely three months since Silas had taken Mr Ahari's hand and been pulled from his grave. 'That's not so soon. Don't look so glum, Sickle. You may well be happy to see the end of this place by that time anyway.'

'I suppose so.' Silas had forced a smile.

They passed quite a few carriages and four, some travellers on foot, and a growler or two shepherding people between Exeter and Plymouth, a port town which lay further southwest. According to Pitch it did not bear visiting.

'The stench of fish is appalling,' he declared.

'It seems you have seen much in your year here, since you came into the Lady Satine's employ,' Silas said.

'And by "employ" you mean "servitude," of course,' Pitch snorted. '- But I've actually hardly travelled at all this time...my last trip to Plymouth was ten years ago at least. It came long before all this nonsense about doing my duty for the Order. There was a time when I had a choice as to whether I could stay or go.'

'Can everyone in Arcadia visit here so readily?'

'No, certainly not. And those that can, those in the elite ranks of White Mountain, are not quick to show a taste for a visit, I assure you.' He tutted. 'They'd never deign to admit they had a taste for a place so common. Arcadia is nothing without its snobbery. To come here is considered akin to a gentleman visiting the East End and its houses of ill-repute. The dignified and noble may be *able* to visit, but that is not to say they would ever admit to such a thing. I suppose your world has that in common with mine. The more respectable you appear, the more likely it is you have sordid and dirty secrets to hide.' He studied his reins more closely than they seemed to deserve.

After a glance to ensure they were still alone on the road, Silas urged Lalassu closer to Sanu and her rider. 'So, if only the elite can come here, was it your rank in the prince's legion that allowed your visits?'

Pitch jerked as though bitten by a bee. 'My rank...in the prince's legion?'

Silas nodded. Sybilla had cautioned him not to speak about any of this, but he found he could not keep his promise. He wished Pitch to know that he knew his truth, that he knew he was a deserter and did not judge him for it. Perhaps that would help the daemon from judging himself so harshly. 'I likely should not say anything...but I want you to know that your secret is very safe with me, and it makes no difference what choice you made.'

'My secret? My choice?' Pitch regarded him with something far too close to anger.

Silas righted himself in the saddle, wondering if he should pretend this conversation had never begun. 'Sybilla told me something of your past. I kept badgering her, and I suppose in the end she grew tired of my questions.' He ran his tongue over his bottom lip, realising too late that Lalassu could hear him and his words would be relayed straight back to the Lady Satine. He might have just gotten Sybilla into a great deal of trouble. But so be it. He didn't understand why knowing the truth was so frowned upon anyway. 'I was worried for you...don't sigh like that...you were terribly unwell and I...' Was frightened that he had lost the daemon and was alone again. But there was no way he could be that painfully forthright. 'I just wanted an explanation, so Sybilla gave me one.' He lowered his voice. 'I know you were a part of the Berserker Prince's legion, I know that you ran from it after the Seraph was killed...it must have been truly awful to have your own commander betray you so.'

Pitch returned his heated gaze to the road ahead. 'You cannot imagine.' His fingers gripped at the cantle like the claws of the owl they had rescued. 'So, I am a deserter of rank from the mad prince's legion.'

Was he asking? Silas cast him a sideways glance. It sounded more like Pitch was announcing it to himself, learning something new. 'That is what Sybilla told me, well most of it, not the rank part perhaps, that is just my summation. But perhaps she was not honest –'

'No, no. It is quite right. Very honest.'

'I mentioned what the boggart had said and how it had upset you so –'

'Fucking boggart,' he muttered.

'But it means nothing to me.'

'The boggart? I should hope not. Should have drowned the wretched thing.'

'No...the desertion,' Silas whispered.

'You are quite ridiculous you know, whispering like that. Who is near us to hear, aside from these nags, and they know full well what a loathsome thing I am.'

Well, that had not gone as Silas planned. He'd intended to show solidarity and indifference to Pitch's wrongdoings. Instead he seemed to have plunged the daemon into another of his low moods.

'You may be incredibly vile at times,' he said carefully, 'but I would not say loathsome.'

Pitch stared ahead, green eyes narrowed, not a twitch to indicate if he noted Silas's attempt at humour.

They plodded on for a while, both lost in their thoughts, until Silas could handle it no longer and changed the tack of the ill-fated conversation entirely.

'Have you been to Scotland by any chance in your travels?'

That did not seem to be the question Pitch was expecting, for he eyed Silas with some bemusement. 'Are you hoping for recommendations on places to stay?'

'No.' Silas shrugged. 'I had the strangest feeling when I saw a painting of Edinburgh Castle that I might have visited it once before...and the lake I saw in my...' What did one call such a thing? It had not been a dream, for he'd not been sleeping. 'Well, the vision that came to me. I thought I might see such a sight in the Lake District as we rode through, but the landscape is not quite the same as what I recall. I just...I just don't think that was the place. So I wondered if perhaps it was a loch I saw.'

'Right, so you are an authority on terrain after a day or two spent riding through it? That talent should serve us well.'

Silas scowled. He might as well keep that expression on his face permanently. 'That is really not helpful.'

'I don't see how I can be helpful based on your vague sense of having been to Edinburgh. I mean really, what does it tell you anyway? At best that you liked to join a queue? Or perhaps had a taste for rowboats and haggis? None of those seem very useful. Maybe the lake you saw was actually a loch. Wonderful. There are only a few hundred of those in Scotland. I'm sure it will be no trouble at all to narrow down your residence...if that's even what it was. Maybe what you recall was simply a sojourn north for a holiday, and you had a tryst with that woman in lavender that went terribly awry.' He gave a theatrical shudder. 'Oh Silas, you sly dog you. I wonder if you died with your prick hanging out?'

'Christ, Pitch, enough. Must you always devolve a conversation so?'

'When you have that woeful look upon your face,' he said, 'yes, I must.' Pitch made an adjustment to the corset at his hips. How he could enjoy riding with such a bone cage wrapped about him, Silas did not know.

'Woeful?'

'Sickle, my dear, I know it must be trying to recall nothing at all of your past, but be ever so careful about what you wish for. I know many a man who'd very much enjoy the empty spaces you have in your head. A past is not always a precious thing that should be held on to.'

Silas watched the daemon, who studied the road ahead with far more fixation than was required. The road ran straight for as far as the eye could see, with the windswept landscape low and sparse. 'I suppose you may be right.'

'There is no supposing about it.' There was nothing betrayed by his expression to suggest that Pitch was thinking of himself when he spoke, but Silas had no doubt of it. 'If you are very desperate to learn some more, then I am quite happy to help you next time you are in the bathtub.'

Now there was an image indeed: a steam-filled room and Pitch working a cloth along his back. For perhaps the first time, Silas did not recoil from the idea of being waist deep in water.

'Did you not say that you think drowning to be what killed you?' Pitch continued. 'I could hold you under and see what memories we can startle from you.'

Silas shuddered, all pleasantness gone. 'No thank you. I don't wish to know that badly.' A lie, of course, and he was sure Pitch knew it. The daemon continued to watch him even after Silas had turned away. His cheek twinged, right at the spot Pitch had scorched him as he sought to run the skriker out of the cemetery. The evidence of the mark itself was long gone. It had begun to heal even as they had sat together afterwards in comfortable silence, stuffing themselves with delights from the Mustow Green baker. But he felt it every now and then, as though the burn lingered beneath the skin. The image of Pitch, faced filled with the horror of what he'd done, lingered too.

'Silas?'

'Hmm? Yes?'

'Still lost in the lochs of Scotland are we, pining over a long-lost love?'

'No. I was just...' He searched for a roundabout in the conversation. The mention of lost loves, oddly, brought him to Edward Charters. Actually Silas thought too often on the moment he'd witnessed at The Moon Inn between Pitch and the lieutenant. He recalled their conversation as clearly as every touch and thrust of their coupling. *Does he still haunt you?* Pitch had asked Charters. *You and he both,* was the reply. At the baron's ball it was the lieutenant himself who had spoken to Silas about a creature of exquisite beauty and perfection, a radiance that blinded his mind's eye, and now Silas wondered on that radiance anew. 'I was thinking about the lieutenant, actually, and what he said to me about believing himself going mad because –'

Pitch sat up straight in the saddle. 'Because he'd come to know exquisite pleasure at my hands? It does tend to happen. He was simply overwhelmed by my glorious self, I assure you. It is no small thing to lie with a daemon, and perhaps I overdid it with him, for he was so talented with that lovely mouth of his.' Pitch suddenly brought Sanu to a halt, jumping off and drawing the reins over his mount's head, tossing them haphazardly over a low shrub at the side of the road. 'Do you need to relieve yourself, Silas? You seem rather full in the cheeks.'

And with that he limped his way into the light smattering of trees that spread out from the road. 'There will be no stopping again for some time,' Pitch called. 'I suggest you take advantage now, or I shall not be held responsible for you wetting your trousers.'

Silas stared down at his hand upon Lalassu's neck, and the penny dropped. 'Very well.'

He dismounted, leaving the pale horse's reins looped over his saddle. It was not as if she would canter off and leave him, but she *would* have the capacity to relay their conversation to Lady Satine. Silas followed after Pitch, who, despite not taking his cane, had moved quite a distance away from the road. And actually *was* relieving himself, darkening the bark of a sycamore.

'Oh, I'm sorry. I misunderstood.' Silas turned away. 'I thought you wished to speak in private.'

'My clever little ankou, you grow brighter every day,' Pitch said. 'That is not to say I did not wish to take a piss as well. Don't you?'

'Actually no. I'm fine.' He folded his arms, staring back towards the road where the horses were just visible among the trees. Both the mares had moved straight to cropping at the thin layer of grass on offer. 'What is it you wished to say?' He tried to ignore the trickling sound, and the fact that he'd caught a glimpse of Pitch's member before he'd turned away. A flash of marble white against the darkness of a woods made full of shadows by the thick canopy.

'It is more what I wished you *not* to say in the company of Satty's nags.'

Silas almost turned at that. 'Whatever do you mean?'

'What were you going to ask me about Mr Charters?'

Silas dug his boot into the giving ground, the darkness of soil and flecks of decay clinging to the leather. 'Well, it is foolish I'm sure.'

'Saying foolish things has never bothered you before.'

'Fine, I was going to ask if perhaps it was someone from Arcadia who had possessed the poor man. Someone of rank who could not be seen to be visiting here. An angel, perhaps? Mr Charters described the creature as being of radiant light and beauty, but maybe I'm relying too heavily on human mythology.' He rushed the words free. 'Perhaps angels are slovenly and made of scales and wretched things. Well, actually, I know that can't be true...for Sybilla has no scales...at least, none I see. Bloody hell, is Sybilla possessing some unfortunate woman's body, just as Lady Satine did to poor Clarence? Is that how it is done for all of you?' Christ almighty, why could he not shut up? He felt so inordinately nervous and keenly aware of the daemon at his back. Was that body Pitch's own design? Or was some terrified young lad a prisoner in his own flesh as the daemon did with him what he willed. Silas felt a roil of nausea. He'd fondled the man, feasted on his lips. What if someone had screamed from deep down at him to stop? 'Oh god,' he whispered. 'Pitch, did I –'

'Calm yourself, Sickle. You touched what is mine, and mine alone. I have not stolen or borrowed, neither has Sybilla,' he said, doing so in a way that was far gentler than Silas had expected. 'Those who choose to do so can create an original appearance, as I and the Valkyrie have done.

But those who wish to remain more finely concealed will take over the body of a human. Hide beneath the facade, as it were.'

'And that was what was done to Mr Charters.'

The pause was less than a heartbeat. 'That is what was done to Mr Charters.'

'By an angel?'

'Yes.' A reply thin as the breeze and whipped away quickly.

Silas could not help but flinch at the idea of the charming young man being used so. 'Does it cause the lieutenant any pain? Aside from the distress of his dreams...and mind.'

Which were both awful enough.

'They are an unfortunate side effect, one I was not warned to expect, but I suppose it makes sense, considering who he...' Pitch's words died quietly. The rustle of clothing took hold of the silence. 'Anyway, I'm sure it will settle in time. Edward has not been a vessel in a long time. He does not even know me in this form. It is entirely different to what he knew when...well, before. We were lovers once, if that will ease the knots I see in your shoulders there, Silas. I had lain with Edward many a time before...before he was a vessel, and he'd done so willingly. He's a pleasant chap, a decent fuck, and yes, fine, I can hear it being said in your mind now, he likely deserved better than this.' Silas had not been thinking that in particular. His thoughts were a whirlpool, but he'd not disagree. 'I have made things difficult by seeking him out anew. I didn't expect his attachment to me. I should have left well enough alone. Then you'd not have been given so much food for thought through your little peephole. But I assure you, it is well and truly over with. The one who used him...' His voice sharpened to a wavering point. 'They are gone.'

In the distance the rumble of carriage wheels announced approaching traffic. Silas could feel the end of this clandestine meeting in the woods approaching, and he was not yet ready for it.

'Will they return?' Silas still stood facing away from the daemon.

Another pause allowed birdsong to fill the air. 'No.' The single word was heavy as an anchor, dropping into the depths.

'Was it Raph...the one you call for in your sleep at times?'

Pitch made a sound too short-lived to decipher. 'Gods...I don'-t fucking *call* for him. You make me sound dreadfully needy.'

But that wasn't it. It wasn't *need*, per se. Silas swallowed against a dry throat. There was a mournfulness in the cries he'd heard. An unmissable sadness.

Regret, perhaps.

*They are gone.* He'd said it with such finality.

A cold trickle ran its way along Silas's spine.

He turned about. Pitch leaned back against the tree, his arms to his sides, his hands splayed against the sycamore as though it were keeping him upright.

'I've heard you speak of one called Raphael...' Really it was more cursing than speaking. Pitch had used the name in vain many a time. 'An Archangel. I wonder if –'

Pitch made a choked sound. 'Yes, yes, that's it. I was fucking an Archangel, and of course he wished none to know about it. So take that as fair warning, Silas. Not a word, you hear? He has a trumpet, and he knows what to do with it. He could make your life, and your arsehole, very uncomfortable.'

The words spilled from him, his face bright with relief, chasing away the consternation of earlier. But he spoke lies, Silas knew. For Pitch had only ever uttered Raphael's name in a curse. There had been no lament, certainly no intimacy, as there was when he whispered to Raph in his dreams. Silas glanced towards the road. The carriage was much closer now, the clink of the tracers like a rising song reminding him that there were more important things to be chasing than the truth from an evasive daemon. Still...he did not wish to let it go.

'Shall we return to the horses?' Pitch made his way without waiting for an answer but did not move so quick as he might have with the cane.

'I do not think it was Raphael,' Silas said.

The daemon went as still as the trees surrounding him. The carriage would pass by before they could reach the road. Silas hoped they'd not stop to see to the loose horses. 'You told me once that, and I use your words, Lord Enoch's precious Seraphim must not debase themselves with daemonkind.'

Pitch's fingers curled into fists, but he stayed silent. Silas took a breath.

There was another whose name might be shortened in such a way. The fallen angel on the Hellfield. Was not Pitch a daemon soldier who had abandoned his legion after seeing him fall? Did his cry in the mines, as the fae took hold of his dark past, lead Ottelie to speak of a great loss? And now there was Pitch's own words...*They are gone.*

The carriage's passing was a riotous affair of noise. The ground rumbled, even where they stood at a distance from the road. Tiny birds flitted from their hiding places to flee, and the grinding rumble of the wheels seemed to bounce from trunk to trunk in their thicket. It was not the Lady Howard's carriage of course. The bandalore was restful in his pocket, but it was a calamitous reminder that they must keep moving.

Soon. But not yet.

'It's not Archangel Raphael at all, is it?' Silas's pulse skittered, and he doubted he'd be heard over the din. 'I believe it is a Seraphim...Seraphiel...that you call for –'

The daemon's turn of foot was astonishing. He whirled about and fairly threw himself across the space that existed between them. His hand was planted across Silas's lips before the ankou could draw breath. Eyes wide, he sought to step back and found the solid, imposing trunk of the sycamore. The earth was damp and sank beneath his heels. He grabbed at the daemon's wrist, his cries muffled by the slender hand across his lips. There were no flames, a good thing considering, but there was a glow coming from Pitch's hand that had Silas blinking.

'Do I need to cut your tongue out to keep you quiet?' Pitch pressed so hard against Silas's mouth that the ankou feared a tooth was about to break. The passing carriage did not slow where the horses grazed with their reins slack about their necks, but it did hit a pothole, causing enough of a horrendous bang to distract Pitch a moment, his tight hold loosening as he glanced over his shoulder. Silas planted his hands against Pitch's chest and shoved him hard.

Caught off-guard, the daemon landed on his arse, a brief cry of shock leaving him.

'What the fuck did you do that for?' His eyes blazed green, thankfully devoid of fire just yet. He shouted over the rumble of the coach, which Silas glimpsed now through the trees. A giant damn thing with six in front, racing at a pace that marked it as a passenger coach.

'I could ask you the same bloody thing.' Silas wiped at his lips. 'That was completely uncalled for. I meant no harm in asking...I'm just trying to understand –'

'What?' Pitch threw up his arms. 'Trying to understand what, Silas? He is dead...he is fucking dead, and I...' He cut himself off with an angry growl, and Silas closed the distance between them, his hands lifting to touch him but thinking better of it.

'And you are so terribly sad for it,' Silas said in the returning quiet. 'There is nothing wrong in that. Did you...did you love him?'

'Love him? Oh fuck, Silas, stop talking, by the grace of all the gods. It was never like that. And do not presume to know what is wrong or right about me, for I barely know myself.' Pitch slid his fingers into his hair, resetting it from where it tangled about his ears. At least the golden sheen was gone from his skin. 'Stop looking at me like you fear I'll splinter.'

'I know you will not splinter, but I just –'

'Stop. I don't need comforting, Silas, so you can keep your furrowed brow clear, and your pitying hands away. You certainly cannot remedy this with a listening ear and a cup of fucking tea. Forget all this, for your sake and mine. Not a word of it, you understand? Your detective work will do you no favours. Do not mention that name to me again. Are we clear?'

Sybilla had warned him. He supposed he was lucky to walk away with only a split lip.

'We are clear.'

Pitch was so brimming with the pins and needles of grief that there was little wonder he slept so badly. The pain was so tangible, like a rough brush against the back of Silas's mind.

'Do not study me too deeply, Silas. You'll not like what you find. I assure you. Now, can we be on our way to find this fucking carriage of yours? I'm in the mood for breaking bones.'

He traipsed back to the horses, emerging into the light. He was a vision of angry loveliness, with his coat splaying behind him and the weak rays of sun that fell catching at his hair, but his shout was not quite so pleasant. He called out to Sanu in no uncertain, or elegant, terms. The mare ignored him, of course, keeping her head down to the grass and her tail to her rider. Silas watched him. With all he'd seen the daemon do, with how secretly Pitch was kept here with his tongue tied and his back marked, there had really been no doubt he was far more than a mere soldier. Tobias Astaroth was significant. And could never have been just one of faceless hundreds, likely thousands, who might have swelled the Berserker Prince's legions. But even if he had been a general, or whichever official rank was highest in Arcadia, how had he ended up in the bed of one of the most powerful angels in Arcadia?

There was a missing piece here, Silas knew it. And he thought he saw the shape of that piece in Pitch's fear of Silas getting in his way. The daemon was terrified that his flame would cause damage where none was intended.

That the wrong person would be struck down by his rage.

*I didn't see him...I didn't see him in the way.* That is what Pitch had muttered into the dirt in the graveyard outside Mustow Green, paralysed by his own horror. Silas had thought himself to be the man Pitch spoke of, but now...now he wondered.

Silas tried to calm his maddened pulse with measured breaths. 'What was his name,' Silas called. 'The Berserker Prince. What was his true name?'

The daemon stumbled, but that was not so unusual when he insisted on walking without the cane. 'Of fucking gods, Mercer. Enough. How does that prick's name matter in any shape or form?'

Silas suspected it mattered very much. The daemon had spoken so many other names readily.

Pitch snatched at Sanu's reins, gathering them roughly and hauling himself into the saddle, muttering beneath his breath.

A raven cawed from a branch nearby. The sound seemed to tangle itself around Silas's ribs. He hurried back into the light, away from thoughts of downed angels and mad princes, back to where the pale horse waited as his guardian rode off without him.

# CHAPTER 9

When Pitch took up his ill-fated attempts at song a while later, a bawdy tune about a fishwife and a butcher that was frightening birds out of the shrubbery, Silas was far too distracted at first to insist that he shut up.

It was bad enough to know that Pitch's lover had been an angel of the highest order, probably as masterful between the sheets as he was at all other things. He scowled at Lalassu's mane. It was a wonder Pitch hadn't laughed in Silas's face when he clambered onto that bed at Harvington Hall, boots on and hands shaking, seeking to take the place of a creature such as the Seraphim must have been. Silas doubted the guardian of the Lord of Arcadia had been anything short of perfection.

But regardless of what Seraphiel might have *been*, he *was* no longer. Struck down by the Berserker Prince.

Silas stared at Pitch's back. The daemon rode ahead, torturing the ears of every forest creature for miles around. Silas must be mad. Truly. To entertain for one moment the notion that the irascible, infuriating, intolerable man he rode with might be just such a prince. What kingdom would have him?

'Truly, will you stop?' he shouted. 'I've had enough.'

Pitch glanced over his shoulder, eyes narrowed. 'No need to bellow about it. If you have no ear for song, that is hardly my fault.'

'That is not song, it is travesty. I would just like a moment of peace.'

'Wouldn't we all.'

93

After that Pitch stayed silent a long while. So long that Silas began to feel guilty for his outburst and spoke of the first thing that came to mind.

'Tell me about Azazel's magick. What do you know of it?'

'Oh gods, are you sure you wouldn't rather I sing?'

'Quite sure.'

Pitch offered up one of his languid sighs. 'I know he is a master cultivator.'

'A cultivator?'

'You would call them a sorcerer or sorceress here. Arcadia calls them cultivators. Stupid, isn't it? Sounds like they are farmers with a talent for tilling the land. But it is a term given to those who work and manipulate divine magick. There are many angels who can draw on the power of their magick, but not so many that can bend it to their will and shape it into new forms. Azazel had quite the talent, even more so than some of the Archangels, even though he is ranked well beneath them. You can imagine how that caused no end of grievances. You should see Gabriel's face when Azazel is mentioned. It was already a horror, but his glower magnifies his ugliness quite magnificently.'

Silas was certain he did not wish to see Archangel Gabriel's face in a rage. 'So is it only the angels that have this magick? What of the daemons? Do they...do you,' Silas corrected himself, 'have magick?'

Pitch laughed, more an expulsion of air through nostrils than anything else. 'We do not. We have the flame instead, straight from the creation fire that burns beneath Enoch's Ophanim Throne. Aren't we just so lucky?' His snide delivery suggested he thought the opposite. 'Though with the flame, as with divine magick, some were served greater portions than others. There is a randomness in creation that even the gods do not seem to have control over.'

Silas nodded, like it made sense at all. 'Your portion must have been large, then. I mean, your portion of the flame. Your talents seem considerable. You were quite...magnificent...at the castle, that is...with your talent...it seems formidable to me...' Bloody hell, his cheeks felt lit by the damn flame itself.

Pitch narrowed in on his discomfort like a hawk. 'You are quite red in the cheeks, you know.'

'I'm very aware.'

The daemon chuckled, soft and teasing. 'Well it is very nice of you to say. And you are not lacking in talent yourself, my dear Sickle. Perhaps you worked with your hands in your past life, for your fingers are so nimble. With your trinket, I mean, of course.' That interminable grin, the motion that pulled at one side of his mouth, sent a further blush to Silas's cheeks.

He worried at a strand of Lalassu's mane. 'I am much improved with the bandalore, I agree,' he said crisply. 'I feel as though I'm getting the knack of it.'

'Indeed.'

Silas damned every sharp line, every chiselled feature upon Pitch's face. 'Do you think the magick will grow much stronger here?' He thought that an elegant diversion back to more serious and sensible things.

Pitch rubbed at his thigh absently, a languid movement that would have proved far more distracting if Silas had not known it was the leg that caused the daemon's limp and was likely paining him. 'How would I know? Depends, I suppose, on what sort of grimoire they have.'

'These are books of magick?' When a nod came, Silas continued. 'Sybilla spoke of these...of Azazel using them to teach humankind.'

Far up ahead on the side of the road, a rider had dismounted, allowing his bay to graze into the brambles.

'It is one thing to know that magick exists,' Pitch said. 'You can *see* the power of a storm, *feel* the heat of the sun, but it would be something else entirely if you were able to control that storm or cause the sun to shine brighter. Once Azazel found humans who could sense divine magick's touch, he had to teach them the language they would need to work it and shape it into forms that were useful. The grimoires were his lesson books. Azazel was quite the teacher, clearly. And he's been a thorn in Arcadia's side ever since. The bastard can cultivate a seal like no one else, which has been very useful in keeping Elyssiam from being blasted apart. Between his divine magick, Samyaza's surviving Nephilim, and Arcadians who have defected to Elyssiam because they are tired of Lord Enoch's lofty expectations and heavy hand, I doubt the fucking Severance War will ever bloody end. It is at something of an impasse. A lot of threats and taunts and waving of halos but very little ground being won on either side.'

The rider up ahead was running his hand down along the horse's back near leg, coaxing it to lift a hoof. Perhaps his mount had thrown a shoe.

'Now you've said that halos are not what I imagine,' Silas said. 'No rings of light about the head, so what are they, then? A weapon of some kind?'

The daemon shrugged his shoulders as though something under his coat tickled at the back of his neck. 'You are so much cleverer, Sickle, since you've had your hands down my pants.'

It was the first mention Pitch had made of the incident in the abandoned mansion. And of course it was referred to with a derisive laugh. Apparently they were not going to have a mature conversation about the complexity of that moment.

'I dare say I was quite smart before then,' Silas grumbled. 'I've been left in the dark about so many things, I might appear a dullard, but I am not. Do you have one?'

'A dullard? Yes, you are my one and only.'

Sweet mercy, this creature would drive him to distraction. 'I meant a halo, of course. Now it is your turn to be the dullard.' He smiled, pleased with his jibe.

'It is a weapon of the angels, you fool,' Pitch snapped. 'And no. I do not have one.' He touched his fingers to the small of his back, shrinking into his coat again.

'Is everything all right? If your back bothers you, I have more of the amuletum –'

'Silas, gods, shut up.'

And most likely he should have done as he was told. Not so long ago, Silas had been pinned to a tree by a furious daemon. But he could not help himself. 'Is that how you were injured perhaps? A halo? Mention of it seems to –'

'Upset me? Irritate me?' Pitch said, though not so snappish as before. 'And yet you still continue to babble on about it. Would you like me to prattle on about ever dreary detail of my life before I rode at your side? Gods man, you would beg me to kill you again, I assure you, the boredom would be so great.'

They were drawing ever closer to the dismounted rider who appeared not to have noticed them as yet, though how he could have missed the heavy clop of the horses, Silas wasn't sure. He searched for sign of a shadow at the man's feet, but with some distance yet to cover, and the grass and the horse's own shadow thrown long, it was hard to make out for certain.

'I dare say there are many things to be said about your life, but boring is not going to be amongst them,' Silas replied.

Since their conversation by the tree, he'd been picturing how the daemon might have looked upon the Hellfield, wild with a hunger for the battle. Silas had decided Pitch would be clad in the most intricate armour, broad in the shoulders and no doubt tight about his waist as he preferred. The metal surface would radiate with the fierceness of the sun when the daemon used his flame. Those arches of fire Silas had seen at Goodrich Castle would rise into the air about him, and his enemies would be forced to take notice. Even the Nephilim, giants supposedly, would stare down in awe. It was not hard at all to imagine how regal...how princely...Pitch might look.

Silas adjusted himself in the saddle. Clearly he'd not had enough sleep last night.

'Yes,' Pitch said. Just that single word.

'Yes?' Silas frowned.

'Yes to your question.'

Silas shuffled backwards through the conversation. His mouth rounded in surprise. 'Yes, it was a halo that hurt you?'

Pitch was very still in the saddle. And he did not reply. But Silas had his answer.

'Thank you for confiding in me,' Silas said, hoping the daemon heard his sincerity. 'And I'm sorry.' He wasn't sure what for, not exactly, but it felt like the right thing to say.

Pitch lifted one shoulder, dismissive. As though he couldn't have cared less either way.

Lalassu threw her head up, and Silas had to wave his hand to stop the long length of her mane catching him in the face. 'Easy there, girl.'

The bandalore released a note. A lone sound that soared upwards and then plummeted down, like an eagle set on its prey. But the timbre of the note was not so predatory as that.

Silas inhaled sharply.

'What is it?' Pitch reined in Sanu, waiting for Silas to catch up.

The note continued its downward spiral, steady on its course. And Silas felt its fall, saw its target as clearly as he saw the road ahead. The tune aimed for the man up ahead. The traveller had most definitely spied their approach now. And Silas knew why. His pulse quickened, though it was excitement and not fear that tripped it. How delightful that note was, unlike any he'd heard since the first time he'd held the bandalore. A soulful note that gave him cause to shiver, but not in any terrible way.

He stared at the man. A plain enough fellow, with close-cut straight auburn hair struck through with some darker strands. His deep brown suede suit didn't appear suitable for riding any great distance.

'Oh my word,' Silas breathed.

'What has come over you?' Pitch said. 'You are devouring him with your eyes. I can hold back, if you'd like some alone time.'

'Ankou.'

'That is what you are, yes.' The daemon feigned patience.

'Not me.' Silas scowled, sinking his fingers into Lalassu's mane, grabbing hold there as though it might ground him. '*He* is an ankou.'

# Chapter 10

The gentleman waved as they approached, with Silas encouraging Lalassu into a trot in his eagerness. Pitch was not so keen, and he and Sanu lagged a few lengths behind. The sun peeked from a gap in the clouds, as though it too thought the moment wondrous enough to show itself.

'Hello there,' the man called, the light catching at the spectacles he wore. Silas wondered if they were for show, as he couldn't imagine seeing the world more precisely than he did now. Surely the goddess would not release a half-blind ankou upon the world?

The glasses did not hold his attention long though. Silas stared, in no small amount of awe, at the tiny silver threads that flowed out from the man's form like ribbons from a maypole, weaving in the air like a snake would wind along the ground.

Silas could barely take a steady breath. He felt as though he too wore one of Pitch's confounded corset vests. The piskies had spoken of seeing the hues of a natural, and Silas could only surmise that that was what he saw now. The creatures had underplayed the spectacle, saying nothing of how intricate and beautiful it was, as though the man were made of these threads somehow and was fraying at the edges.

Was this how Silas appeared to them all too?

An ankou.

Silas knew it as clearly as he knew the horse beneath him and the daemon behind. And the bandalore's note had heralded it. The man peered up at him, shading his eyes with one hand while the other tapped against his leg in a restless pattern.

'Is everything all right?' Silas said for lack of knowing what else to say. Did the man see him for who he was? He showed no sign of it yet. So how did one go about this? Did they just blurt it out? Hello, nice to meet you, I'm death's messenger too.

'Thank you so much for stopping. Very kind of you.' He spoke well, someone of means, his accent heavy with the rolling lilt of the West Country. 'I, ah, well my horse isn't doing well you see.' The horse didn't seem to know it, munching away at the grass that had now caught Lalassu's eye. 'I thought her lame to begin with, but I dare say it's her back. She's getting on. Not quite so magnificent as your steed there, my good chap.'

Lalassu was sublime, but Silas did not wish to speak about their horses. Was it custom for ankou to ignore one another on meeting? Christ, was this another thing he'd not been told?

'Thank you,' he said. 'She is a beauty, she is a beauty, isn't she?' Silas drew Lalassu to a halt, and she obliged with her usual promptness. The mare stretched her neck to nuzzle at the man's shoulder. He flinched at the touch.

'She won't harm you.' Silas hurried his assurance. 'Her size tends to intimidate though, I'm afraid.' And how well he knew that feeling.

'No, no, I'm sure she's very friendly.' The man's smile was not so steady as his voice. 'I'm just a little twitchy, as I should have returned home some time ago. They'll be wondering where I am.'

They? Silas had never stopped to wonder on the living arrangements of other ankou. He had Holly Village, which he supposed was as close to a home as he could manage, but then he was not a run-of-the-mill ankou, according to Lady Satine.

'Are you far from home?' Silas searched for sign that the man recognised him. He was being studied, that much was certain, but so far there was nothing to say he knew another of his kind. Perhaps Silas had been mistaken after all? He shook himself inwardly. No. This man was ankou. Every fibre heralded it. The thin threads that waved lazily at the air around him marked it as so.

'No actually, I'm not far at all.' His tapping hand stilled, fingers clutching at the material of his grey trouser leg. 'We are barely a quarter-hour ride I'd say. I could walk really, but I thought I'd rest her a moment and see.'

He was not a mere slip of a man either. Not so imposing as Silas, who was far more substantial in girth and broader of shoulder, but tall nonetheless. And his frame, though hidden beneath a rather frumpish fit of material, was solid. With his outstanding mutton chops and thin moustache, he reminded Silas a little of one of the boxers from the barn in Bishop's Castle. Thinking of that dire place had Silas glancing back to see where the daemon was. Pitch had come to a halt a length away, watching them both quietly.

'His horse is not riding well,' Silas told him.

'I heard,' Pitch said with undisguised disinterest. Which irritated Silas no end. He supposed he shouldn't expect the daemon to care one iota if they'd found another ankou or not. But still. It would have been nice if he at least pretended it was interesting.

'Good day to you.' The man squinted as the sun defied its cloud prison. He nodded at Pitch, and Silas thought he saw something flicker within his smile. A hesitancy that made it twitch strangely. But then, many a man had been brought undone by the daemon's malachite stare. 'Goodness, this is quite...well...let me introduce myself. I'm Mr Balthazar Crane.'

Pitch gave him a sharp nod but did not offer his name in return.

'My apologies,' Silas said. 'I've been remiss with introductions. I'm Silas –'

Mr Crane, eyes still shaded, pulled his gaze from the daemon. 'Mercer. You are Silas Mercer, the ankou-on-the-pale-horse, and Tobias Astaroth. Your reputations precede you both, gentlemen. This is all quite exciting really.' He wrung his hands. 'I never thought I'd come across you both. How wonderful it is to meet you. Excuse me if I appear a little star-struck. It is quite...ah, it is quite overwhelming to meet you, both of you.' He wiped at a thin line of sweat on his brow. He must have worked himself up with concerns over his mount, for the day was not warm at all.

'Oh...' Silas said. 'You do recognise me, then?'

'Clearly he does,' Pitch said, dry as a drought-stricken field. 'He just named you.'

'It's just that you said nothing of it when we first met, Mr Crane.' Silas spoke to the man, who had given up trying to stare into the sunlight and peered down at his shoes instead. 'I thought maybe there was etiquette I'd missed, that maybe I should not acknowledge our...natural state too openly.'

'Oh gods no.' Mr Crane laughed, a shrill sound. 'Never mind me, I'm behaving awfully really. I was just...well, it is one thing to hear of you, but another entirely to have you right here. And your hues are so...goodness, I suppose you cannot see yourself. But they are quite astonishing.'

'Do not let your head swell, Silas. He exaggerates.' Pitch snorted. 'You have a vague smudge of black about you, nothing more.'

Silas glanced at him. 'Really? You never mentioned it before.'

'Why would I? There are far more interesting things attached to you.' Pitch winked, and Silas wished he could strike the bastard there and then. He turned back to Mr Crane, who was scowling quite intently.

'That's not what I see at all,' he declared. 'And I've met only one other ankou before. I wondered if...if there was a chance...that I'd...I'd made a mistake with you.' He scratched at his ear, shaking his head.

'Gods,' Pitch sighed. 'Do all ankou trip over their tongues? Whatever are you on about, man?' He nudged Sanu closer. Mr Crane's head jerked up, his eyes widening.

'Nothing...nothing at all.' He shoved at his glasses. 'I've so very rarely come across another ankou, as I said. And I know, Mr Mercer, that you are the greater among us. Forgive me for being so tongue-tied.'

'There is nothing to forgive, and please, call me Silas.'

'You can call me Mr Astaroth.' Pitch wheeled Sanu about, doing so with no discernible touch of the reins. 'We should be moving on, Silas. Don't you have a carriage to deal with?'

But there was no way Silas was about to move on so easily. 'Can we escort you home, Mr Crane?' he asked. 'Lalassu could likely carry us both if it is a short distance.' The mare raised her head at her name and snorted.

'Can he not wait until another carriage passes by and flag them down?' Pitch said, having already urged Sanu back onto the road. The red horse whipped her tail back and forth, as impatient as her rider. 'Or better yet, walk as he said he could do?'

Mr Crane wrung his hands. 'The next carriage is at least a couple of hours away, I'm afraid,' he said in a small voice, casting nervous glances at the daemon. 'Would it be a terrible bother, Mr...Silas?'

'Yes.' That came from Pitch.

'No,' Silas declared. 'No bother at all.'

'Oh for fuck's sake,' Pitch said with a flick of his white coat that set the gold thread shimmering. 'We are not a taxi service.'

'Thank you so much, Silas.'

Balthazar Crane hurried over to his horse, which had grazed its way into the unfenced field they had stopped beside. While his back was turned, Silas urged Lalassu to the daemon's side.

'Will you stop it? This won't take a moment. He said he's not far. And I'd like to speak with him. Who knows when I might meet another ankou? Mr Crane himself said it is rare.'

'I don't like Mr Crane.'

'Do you like anybody?'

'You are tolerable.'

That gave Silas pause. But likely the daemon had said it to exact such a reaction. 'Pitch, I'd like to help him.'

'He is far too sweaty.'

That was not untrue. 'Perhaps because you are glaring at him the way you do. I'm not sure you know how disconcerting it is.'

Mr Crane had his horse's reins, but the bay was reluctant to finish its meal.

'Oh, I'm well aware,' Pitch drawled. 'It's entirely the point of the glare. He seems far too skittish too, don't you think?'

Silas heaved a frustrated sigh. 'Bloody hell. Fine, you can continue on. I'll take him to his residence and then catch up to you.'

Pitch cocked his head, eyeing Silas with disbelief. 'Are you that excited by this insipid fool that all the blood has gone from your head to your cock? What did I say at Castle Combe? You cannot traipse about without me, or without me knowing where you have gone. And where the blazes would I be going anyway? You are the one with the hound for a horse. Let's be done with this, then. You can stroke one another till you've had your fill, and then we'll be on our way.'

There was no point in acknowledging any of what Pitch said, save for the part where the daemon agreed to give the ankou a ride back to his residence. Besides, Mr Crane was now almost with them, leading his horse, who came reluctantly, the bit clamped between its jaws, straining against the length of the reins.

Silas offered his arm so Mr Crane would have leverage to lift himself onto Lalassu's back. The man managed her height easily. With their arms interlocked, and his weight bracing against Silas for a brief moment, he swung himself up and over with no struggle, as though lifted by other means. Very likely he was. Silas knew himself how readily he could find the impetus to lift onto Lalassu's back. As Silas had suspected, the mare did not baulk at the extra weight, though her ears were twisted back all the while, and she did prance about a little as he settled.

One thing Silas had not accounted for was how very close Mr Crane would be and that he would need to hold on to maintain his seat. Silas glanced down at the hand about his waist. Not so thick as Silas's own, but with nails far more tended, no trace of the road or reins beneath them. Mr Crane held on lightly with one hand, the other keeping a hold of his own horse's reins, the animal plodding along behind. It was odd to have a stranger so close. The heat of him was evident at Silas's back, and when Mr Crane turned his head, Silas felt his chin brush at his coat.

The last person who had shared a ride in such a way now travelled just up ahead. Once or twice Pitch glanced over his shoulder, his hair sliding across his face, making it difficult for Silas to discern the looks he cast. He thought once he spotted emerald eyes narrowed and unhappy, but considering Pitch did not wish to make this side journey at all, it was likely the delay that irritated him and not anything so trivial as displeasure at another man wrapped about Silas. The landscape changed over the next subtle rise in the road, the open expanse swallowed up by woodlands some ways ahead.

'I'm afraid I've upset Mr Astaroth.' Mr Crane spoke against Silas's neck, his breath causing an unwanted shiver.

'It is easily done. Don't mind him.'

Mr Crane shifted, and his arms tightened at Silas's side briefly. He thought the man trembled.

'The daemons are so variable in their tempers, are they not?'

'You've met daemons before?'

There was a soft sound, perhaps a sigh. 'One or two. I've heard tell that Mr Astaroth wiped out an entire cluster of bluecaps while in a rage.'

Silas frowned and repeated much of what he had told the ghosts at Castle Combe. 'That is not the entire truth. They had done some terrible things, and I'm afraid they went some way to bringing their demise upon themselves. You must have heard too of the Verderer. The spirit of the Forest of Dean was not itself, and in turn, no creature of the woods was spared. I hope the rumours also say what he did to protect me and the spirit. A new, strong Verderer guards the forest again, thanks to him.'

'And you.'

Silas nodded.

'I'm sorry,' Mr Crane said. 'I didn't mean to offend you. You have formed a solid partnership it seems.'

Oh the ankou did not know the half of it. Silas watched Pitch ride on ahead, with his shoulders held back, arse shifting up and down as he rose to Sanu's trot. Silas scratched at the roughness of his beard, trying to rub away the indecent nature of his thoughts.

'We are working well together,' he said.

'And he is very protective of you.'

Silas hesitated, not sure if it was a question. 'We do our best to protect one another.'

'There is much to shield yourself against, I imagine,' Mr Crane said quietly. His fingers tightened upon Silas's coat. 'With the Blight running so strong.'

'Indeed.'

Mr Crane did not speak again, not until they had travelled through a light dusting of woodlands and he pointed to a narrow road that branched off the main thoroughfare to the right.

'There,' he whispered. 'That is the road to my house.'

'Along that side trail?'

There was a pause. 'Yes. Gidleigh Park House is just a little ways along.'

'Pitch, hold on!' Silas called out. 'You have passed the turn-off.'

The daemon was slow to wheel Sanu about, his lips moving with mutterings that did not reach Silas.

The road to the ankou's home curved up ahead, giving the appearance that it disappeared altogether into the woodlands. Lalassu slowed, and he had to use his heels gently to push her on. Perhaps she too was reminded of the last time such a road had lain before them, when they'd entered the Forest of Dean. But his unease lifted not long after, for around that first curve, the woodlands pulled back from the road and Mr Crane's residence came into view.

# CHAPTER 11

Gidleigh Park House rested upon the slope of a hill that was rich with evergreens. The house was in fact a length of Tudor-style buildings, with their broad, dark beams offset against the bleached white of their walls. It was a simple enough structure, more of a hunting lodge style than the elaborate build of Harvington Hall. The black-and-white facade stood out from the greenery, like a focused point in an oil painting. They approached from a road that wound around to the left, hiding the river until Silas was almost upon it. He eyed it with much wariness. This river was no wider than the one beneath the boggart's bridge but clearly much deeper. All at once he was dry-mouthed with reticence.

'Everything all right, Silas?' Mr Crane must have felt him tense.

Pitch trotted up behind them, pulling Sanu into line alongside Lalassu, who had slowed into a barely moving walk, as though sensing her rider's unease.

'He's fine, don't worry yourself about it,' Pitch said with some sharpness. 'You are here now, safe and sound. Silas, best you let your passenger go, so we can be on our way.'

Silas pulled his gaze from the river, whose surface swirled with tiny whirlpools caused by the significant current.

'Yes, yes. Of course.' He studied the approaching bridge, a low-set timber affair with railings of a criss-cross design that allowed easy view of the river below. Most unlikely to have a boggart beneath it, he assured himself. Christ's sake, how many bridges had he crossed now? A dozen at least, and he'd traversed the walkway over the moat at Harvington Hall more times than he could count. He really thought himself to have triumphed over this unfortunate phobia. But here he was, skin crawling, throat tight. Ludicrous behaviour that would give Pitch no end of pleasure if Silas did not get ahold of himself.

The water splashed wildly up against the barrel of the bridge. He could hear the calamity as they drew closer, as though there were obstacles, rocks perhaps, beneath the surface there.

Silas urged Lalassu on with a light nudge. The mare set off across the bridge that was wide enough for Pitch to remain at his side.

'I'm quite fine,' Silas said gruffly. 'You can ride on.'

'I'm aware. But I thought I'd stay here. We've no rush. You can take it slowly.'

Silas left his scrutiny of the flowing waters to glance at his guardian. There was nothing snide lurking in Pitch's features. His smile was a whisper of a thing and without any trace of malice. The daemon's calm demeanour loosened the knot in Silas's gut.

'You don't like the water much,' Balthazar Crane said at his back.

To Silas's ear it sounded more of a statement, and he felt foolish, all at once, for his trepidation. 'No. I don't think I do.' He sought to laugh off his foolishness, but even to his own ears, the sound was fragile. But Silas decided if ever there were the right person to speak to about his aversion, and the turbulent memories it jogged, then it was another ankou. 'I wonder if you have...'

A gleam beneath the water's surface caught his eye. Flashing movement, too large to be a fish. Silas opened and closed his eyes. The rippling shape was still there but distorted by the glint of sunshine on the water's surface. He thought, for just a blink, that he saw limbs, arms perhaps, spread wide, lifting towards him.

'What were you going to say?' Mr Crane asked.

There. There it was again. A very definite flash of silver, right where the water seemed to bulge upward, as though something sought to jettison from beneath. He was very near to calling Pitch's attention to it when the water seemed to darken, as though a cloud's shadow flitted over the surface, and the strange display filtered away into the current. Silas glanced up to find that the sky was the clearest it had been all day, with the clouds down low and distant on the horizon.

'Ah, I was just...are there trout in the river? Eels perhaps?'

Pitch regarded him with no small amount of exasperation. 'We don't have time for fishing, Silas.'

'I couldn't say,' Mr Crane answered. 'I'm not all that familiar with this river.'

'You're not familiar with the river that you must cross every day?' Pitch said, arching a brow.

Silas felt Mr Crane shift, and his hands slid from Silas's waist. 'That's not what I meant to say...I'm not a fisherman, so I'm not familiar with the type of seafood on offer. Hardly time for fishing, as you said. I've been terribly busy. You gentlemen know as well as any that things are not as they should be. I have no idea how it is for daemons, but Mr Mercer would know very well what a challenge the Blight has been of late.'

'We are *both* very well aware.' Pitch's caustic tone and the ankou's talk of the Blight finally pulled Silas from his ponderings.

The bridge was behind them now, and whatever it was he'd seen in the river had not shown itself again. 'The Blight has certainly caused us much havoc,' Silas said. 'We ride to its doings even now.'

'Go ahead, Silas,' Pitch sighed. 'Tell the utter stranger of all our plans.'

'He is ankou, Pitch,' Silas said, exasperated. 'You must know, Mr Crane, of the talk of a teratism in these parts? The carriage that is running amuck.'

'You seek the Lady Howard's carriage, of course,' Mr Crane said quickly. 'And there is need of you, no doubt. If you stop in for a tea, I can tell you what I know of her.'

'That would be very helpful.' Silas was eager, both to speak with the ankou and to delay the encounter with the carriage. Though he'd perish before he'd admit that. 'I believe she has been a fixture on the road from Tavistock to Okehampton Castle for years and years and not too much trouble until now. Have you seen her carriage yourself?'

'I have, once or twice, but I stayed clear. The teratisms are too much for my blade, and it is not for me to tangle with them. We wondered how long it might be before you arrived.'

'We?' Pitch cut his word through the space between the horses.

Silas noted the jerk of Mr Crane's hands. 'Well, I don't live here alone, of course. That would be terribly lonely. There are naturals among the purebreds in the household staff. The Blight might not affect them directly, but that is not to say some of them don't sense its disturbance.'

Mr Crane did not ask Silas to pull Lalassu up so he could dismount. He simply slid from the mare's back, hitting the ground with a barely perceptible thud. The removal of his warmth at Silas's back caused the ankou to shudder. As too did the icy stare Pitch was sending the man's way.

'We really don't have time for tea and gossip.' Pitch drew Sanu to a halt. 'Come along, Silas.'

He shook his head. 'I'd like to stay a moment or two.'

Pitch cast aside Silas's wishes with a wave. 'And I'd like to be done with your teratism and out of this saddle before my balls are rubbed raw, so let's move on.'

'A shame you will not stay.' Mr Crane led his horse forward, pulling her past Lalassu. The bay had endured the journey well, with no obvious sign of being lame or unwell. 'My housekeeper could tend to that stain upon your coat, and my chef is practising her desserts for a dance we are to hold just next week. She has baked so many pastries of late, I fear I shall turn into one if I eat another.'

That lifted Pitch's head. 'Pastries?'

'Lemon tarts and eclairs are her speciality, but she does a wondrous strawberry shortcake, too.'

Forget Azazel's magick, the daemon needed only the mention of sweet treats to be spellbound. 'Really?' he said, more breathless than the word deserved.

'So just one cup of tea, and then we'll be off.' Silas nodded at Pitch, as though doing so would urge him to agree.

'Well, I suppose we might stop very briefly,' Pitch returned. 'They did a terrible job of tending to my coat at the last place. I do hope your laundress is more skilled.'

'Oh very much so. How wonderful. I'm so glad you will stay.-' Balthazar Crane sounded more relieved than glad. 'Come, come then. Let the stable boy attend to the horses and follow me, gentlemen. I'm sure Mrs Vellan has seen us arrive and has the kitchen preparing for us, even as we speak.'

The house did not seem as though it held a living soul, let alone a bustling kitchen. The splashing of the river behind them was by far the loudest sound about. Silas tried to recall if it had been so noisy when they crossed it not a few minutes ago.

At mention of him, the stable boy seemed to emerge as though from thin air, stepping out from behind several elegant conifers that concealed the easterly edge of the house. Silas could see the hint of a building further back towards where the woods settled dark and deep upon the hillside. The building was a miniature version of the house, with its dark beams and crisp white walls. Stables, he presumed.

The young lad, hovering at the edge of manhood and not really a boy at all, seemed very smartly dressed for a stablehand, with a red handkerchief poking from the chest pocket of his stiffly starched white shirt. His mousy hair was slicked back, damp against his head.

There was an oddness about the place, about the ankou too, if Silas were honest. But the same could have been said for Old Bess and his Sanctuary.

'Thank you.' Silas dismounted and handed the lad Lalassu's reins.

The skinny youth was dwarfed by both horse and dismounted rider and seemed well aware of it. He jerked forward in a hurried bow but said nothing. He seemed too overawed to meet Silas's eye, keeping his gaze firmly down. And when their hands brushed with the exchange of reins, the poor thing nearly came out of his skin, he jumped so hard.

Silas frowned, a flicker of concern rising. But it could be simply that he was an imposing man. One of his shoulders was nearly as big as the lad's head. Or perhaps, more vile an idea, it was that Mr Crane was not so congenial a master when there were no guests about. If he were the true master of this place. It did puzzle Silas how an ankou with just one year of existence could secure such a grand residence in such a short time. Silas was keen to question him on it.

Pitch tossed Sanu's reins to the boy, who, though timid, was evidently well versed with dealing with horses and impetuous riders. He held the reins of all three animals, rubbing their noses and digging into his pockets for sugar cubes, which he offered to each in turn, talking quietly to them as they nuzzled his open palm greedily.

'Not too many of those for the red nag,' Pitch called, already heading up towards the house, whose entrance lay up a short flight of stairs built into the slope of the land. 'I don't fancy having to keep her reined in for the rest of the afternoon because her blood is filled with sugar.'

'Your cane, Pitch,' Silas called. 'Will you not need it?'

'If I did, I would have brought it with me.' He clasped his hands behind his back and walked on.

Silas could see the taut pull of his shoulders. He recognised that stance well. The daemon was spending much effort in keeping his limp to a minimum. Silas quickly withdrew the contracted cane from his saddlebag. He would hand it over wordlessly later on, when the daemon's face was pinched with discomfort. Silas would receive no thanks for his foresight, of course. He never did.

'Shall we, Mr Mercer?' Balthazar Crane swept a hand towards the door.

The stable boy led all three horses off towards the stables, and they followed without issue.

'Very well then.' Silas smiled and followed after Pitch and Mr Crane.

The front door, a blackened wood with a great brass knocker at its centre, swung open. A woman stood there, her hands planted one over the other on her stomach. Her grey hair was pulled back from her face so tightly that it caused the skin on her cheeks to stretch. She had a thin mouth, puckered with deep lines, as though she'd pursed them too often, and beneath her eyes lay smudges of ashen skin. Sleep had eluded her for some time.

'Welcome back, Mr Crane. And hello to you, gentlemen.' She cleared her throat. 'I'm Mrs Vellan.'

Her shadow played at the edges of her skirt. A purebred, certainly.

'You must have been worried about me, Mrs Vellan.' There was an odd emphasis on the ankou's words. The woman bobbed, dipping her head.

'We were beginning to wonder what had become of you, that is certain. But I'm very relieved to see all is well.' If relief made one tug at one's skirts, she was very relieved indeed. What a curiously jittery household this was. It gave Silas cause to regard Mr Crane with a more scrutinising eye. There was nothing that said an ankou could not be a tyrant, he supposed.

Mr Crane was nodding tersely. 'These gentlemen are from the Order, Mrs Vellan, a very fine establishment based in London.'

Mrs Vellan bothered at her lip, her gaze dropping to the floor. 'Yes, sir. Very fine indeed.'

'They are in ever so much of a hurry, with important work to do. So do bring tea and sweets as quickly as you can.' He moved to dismiss her but hesitated. 'Oh, and could you take Mr Astaroth's coat and see what the laundress can do with that stain upon the collar. Blood, you see.'

The woman's eyes flew up to fix on her master. 'The laundress?'

'Yes. Mrs Vellan, Badh, our laundress. Take her the coat. Do get your wits about you.'

Recognition seemed to dawn at last, and she nodded. 'Yes, yes, of course.'

Pitch shrugged off his splendid coat, draping it from one finger to hand it to Mrs Vellan. With another sharp bob, she took it and was gone in a whisper of pale green linen and petticoats. Her house keys at her waist jingled as she scurried down the corridor.

'Excuse her. She's getting on, I'm afraid.' Mr Crane winced. 'Please come in, gentlemen. We'll use the reading room I think. It's very pleasant at this time of day.' He moved on ahead when Pitch declined his invitation to go first.

'You lead the way. It is your house, I have no idea where to go.'

As Mr Crane moved inside and into the dullness of the corridor, Pitch touched a hand to Silas's arm, urging him to wait. When a short distance opened between them and their host, he whispered, 'These had best be damned good pastries. I don't like your ankou at all. He's irksome, and there is something snakish about him. You have terrible taste in companions, I must say.'

'I wholeheartedly agree.' Silas stared meaningfully at the daemon.

'Touché.' Pitch's eyes danced with jade mischief.

'But you are right,' Silas said, watching Mr Crane disappear into a room down the far end of the corridor. 'There is something uncomfortable here.'

'And you still wish to speak with him.'

A statement, not a question.

Silas shot Pitch a grateful glance. 'I do. And would Lalassu and Sanu not have alerted us if there were any grave danger?'

'The only grave danger we face, I fear, is that of dying of boredom. Go, chat with your dead man, and let's be done with it.'

'Thank you.' Silas smiled.

'Oh gods, stop looking so grateful for nothing at all. Go on.' Pitch planted his hand firmly against Silas's arse and squeezed. With a sputter and flush of heat, Silas stepped over the threshold.

# CHAPTER 12

The pastries were very good, and Pitch found his appetite roaring its return louder with each morsel he ate. He'd not taxed himself too badly setting the abandoned mansion alight, but that was not to say the use of the flame hadn' depleted him somewhat. Not that he'd admit that to Silas. It was bad enough he'd acted like a man possessed in that room of witch bottles, coming apart at the sight of some mangled bird carcasses and a forlorn owl. Pitch felt as though he knew himself less and less each day in this infernal world.

He bit into an eclair, eyes rolling at the sweetness that dissolved on his tongue. Here was sign that the gods weren't all terrible bastards, for one of them at least had made such a miraculous thing as milk, which could be churned into this creamy delight that stained his lips.

'There is plenty more, Mr Astaroth.' Mr Crane paused in his conversation with Silas. 'Do not hold back.'

'Oh he needs no invitation for that,' Silas said, his bemusement causing his eyes to shimmer. 'But you have a little something' – he touched his chin – 'just there. Cream, I think.'

Pitch wiped a finger across his chin and licked the offending smudge away slowly. 'Are you not having any more, Sickle?' He did not normally use the nickname he'd chosen for the ankou when others were around, but he was bloated with saccharine goodness, and his head was light with being overfilled. And he was enjoying seeing the ankou's bustling enthusiasm as he spoke with Mr Crane on matters pertaining to death's messengers. Silas seemed delighted to have met one of his kind, and his delight smoothed much of the tension from his face. The pair had spent some time comparing the most horrendous of the wounds they'd witnessed upon a lost soul, a conversation that involved split skulls and hanging entrails, but it did not put Pitch off his food in the slightest.

'I wouldn't wish to deprive you,' Silas said, at ease now that they had all settled with cups of tea and cakes delivered by the curt Mrs Vellan. 'You appear to be enjoying the pastries very much.' He smiled. A genuine curve of his mouth that was rather nice to look at.

What a dolt Silas was. So pleased that *Pitch* was pleased. He couldn't seem to help himself; he insisted on fussing no matter how many times Pitch reprimanded him. He'd brought the cane with him, setting it without a word beside Pitch as they took their seats. What a buffoon. Quite a handsome buffoon, mind, whose solid hips barely fit him into the armchair he'd taken near the window. Those very same hips had pressed Pitch against a table not a day ago.

The daemon coughed, blaming a flake of golden pastry. 'These are not the worst pastries I've had,' he acquiesced. He crossed his legs, noting the stiffness that had grown between them. Not a solid jutting length, mind, just a subtle strengthening of pleasure that sometimes came when he overindulged on sweets. Sating an incubus appetite was best done through carnal exploits. Sugar and alcohol were pale rivals for a feed. Usually. Here though, he had to admit, he was quite warm in the cheeks with his fill.

Pitch picked up another eclair. Just one more. He touched his lips to the rounded end, watching Silas across from him. His beard needed a trim, and his hair refused to remain in any of the ties he used to bind it. Bess had tidied him up barely a week ago, yet the ankou had a rugged look about him once more, like a wild highwayman. His beard had rasped Pitch's skin when they kissed, leaving the skin burning long after the blasted piskies had ruined things.

No, Pitch admonished himself. Not ruined. They had been a welcome interruption. He'd been intolerably needy that day.

Still, it did no harm to think on that encounter. Especially here, where he had no interest in the conversation at all. He had to amuse himself somehow, so why not steal an opportunity to study the ankou...-

*his* ankou, not the stranger. Pitch pressed his sticky fingertips into the serviette on his lap, irritated at the stupidity of his own thoughts. His ankou? What nonsense was that?

He touched his tongue at a bulge of cream that fought its way free of the pastry and returned to his study of Silas.

The man was a far hairier specimen than Pitch thought he preferred. Seraphiel had always insisted that both the lieutenant and Pitch were clean-shaved, and Pitch had been happy to go along with whatever the Seraphim desired. Enoch's favourite angel was dirtying himself well enough by lying with a daemon. It was not unreasonable that he wanted him as cleaned up as possible in every other way.

Raph would have despised Silas's rambunctious curls.

Well, that would have been the Seraphim's loss.

Pitch surprised himself with the thought. He so rarely thought of Raph with anything but wretchedness.

But it had happened more than once now when the Silas was around.

Pitch eased the eclair deeper into his mouth, rounding his lips over the hard icing of chocolate, enjoying the memory of his fingers digging into the swirls of hair that covered Silas's chest. His prick twitched, his baser needs clamouring for his attention. He eased the eclair out of his mouth before pushing it back in over his teeth and tongue.

By the Archangels' pristine orifices, how was it possible that he had only a vague idea of what awaited him beneath Silas's trousers? Had he even seen the ankou's cock in passing? No. He'd been too busy simpering beneath those stupidly broad hands, leaking at the touch of tender fingers.

Pitch could make the discovery now, could he not? Stride across this room and kneel between those ludicrously thick thighs. Tease down those trousers and taste what lay beneath. Make Silas shudder.

Pitch's teeth scraped the chocolate from the top of the eclair, the pastry dampening in his mouth. His breath came in quick successions, and his body was warm with that wonderful glow he knew so well. Desire. Simple, powerful, and so very hungry here. The ever-scratching presence at his core was blanketed by it, subdued by brazen want. He shifted his feet, damning the tiresome conversation the ankou shared. He wanted

Silas's attention on him. He wanted the ankou's...*his* ankou's...lips upon him. And he wanted it now.

'So, you can imagine how...' Silas glanced over at him, midsentence. He appeared to lose his train of thought, tugging at his collar. He turned back to Mr Crane, who was distracted with pouring them another cup of tea. 'Ah, you can imagine how strange it was...my...that was my first encounter with a...with a...' Silas abandoned his efforts to keep his gaze away. He turned back to Pitch, giving him the oddest look.

*What are you doing?* he mouthed.

Pitch scowled. What was the oaf on about? Gods, why must he ruin a perfectly delicious moment with his nagging? A sliver of cream ran from the corner of Pitch's mouth, warm and thick and somewhat uncomfortable.

He froze. What the fuck *was* he doing? He had the eclair pushed into his gob so far it touched at the back of his throat. And he was far too breathless, too filled with a need that bloomed hard within him. He slipped the eclair from his mouth and let it drop onto the plate. The pastry was sodden by his saliva, the cream oozing from punctures in the crust.

Bloody tits-on-a-manticore. He'd been sucking off a pastry.

Actually he'd been sucking off Silas. Pinning him down in his thoughts, stripping off that blasted coat the ankou loved so much and exploring what lay beneath. And Pitch didn't wish to stop.

Gods damn it. How had he gotten so dangerously ardent?

Pitch brushed at crumbs that had fallen into his lap, wincing as his fingers found a prick so strained that if Silas were to look at him a certain way, the daemon would likely scream out a release, here and now. Right in front of the ankou and his newfound chum. Wonderful.

Pitch rose to his feet. The compacted cane rolled into the depression between the cushions, but he was too eager to leave the room to bother with retrieving it. Pitch fussed with his vest in a vain attempt to hide the turret in his trousers. His skin was tingling, and his belly was tight with need. He kept his gaze away from Silas. Not simply because he feared he might see a hint of repulsion on the ankou's face, but because he was frightened that he'd lose a hold of the fire in his belly, and he might find himself taking matters into his own hands. Whether Sickle wanted it or not.

'I wonder if you have a water closet?' he said, hoarse and hurried.

'Yes, of course.' Mr Crane's expression bothered him, though not half as much as his own need to get his hands upon himself. The ankou pointed to the door. 'I'll have Mrs Vellan show you. It's rather a maze upstairs.' Before Pitch could protest, Mr Crane called out, 'Mrs Vellan?'

She appeared right away as though she'd been hovering in the hallway all this time.

'Yes, Mr Crane?'

'Take Mr Astaroth to the water closet, will you?'

Her hesitation was infinitesimal. 'Yes, Mr Crane.'

Their exchange was underlaid with a note of tension that Pitch did not like. He also did not like a chaperon, not while he blazed with a hunger like this. He was racked with a desperation that had flared out of nowhere and was disturbing in its intensity. Had he starved himself of pleasure too long? It had been what, a week, maybe more, since he'd rutted on the stairwell at the hall and been interrupted by that insufferable hag, Tyvain. The encounter had been dreary, unsatisfying...and unnecessary. He'd still been well aglow from his encounter with Silas. Since then, there'd been nothing save for the fumble with the ankou yesterday in the mansion.

'This way, Mr Astaroth.'

With a tight nod, Pitch hurried out of the room. He felt Silas's stare every step of the way. He was sure the ankou was frowning, likely thinking Pitch had gone mad. Maybe he had. But he'd think more on that after he'd given himself a thorough seeing to and could think straight again.

# CHAPTER 13

Pitch followed after the housekeeper, thinking absently on how the corridor now seemed filled with that strange silence he'd noted on arriving at the house. He grimaced at how movement made the fabric of his trousers rub at hard places.

Gods, this really was ill-timed. When last he'd been so overcome by his incubus blood, the overwhelming desire had made sense. He'd been starving himself, denying his every craving while chained to the bed in the hall. When he'd abandoned his attempts to fade away, the moment Silas clambered into his bed, his appetite had been ferocious.

But what the fuck had him frothing at the mouth, almost literally, here?

Pitch followed the housekeeper, who moved with brisk, short steps, to the stairs at the end of the corridor. Her skirt ran behind her, trailing like a faded green river.

'This way, sir.'

Why was she whispering? Perhaps she felt it, the tug at her senses, the quickening between her legs that came when a creature like Pitch set his sights on hidden desires. But he was doing no such thing here. He held no taste for the woman leading him up the stairs.

He wiped his hand across his chin and found it damp with sweat. His body hummed with the need to turn around and return to where his desire truly lay. Back in the parlour, with a cup of tea in hand. No doubt already putting a needy daemon out of mind while chatting of death and scythes.

'Christ almighty.' Pitch stole Silas's curse. 'Get ahold of yourself, man.'

The stairs were a bloody nightmare. He used one hand to wrap his coat in such a way his want was not jutting out like a signal post while the other traced the banister. At least the blazing heat of lust made him more pliable, and he was able to keep up with Mrs Vellan's rather cracking pace, the pull of his hip a distant concern.

The upstairs was darker than below, with most of the doors along the hallway closed off. There was no runner on the floor, so their footsteps seemed overly loud on the dark wood.

'Just point the way. I don't need my hand held.' He was sharp about it, far too warm beneath his shirt, far too hard beneath his fall-fronts.

Mrs Vellan jumped, an actual lift that must have taken her off her feet a moment. 'Of course, sir.' Her voice quivered. A few more paces and she stopped outside one of the multiple, unremarkable doorways. 'Here...this is it.' She gestured.

Her hand shook as it hung in the air. She dove it back to her skirt, scrunching a handful of material. She did that quite a lot, now he came to think of it. But he was barely able to think at all.

'Thank you. You can go.' Pitch fairly threw himself at the door.

His arousal was mind-numbing, ball pinching, an ache that was growing harder and much too painful. Far too encompassing to have come from a pile of sticky sweets.

Through the turbulence, a singular thought pushed its way clear. This was wrong. This torrent of arousal was his, yes, but he knew his lust well, and he *knew* a couple of eclairs and a few minutes spent undressing Silas in his mind should not have rendered him so ferociously ravenous.

Fuck.

Was there something amiss? Or was this another of his growing list of peculiarities? He'd been breaking apart for a long while, even before the Blight ran its interference with him. Long before they had needled him with whatever the blazes amuletum was to try to hold him together. Likely this wayward arousal was simply Pitch losing another piece of himself.

Silas was with an ankou, another of his kind. They served the same mistress. And Lalassu and Sanu had not baulked at coming here. Mr Crane was odd, yes. But that hardly made him a threat.

'Shit, shit.' Pitch grasped the handle, using the cold press of metal to steady himself.

This wretched mess was all him. Pathetically, him.

'Go,' he hissed at the housekeeper who still hovered nearby. 'Get away.'

His fingers twitched to reach for her, to devour her, even though she'd make a poor substitute for the true prize.

'Mr Astaroth...' Her voice trembled. Was the damn woman crying? 'I don't think...'

'Piss off.' The words were squeezed from him, his body cramping with the effort it took not to lunge for her.

The handle turned in his grasp. Pitch moved to step back, fighting his way through the foggy hold of urgent desires. The door swung open. A hand reached for him, grabbing hold of his wrist. The grip was painfully tight against skin inflamed with mindless want.

'Let me help you.' The whisper was a caress, a touch that promised relief. He shuddered.

She was beautiful. She was...something else...all his senses were muddled, colliding with one another.

She was raven-haired, eyes the colour of a winter puddle with the ice thin across the top. Her robe, a satin fabric of brilliant red was loose about her chest, her breasts fighting their way free of the folds.

'No...I am fine...' Pitch shook his head. He wasn't fine.

'Lie with me.'

The pressure at his wrist strengthened, and he stepped forward. Over the threshold.

He fell into a pair of waiting arms, and as they encircled him, keeping him from falling to his knees, he felt the shift of something deep within. Beneath the heavy shroud of his arousal, the wildness at his heart stirred. But it was muted, so distant and shrouded beneath the clamouring of his incubus needs. He lost touch with it far too easily, as though it were a leviathan testing the surface only to shrink back to the depths.

'There, there.' The woman murmured at his ear, and the sound of it sent a thrill of pleasure racing down into the small of his back. A scent caressed his nostrils, clearer now.

Daemon. She was daemon. But with a sour note he couldn't place. Somewhere in his addled mind, he felt relief. A daemon would not be so readily enchanted if his desires swept from his control as they sought to do. She would not be so easily overcome as a human, or a once-human man.

Pitch winced.

Fingers caressed his back, trailing their way up and down the length of his spine, and his cock jerked, leaking warmth. Despite himself, he groaned and leaned into the hard body that held him.

'That's right, let it all go. You seem to be in need of respite, Tobias.'

He shook his head, struggling to get his bearings and find his senses. The room he'd just been pressed into was dim, but it did not help matters that he was nearly buried in her robe and breasts. He knew the softness, the pliable give of a woman's chest. He had a preference for the harder lines of a man, but right this instant, he likely would have fucked the damned keyhole to bring relief.

Who was she? He felt a coarse rub of something at his legs, as though she wore something else beneath the robe. His thoughts stuttered, much like the candles in the room he noted as he lifted his head to try to see where he was. Light fingers found his cheek, brushing it. He shivered and moaned like the whore he was willing to be.

'Who are you?' Gods he could barely work a word free.

There was long dark hair, the same hue as Silas's but dead straight.

Silas. Shit. Pitch couldn't let the ankou see him like this. He'd seen far too much of Pitch's baser, uglier side already.

'I am someone who can work you out of a very tight spot.' She answered a question he'd forgotten he'd asked. Her hands were working at the buttons of his fall-fronts. He wanted to scream at her to hurry up and yet roar at her to stop. 'How very hungry you are, my pretty daemon.'

He intended to demand she let go of him, but instead his hips moved forward. The woman shifted away from him, and, damn him, he whimpered, following after her as she hooked a finger into the pleat of his corset vest and led him forward. The room seemed hazy, likely from the multitude of fucking candles set about the room. Who needed so many of the damned things? He blinked, trying to clear his vision and his mind. There was no furniture in the room. The hearth was filled to bursting with lit candles, while more had been set upon the bare floors and ringed the grand white rug that lay at the centre of the room. He squinted. It was not a rug at all but an animal pelt, and likely more than one stitched together, considering its grand size.

He shouldn't go to the rug. He mustn't.

The last of his common sense was shouting at him, but the woman had him unbuttoned. When had that happened? Her fingers were on his cock. Wrapped about its length. The air fled his lungs.

Rough. Gods, she was rough with him. Jerking him forward, leading him by his prick.

Pitch's throat was tight, the room stifling.

He wanted this. He abhorred this.

A pressure touched at the backs of his knees. He sank down, pressed onto his back. The rug was cold; he felt it even through the layers of his clothing. Like it was a slab of godsdamned ice. Hands fell upon his corset vest, making light work of the buttons, not tearing it open, for which he was grateful. It was tugged free and cast aside. His shirt didn't receive such subtle treatment though, and was torn open like the wrapping on a parcel.

Pitch was sick and craving. He was a fucking mess. Never more so than now.

'I don't want this.' He denied it even as he arched his hips up against the hands that worked at his member. The rub of skin was harsh; she was not being gentle with him. So few were. Desire made people lose themselves. They forgot him. Seraphiel had been no different. The angel had liked to press him down, as the woman did here. He'd thrilled at having the prince submit to him, surrender, and bend as he desired.

But Silas was not the same.

Silas.

This time Pitch's moan came from another place. One of fear.

Silas was not safe. Not with his splintering guardian and not with that fucking ankou. Pitch's inner thoughts rose like bubbles of air in water, disappearing as they reached the surface.

He could not shift his legs, nor even wiggle his toes. Gods, this was too much like the bluecaps, working their needle points into his mind. Stealing things from him.

Only here he *wanted* her to take from him. He wanted to scream into his release...but, just as much, just as fervently, he wanted to get the fuck out of here.

A weight settled over his hips, hands still fondling him. He strained into the touch, lust and desire and a vicious hunger rising up to take hold of all coherent thought and pummel it into mush. Where her thighs met his hips, there was the rough scrape of material again...as though she wore clothing of a weave thick and coarse.

'Shall I take you now?' she whispered. Raven hair, sculpted beauty, harsh grey eyes. Not an inch of humanity about her. 'Hmmm? Shall I give you what you desire?'

She loomed above him, naked and glorious. Small jutting breasts, like knife points. Dangerous.

'Yes.' He choked, despising himself. 'No...no.'

Her laughter was pieces of glass. 'Goodness. I'm impressed you cannot still decide, with all that you consumed, and with me so close. But it's not me you want straddled over you at all, is it? I'm impressed you got yourself out of that room before you took command of that friend of yours. How convenient it was, to have him here. My, my how you crave him. Gracious me how you crave him. It has made this so much easier than I imagined.'

All at once, through the haze, through the heat, Pitch understood what this was.

Fucking gods. The daemon had him enchanted.

She was playing him all too well at his own game. Better even. For Pitch's lusts were not for her, but she commanded them anyway. Redirected his hunger to her.

The woman took hold, readying her wet heat to consume him. He twisted his hips, seeking to move away...or move closer. His damned hip sang with the tight clench of angry muscle. His body, ravenous, betrayed him. He rose up to meet her, seeking the release he'd find in the depths between her legs. Curse her. Damn her to every miserable crevice in the Hellfield. She should not be able to work him so. And he should be able to stop her, not strain towards her like she were something he coveted.

She had him by the veritable balls.

'Someone approaches.' A small and tiny whisper. Another witness to his slow collapse. They were not alone in the room. 'The Horseman is coming.'

Pitch heard it all through the pounding of his pulse. Damning the rigid part of himself that quivered in a stranger's grasp, but all the while desperate for her to work him.

Put him out of his misery.

'Oh, is he looking for you?' Her grin was dastardly as she peered down at him. 'How very sweet. Perhaps we should bring Mr Mercer in here? You would like that, wouldn't you, my dear?' Her fingers were unkind as they cupped him and toyed with him.

Pitch moaned and arched his back. Like it? He was ready to come apart just *thinking* on having Silas between his legs. Heavy footsteps approached the room.

'Keep him away,' the daemon said through clenched teeth.

'Pitch? Are you about?' The ankou's rumbling voice came from far too close by – and was a nightmare for Pitch's frustrations. Heat whipped through his belly and sent tendrils into stiff and aching places. He was nothing but incubus right now, that ancient part of his daemonic lineage that consumed all sensibilities. Pitch was holding on to himself by the merest thread.

And she was responsible. Toying with him as though he were the lowliest of daemons, vulnerable to enchantment as readily as any human. No one should be able to make a Dominion prince so pliable, so surrendered. He'd not even struggled to find his way from beneath her.

The sound of hurried footsteps came from beyond the door.

'Mr Mercer...can I...can I help you?' Mrs Vellan was harried.

Pitch whimpered. Fingers caressed his belly, and he shivered despite all attempts to do otherwise.

The woman above him held her wicked smile, poised. One movement away from taking him. Her daemonic scent was eye-watering, the drag of her enchantment tying him in knots. Who the fuck was she that she could hold him in such a vice grip?

'I was just wondering if Mr Astaroth is all right,' Silas said.

To hear his voice did untoward things to Pitch's thoughts. The woman pressed her hand over Pitch's mouth. The sour tinge of her scent was upon her skin as well.

'Mr Astaroth is quite fine, sir.' Mrs Vellan's stuttering would convince no one. 'How about we get you back downstairs, then?'

'Where is he?' The oaf was bullheaded at the worst of times. 'He seemed quite unwell when he left the room. Can you not just direct me to where he is?'

'The thing is...I'm afraid...well, it's a delicate matter. Mr Astaroth is rather...he's rather...he's in some company, and rather busy.'

'Company? I don't understand...oh. I see.' How could such a large man sound so tiny? 'Well, tell Mr Astaroth when he is done, we will take our leave.'

Pitch knew the nuances of Silas's tone well. He was angry, confused...but there was something else. He was pained in some way. Heavy footsteps beat a path along the corridor. Leaving Pitch behind.

A good thing. He must cling to that.

'Silas,' he whispered.

'Shall we call him back?' The daemon's tongue brushed Pitch's ear. 'You could watch me play with him, if you like?'

Pitch's frantic pulse grew madder. 'Touch him and I'll kill you twice over.'

The woman's smile did not falter. 'I understand. You don't like others playing with your things. I'd not share him either if he were mine. A pity I could not have tasted him too, but Mr Crane needs to move him along. One should never keep a sorceress waiting. It is just bad manners.' She lowered her face to his chest and took a long, deep breath. 'You smell ever so curious, has anyone ever told you? You are all kinds of sour and sweet, or perhaps it's just been an age too long since I've tasted daemon. Either way, you make it rather easy to get the juices flowing, I'll say.'

Pitch wriggled beneath her, his body and mind caught in the weave of her web. A sorceress? What was this bitch on about? He needed to...needed to what? He rolled his head back and forth. Why was he here?

Damn it, everything was growing so fucking hazy. The woman sighed and traced a fingernail down the centre of his chest. He bucked, his eyes fluttering closed. That thread he clung to grew thinner.

'Let's have some fun, shall we?' She dug a fingertip into his nipple, and sweet agony fired across his chest.

The daemon bore down on him, sinking over him. Vanishing his rigid prick deep within.

He cried out. As much from the shock of it as the pleasure.

The relief was a torrent, chaotic and jarring. He drove into her, his cries wrung from him, his body, his traitorous body bucking and spasming as she worked him up and down. She'd woven him tightly in her enchantment, binding him there like a fly stuck upon a web, calling on the base depths of his nature with a song he could not ignore. She stole from his body, every bit as much as the bluecaps' had stolen from his mind.

This time, though, there was no fiery rage, or foolish ankou, to rescue the daemon from himself.

# CHAPTER 14

Silas raced down the stairs, fleeing the sounds that had escaped from one of the rooms and pursued him. He almost collided with the ankou who waited on him at the bottom of the staircase.

'Mr Mercer, did you get lost?' Mr Crane peered through his glasses with something that might have been irritation. 'I told you the library was across the hall. Whatever are you doing upstairs?'

Silas had to catch himself and wipe the stern frown from his face so that the other ankou would not see. It would be unseemly to be found pouty and disconcerted by a wanton daemon satisfying an appetite. Damn the bloody bastard. He'd been worried at the glazed look in Pitch-'s eye, the stumbled exit from the parlour, the entirely odd exhibition with the chocolate eclair. Granted, that part was only bothersome for how stirring it was. The sight of pillowy lips spreading to take in the girth of the pastry had made parts of Silas tingle. But the appeal had dimmed when he saw the confusion on Pitch's face. The daemon had dropped the eclair like it burned him the moment he realised what he was doing. As though he hadn't realised it before.

When Mr Crane excused himself to tend to some business and suggested Silas might enjoy perusing the book collection in the library while he waited, it had been the perfect moment to make a furtive trip upstairs. Just to confirm that Pitch had simply been looking for a reason to excuse himself from the room and a conversation he no doubt had been bored to tears with.

'My apologies, Mr Crane,' Silas said tightly. 'I was concerned about my companion. He did not seem quite himself.'

'I told you that Mrs Vellan would take care of him. Besides, I thought he seemed exactly himself.' Balthazar Crane's smile was tentative, the silver threads in his aura faint and drifting gently. 'Are daemons not rather slaves to their appetites, especially when in human form? And your Mr Astaroth is quite the ravenous type, they say.'

Silas frowned, though not, for once, at the suggestion that Pitch was *his* in any way. 'So far as you knew, he had asked to use the water closet. Why do you assume he is...' He couldn't bring himself to say it. The cries coming from that room rang in his ears, taunting him. Christ almighty, he was an idiot to be so rattled. What did Silas expect? That a rushed kiss and clumsy fondle on a kitchen table would be enough to satisfy the daemon's need? Silas had known this moment would come. He'd been braced and ready for it since they set out from Harvington Hall. But, stupidly, far too eagerly, he'd thought it would happen *with* him.

Mr Crane was regarding him. 'Why do I assume he is seeking pleasure? I would have been blind not to see how worked up he was in that parlour. With the way he was looking at you...I was wondering if I should have put a few pitchers of iced water in the room.'

Silas warmed. He'd not been blind. He'd seen the radiance in those green eyes. He could see nothing else. 'That look was not reserved for me, I assure you. He shares it about very easily when the mood is upon him.' Christ, he sounded bitter.

Maybe Mr Crane noted it, for there was a slyness behind his smile. 'He did not share it with me.' He let the words hang there a moment. 'But it would seem some among my household were to his tastes.' He waved off Silas's attempt at an apology. 'Pay it no mind, Mr Mercer. I have no quarrel with it. But really, Mr Astaroth must be quite the trial to journey with. I feel rather sorry for you.'

'He is not a trial,' Silas said, too quickly and with too much conviction. 'There is no reason to feel such pity, Mr Crane.' The silence was weighty.

Wonderful. Now he was behaving badly in front of the first ankou he-'d crossed paths with. He sighed. 'I'm sorry. It has been a dreadful...well, a dreadful few weeks, and now with this next teratism so close, I'm more short-tempered than I should be. I suppose I'm rather nervous, if I am honest.' He hadn't gone so far as to mention to his fellow ankou about the lost souls begging him to send them on their way. He could not say why, only that he felt no more settled here in this house than he had done anywhere along the road. 'I apologise.'

'And I am very glad, and honoured, that you are so frank with me. You have serious responsibilities indeed. I am quite glad that I do not need to deal with the monstrosities created by the Blight.' The ankou's gaze seemed drawn to the staircase. 'Here, I have an idea. Let us go for a walk, shall we?' Mr Crane moved away from the stairs. 'There is a very pleasant trail through the woods that will take us to a splendid greensward, not far from here. It would be a lovely stroll on such a mild afternoon, and it is a place I find most relaxing to visit.'

He guided Silas away from the staircase as he spoke, but not before Silas caught again the faint sound of pleasure coming from above. At least, he supposed it was pleasure. He was not going to stand about so he could decipher the distant grunts and cries.

'Yes. Yes, that sounds a splendid idea.' Silas hurried ahead, making his way to the front door even though he had no idea if that was where they were going.

Mrs Vellan stepped out of a room up ahead, wringing her hands, her head down. She must have used the servants stairs, for he'd not noticed her coming down behind him. But then, he probably wouldn't have noticed a bear following him, he'd been so distracted.

She seemed not to notice them at first, gasping when Mr Crane spoke.

'Mrs Vellan.' He was crisp and precise. 'Is all well?'

She bobbed in a hurried curtsy, her face pale. 'Yes, yes. All very well, sir.'

'Good, good.' Silas had the distinct sense that much of the conversation between them was unspoken. 'We are going for a stroll.'

'Very good, sir.' Her voice barely stretched the distance between them.

'Come along, Mr Mercer,' Mr Crane declared. 'I should like to hear more on the effects of the Blight on the lost souls. It truly sounds dreadful.'

Right now Silas was happy for any distraction from what was going on upstairs. His anger was a tight knot beneath his ribs.

They left the house, stepping out into a cheery but very brisk afternoon. Mr Crane led him over the road they had arrived on and uncomfortably close to the churning river once more. It was a good thing, actually, that Silas was so irritated, for he found his attentions elsewhere than upon the water. He barely even glanced at it as they moved deeper into the woodlands that flanked the house.

'Mr Mercer?'

Silas started, nearly tripping over a tree root. 'I beg your pardon?'

'I was just asking if you know what it is that saw you become a Horseman?'

'What it is?' Silas said, somewhat confused.

'Well, why you were chosen, rather than say, me? I'm ever so curious.'

'Ah, I see. I'm as curious as you, I haven't a clue I'm afraid. Was it Mr Ahari who...'

'Saw me out of my grave? Yes. Congenial enough chap, but he doesn't have a lot to say. Seems to prefer to leave one in the dark.' It was said with some heat, an irritation that Silas could relate to. 'He declared it was innate to me, this whole ankou thing, and I suppose he was right in the end. But blast him, could he not have spared a few moments more of his time to make it a little easier?'

'I am with you there.' Silas smiled as Mr Crane held back the thin branches of a goat willow, waiting for Silas to pass before letting it spring back across the path. 'He seems to go to great pains to say very little at all. I have the sense I am being tested most of the time. And have no idea if I am succeeding or failing at the task I've been set.'

'It seems you are doing very well indeed, for you are still on your feet, despite what has been sent your way. What with the Verderer and the revenants.'

Silas stared at the man's back. The silver threads moved quicker than before, weaving quiet patterns in the air. 'You know of the revenants?'

He thought he saw the man tense, but it may have just been borne from the ankou's attempts to stretch over a muddy patch of ground.

'Yes. Of course. News came from the Order.' Silas supposed it made sense that the other ankou would be warned they might be in danger of attack. 'It must have been dreadful.'

'I can't say I recommend it. Though in the end, they are not so hard to dispatch.' Especially when one had the assistance of a red-eyed beast. He kept the skriker to himself though, just as he did the encounter with the three souls in Castle Combe. 'I truly hope that might be the last of them.' He hesitated, unsure if he should speak about magick with his fellow ankou. How much did the fellow already know? More importantly, how much should Silas tell?

'Times are strange indeed, are they not?' Mr Crane said. 'The Blight has never been stronger, I'm told.'

The path they travelled wound through a forest sublime with its mosses and parsley ferns. The cool air touched at the back of Silas's neck.

'What do you know of it?' Silas asked.

'The Blight?'

'Yes. Have you been told of its origins?'

'A consequence of war...' Mr Crane glanced over his shoulder. 'A foul and bloody angels' war at that.'

'So you know of Samyaza, and the Watchers?'

'I do,' Mr Crane said simply.

Silas frowned at his feet, taking care around a collection of partially concealed roots in his path. He wondered who had told Mr Crane. Pitch had been the one to tell him of the rebellion. Without the daemon, Silas was not sure anyone at the Order would have enlightened him.

'But do you know what it is exactly?' he asked. 'Why it is that it affects human souls in such a way? I've not been able to discover it.'

'So the Order has not seen fit to speak of it even to their most esteemed of ankou, then?' The man's disdain was rich and evident.

'Mr Ahari told me it was a chaos at the heart of this world.' He knit his brow. 'And the Lady Satine, she said...' In truth not much at all, not of the origins of the Blight at least. 'She said that it had strengthened of late, but she did not know why.'

Mr Crane made a small sound, a huff of breath that Silas could not decipher. 'I doubt that very much.'

'That it has strengthened?'

'That she does not know why. Have you not noticed how very little we are told by the Order, Silas?'

Silas shrugged, oddly uncomfortable with the other ankou's criticism but unable to deny he had a point. 'I have noticed, very much so. It is vexing.'

'It is their way. To keep us in the dark because they do not deem us important enough for the truth.' He was scathing, kicking at the path as he walked. 'We are beholden to a goddess that tortures us with another year of life, claiming it in her name, and then casting us aside when her will is done. It is like showing a starving man a feast but keeping him at arm's length until he slowly starves away.' He stopped, turning to face Silas, who was caught off-guard by the sudden halt and took a hasty step back. 'I have but a month to go until Izanami is done with me.' He shuddered. 'A mere month and I will be stripped from this world again.' His voice cracked, and Silas thought he understood some of what was making the man seem so discomforted. He himself fought very hard not to think on the brevity of his second life.

'I'm sorry.'

'Don't be. It will happen to you, and it will be upon you before you know it. And you may find yourself making a desperate choice...' Mr Crane shook himself. 'Do you remember anything of your life, Silas? Is a Horseman given that pleasure at least, or is that stolen from you, as it was stolen from me?'

The light caught the ankou's glasses in such a way that his eyes were hidden behind a glare on the lens. The man seemed larger, the fine silver threads surrounding him seeming to stir and reach wider. Silas could have told the ankou the truth, that he had seen a fragment of his past, but instinct held his tongue once more. He was conscious, all at once, of how far from the house they had strolled. How far from Pitch and Lalassu he was.

Silas reassured himself, not for the first time, that if there were anything to fear here, the mare would have known it. He ignored the tiny voice that said she had not been there for him when the ash-men attacked, that the horse was not infallible.

'I don't recall anything of my life,' Silas said. 'I wish I could tell you otherwise.'

Mr Crane studied him for a long moment. 'Nothing of your death?'

Silas stared back. 'I...' He hesitated. 'What of you? Do you recall anything of it?'

Mr Crane's lips parted, but his words did not come straightaway. 'No...no I do not. And I suppose the goddess shows us a small mercy there, for we do not come from happy endings.'

'That much I do know,' Silas said quietly. Murder, regret, or grief. That was what held a soul so readily to the world. And he was not sure yet which of these kept him.

Mr Crane lowered his head, sweeping a hand through his hair. '- Forgive me, Silas. I am making you uncomfortable, and that was not my intention at all. I am very much looking forward to taking you to the greensward. I truly hope you find it enlightening.'

How a swathe of turf could be enlightening, Silas could only imagine. But the walk so far had been pleasant, at least so far as the scenery went.

They walked on a few steps in silence. Looking over his shoulder, Silas could see no hint of the house they had left behind. The forest was dense, with no sign of the greensward the ankou spoke of. If there was a wide expanse of grass here, it was well hidden. With his anger at Pitch well and truly cooled, Silas wondered if they should perhaps turn back. The daemon must be done with his infernal cavorting by now. Silas's belly clenched. Perhaps he was not quite ready to return. Let Pitch fume a while when he learned that Silas had gone expressly against his wishes, and left without telling him.

'So you did not say what you knew of the Blight, Mr Crane. In your time as ankou, has it been made any clearer to you?'

'Only when I found the right people to speak with, Mr Mercer.' He brushed at the low hang of a birch's slender, barren branches. 'There are those who wish us to know the truth behind the Blight.'

Silas's pulse seemed to stagger at that. 'And what might that truth be, Mr Crane?'

They stepped around a wych elm, and the way ahead opened up before the ankou could answer. A wide expanse of low, undulating hills covered in short brown grass ran for as far as the eye could see. He spied the dark curves of a riverbank further in the distance, winding its way through the brown and yellow landscape, but something drew his gaze westward, a tug on his senses like the buzzing of a fly in the corner of his eye.

An expansive circle of bright green shone under the midafternoon sun, far too meticulously rounded to be a naturally grown patch of turf. And far too healthy compared to the drab colours that surrounded it. The circle had something dotted around its edges, stones perhaps, or the stumps of fallen trees. But it was clear what this was.

The greensward.

And Silas did not wish to take another step towards it.

He pressed his hand to his pocket. Reassuring himself that the bandalore was with him. Gooseflesh crawled where the breeze touched his bare skin. Mr Crane was watching him.

'Don't be afraid, Silas. There is no need for it. I want you to see the truth as it's been shown to me. I want to offer you the chance to take control of the life that should be yours. You need not be beholden to the Order, or to the goddess. Another can take her place.' He was bright-eyed with a rising passion.

Shit. Silas had trusted far too blindly here. 'I think it best we return to the house now, Mr Crane.'

'Not yet. Not yet. There is so much for you to learn. Come with me, Silas. Let me show you how foolish they are.' He thrust his hand towards the greensward, which lay a good distance yet from where they stood, but not far enough so far as Silas was concerned. 'Come and learn. The Blight is not chaos, it is power. One that they cannot subdue. No matter how hard they may try or how powerful they believe themselves to be, they will all learn that they were never enough.'

Silas tore his gaze from the greensward. *You are not enough.* Those words were all too familiar. Hissed into his ear as the ash-men sought to take the bandalore from him.

'Balthazar, what have you done?'

Mr Crane laughed, and it was a pitched and crooked sound. 'Saved myself. Freed myself.' He stepped up to Silas, and it took every effort not to flinch away. 'And I want to help you do the same. Come, and you will see. They promised me you would have a chance.'

'A chance? To do what?'

'Survive, Mr Mercer.'

Bloody hell, Silas was every inch the idiot Pitch claimed him to be. Following after this stranger, letting himself be distracted by something so ridiculous as the daemon's ill-timed need for rutting.

The heat drained from him. Ill-timed, or perfectly timed? '-You manipulated him.' His mind raced. 'The food...you laced those pastries...' With something that might make a daemon wobbly on his feet and glassy-eyed. 'What the hell have you done to him?'

'I'm not sure that should be your biggest concern right now,' the ankou replied. 'And besides, there are far more unpleasant ways to be subdued. Mr Astaroth will be quite fine, so long as you do as I ask.'

Silas spun on his heels, entirely done with Mr Crane. 'Fuck you.' He was also done with niceties. 'If Pitch is harmed –'

'He won't be. A little exhausted perhaps...but otherwise intact. So long as you do as you are told. If you wish to ensure the safety of your daemon, then you will come with me. Test me, and he will suffer. As will dear old Mrs Vellan and her son. We, as ankou, may not be able to kill humans who are not yet marked for death, but I certainly know plenty who can.' His smile was strange, twitching and unable to settle into place. 'Come along now, Mr Mercer.' The ankou spread his arm as though presenting Silas with a gift, gesturing towards the swathe of green that shone as though spotlighted from above. 'And prepare to have your eyes widened.'

# CHAPTER 15

The distance to the greensward was deceptive and further than it appeared. More than once Silas considered fleeing back to the house. He was sick with the thought of having left Pitch there alone. He had given the daemon his word to never set off again without telling him.

Christ almighty. Silas should have known, damn it. But he'd been too busy playing the jealous fool to see that all was not well. That look on Pitch's face should have told him. The naked longing that had been clearly directed at Silas. That was not how the daemon played his games. He was never that vulnerable. That readable. Silas gritted his teeth. Such a longing had never surfaced before because it did not exist to surface. Pitch had been exploited somehow, made a liar of.

A fresh horror struck Silas. Had he misconstrued those sounds he'd heard? The ones he had flinched from?

For the first time the bandalore hummed. At least, that is what it seemed to try to do, but the notes at the back of Silas's mind came as though from beneath a dozen blankets.

The churn of unease took him harder. But he hardly needed the scythe's late warning to tell him all was not well. Why had it taken so bloody long to stir? Or had they meddled with the bandalore every bit as much as they had meddled with the daemon?

The greensward was just up ahead. His pulse thundered. A patch of skin on the back of his hand itched terribly. He might need to stop a moment if his stomach did not stop roiling. There could be no denying the signals his body gave him.

Go no further.

Mr Crane reached the brilliant carpet of spring-fresh grass. He did not glance back to see if Silas followed. He simply waited, hands behind his back, like a landowner surveying his acreage.

It was stones, Silas saw now, and not tree stumps that circled the greensward. Oval shapes that were placed at regular intervals about the circumference, most of them sitting lopsided and covered in pale lichen. These were not new additions certainly. Time and the elements had marked them well.

Silas blinked. There was a shimmer in the air about each of the stones, like tiny dust motes caught in the light filtering into a room.

'What is that?' He was several paces back from the circle, and that was far too close. The bandalore seemed to strain to call to him, sending its song out over a massive divide that weakened the sound.

'Come and see,' Mr Crane replied.

Silas knew it was the very last thing he should do. He shook his head. 'Balthazar, whatever this is, I can assure you it is most unwise. Do you not think the Order will come for you if we are harmed? I'm sure by now they know already that things are amiss –'

'Because of your horses?' He smiled, so very sure of himself. 'The ones that are in the deepest of sleeps in the stables, dreaming of wide pastures and salt licks?'

Silas stood on unsteady ground, in every way. He might have accused the ankou of lying were it not for the fact that Lalassu was nowhere to be found. The horse that had sensed the approach of the necromancer's wagon was not making the earth shudder with her approach. There was no chance she would not be menacing this insane man right now if she were able.

'Mr Crane,' Silas said, feeling all the more desperate. 'This is madness. Whatever you intend here –'

'Madness? To wish to serve masters who will deem me worthy of more than being a servant? I think not, Mr Mercer.' He jerked his chin towards the circle. 'The Horseman is hesitating. Give him some encouragement.'

'Who are you talking –'

A scream came from within the circle. Throaty, anguished, and crackling beneath its own weight.

'Help me.' A youthful voice, weighted by manhood.

The sounds seemed to be right in front of him, but Silas could see no sign of any life. Not even a darting bird or flitting insect passed across the circle of bright, uniform blades of grass. For a terrible, terrible moment he thought it was Pitch who called out, then he felt all the worse for the flicker of relief that came with realising it was not the daemon's voice.

Silas took an unwilling step forward. 'Who is that?'

'Did I not make it clear there will be suffering if you do not follow me? Step into the circle, Silas.'

'No.'

This time the scream dragged on, as though using all the air in the wretched man's lungs. It came again from right in front of him, so damned close that Silas staggered back, bile burning at the back of his throat. But he saw nothing. No one in agony. No one writhing beneath the torment inflicted on them.

'Stop. Stop! Christ, Balthazar.'

'Step into the circle, Silas.' He bit down on each word. 'Enter the greensward, and they might leave him with some skin upon his bones. Mrs Vellan might still recognise her son.'

Silas had to press his lips to keep from retching. The muffled call of the bandalore sought to push its way clear, as though Silas still needed warning that here was a bad place. Balthazar Crane watched him through smudged lenses. He might have spoken firmly, without a waver, but he did not stand so surely. The ankou shifted from foot to foot, and the fingers he raised to push back his spectacles shook hard.

'Please, Silas,' he whispered. 'Let them show you how it could be. Do you not wish to see the truth?' If he were a piece of porcelain, he would have cracked with those words. The ankou could not have looked more frail, more desperate.

'You cannot force me onto the greensward, can you?' Silas said, as certain of it as he was that he should listen to his instincts, his bandalore, and flee this place. But he could not heed that warning. Not after hearing those screams and knowing that Pitch was a hostage in that blasted house.

'I can,' Balthazar returned. 'But it is better that I don't, they say. Your surrender will...strengthen things. Besides, I do not *want* to force you. My intentions are good. I promise you.'

'Good?' Silas laughed. 'Bloody hell, man, you are likely torturing someone, you have plied my companion with an elixir that has rendered him senseless, and you've sedated our mounts.'

'Because I wanted your full attention, Silas. *They* want your full attention.'

'Who, damn you?'

'Those who can free us.' The shimmer around the stones grew more pronounced as the sun disappeared behind a passing cloud. The strangeness and horror of the situation was made all the more so by the temperate, pleasant day. 'At long last they have risen from the hidden places and will show us the light.'

Silas stared at the other ankou, his throat tight. The world shimmered about him, as though all the solidness had been taken from it. 'You have lost your mind.'

The man's scream came for the third time, more garbled this time, as though he barely had the strength to make a sound.

'I thought you a sympathetic man.' Crane raised his voice. 'The lost souls talk of you as though you are their saviour. They are so disappointed when it is me who appears to them and not you. But it seems the living don't interest you so well. Perhaps you will be more readily convinced if we bring your daemon here and let Nemain play with him instead?'

Silas hesitated. Not because he wished them to lay a hand on Pitch. Christ, the very thought had him clenching his fists so hard his knuckles ached. But because it would mean that Silas could see for himself if he was well.

He shook off the notion as soon as it rose. 'No. Do not bring him into this, any more than you have. If I listen, you will let that man and Tobias go, with no more harm done to them.'

'Of course.' Crane was a terrible liar. The sweat alone on his brow would have betrayed him, a misplaced heat on a cool day.

Silas breathed in. There was no doubt moving forward was an absolutely terrible idea, but all he had of use to him was time.

Time for Pitch to find a way to fight off whatever beguiling trap held him; time, perhaps, for the Lady Satine to notice how quiet her mares were and become concerned. Silas surveyed the sparse surrounds from beneath a furrowed brow. There was the skriker too. The beast had found him once before in a time of need. Dear God, let that creature find him again.

Silas pressed forward before he became cemented to the spot. The bandalore's notes were incessant, though with each step they seemed to grow fainter still. He slipped his hand into his pocket. The bandalore's string did not reach to meet him, but at least he held its solid discs in his grasp. With pulse quickening, he strode between the stones and into a swirl of glittering air so thick he had to blink madly to keep his eye on the way ahead. He was struck with the most uncomfortable sense of something hooking into his chest and pulling at him. As though claws had found their way around his ribs. His head pounded with an ache, right at his forehead, and white spots blotted his view of the world.

Silas uttered a shocked cry, stumbling ungraciously onto the all-too-green swathe of grass. Falling to his knees upon the greensward, with a weight bearing down on him that made all thought of rising seem impossible, he released the bandalore to clutch at his head, squeezing his eyes open and shut, trying to make out his surrounds.

A darkened patch before him stole the greenness from the landscape. His vision was too blurred, his head too cluttered to make sense of what he was looking at. But there was no such confusion about the figures that stood to the side of the spread of darkness.

Three that he could make out. The middle seemed closest, a figure in all shades of shadow and grey. Someone was groaning to his right, but they were little more than a heap of white upon the ground.

'Take him, not too rough now.' The voice was unpleasant on the ear, but more so what followed.

There was an explosion of laughter. Youthful voices, squealing with delight. A shiver of familiarity ran through him. Silas lifted his hand to retrieve the bandalore, but he was far too slow. His arm was grabbed and wrenched behind his back as though he were but a puny boy fighting a giant.

'No daemon around this time to save you,' a child whispered.

The hands came at him from every angle. How many of these infernal sods were there? Grasping at him, pulling at the lengths of his coat. Drawing him down.

'Let me go,' Silas roared, flailing about with all the strength he could draw, which here, upon the greensward, seemed to be pathetically inadequate. His coat was heavy as a fisherman's net full of a day's catch. Silas threw his mindfulness towards the bandalore, shouting at the scythe to heed his call and come to him. But he had the sense of shouting across a chasm, and he could not make himself loud enough to be heard.

Hands found him, with sharp nails that pierced through his coat and stabbed into his upper arms. Strands of hair whipped against his face, blinding him again just as the strange dust had begun to clear.

And the laughter. Good god, it was dreadful. Punching at his senses. Tickling at his memories.

Silas sought to swing his arms. He may as well have coated them in mud and hung anchors from them for all the momentum he could achieve. Getting to his feet was an impossibility.

His terrible idea now seemed ten times more so.

A kick to his gut sent him jerking backwards. He braced for a fall, but his back landed against a solid mass. Pincers found his shoulders, sinking through the fabric of coat and shirt alike, and dragging from him a howl of protest. All at once there were flapping wings landing upon his face. His world became a flurry of feathers that reeked of foul and foetid things. He flung his head this way and that, trying to make sense of the chaos that had descended on his world.

A pair of massive birds, greater than vultures, with long crooked necks and eyes too wide for their tiny heads, flanked him. His pulse, already thundering, picked up its pace. Dear god, he knew these creatures with their filthy wings and their bald heads. They had tried to tear him apart in the cemetery beside Holly Village.

'Harpies,' he breathed.

# CHAPTER 16

H e did not wish to be here. That was all Pitch knew for sure through the deluge of lust and greed that enveloped him, and through the grunt and heave and thrust of bodies. He did not wish to be here, not truly, but if he were set free right then, he was not sure he would run. Or fight.

His appetite raged.

The daemonkind woman, a succubus of the like he'd never encountered in Arcadia, was a beauty to behold, with her skin the hue of a farm girl's but as smooth as marble, her wayward black curls bouncing upon her shoulders, shrouding her wide brown nipples in a moving veil. She had her hands planted against his shoulders, forcing him down, making it difficult for him to find the rhythm of their union. But then, she did not wish him to mark the pentameter of this dance. He was not allowed to lead here. Throat tight with the cries he tried to stifle, Pitch found himself comparing her to another who had liked to hold him down, dictating every move. Seraphiel had not been an easy lover. Thorough, and enduring, yes, the perfect partner if one enjoyed a decent sprinkling of pain with their pleasure. Raph had come at carnal pleasure like he'd done most things. Head on. With purpose. Slightly distracted and distant, as though his mind were already moving on to something else, even when he was buried to the hilt in his lover.

Like him, this daemon sought to dominate, to own. But where Raph had been seemingly unaware of his own devastating strength, this daemon was very much aware of hers and its effect on him. She was the clear master and intent on making him a slave to her enchantment. She had crossed a boundary by doing so. Daemons did not, as a rule, manipulate each other. Not without consent. But he should have been able to make light work of her advances. He should not have been so easily made a servant to his desires.

For all his efforts, Pitch could not seem to reverse the tables. He was weakened where he should be strong. The restlessness within was tangled up in her, stirring lazily as though half-asleep. She had him sedated, every bit as much as aroused.

He did not wish to be here.

Pitch threw back his head, body straining with her attentions. Trying to send his thoughts anywhere else but between his damned legs.

He stared up. The ceiling was carved full of sigils.

Fucking magick. He'd never seen humankind's sorcery in reality. If it had been there in years past, he'd taken no notice. But there were some faint resemblances to the divine markings of the angelics in the works above him, and *that* he had seen plenty of. Mostly in Raph's Sanctuary, in that damned room the angel couldn't seem to tear himself away from, a cluttered workshop of some kind where he'd tinkered like an obsessed chemist, leaving Pitch wandering the hallways and eating himself senseless for hours as the Seraphim worked. It had caught him by surprise, how lonely it would be to be desired by a great and mighty angel. He'd not even been allowed to leave the Sanctuary, couldn't have found it now if he'd wanted too. He'd admit it to no one, but he'd been held there like a captured fucking bride.

'Get off me,' he hissed, only to have his mouth betray him a moment later with a groan as she twisted her hips to devour him more deeply.

'I know you can handle more, Mr Astaroth.' Her breath held hints of mint and lemon.

'I said stop.' He was saying it, he could hear the words coming out of his mouth, but his body took no notice. He met her thrusts. He was shuddering already with the build of another release. Gods, her enchantment was formidable. It felt as though it touched at every desire he'd ever known. He had his fair share of incubus blood. It caused him no end of cravings, for sex, for the fight, for sweeter things, but this creature, she put him to shame. If this were not an outright assault, he might have been awed by how she played with him like he were the most malleable of humankind.

But it *was* an assault. He had been waylaid, blindsided, and he did not wish to be here.

There was somewhere else he should be. If he could only calm himself a moment to think clearly on where that was.

'I'm not quite done with riling you up, pretty one.' A bead of sweat dripped from her chin, and when it struck his cheek, his stomach roiled. He shook his head. His hair was plastered to the sides of his face and would not budge.

'Gods, I said...' He hesitated. He said what? Pitch winced; this arousal had needle points.

She lifted his hands from where he pressed them at her thighs in a weak attempt to fend her off. He would have laughed at himself were he not so bloody horrified at his inability to end this. The woman pressed his hands above his head, down onto the rug, which seemed to only have grown colder against Pitch's back.

'We can't stop yet, I'm afraid. I need you here a little longer.' Her breasts glanced against his chest. Her mouth came far too close to his. The waft of lemon rose over the mint now, and his head spun.

Needed him here longer? Why would she say that? Pitch squeezed his eyes shut. Gods damn the bitch to any hell that would have her. She had him rigid, coiled, and so very nearly blinded by need.

'Careful, Onoskolis.' That other voice again. A quiet observer to his downfall.

Pitch sought to tilt his head, to follow the sound which came from behind. Onoskolis? The name wasn't familiar, but there *was* something familiar about the other voice. 'Don't take from him too deeply, or you'll end up no better than our kin.'

The daemon woman's laughter snapped at the air. 'Your queen was greedy to begin with, always had been, and it made you all weak.'

'Watch your dirty mouth.'

She moved languidly now atop him, taking her sweet time with his pleasure. Time...what did she need time for?

146

'What? I can't speak the truth?' said the daemon, Onoskolis. 'Your queen's greed led you all to feast on one of daemonkind, and you thought that would end well for you?' She tutted, and there was some fierce muttering from the other speaker Pitch could not make out. 'I suppose you were all mad at the time, but it was hardly going to take much to make the bluecaps mindless, was it?'

Bluecaps. Fuck, this day got worse. There was a godsdamned bluecap here, watching him being ridden like a show pony. Another good reason Pitch should not be here. He should be...elsewhere...someone was waiting on him. He'd not come here alone. Had he?

No.

He was not alone.

Through the haze, the muddle that was his mind, Pitch found a real flicker of pleasure. A faint and ill-defined thought of another, and with that thought, the tension, the brace of his body against assault, eased ever so slightly.

'That's it, Mr Astaroth,' Onoskolis murmured against his ear. 'It is far more satisfying if you do not fight me. This need not be so terrible.'

'Piss off.'

She patted his cheek. 'Not yet.'

'I did not feed on him, I'll have you know,' the bluecap declared, voice squeaking with indignation. 'Many of us did not follow Her Majesty's lead, but still he brought the walls down upon us. He slaughtered us all.'

'Well, not all, you're still with us to tell the tale. You should probably have thanked the ankou before Mr Crane took him away. If not for you having to lead Mr Mercer out of the mine and missing the entertainment, you'd have been biting into our pretty daemon here just like all the others. And died with them too. How terrible.' Her laughter, scoured with disdain, said she did not think it so terrible at all. She truly had an unpleasant laugh. It shook her whole body, her muscles tightening around his prick. 'If your queen had tried such a thing with me, I would have done the very same, and that mine would be no less ruined than it is now.'

'Her Majesty wasn't to blame, not entirely.' The bluecap seethed. 'She wasn't in her right mind, as you know. But they'd have survived what was done to the Verderer and the forest if it weren't for this bastard.'

Pitch barely heard them past the mention of one name. Mr Mercer. He knew that name. He could breathe easier just thinking it.

Gods. Silas.

Silas Mercer.

How stupefied had they made him if Pitch could forget the ankou for even a moment?

*Mr Crane took him away.*

For Mr Crane's sake, he best have done so simply to show Silas the thrills of the nearest graveyard. For anything else was going to cost him his miserable second life.

# CHAPTER 17

'Get your bloody hands off me,' Silas shouted.

His head throbbed. Behind his eyes was worst of all, as though something writhed about in his skull and sought escape.

A pair of harpies, in their vile and natural state, alighted on his shoulders. And they drove their exposed talons through the soft flesh below where his collar bone reached to meet his arm. Silas's scream rose over the maelstrom of birdlike screeches around him. The pain made him light-headed, the world a spinning top. He collapsed to his knees, seeking to pull away from the agony that beset his shoulders.

Instead, fresh pain was wrought upon him.

Wings scraped his back, tension pulled his coat taut behind him. There was a pressure at his calves. And then nothing but hot, splicing pain. Knife-like claws tore through the bulge of calf muscle, pinning his legs to the damp ground. Silas's mouth was rounded, wide open with a desperate, silent cry.

'Do hold still, Mr Mercer.' The voice was like the clanging of a church bell, resolute and booming about the space as though he were in an enclosed room and not the openness of the countryside. 'I'm sure you'd not like to see our friend here wounded any further. I hear you are a congenial chap that way.'

Silas pressed trembling lips tight. His body shook, and his shoulders burned where the talons impaled him. His arms dangled like a scarecrow's whose legs had buckled beneath him. The harpies' harsh wings impeded his view of the surroundings and filled his nostrils with a stench that made his eyes water.

'Is Pitch here?' His tongue was thick in his mouth.

'Oh no, no. He's quite occupied with other things right now.' The harpies cackled at that. 'We have another guest with us, one who is feeling rather sorry for himself right now. Much like you.'

Mrs Vellan's son.

'I was promised he would be safe...my companion too, if I came to you.'

'A good thing for us you are so very concerned about others, isn't it?' The timbre was deep. It forced itself upon the ears, sending any other sound fleeing. 'This might have been more troublesome if it were your daemon friend we had to deal with, for I doubt Mr Astaroth would care a whit if we gutted this fellow right in front of him. Do give Mr Mercer a little space, will you? I think he understands now there is little point in seeking to escape.'

The harpies upon Silas's shoulders drew their talons clear. He choked on his cry. The wretched creatures lifted away. One of them glanced their wing against his chin, opening the skin.

Silas grunted but clenched his jaw, refusing to scream again. Blood flowed, warm and sickly, from the punctures in his flesh and the slice on his cheek. The stifled cry brought tears to his eyes. Tears that at last shifted the blur caused by the odd dust he'd struck on entering the circle. He had his first clear glimpse of his surrounds. The smear of darkness he'd spied earlier was a pond. Lily pads with torn edges drifted atop the water, bumping against clumps of yellow froth floating like scrambled eggs upon the surface. The pond was modest in size, he could have cast a fishing line from one bank to the other without too much effort, but there was no telling how deep it might be. He could see no hint of the bottom from where he knelt. It was like looking at a giant vat of gravy. The water was thick and impenetrable with silt.

And he was far closer to it than he liked.

If he were pushed onto all fours, his hands would sink into the putrid water.

He sucked in an unsteady breath. It would not do to allow them to see any hint of the panic that held him.

Silas pulled his gaze from the pond to the far bank. The figures he'd glimpsed before and three harpies in their vagabond, childlike forms gathered near the bundle of white that had caught his eye when first he'd found his way into this ring of horrors. Silas could not decide where to look first: at the unfortunate lad who lay curled in on himself on the ground, his face battered terribly, crimson smearing most of it; or the masked and cloaked figure who stood over him. They were tall, but that was all he could tell of their appearance, for the cloak they wore draped like a covered statue in a summer house closed for the winter months and hinted at no detail of what lay beneath. The cloak was a dense material. Leather, Silas would say at a guess, though black as the deep shade of night. Their mask covered their face almost entirely too, leaving only the lips bare, dangling blue-black feathers hanging on either side of their lips like a partly opened curtain.

Two more figures in identical dress stood behind, one considerably taller and broader than the other. He thought at first one had a harpy perched on their shoulder, but he blinked again and saw it for what it was. A raven.

'What have you done to him?' Silas rasped.

He studied the prostrate figure. The lad shifted, rolling back on his hip, groaning. The short-lived movement revealed a hint of red at his breast. A handkerchief, bright as a summer apple.

Christ. There was no doubt of it, then. This was the stable boy, the youngster who must have barely made his way through his teens, who lay injured. Mrs Vellan's son.

Silas swayed back, and the harpies at his back reminded him all too well of his circumstances. Their beaks snapped at his shoulder blades, and their talons, embedded in his calves, rang a new song of vicious woe through his senses. He hissed through the pain, tilting forward where his punctured shoulders joined the chorus. Bloody hell, he'd not known anything like it. His vision tilted, threatened to blacken entirely. The two harpies who had ruined his shoulders danced alongside him, cackling their delight in his misery.

'Like I said, Mr Mercer,' the deep voice came from the stout figure beside the slighter one paired with the raven. 'It is best you stay still.'

A sharp whistle sounded, and the harpies at Silas's side, their talons dark with his blood, stretched their tattered, ugly wings and soared low over the ground to settle beside the figure with the raven. That bird tilted its head to peer down at them. The harpies danced their claws against the turf like soldiers readying to march. They were massive creatures, half as high as the figure they settled by, though in truth that person was not so imposing themselves. The top of their head would barely have reached Silas's chest.

'I should tell you,' he said, seeking to sound menacing, 'that you are interfering in the affairs of the Order, and they will not thank you for it.'

'And how often does the Order thank you, Mr Mercer?' The hulking figure spoke, a rumbling depth to their tone that caused Silas unwelcome shivers. 'I doubt they spare such trivial things as a thank-you for their servants, do they? You simply do as you are told. Do you not?'

Silas glared. The other ankou had spoken of such things, of taking control, of not being beholden to the Order. Or the goddess.

But why did Balthazar Crane seek such things?

Did the ankou not feel the scythe to be a part of him, as Silas did?

To imagine being without the bandalore, even when it was quiet as a long-forgotten tomb, as it was now, was incomprehensible to him. Had *become* incomprehensible. The sense that the scythe was an extension of all that he was, another limb, a vital organ Silas could not exist without, had come upon him gradually. Strengthening with each strike of the blade. Stealthy as a sunrise.

Until he found himself here, as clearheaded about his place as the pain would allow.

'I do not need the Order's thanks,' Silas declared, meaning it well. 'I have that from those I save. And so long as the Order has me protecting lost souls, then yes, I will do exactly as I am told.'

The man sniffed and laughed at the same time, giving the sound a disturbing quality. 'How very noble of you. A pity the Order is not so. They are witch hunters, do you know? Murderers of innocents, so as to protect their secret.' The figure at his side made their first movement of note, a shuffle that set the folds of their cloak swaying. 'You are complicit in that too, Mr Mercer. But you murder the dead, while they take care of the living.'

'Now you are talking foolish nonsense.' Granted, some of it may be true. Sybilla had...dealt...with the emergence of Azazel's magick for centuries. But with cause. The maleficium would ultimately corrupt those who used it and put the innocent in danger.

'Are you so sure?'

'Iblis.' The interruption came from the second figure. 'I would like to begin.' A woman Silas would wager, from the high tilt of the voice.

'Of course. Forgive me.' The man, Iblis, pulled his hand from beneath the folds of his coat and set it on the empty shoulder of the woman who stood beside him. The raven leaned out, head turning in that jerky way that birds had to set one eye upon the man's hand on its mistress's shoulder. 'You know full well what damage the Order can do. I simply wished Mr Mercer to know what sort of organisation he is a part of before you dealt with him.'

The man pulled his hand away, the bird watching him all the while. The harpies surrounding them snapped at one another, ruffling feathers and growling like an angry mob.

'And what exactly do you intend for me?' Silas spoke with a brazenness he did not feel. He was parched by discomfort. The pressure behind his eyes was staggering. And he was not sure how much longer he could stay upright on his knees.

'I intend to take your scythe,' the woman said, hushed, as though she spoke at a funeral.

Wretched as he may feel, with blood streaming from his wounds and the brittle sear of pain at his legs, Silas could not help but laugh. 'You wish to take the scythe?' Christ, laughing was a terrible idea for his wounds. 'Did you not already learn through your walking corpses that such a thing is impossible?'

It was, wasn't it? No one could take the scythe from death's messenger, surely? The ash-men had tried in their crude fashion to do so, but they were mere puppets.

'Those revenants were not mine. And I am stronger than my siblings. Nothing is impossible, Silas,' said the woman with the raven. 'Difficult, maybe. But I assure you, not impossible. I will take your scythe, and we will see what it is that makes you unique among the ankou.'

She edged her arms from the cloak, slipping the fabric back over her shoulders, revealing more layers of dark material beneath. There was no belt or cinching to define a waist; there was no form to her at all. Just layers and layers of the dense fabric. She held a thin blade. Silas noted the swirl of dust about it, the same he'd seen around the stones.

'Does the Order truly believe magick can be subdued? That they could slay innocents for centuries and there would be no repercussions? This is *my* magick, my mother's before me, and hers before that. A gift.' She drew a sharp breath. 'Do you know where our gift comes from, Mr Mercer?' He said nothing. 'An angel. A magnificent and glorious angel, and by the grace of the goddess Morrigan his legacy has survived. I have endured. My family endured, generation after generation, growing stronger. We survived to honour Azazel. And now I walk in his light. The Order has tried very hard to extinguish that light, Mr Mercer.'

'Come along now, Nemain.' Iblis was strangely gentle, but his voice held no less of a command. 'We should begin and not dally.'

'I am focused, Iblis. I assure you. But I have waited a long while to speak my mind,' she said. The raven cawed, the sharp sound making Silas's skin crawl all over again.

Bloody hell, it was becoming a monstrous struggle to keep upright, to keep his head clear. His thoughts were worms, sliding from sharp edges in his mind, but one word stuck fast. Morrigan. He'd heard that name before. But where?

'You have waited a very long while, indeed,' Iblis said carefully. 'And I have kept you safe for equally as long. Now let us do what we set out to do. Focus upon that.'

The woman rounded on him. 'I appreciate your guidance, Iblis. You protected my family when all others would have seen us slain. For that I am indebted to you, we all are, but do not mollycoddle me. I am well aware of the need for focus, and I have it. See for yourself how helpless the pale Horseman is.' She laughed, and there was much unsteadiness about it. 'Lady Satine's precious little rider is here. Death's own servant is on his knees before us, thanks to my magick.' She waved the knife about to mark her words. The harpies at her side and at Silas's back cackled. The raven sat, unperturbed by her vigour. 'Macha couldn't manage her bloody corpses well enough to capture Mr Mercer, but I have done so.'

Iblis raised his hands. 'You are formidable. The angel has blessed you, and the goddess watches over you.' His head shifted, and though Silas could not see the man's eyes, he felt his attention had moved to the raven. 'You are the lighthouse in this darkness, and it is through your glow that we will find what we search for, but let us not tempt the fates and linger here too long. Badh can likely only hold the daemon and the horses so long.'

Two of the harpy children that stood by him, clad in their rip-weary rags, toed the grass with dirty bare feet as though terribly bored with all the misery.

'Even if they are free, they cannot find him here,' she snapped. The woman was just as restless, shifting back and forth on her feet. Her irritation reminded Silas of Pitch in some ways, how it lurked dangerously beneath the surface. He winced to think on the daemon.

'But *we* must leave eventually,' Iblis soothed. 'It is us I worry they will find. So shall we begin?'

The raven's drawl crept along the air. The woman nodded. 'We shall.'

Silas licked his dry lips. The pounding in his head was like a builder-'s hammer against a nail. It was increasingly difficult to focus on the conversation, but the name exploded from the back of his skull like it had been sent from a slingshot. Morrigan. The goddess who had aided Samyaza and the Watchers when they arrived in this world. Sheltering them while they constructed their man-made monstrosities.

The woman and her raven made their way about the pond, past the silent figure who still stood over the barely conscious lad. It was astounding how formidable a presence she was, despite her stature being so diminutive. The raven played no small part in making her seem much larger, the knife a part in making her more dangerous. She took her time to come to him. By the time she was close, Silas was swaying on his knees, aching to his core.

'Mr Mercer, I want you to know who I am so my name might play on your lips as you scream for your freedom.' She tilted her chin, her declaration announced with the pride of a conqueror.

'I already know who you are,' Silas's breath was stolen from him with each word, the pain dragging them forth. 'You are someone I do not like at all.'

'That hardly concerns me. I am not here to be liked. I am here to serve my master.' She bent down to speak at his ear. The raven shifted with her, the bird's sharpened beak discomfortingly close to Silas's eyes. 'I am the sorceress Nemain. Azazel's magick runs thick in my veins, as it does my siblings'. The Order has not met the likes of us, I assure you. And they will imprison him no longer. Our master shall be found.'

The pounding in Silas's head marked the tempo of her mad words. 'If you speak of Azazel, you are in the wrong world, I'm afraid.' He tried to smile and was not sure if his mouth moved in such a way. He was growing numb all over. 'He was banished from this world and cannot return.'

'You misunderstand me, Mr Mercer.' She studied him from behind darkened eyes. The tip of her blade touched the underside of his chin. 'It is not Azazel I speak of at all. It is the Watcher King Samyaza who calls to us.'

He squeezed his eyes shut against the thump of his skull. Samyaza? What new madness was this? Silas shook his head and regretted it instantly. He was shivering now, the headache consuming him. He had the terrible sense of an onslaught, a tidal wave approaching. 'Samyaza was destroyed...' He was surprised the words formed at all. 'The Seraphim destroyed him. Long before you or I drew breath in this world.'

The woman leaned in very close, and the raven's feathers brushed his cheek. He nearly cried out; the touch of them burned. 'Do you truly think that one such as he, for all his might, could be entirely vanquished? And he is stronger now than ever. Do you know of the Berserker Prince, Mr Mercer?' Silas tensed, lips pressed. 'We owe much to his fits of rage, for it was when he struck down the Seraphim that our master's voice found its freedom. The Watcher King calls to us.'

The harpies weighted upon each of his thighs cackled and shifted, burying their talons deeper into his flesh.

Silas lifted his head, but it was a weight he could barely handle, and he could not shape any words with his useless tongue.

'You hear him, you see what he creates,' she continued, tapping the knife tip against his chin. 'The Blight carries our master's messages, and you keep trying to silence him, Mr Mercer. You keep swinging that fucking blade about and destroying his creations. I am here to make you stop.'

She stepped back, but not before the raven snapped at Silas's ear, tearing at the lobe. The pain was insignificant compared to what he endured already, and he barely flinched.

Christ almighty, did this mad woman suggest the Watcher King somehow yet lived?

Nemain turned, calling out to the cloaked figure who still stood over Mrs Vellan's battered son. 'Bring him to the edge of the water.'

They gave her a sharp nod and dragged the weakly struggling man to the pond, almost directly opposite to where Silas knelt, impaled and captive. The harpies who had been on Silas's shoulders earlier wobbled about the terrified lad, weaving their heads about on sinewy, snakelike necks. The cloaked figure shoved the young man down onto his knees, where the water lapped at his thighs, and jerked his head back so that his throat was exposed. A terrible, sick curl of dread crept through Silas.

'What are you doing?' he rasped, unsure if his words would even reach the woman's ears. 'Leave him, damn you. You have me here, is that not enough?'

'Of course not. Did I not say I want to see what your scythe can tell me? I want to strip away your layers, Mr Mercer, and find the heart of the man beneath. And for that, I'll need the lifeblood of a man.' Nemain joined the cloaked man where he stood with his sobbing hostage. The other man, the one who had cautioned her to take care, watched on silently from where he stood near one of the lilting stones that formed the diabolical circle. The harpy children waited by him, one of them scratching at the tangled, oily mess that was their head of hair.

As Nemain drew near with her blade, the lad found a new strength, flailing his arms in feeble protest, his shifting about sinking him lower into the mud.

'Help me! Please help me.'

A stain spread upon the crotch of his trousers as his terror bloomed large. He saw his fate, as clearly as Silas did.

'Stop. I beg you!' Silas shouted, and the pressure behind his eyes dealt him a cruel blow. He swayed, and the harpies at his back dug their talons deeper into his calves. 'Let him go. You have me...' He gasped as every inch of skin fired with pain. 'You promised...if I came to you...'

'I never promised you his freedom. That was not me.'

It was Mr Crane who had made such a false promise.

The ankou had promised that Pitch would be safe, too, if Silas played his part.

Bloody hell, that bastard's words were not worth the spit it took to form them.

A knot pressed at the back of Silas's throat. He looked to the heavens where all the gods seemed to have found better things to do than follow his plight. Christ, did Izanami not see what was happening? One of her own ankou had turned betrayer, and Silas was laid out like a sacrifice while his guardian may be...Silas froze that thought. He could not allow it to take shape. Pitch was no mere daemon. They could not harm him. *God, do not let them harm him.* Silas had walked away from the daemon a second time, left him alone when he was vulnerable. No matter how these next moments played out, he'd never forgive himself for that.

'I'm begging you.' Silas doubted that would make a lick of difference here, but he was desperate. Maybe the goddess was ignoring him because she was ashamed of how bloody easily he had been duped into being here. 'You don't need this man's blood on your hands. He is innocent.'

Nemain glanced up at him from where she held the tip of the blade to the whimpering man's throat. She was smiling. No, she was grinning. 'Mr Mercer, his blood on my hands is exactly what I need. For what is death magick without death?'

'Help me.' The lad's fright-widened eyes found Silas. He shook so hard that he was liable to cut his own throat from all the moving about. 'I don't want to die.'

All the harpies were raucous at that, cackling like a deranged flock of geese. Silas winced.

Nemain gave the ankou no chance to utter a single consoling word. She drew the blade across the man's throat, slicing him open in one swift movement. 'Let him go.'

The cloaked figure released their hold, and the young man fell forward, gasping, choking, making all manner of dreadful sounds as the life drained from him. He landed face-first in the pond, his blood fanning out around his head in an awful halo.

'No! What have you done?' Silas's guttural cry was wretched, searing his throat like it was made of thorns. His skull felt cracked, fit to splinter wide open, the unbearable pressure behind his eyes making him breathless. 'He had no part in this.'

'The irony is that is exactly why he had a part in this.' The sorceress tucked her blade away beneath copious layers and made her way around the pond, her cloak dragging through the muddied edges, the raven sitting quietly upon her shoulder. 'The blood of an innocent has a power of its own.'

Nemain's fingers glistened with that blood. She took her time circumnavigating the pond, as though not bothered by a care in the world. She returned to stand before Silas.

'Hold him still,' she ordered.

The harpies flew from the far side of the body of water to join their brethren who still anchored Silas to the ground. The pair were in their childlike form and ran, giggling, hand in hand to join their brethren. The sound turned his stomach and made his flesh crawl. Hands and claws fought for purchase on his body, taking his arms, pulling them by his sides. The sorceress once again had the blade at his chin. Silas shook his head, trying to fend her off. The metal scored his skin, burning sure as any flame.

Christ, what he wouldn't do right now to see Pitch's flames purge this damned place to ash. But now he feared what might happen if the daemon *did* appear. If Silas was right, if Pitch was all he imagined him to be, then what might these cretins do with the very prince whose wild actions they believed had stirred their master?

Nemain pushed back the hair that was caked to his forehead by sweat and grime. And she traced her finger through the blood that clung to her blade. She touched her saturated finger to Silas's brow, sweeping it about, marking him with the blood of the housekeeper's young son.

Her lips moved with words he did not recognise, slippery words that kept her lips pressed close together, the air whistling between them.

The bandalore's note came as if from the heavens, as far away as any of the help he had prayed for.

The raven shrugged its wings and let loose with croaking that made Silas's blood run cold beneath the oozing warmth across his brow.

Nemain ran her tongue across her teeth. 'You don't like the water, do you, Mr Mercer?'

The wave of panic that swept him held ice and jagged pieces. 'I care neither way for it.'

Her lip twitched. 'Terrible liar. I hear from good sources that you are uncommonly fearful of a shallow stream. And prone to refusing a bath when it is offered to you. They remarked upon that with much amusement at The Moon Inn.'

Silas's shudders were impossible to hide, but he refused to look her in the eye. He stared beyond her to where the pond was almost completely stained now by the spread of the stable boy's blood, shifted from hickory brown to a putrid claylike red. 'You are misinformed.' His heartbeat was in time with the thumping inside his head, loud in his ears.

That fucking boggart, the very bane of their lives. But that creature had not betrayed them alone. Bloody hell, was it Mabel at the inn who had tattled such tales? He had a vague recollection that she'd been annoyed at his refusal to accept the tub. Maybe she'd been seeking an excuse to be in the room where the peephole into Pitch's lodgings lay.

The sorceress stroked her bloodied fingers down the side of his face, tracing crimson marks there.

'Oh, I think not,' Nemain said, an air of satisfaction about her. 'Your boggart friend took some convincing to speak to us of the Horseman who had ridden over his bridge. But he found his tongue in time when we threatened to take it from him. He spat your fear at the very last. He said you had flailed about with terror in a puddle that would not have drowned a dog, and the daemon had to beat the calm back into you. I knew it then that we had it. That place where you are weakest. A pity the boggart was not persuaded to join us. He made a wonderful storyteller, wonderfully dramatic. But it was not to be.' Nemain moved lower and lower as she spoke, and he saw too late where she was headed. Not that he could have prevented her from slipping a hand into his pocket, for he was overwhelmed with harpies, who were not careful at all in the way they handled him. He fought to breathe as they bustled and shoved and pinched.

The sorceress raised the bandalore so it was level with her eyes, which were covered behind a thin gauze upon the peepholes in her mask. She peered at him over the top of the discs.

'Now shall we see what your pretty toy can sing to us?' she said. 'For I believe you are a piece of the riddle I intend to solve, Mr Mercer. In you, we may find the way to our master. Shall we see what we can learn of our Horseman, then?'

The scythe sang out a morose note, much more verbose this time. A plaintive sound that rose like a flare above him. The two other cloaked figures watched from their places beyond the pond.

'Call on the panlong,' she said.

The harpies grew excited at that, their jarring, crackling cries rising.

The cloaked figure who had stood over the stable boy as he lost his life raised their fingers to their lips. Another pitched whistle rang out, this very different from the last, more melodic and alluring.

The pond water grew unsettled, a swirling at the centre that tugged at the dead body floating about. All at once the waters broke open, and a creature lifted from the depths. A massive serpent, silvery body thick as the trunk of a birch, with onyx antler-like protrusions jutting from its flattened triangular skull. It had enormous eyes, the size of dinner plates, bulging from the side of its head, and its nostrils were large enough to swallow a man's hand.

'No!' Silas fought against his foul capturers, their bladed feathers tearing at his clothing and flesh. 'Do not do this.'

The whistle erupted again. One short burst of sound, a signal of some kind, for the next moment all Silas could see was the flash of silver-scaled flesh coming with the strike of a hideous green-grey tongue before it.

The harpies were losing their minds with hysterical laughter that drowned out the desperate notes of the bandalore.

'Stop this!' he shouted. 'You will regret this.'

But it was he who had regrets. God damn it all, why had he not listened to Pitch and ridden on the moment the ankou was delivered?

The panlong flew at him, darting a tongue as grey and foetid as a corpse towards him. The harpies scattered. The ones so long at his calves tore their talons free and rose into the air with screams of what may have been delight or terror.

The panlong's tongue circled his waist, dragging him into the water.

Silas loosened his own scream to join them, one that scraped all the way from the pit of his stomach to the tip of his tongue.

He crashed into the water, and the panlong's coils found him, wrapping about, pinning his arms to his sides, crushing his ribs.

The water seared his nostrils, finding its way into his ears and mouth, punching at him. Demanding entrance. His eyes burned, blinking madly into darkness.

Oh god, this darkness. He could not bear it.

He was pinned and bound. He could not flail, he could not struggle, he could not fight.

The weight of the world was upon him. Drowning him.

*You don't like the water do you, Mr Mercer?*

He despised it. Feared it above all else.

For it was where it had all begun. It was where it had all ended.

And here he was, as the sorceress had said, at the place where he was weakest.

# CHAPTER 18

Pitch arched his back. But it was like trying to shift a mountain, and his arse barely left the ground before she was sinking her nails into his belly, forcing him back down.

'Where do you think you're going then, sweet one?'

'Get off me,' he spat. 'Where is the ankou?'

'Which one? I suppose it doesn't matter really, they are both in the same place.' She purred. 'My goodness, you can squirm about like that all you like, my dear. It is exquisite.'

Pitch slumped against the rug, hissing at the icy bite of it.

'Oh, you're no fun at all,' Onoskolis pouted.

She tossed her head, and it was as though her hair came alive, swaying and shifting like a thick flock of starlings. The waves parted at two places upon her crown, exposing protrusions of bone. Where there had been nothing of note before, now, jutting from the dark lengths were twin horns, undulating like ocean waves over the curve of her skull, reaching so far back he could not see their tips from where he lay.

The rub of something coarse bothered him again, and he tore his gaze from her head to her hips.

One leg was normal, a slender and defined limb that might have caught his eye any other time, but he could not say the same of the other. Supple skin had been replaced with a rough coat of brown-black hair that would not have been out of place on a donkey. He tilted his head, following the line of the limb, tracing where it ran from a bulging hip down to the base where the foot had been replaced by a hoof.

'What? Did you not wish to see who truly has you pinned down and begging?' Onoskolis caressed his cheek. Pitch snapped his teeth, trying to catch one of her fingers. Perhaps two if he was lucky. He'd bite the fucking things off. 'Did you not think an Alp capable of such things?' She clucked her tongue. 'As arrogant as they say, aren't you?'

Alp were irksome lesser, very lesser, daemons. Irritating as rats, though half as prolific, thank the gods. They were present in this world, he knew. It was they who terrified the humans in their beds, crouching upon their chests while they slept. The unfortunates would wake to find they were held down by a mammoth weight, barely able to breath. Their bodies refusing to move until the Alp grew bored and crept away.

But by Gabriel's tits, how was this creature managing such a feat with him? To paralyse any other daemon should have been impossible; to restrain a Dominion, utterly unthinkable. And her enchantment...no Alp he'd ever known had such strength. She had not only rendered him near mindless, utterly pliable, but she'd also starved him of any nourishment. He'd not been allowed to feed, while she gorged herself on pleasure.

He let his head fall back, his eyes drawn to the sigils overhead once more.

There must lie his answer.

Pitch's lids fluttered, in danger of closing. He was drained dry.

'If you do not get off his cock soon, I'll stab the both of you.' The bluecap tried for a threatening growl but failed. 'You are not here for your own pleasure.'

'That is where you are quite wrong, Stelanza,' the Alp said. 'My pleasure was certainly a part of the deal, and by all the gods, there is no greater pleasure than this sweet daemon. He's making my eyes water. What is your rush? They will need time for what they have planned. You'll get your chance to use your blade. Stop fretting your ugly fae head about it. He'll not be around much longer to enjoy. I intend to take my time.'

Pitch lay slack and exhausted. He'd felt nearly as boneless as this when he'd been tied to that infernal bed. But that had been of his own choosing. Onoskolis's enchantment still tickled at his senses, a taunt that she was not yet done with him.

But he was very, very done with her.

'Our bluecap is getting restless,' she said from her perch upon him. 'I suppose it's time to take my fill, what do you say?'

'You have already forfeited your life, go ahead.' Pitch could not have harmed a sparrow right then, but he'd not stay on his back forever. She would die very poorly when he was on his feet. 'I will kill you either way.'

'I'm afraid you won't be capable of doing any such thing.' Her thrust was unkind, too hard upon sensitive flesh. 'It is a waste, I'll say, but you'll be dead very shortly. And that is nothing to do with your performance, my dear, so do not fret. It is simply how it is meant to be. You have become a problem for us, and my masters have no tolerance for such problems.'

She freed one hand to drag a long nail down the side of his face. Gods, he was so very tired of this bitch touching him. Pitch bucked his hips. The strength of the movement caught her off-guard, and he slipped free from her imprisoning depths. Snarling, she ground down against him, pressing his freed cock against his hip bone. It was painful, but the freedom was sweeter than a thousand strawberry tarts.

'Oh come now, it has not been so bad as that, has it? Could you imagine a more pleasurable way to go than this?' She frowned. 'Far nicer than what awaits that ankou fellow, I'm sure. Nemain is quite determined to have her way with him, and I assure you, it will not involve him spread upon his back. I dare say he'll likely be screaming for his mother by now.' She gestured at the ceiling. 'I've seen you admiring Badh's work. And you have Macha to thank for those horses sleeping like stones in the stables. The Morrigan's little trio of sorcerers are formidable. They are going to cause the Order the worst headache they-'ve had in centuries.'

Onoskolis clearly enjoyed the idea. Even the bluecap, Stelanza, laughed quietly from whatever dark corner they lurked in.

He heard them both from a distance. His mind caught upon the threat to Silas.

Pitch's pulse thudded an impractical beat. *He'll be screaming for his mother.*

At long, long last a roil of unsteadiness flooded his belly. As though the beast at his core finally stirred from its slumber.

The door handle rattled, and the door was flung open.

'It is done, she has him,' a new voice declared. 'Simpering fool didn't need much convincing. One human scream and a threat to this arsehole here, and onto the greensward the ankou went.' The sex of the speaker was hard to determine, gruff and breathless as they were.

Pitch rolled his head, biting so hard at his lip he tasted copper. The speaker stood in the doorway, clad in a cloak made of a strange heavy fabric. It appeared to be leather but shifted with the airiness of a finer thread. They wore a mask of feathers across their face and looked utterly ridiculous. Their covered gaze ran along the length of Pitch's body and lingered where the Alp had hooked her vile hoof over his ankle. Pitch sensed the new arrival's reticence. The quick flick of a tongue against narrow lips suggested unease. Perhaps they had not seen the Alp in her true form. Perhaps they pitied him.

The beast coiled tighter in his belly.

'Wonderful,' Onoskolis replied. 'We've been having a lovely time here too. The daemon has been quite the mouthful, I must say.'

Pitch ground his teeth. He'd not waste another breath on the Alp.

'Spare me the details, if you don't mind.' The rough grunt of a man. 'He doesn't seem all that much to me.'

*Onto the greensward he went.* By Enoch's fucking balls, if Silas had so much as a grazed knee, there would be carnage.

The beast rolled about in languid agreement, still too dozy by half.

'Perhaps you'd like to try him and see, Badh,' Onoskolis purred. 'I was going to finish up, but I can wait a few moments more if you'd like to indulge.'

If she intended to make Pitch fearful, she failed. And her invitation had the man recoiling.

'Don't be a fool...' he stuttered. 'That is to say, I appreciate the offer, it is most kind.' Sorcerer or not, this quivering idiot was uncomfortable in the company of daemons. 'But I've neither time nor taste for the likes of him.'

'Liar. I'm to the taste of everyone.' Pitch's thick tongue mixed his words into a slurry, but he'd been insulted enough this day.

Though he could not see all of the man's grimace for the ludicrous mask he wore, it was there. So this was the fool who had made the sigils that imprisoned him? His chin was far too square for Pitch's liking, the top lip uneven where an old scar ruined it. He wondered how wide those lips could spread when the arsehole screamed for his life.

Whatever else Badh was, he was human, first and foremost, casting a shadow that stretched across the floor to where the candles circled the rug. Considering what very little light came from the hallway beyond him, his shadow was oddly large. Still, unremarkable as he appeared, this Badh knew how to give a sigil some backbone.

'Finish with him now,' the sorcerer said. 'The ankou is dealt with and should not bother us again. It is time to go and collect the remaining souls from Lady Howard and be done with this place. The Order won't be blinded forever. Stelanza, you have the Gu?'

A prickle of unease ran with Pitch's ire. What the blazes were they doing with such a thing?

'Of course I have it,' the bluecap replied. 'I've been holding this blasted knife for an hour. But she is making me wait.'

'Don't bandy it about like that,' Badh said, irritated. 'A drop in the wrong place, and he will not be the only corpse we leave behind.'

How the fuck had these cretins gotten ahold of Gu? That nefarious poison came from creatures that existed only in Arcadia. Four rare species who did not think much of having their venom extracted to make Gu, and it was no minor feat to capture them to do so. It was one small mercy that Gu was so bloody difficult to secure, for the poison itself showed no such mercy when used upon a daemon who had no access to the antidote.

'I'd grow sick, but I'd not die,' the bluecap huffed. 'It is you and Onoskolis who should be concerned with such things. Now tell her to get on with it. Do you have any idea how sickening it has been to watch her play with him this past hour?'

Onoskolis grinned from where she sat still perched upon Pitch like an eagle upon her prey. 'And I could play an hour more, easily.'

An hour...he'd been subjugated here for an hour? Fuck. There was no telling how far they could have gone with Silas by now.

'Onoskolis, you wished time with him, and you've had it.' Badh was careful. The sorcerer was afraid of the Alp, that was clear. And with the way the shift of his head suggested his hidden gaze moved to Pitch every now and then, she was not the only daemon he feared. Wise man. 'But we must move quickly now. The horses are fighting the draughts Macha gave them. They won't be kept quiet much longer.'

'Don't see why you didn't kill the damned things,' the bluecap returned. 'There's enough of this poison for them too.'

'Those beasts are djinn and fortified by the Lady Satine herself,' Badh said. 'If the Gu was capable of killing them, and that is doubtful, it would be like lighting an enormous signal fire for the Order to see. Sleep is one thing, death entirely another.' Badh tilted his head. He was likely looking at Pitch, but it was hard to make out his eyes beneath their thin veil of chiffon-like material. 'But it will take them longer to realise their guardian daemon is no more. Perhaps they shall even thank us for it. I've been told, Mr Astaroth, that you have been quite the bother.' The sorcerer's smile was less well hidden than his eyes. He had remarkably good teeth. 'Get on with it now. Render us one daemon less to worry about, won't you, Onoskolis? And we shall light our own signal fire so the Order will know the Morrigan has risen and is not to be trifled with.'

Fucking gods, this idiot enjoyed the sound of his own voice.

'Yes,' Pitch snarled. 'Do get on with it, Onoskolis.' He stared up at her, pouring every inch of his slowly returning rage into the gaze. Pitch shifted his feet, rolling his ankles. He was coming too, emerging from whatever stinking cocoon they'd locked him in. He had no idea why, and it didn't matter a damn.

'Hush now. You are much prettier when you don't speak.' She touched a finger to his lips, and he had to battle himself not to bite her fucking finger off. Patience was required here. His strength was dribbling back to him.

'Meet me at the agreed place when you are done. I'll wait ten minutes, no more.'

Badh spun about, and Pitch caught a glimpse beneath his cloak. More layers were revealed, as dark as the rest, save for one gleam of colour: a flash of dull gold, which clung to the edges of a small book dangling within the folds. A grimoire, likely. Or maybe something more innocuous. A prayer book, perhaps. And well that Badh should start praying.

The door slammed shut.

Onoskolis moved fast, catching him unawares with his mind still on the golden book. She threw her weight along his length, and her mouth covered his, eating at his cry of pain.

The Alp devoured him. Her tongue defiled his lips, pushing them open as though they were the folds of an envelope, delicate and easily torn. She spread him wide, making him gag on the invading, slippery flesh. The Alp pulled away, leaving him gasping. She planted a widened hand on his cheek and wrenched his head to the side.

'Fuck,' he grunted. His struggle was pathetic, infuriating.

Onoskolis grinned, her breath searing his cheek, and dove her mouth down onto his neck. She sank her teeth into him, what felt like a thousand dagger tips piercing his skin. He kicked out, his heels skimming the rug, unable to gain any traction.

Gods damn this bitch to the deepest abaddon. He'd forgotten the dhampir were not the only supernatural race with a taste for blood. The Alp craved it too.

She was feeding on him anew.

Onoskolis's claws dug into the side of his face, the heat of escaping blood warming his skin.

Fearsome rage slithered through him, clumsy but stronger than before. The beast at his core shook itself like a fight-stunned stag recovering his senses.

But it was not the rousing beast that freed him.

Onoskolis dislodged her fangs and threw herself back with an almighty scream. She scrambled off him, leaving him open and exposed, damp and damaged, but free at last.

'Gods!' She scratched at her lips as though they'd just found acid and burned. 'What in the gods' names...he is no daemon. The knife...give me the knife, damn you.'

But the bluecap had waited too long to share now. 'No. Get out of the way.'

'Hurry up, you fool!' The daemon coughed, rubbing at her mouth. 'Kill him.'

Pitch grunted, trying to set his world right. It was still cotton covered, muddled and out of kilter. *He is no daemon?* The stupid cow had gone mad, and no one was more deserving of it. He rolled onto his side, and the bluecap came at him. A slender figure of blue, slight as the blade she carried. He threw up his hand, warding off the blow aimed at his chest, and the blade sliced across his forearm instead, carving easily through his shirt and a good portion of his skin. The Gu ploughed into his body, putting all old pains to shame.

His blood bubbled. The poison raced up his arms, trying to tear open the veins, searing as salt against an open wound. He roared, and his wild heart roared with him.

'More. Give him more,' Onoskolis screamed. 'Give me the fucking knife.'

Pitch rocked to his knees, upright for the first time in what felt like lifetimes, swaying like a sailor on the open sea. He grabbed at his open trousers with clumsy hands. Gods, he was in no state to button himself up, but if he tried to move like this, he'd end up flat on his face again.

'He's moving! Why is he moving?' The screech from the bluecap stung his ears. 'They said the sigils would hold him.'

'Badh said they would hold a daemon. He's not...he's not...there's something wrong.' All trace of her overweening nature had vanished. 'He's not right. He tastes like no daemon I've known.' Served her right for taking a meal where it was not offered. He hoped he tasted like rotten meat and excrement. She deserved no less. 'This is not...stab him again...you need to aim for the heart, damn it.'

What Pitch *needed* was to be on his feet, but by the gods that seemed a long way to travel when one's limbs were made of lead. The bluecap dared another swipe at him, and a fresh lick of pain tore across his shoulder. He spat his fury, new veins coming alight with an agony that made him shake like he'd been locked in an icehouse.

He bellowed, and it was a dreadful sound, thick with a rage that bubbled every bit as much as the Gu in his veins.

It was not enough that he was red and raw where he ought not to be. Now they sought to boil him from the inside. He was drained, he was poisoned, he could not get his fucking fingers to work themselves properly around his godsdamned buttons. Wouldn't this just be a sight to see for all those in Arcadia who despised him? The daemon prince was going to die on his knees.

They should so wish. But he was not done yet. The ankou needed him.

'Where...is...Silas?' The words flew with spittle and frustration. His flame would not ignite as it should.

'Why won't he die? You said this would kill him!' the bluecap screeched. 'Will the sigils hold?'

'Forget the fucking sigils.' Onoskolis was no longer smug. She was shouting like a madwoman. 'We need to go.'

One more button.

He was as unsteady as he'd ever been. But Pitch knew unsteadiness well; he was accustomed to fighting his true nature, to settling the beast. To dealing with torment of the mind as well. Seraphiel's death had threatened to topple him into the madness that had long plagued him.

That madness had painted the angel as a monster in his mind's eye. A blazing threat that descended upon him in a blaze of halo and rage. He'd feared for his life, in his delusional state, and thought the Seraphim intent on destroying him.

The madness had caused Pitch...Vassago...to raise his vestige and strike. To rain down a flame that had made the Hellfield incandescent and turned a Seraphim into a falling star.

The moment the light had dimmed, he'd seen what he had done. Vassago had turned his weapon on himself.

It had taken Lucifer and Gabriel both to hold him down. Half his own legion had aided them, surrounding their prince to ensure such an easy escape was impossible.

Pitch shook his head, ridding himself of the fallen prince. Focusing upon the last fucking button on these godsdamned inconvenient trousers.

Onoskolis and the bluecap were shouting, the Alp still trying to convince the bluecap they should run. 'He is too much for us. They have underestimated the red rider, and it is us who will pay if we don't go now.'

She was only partly right. Onoskolis would pay, whether she left or not.

The last button slid into its place. Pitch slumped onto his heels, exhausted by such a simple effort.

But at his fingertips, the faint semblance of a glow. The flame burning at last.

No delusion plagued him here. Pitch knew exactly who his enemy was and what they had taken from him.

'I asked you nicely once already. Where is my ankou?'

# CHAPTER 19

Silas kicked to the surface once more, spluttering, frantic with fear. His throat was raw from coughing, his chest aching and set to burst. And his coat, damn it all, it may as well be a slab of lead, determined to pull him to the bottom.

His coat?

Silas winced, his eyes stinging with the harsh rub of murky water. There was a wrongness here he could not fathom. An oddness to his attire.

He kicked out at the bottomless darkness, and something kicked back. It struck him in the middle and grabbed at his hips, wrapped about his chest, and tried to squeeze the air from him. It sought to pull him under.

'No! Don't!' The words flew mangled and wrecked from his mouth.

He must not go under again. *Christ almighty, do not go under again.*

Silas shook his head, blinking. The landscape was made shimmering and hazy by the liquid in his eyes, but he was quite sure of what he saw. Far ahead of him, its silhouette was unmistakable. A castle. A flag flapped at the top of the single turret, which dominated the building, the material a hue of royal blue, the wind making light work of the expanse of fabric. He felt that wind here, toying with the surface of the lake he flailed in, urging the water to swell.

Spray flew at him, and he spread his arms, trying to swim about so he'd not be blinded. A jetty lay nearby. Barely a dozen strokes and he might reach it. A rowboat was tied at its end, and the boat drifted and swayed, straining at its rope, throwing its broad end towards him, enticingly close. A few strokes, nothing more. If he were not so laden down by his coat, he might make it.

This was not right. This was not how it usually was. The coat bothered him, almost as much so as drowning.

The wind coaxed up a fresh swell, charging waves that ran along the surface like the charge of a liquid horseman.

Horseman. The word jolted something within him, a rock to flint. But the flame did not ignite.

'Help me!' he spluttered. 'Help!'

Someone stood upon the jetty, a length of wood in their left hand. An oar. They stood it against the ground like a shepherd's staff. Silas's stomach clenched, but his thoughts were scrambled by desperation.

Why were they just standing there? Could they not hear his cries?

The pressure about his ribs, the sense of being wrapped all about, frightened him. This person could help him. Save him. They need only get into the boat and they could reach him.

The water dashed against Silas's face, cutting a raw path up his nostrils. 'Please, help me,' he called.

But they would not. This person would not help him. They never did. The odd thoughts struck him as another blow came from beneath the surface. Straight into his gut.

'I told you to stay away from him,' the stranger cried. 'You brought this on yourself.' A lantern dangled from their other hand, its small flame wiggling madly, its paltry shine unnecessary for the earliness of the evening.

Oh god. Silas sobbed, and the water pushed into his mouth.

He knew that light well. But knew the oar better. He choked on bitterness and gritty wetness. That oar had put him here. He'd felt its weight against his back, catching him unaware.

'You've ruined us all, you bastard.' The shout carried the weight of a man's timbre. 'You sick bastard.'

Silas ground his teeth, straining to lift his arms.

'Please. Help me.' His muscles burned with fatigue as he kicked madly beneath the surface, but it was not enough.

*You are not enough.*

Silas coughed, startled. The thought was out of place, like an audience member speaking through a play. Something scratched at the back of his eyes as though the filth from the churned-up water had made it in there somehow, and he lost hold of the words. They drifted down into the murkiness below. The ink black that wanted to claim him.

That *would* claim him. It was a certainty, cold and etched in stone. He did not survive this.

He never survived.

A wave struck him in the face, and the tightness that held his body captive drew itself in closer.

'You didn't listen, you bastard. You fucking bugger.' The man thrust the lantern before him. He staggered, clutching at the oar. Silas knew him...he knew him...but his name slipped and slithered and ran away. 'I told you it would ruin our family to bend for the likes of him.' The words did not come easily, as though the man's tongue and lips would not work in unison. 'But you didn't listen.' The man thumped the oar against the jetty, a hollow sound that made the very lake tremble. 'Too busy thinking with your prick. Now the lord's son is dead, and he has lost his mind with the grief. You've made our family homeless, you selfish cunt. We are to be cast out.'

Silas's eyes stung, a pang borne of more than silt. These words, laced with hatred and desperation, were not new to him. His head pounded. He knew this man. His throat tightened. The waters were sucking at him, their siren call ready to claim him. Silas would go down for a fourth time, and he'd not resurface.

He knew it. Sure as he knew it was the man on the jetty who'd put him here. In his tomb.

Always the same. Always the same. Silas bellowed his remorse as the past thumped him senseless.

It was always the same.

His death always came this way. Silas scratched at the water, at his own turbulent thoughts. Always?

The tug came again at his coat. The sharp pull of something more than just current and swirl.

The flowing, wretched length of material that was heavy as three anchors. What the blazes was it about this damned coat that had a drowning man pausing to think on it?

Distant cries reached him, and with his chin tilted high to keep his mouth from the waterline, Silas thrashed at the water, pulling his way about. Someone tried to reach him. Sometimes there were many, sometimes few. But here, in this time, it was the woman in lilac, and the young man was with her.

Oh, Christ. Yes. The lad always appeared.

And was always too late.

A sharp pain stabbed at his temples. Silas's cry was a tremulous thing. No one ever reached him in time.

'Help him.' The woman's scream was garbled by the water that filled Silas's ears, his senses, his very being. The water claimed him. As it always did. 'Stop your madness now.'

A hard blow caught him in the ribs. He jerked sideways so hard he was submerged for a moment, only to gasp his way clear again. This god-damned coat dragging him down like it were a leviathan.

Was that what stalked him beneath the surface? A monstrosity that would consume him.

'For god's sake, do something!' the woman shrieked.

'Throw him the oar. Give it to me, let me do it.' The lad spoke, fiery with resolve. And hope. He always was. 'Help him! He's your brother, you vile man.' The cries floated over to where Silas treaded water, but they were protestations against the inevitable. The lake...no, the loch. It was a loch. And she always claimed him. He was hers to consume.

Bloody hell. The remembering hurt so badly. It was breaking him apart, inch by inch.

Another great, searing pain struck behind his eyes, and the loch tilted on its axis, tipping the world with it. Flipping it over and throwing him up into a brand-new world, with all the terrors of the old still intact.

He remained in the water.

Silas never truly left it. Oh god. The return of the memories was too much. As crushing as the deep could be.

The waters were more tumultuous here in this place. In this time. Silas shook with an ancient, cretinous fear.

His arms were heavy, too heavy, much weightier than before. And only one of his legs worked for him. Only one limb agreed to kick at the abyss as it rose up to claim him.

Another boat bobbed on the water beside him, this one far cruder than the other, chipped and shaved from a tree trunk. Although its sides were low to the water, they might as well be the highest mountain peak for all the hope he had of surmounting them. His coat was too damned heavy. And the dragging, clutching, pressure at his chest was relentless. Silas whimpered like an injured dog facing his master's gun. The froth-tipped waves smacked against the sides of the boat and slammed themselves ever harder against him.

A man leaned over the side of the boat. He was clad in thick furs that teased at the underneath of a solid jaw, not unlike Silas's own. For a moment it seemed the man was his rescuer. Reaching for Silas. Trying to save him.

But no one ever saved him. Certainly not this man.

Not this time.

Rough hands found his hair, grasping a handful. Pressing him down. Trying to force him under.

'No. Leave 'im be!' The words cracked with the unreliable timbre of youth. A young man pleading for Silas. For the man Silas had been.

He fought the waters, putting up a futile protest at their all-encompassing presence.

A rough jerk pulled Silas's mouth clear, and he let out an anguished cry. 'Brother, please.'

His own words felt foreign on his tongue; they clattered against his teeth. But Silas knew them to be true. The twisting, painful knots that came with uttering them told him so.

This is how it had *always* been. How could he have forgotten the horror of this? How could he have forgotten the centuries that gaped like chasms in his past?

Christ almighty, he thought his skull would shatter there and then with knowing what this was. He was drowning in memories.

'Do not call me "brother,"' the man hissed. 'You have cursed this land, this family. Since the day you tore your entrance into the world and killed our mother. You are tainted, like all the rest. Now the gods punish us with the rains.'

It was pouring. How had he not seen that before? Silas blinked madly as he tried to wrench his head free of the man's hold. The deluge strengthened. There was barely any telling where the loch began and the rainfall started.

The loch. Present once more. The castle, though, was far off in a much distant future. Silas could not see the shore, the rains were too heavy, the boat too close. But he did not need to see to know what he'd find there: the same contours of the land where it met the waters of the loch.

'You are a monster.' The man spat, jerking Silas's head so hard something crunched in his neck. 'And monster's must die.'

Monster. Was he a monster?

Silas's head was filling, the pressure beneath his skull too immense for such a small space.

'I'm beggin' you...let him up...' The young lad had pleaded for Silas for untold years. Untold deaths. No one listened this first time; no one had listened since.

'Shut up, or you go over with him. He must die. A sacrifice will save us.'

It wouldn't. Such a paltry thing as one man's death, even if he were monstrous, would not save them from the wrath that had descended upon the world to wipe out all the bad things.

The rain would keep on falling. The lands would flood.

Silas's thoughts were bending, contorting, writhing out of shape with all the pressure, within and without. All the while his infernal coat dragged at him. Tension sat upon his chest, making every faltering breath a labour.

Christ, he was so very tired of fighting.

'May the gods take you.' The man shouted at the deities. And one of those gods would hear him. 'Let this death we offer you, this sacrifice in your name, please you. We give him unto you. This blasphemy against all the gods. None is more worthy of death than this wretched creature.' The man grunted, and a great many curses fell from his lips. He did not release his hold on Silas's head, but the force of his hold lessened. 'Sit down, you runt.'

'But he's your brother,' the lad protested.

'He is my mother's murderer and the spawn of the devil who had his way with her. A daemon.'

He had that wrong. Whatever Silas had been...was...he was no devil's child. His sire had been an angel.

A strange whirring tickled at the back of his mind. Thoughts of monsters and daemons and...someone else. Wearing this coat. This damned bloody coat that was here even now. In a world of furs and leather. A wrongness he could still not fathom.

The daggers struck at the backs of Silas's eyes, without warning or mercy. He closed his eyes.

'Now sit down, ya brat,' the murderous brother raged. 'Or I'll throw ya overboard with 'im. The gods demand a sacrifice, and I'll give it to them. This monster is theirs. Let us pray they take all the rest.'

The man, his brother, pressed Silas down beneath the water, where he sobbed, his tears invisible amongst the writhing waves. The past was a marching army, and its heels bore down on him.

Oh, by the goddess, he could not take it.

He saw it now. What he was. What he had been.

Nephilim.

How had he forgotten this moment? Maybe She showed a small mercy and *allowed* Silas to forget.

So why then did the past torture him now? Damn it, why was he wrapped in this blasted coat, like it was his funeral shroud?

*Show me where you are, Silas.*

The whisper was a fresh slap, another blow to add to all the others. But what did it matter if he did not struggle against it? This fight had already been fought. And he always lost.

The struggle left him. His arms slackened, the current tugging them out from his sides while the past crushed him.

Sweet mother of god. He was a monster.

All that held Silas above the water now were his brother's fingers tangled in his hair. His brother, seething with a grief that had cut into him and made armour of his skin and weapons of his bones.

*Tell me where you fell, Silas. Let us see.*

Christ, what did it matter where he was? He was in his tomb.

*Show us the way.*

Despite the knowledge reborn, the desolation and the yawning centuries, something of the voice stirred a great unease. The whisper was as out of place as the bloody coat and made him want to pull free of his brother's grasp and hide in the depths.

A frightened face appeared over the edge of the boat, shivering as the water did. Eyes of cornflower blue that were a bright spot in a sullen world. The lad held his hand outstretched, reaching for Silas.

But no one ever saved him.

'Take it, take it. Hold on.' Muffled cries and desperate words.

Something dangled in the water right above Silas, and though he did not think he possessed the strength, he reached up and found familiar rounded curves. His fingers curled, and his very soul ached. His true soul. The one he had forgotten until the waters came to remind him.

The one created when an angel sought to defy his gods.

Silas clutched the rounded discs.

This bandalore was not made of wood but clay, a token meant for an altar, an offering to the gods and their unsettled, flooding waters. Silas had been made an offering too. A sacrifice offered to subdue the rains. The rains had not ceased, the lord of Arcadia was too incensed for that, but the goddess of death had taken what was offered.

There was a tug against his grip, a struggle to raise him upwards like he was a giant fish caught upon a hook. The young man sought to save him. His attempt was hopeless, of course, but it made Silas's tired soul ache anew, and he wept.

*Show us the way.*

Silas thrashed about, throwing off the voice. No. He would not. Must not.

The world surged and flipped once more. Silas cried out into the deluge and he was thrown back to only slightly calmer waters, where his brother acted out their eternal turmoil unknowingly, standing upon the jetty with his oar once more, striking out at those who pleaded with him to do something, anything to help a drowning man.

A heavy thump landed against Silas's side. His coat swirled about him, as perilous as a fishing net for a creature of the sea.

'I can reach him, let me pass.'

There he was, as always. Stoic and determined, believing in the impossible. The young man with the cornflower-blue eyes. Fated to try to rescue him. Fated to fail at that but tasked by the goddess with something greater. Silas smiled as he lost himself beneath the waters for a moment, remembering those eyes once more. The new keeper of the bandalore had found him already. Charlie was safe at Harvington Hall, oblivious to their calling. When Silas's time was done, the bandalore would find its way into the hands of its keeper, and the wait for the next time the Horseman would be summoned would begin anew.

*Show me what you remember. Who do you see?*

He'd die a thousand more times before he'd give the whisperer that. The loch took hold of his coat-tails and gave them a savage wrench. The violent motion rattled things about in Silas's head, and there it was. The oddness he couldn't fathom.

This coat. Silas had not been wearing this coat when he died.

Not the first time, nor the last.

The coat was out of place, because this was not real.

Not this time.

He let go, letting the waters take him and drag him down into the abyss, where silence and darkness reigned.

No one ever came for him. That was the way of it.

Yet that did not stop the oddest rush of hope filling him. Silas hugged at his coat, thinking of the other who had worn it. And he was not so afraid as he'd once been.

# CHAPTER 20

P itch was a terrible saviour.

He knelt with hands splayed, face scrunched with concentration and nothing to show for it but ludicrously tiny flames dancing behind his fingernails.

'Fuck,' he hissed.

The bluecap was still shrilling about the fact that he wasn't dead, and Pitch was delighted to disappoint her. That being said, living in this instant was torturous. The Gu played along his veins, devouring his waning strength, searching out his weakest points and turning them stiff and rank with decay. Twice he tried to get to his feet; twice his body failed him. On the third try, his foot slipped against the rug, bunching it up at one side and revealing more sigils carved into the floorboards beneath him. There was more material there too. A stark white fabric as though an underlayer had been set down before the rug was placed.

His gaolers held themselves at a distance, ready at the door to scurry away like the pathetic rodents they were.

'Wait. Look. He can't break out...the seals are holding,' the bluecap whispered.

Pitch sent her his most fearsome glare, and the translucent fae with some semblance of a woman's figure shrank back behind the Alp. Gods, he wished he still held the ability to shift into his true daemonic form. The bluecap would have shit her precious crystal britches. Onoskolis held the knife pointed towards him, settling and unsettling her grasp upon it. It was a seemingly innocuous blade, with little sign of the Gu which marked its metal. The poison did not make itself known easily. To the inattentive it appeared as though the blade were wet with water.

Pitch's breath hitched. A vicious tightening of his gut doubled him over. He retched, and black bile shot from his mouth, making a foul map upon the brilliant white of the rug. He heard Onoskolis curse, an Arcadian diatribe so coarse and base he would have been impressed were he not in such a predicament.

'What's wrong?' the bluecap said. 'This is good. He's dying, isn't he?'

'He should be. But I don't think that is what is happening. It may be time to forgo our pride, and leave.'

Why they were still there at all, he had no fucking idea. Perhaps he was a joy to watch.

Another spasm took hold, one so severe Pitch thought his neck might snap. He threw up again, tasting things even worse than the rotten meat and excrement he'd wished on Onoskolis as she fed on him. Gods, it sure as Enoch's arse felt as though he was dying. Pitch raised his hands and cursed all the unholy things in this world and the next. He could not summon more than a pinprick of flame to his fingertips.

Gods damn it. If death was coming for him, he didn't have time for it.

'Go. Go.' Onoskolis pushed the bluecap through the open door. 'We must find Badh. Go.'

She wasn't looking at him so hungrily anymore. The Alp was not so vainglorious now. She could barely trot off on her cloven foot fast enough and looked set to hurl her guts as readily as him. Pitch stared down at the splattering of black on the rug. The simmering glow from his fingers cast odd shadows. His gut twisted, he buckled forward, and more of the repugnant bile poured out of him. He coughed, wiping a hand across his mouth.

Pitch froze there, the back of his hand blackened, his lips tingling. That movement of his hand had come so much more easily. His palms glowed with a brighter fortitude. He was tired to his very marrow, but he was not so weak as before.

He understood it then.

This bout of sickness wasn't his insides liquefying, death charging in. He was repelling the poison. The Gu was being expelled from his body.

Godsdamned magnificent.

A faint scream came from below, somewhere down in the lower levels of the house. Unmistakably human. The howl of a wolf...or something close to it, followed. Heavy, thunderous sounds were next, as though a herd of cattle were running amuck downstairs.

Pitch was still on his fucking knees.

He growled his displeasure and forced himself up onto one foot, then wobbled precariously onto the other. The room tilted and swayed, and a pressure worked at him, like a descending cloud sought to push him back down.

'Fucking sigils.'

His first run-in with divine magick in this world was a decidedly unpleasant affair. How the blazes had these fools become so adept in their magick? More importantly, how had he shattered that bloody magick and set himself free?

More screams rose. And closer. Growing ever closer. The howls resounded, shifting from down low and guttural, rising to a shriek that would have made a wyvern envious.

Pitch bit at the inside of his cheek. At least his pulse was managing more than a sluggish thud, but now he had other troubles. He held his hands before him, patting at the confines of his invisible prison, searching for...what exactly? A hole in the magick? Shit. How did this work? Divine magick manifested very differently in Arcadia. The angels bore it more like shields or arrows. It was the power behind their halos. Usually it was the higher angels who were the most talented at weaving and moulding magick to their will. Seraphiel had been without equal. Or so he liked to think. No one dared to speak of the low-born angel Azazel in the presence of the Seraphim.

But Azazel was proof that chaos always held a card in creation's game, and there was no predicting when it would deal in. Prince Vassago was such proof himself. He'd emerged from the creation process like no other. The strongest...and wildest...by far, of any of the Dominion. Lucifer had sired two other princes among the seven, but Seir and Orobas were pale imitations of the Berserker Prince.

Neither had ever bested him.

But now a few carvings on the floor and the ceiling had Pitch bamboozled and stuck fast.

He tilted his head, the muscles in his neck none too happy, to stare up at the sigils. The designs were simple enough: a shape like a cross there, a vague design of a hammer there, all encircled by intricate swirls and lines. Magick infused with humanity. How the humans had ever survived Azazel's maleficium, he could not fathom. Gods, how *he* had survived his brush with divine magick was an equal mystery.

Pitch hitched his shoulders and winced at the rough tug of damaged skin. The wound did not show, made invisible by whatever blasted ink was burrowed along his spine, but that was not to say it did not declare its presence loud and clear.

'Come on, damn it. Think straight, you fool.'

He stumbled about his confines. Pressing at the air, feeling the resistance there. His legs were trembling, but he stayed upright. And he'd not felt the need to vomit again, yet. There was that at least.

A chaotic pounding erupted beyond the door, a calamity on the staircase. Shouts and cries rang out, all needled with the tinges of panic.

'Onoskolis, don't abandon me!'

A thump shook the whole house, a rumble through the floorboards beneath him. Even the candlelight flickered.

A brutal crunch, a shattering of something fragile, and then the awful shriek resounded again and tried to lift the very roof off the place. Pitch winced, covering his ears, bowing against the sound that must have woken all the dead for miles around.

A flicker of movement by the door drew his eye. A blur of blue raced into the frame. The bluecap froze right in the centre, as though captured in a picture.

'Help me!'

If she was asking for his help, then she'd been driven mad by terror. And Pitch would spare no sympathy. The bluecap fell hard against the floorboards, crystal fingers rending the wood, pulling up splinters. Something had taken ahold of her, seeking to drag her away. She was a flurry of fight and desperation. Thin veins of black raced through her sapphire-blue form, stark and ugly. She cried out, one last time, looking to him, of all people, to save her.

The bluecap shattered into hundreds of tiny fragments.

Her remains scattered like hail upon a porch, pellets of midnight blue going every which way. Some rolled into the room, all the way up to where the border of candles marked the rug, where they settled and at once melted, spreading sky-blue stains across the timber.

Pitch stared, shocked into stillness. The bluecap's killer stepped into the doorway.

A scraggly, panting, red-eyed beast.

# CHAPTER 21

'Forneus?' Pitch said, incredulous though finding time in the chaos to still be amused at naming such a creature after his Arcadian valet. The hydra would have despised it no end. What the –'

The enormous creature paid him no mind. Its disconcerting red eye was fixed on the rug at Pitch's feet, drool running from the coarse fur around its jaws. The skriker barked, a sound like trapped thunder, and nipped with long teeth at the edge of the furs that formed a makeshift, albeit soft, prison for Pitch.

Gods, the creature still stank to all the heavens. Combined with the reek of Pitch's own expulsions, this room had become more intolerable than before. He pressed his splayed hands against the unseen barrier that held him, leaning his weight against it.

The hound sank down low on its front legs, paws double the size of Pitch's hands, and nudged its nose towards the nearest candle. The beast huffed, causing the long hair about its snout to flare, but the candle was resolute. It bent and shuddered but was not extinguished. The skriker tried again, its ribs widening with the depth of the breath it took. This time it breathed long and ragged, air streaming from its nostrils until it seemed impossible any more could have been in its lungs. Again the flame flickered, though its dance this time was far more frantic. The single teardrop of light split down its centre, and two mirroring flames held fast to the wick, bending on either side as though trying to avoid what the skriker delivered. It was no escape. With one last great shudder, the

187

flames blinked out, and white smoke trailed away from the blackened wick.

The pressure against Pitch's hands softened as though he leaned into a rock wall that had suddenly become soft and pliable as mud.

Not pliable enough though. He could not force his foot far enough forward to slip off the rug.

'Hurry up,' he snapped at the hound. 'You should be with your master, not here.'

Forneus had not yet looked at him once. The beast shifted down onto his belly, touching the tip of an onyx nose that glistened in the remaining candlelight to the fur Pitch had been forced down upon. The skriker tossed its head with a whelp and wriggled back away from where he'd managed to flip a corner of the fur to expose the snowy-white material beneath.

Pitch furrowed his brow. 'What the fuck are you doing? This is no time for playing about.' He was being exceedingly ungrateful towards what was likely his rescuer, but he'd spent far too much time in this wretched room already. And Silas had spent too much time out of his sight.

Forneus edged in again, his snout pressing beneath the rumpled fabric, a growl coming from him. His pointed fangs found purchase on the material, and the creature pulled back. The beast whimpered.

'What is it?' Pitch swayed as he leaned down to see what it was the hound was so intent on. Forneus growled, foreboding as a gorgon with a bone, and Pitch had sense enough to pull his hand away. 'Well, hurry up with it, then. And by the gods you'd best be helping me and not trying to make a meal of me. Your master will wish to see all parts of me remain intact. He's growing partial to them I think. Foolish dolt he is.' Pitch swallowed.

'Hurry, Forneus,' he whispered. 'He is quite alone.'

The hound's larger red eye brightened, fixed on Pitch, and the skriker bared his teeth all the way back to the very last molar. Forneus bunched his haunches and heaved back. The beast yelped, and there was no doubt of the pain. His claws scrabbled for purchase on the slippery wood, as though the weight of the fabric were ten times what it appeared. Forneus snarled, and Pitch was sure his eyes held tinges of orange that had not been there before.

The fabric whipped from beneath the fur.

Pitch's own coat flew out, spreading like a great white wing and fluttering to cover Forneus's head. The gold embroidery glinted with the soft hue of candlelight.

'What the bloody blazes is that –' Pitch tumbled forward, the pressure around him vanishing. He could hear its extinction as much as feel it. It caused the hair on the back of his neck to stand and a strange tremor to run through him. He barely stopped himself from collapsing on top of Silas's pet, who was whimpering beneath his canopy of delicate gold thread and exquisite tailoring. Whatever place his coat had held in the magickal workings at play here, it was done with, thanks to a mangy, dribbling hound. Perhaps Forneus was not so irksome after all.

'If those bastards have put so much as a smudge on my coat, I swear I will...' He stopped himself. Shook himself. He was free. However the bloody mutt had done it, it was done.

Which meant this was now the very *last* place that Pitch should be.

'Where is he?' He pulled his coat off the hound's head, leaving the coarse hair on its broad head standing up at an odd angle and one ragged ear flopping back, exposing the pink skin within the folds. 'Where is Silas?'

The beast snarled, and Pitch wondered if he had been right earlier – that Forneus was hungry and daemon was on the menu. He stumbled back, uncertain he could fend off even this mangy creature in his current state. Forneus turned tail and lumbered out the door, his great paws leaving blue prints as they moved through the thin layer of the bluecap's melted remains. Pitch followed after, not caring a damn that he trod through the departed fae. He did wince though, at the mammoth effort it took just to swing his coat about his shoulders and shrug it back on. He was seeing stars by the time both arms were done, but there was something comforting about having the pristine coat on, covering up the ruin that lay beneath. He left the corset vest behind, his favourite until a short time ago. Pitch had no place for it now.

He sought to do up the button on his coat. That was a mistake. The room tilted again, and he slammed a hip into the doorframe. His troublesome hip at that. Gods, he was weak. The Gu was still plaguing him like mites in his veins, and the blade's cuts stung with unrelenting fervour. He stepped from the room, stifling the urge to whimper as he did so. Tea in the parlour seemed lifetimes ago.

How far had they taken Silas from him?

Pitch forced himself forward, one hand tracing the length of the wall as he went. To try walking unaided was ill-advised. He'd be flat on his face in a moment. He limped along after the hound, who loped well ahead, bounding past the closed rooms along the hallway and settling at the top of the stairs.

Though Pitch hurried as best he could, Forneus was already loping down the stairs, taking three at a time, when Pitch at last reached the top step. The daemon eyed the descent.

'Fuck.'

And damn that Alp whore again. She could have at least assaulted him in a ground-floor room. He glowered at the stairs, bit his cheek, and made his move. He cursed them one by one as he made his way. By the time he reached the bottom, he was panting like a geriatric who'd barely walked a day in his life. He shoved his hands against his knees, leaning forward as he sought to catch his breath. If Onoskolis was anywhere nearby, then now was when she should strike. Pitch would have done so. He was injured and vulnerable, a prime target for ambush. But there was no sign of her.

No sign that the house had any other occupants at all.

*He is no daemon.* The words kept clanging in his head.

Fortunate for him that he had tasted so dreadful. If Onoskolis had drained him before they stabbed him with the Gu, there was a chance he'd not be so barely on his feet as he was now. He might still be on his back on that rug. And not so alive.

His gaze travelled the length of the corridor. The front door was wide open...actually no, the door itself was halfway into the foyer, knocked clear of its hinges. The skriker barely fit through the entranceway, his sides near to brushing the frame. The hound tilted its head to peer back, snapping a bark, one that crashed along the walls down to where Pitch wavered on his feet.

'I'm coming, damn it.' Too bloody slowly. Gods damn it all. It was then he recalled that Silas had brought his cane in with them when they arrived. The ankou had adapted to Pitch's regular refusal to use the cane by carrying it himself in his saddlebag or in hand, unafraid to nag the daemon to use it.

A sharp tug caught at Pitch's chest. How afraid was Silas now? Did he think he'd been abandoned? Heat bloomed in Pitch's palms. The flames rose above his skin with renewed strength. Paltry still, there was some way to go before he'd be terrifying, but this was a step in the right direction.

A harsh bark made him jump. Forneus pawed at the threshold, eager to move on.

'Hold up, you flea-bitten mange pit, I need the cane.'

Never in a thousand lifetimes would he ever admit to Silas he had just uttered those words.

Pitch stumbled like a drunkard from one side of the hall to the other, collapsing against the parlour doorway. This was where the nightmare had begun. Pitch dragged unwilling feet to the lounge, offering up silent prayers to any god that bothered to listen, which was likely none, that the cane was still where he'd left it. He nearly threw up all over again when he found the seats empty of anything but overzealous embroidery.

He collapsed onto the cushions, sinking into the join between them. A hard nub pressed against his arse cheek. With a cry he shoved himself clear, digging his hands into the crevice, finding the curved point of the fox's nose. Likely he'd been sitting on the cane when he'd made a fool of himself with the pastries. Pitch snatched it up. It was still in its retracted state. He rose to his feet with a grunt, finding the concealed button that would transform the cane into a usable form. With the stick now taking his faltering weight, Pitch made his way out of the room. He glimpsed the tea set that had been brought in by the housekeeper, Silas's cup still half-full. It would be dreadfully cold now. The ankou was not prone to being irritated about trivial things, but he would, Pitch suspected, be annoyed with cold tea.

Pitch limped his way out the front door. Gods, the house was quiet, and the silence rubbed at him in all the wrong ways. He was tense, every muscle twitching with hesitancy, tight with waiting on another threat to loom out of a hidden place and find him.

The day was so very dull, the clouds smearing the efforts of the dying sun, but he could not suck in enough of that crisp fresh air. The scent was clean, with no tinge of vomit or stolen arousal.

Onoskolis would live only briefly to rue the day she touched him.

'Take me to him, hound.' Pitch held tight to the cane as he negotiated the steps down to the garden path. There were only three, but by the Lucifer's sphincter, he struggled with them.

The skriker ran off to the right. The stables lay left. Pitch hesitated. Did the creature already know those stables were empty? It would account for why the bloody horses had not appeared before now. Or perhaps Satty's precious mares had freed themselves and had galloped away without a second thought for their riders. He sniffed. Sanu may do so, but there was no way Lalassu would abandon Silas. Perhaps, and Pitch's chest lightened at the thought, the mare was with him even now.

A terrifying shriek came from Forneus, the blood-curdling cry that Pitch had heard when he'd still been a prisoner beneath the sigils.

Red eyes fixed on him, jaws parted to allow the dreadful noise to escape. The beast's cry was a call to arms. A demand to follow.

All thought of checking the stables fled. Pitch hobbled his way down the steps, grimacing with how unkind the move was upon a battered body.

He reached the last. Straightened. Footfalls thudded along the hallway he'd just left. And he was sure he heard the rap of a bony hoof in the sound.

Onoskolis had found him.

Pitch spun about, summoning up the flame. It was not easy, and by Enoch's taint it pained him, but Pitch would not, could not, be taken again. Silas had waited too long for him.

The daemon roared, and the flame roared with him, through his hand and into the cane. Mr Ahari's offering transformed itself, the handle reshaped itself into a hilt that fit the curve of Pitch's hand precisely. The wood came alight, glowing like a poker that had been set all the way into a fire, bending in a delicate crescent shape. Pitch brandished it like a sword...no...a sabre. So much like his lost vestige.

The flame poured from the transformed cane, a brilliant ribbon of glorious power.

And his only regret was that the Alp would be incinerated before Pitch could hear her scream.

# CHAPTER 22

T he blaze illuminated the sallow-faced woman who appeared in the
doorway. It was the housekeeper who had led him to that wretched
room.

'No!' Her cry buckled beneath her terror as the flames tore towards
her. 'My son, they have my son.'

'Shit.' Pitch threw his arm wide, dragging the sabre through the air.
Onoskolis may not have appeared, but the thought of her had the flame
burning like wildfire, out of his control in an instant.

And all at once he was back there. Upon the Hellfield. Making a
terrible mistake. The image of Seraphiel in those last moments struck
Pitch like a punch to the heart.

The housekeeper screamed, bringing him back from one desolate
place to another. The stench of burned flesh stifled the air. He stepped
back, and his heel went off the edge of the step. His arm flew up, the sabre
rising, its torrent of fire and daemonic rage striking the face of the house,
searing a gash through beams and brick and windows. Glass popped and
shattered, and he fought to bring himself under control.

Gods, why was that always so difficult for him?

And here he could not even blame the beast for raising its nefarious
head. That wild scratching at his core was still drowsy and browbeaten.
Mr Ahari's cane was a stronger conduit than he'd been ready for. More
like his long-lost vestige than the daemon could have hoped for. But right

now, it was a catastrophic problem. Pitch grappled with his weapon, fighting it as though it were a living thing.

The hapless woman still screamed, clutching a shoulder that had melted into a grotesque sludge of flesh and gown.

Pitch had not seen Seraphiel's injuries that day. Lucifer and Gabriel had been upon him too quickly. But the wounds would have been far worse than this. They must have been to bring down a Seraphim.

The house groaned, timbers relenting under the heat. A section of beam fell. Pitch moved as though in slow motion.

'Look out,' he cried.

There was no chance for her to heed him. She did not even have time to raise her head to his cry.

The massive piece of wood struck Mrs Vellan, silencing her. She fell and would not get up. Crimson flowed over the steps, reflected the lick of flame that was beginning to eat at the house.

'Fuck, fuck!' Pitch shouted at the infuriatingly fair afternoon. He slammed the tip of the sabre into the ground, and it was like blowing out a match. The weapon's glow flickered, faded. The wood reappeared, the hilt shifting beneath his hold, returning itself to the shape of the fox. The gems found their place upon the animal's face, giving it emeralds for eyes. Control was his once more.

A pity it was too fucking late. Again.

Why had the stupid woman crept up on him? He clutched the fox head. The metal was cool. He'd not intended to harm her, though the gods knew she deserved no less.

Mrs Vellan had led him into harm's way, delivered him to the bitch Onoskolis, to be set upon like a morsel before a starving beast. She was human, paltry. A nothing in the scheme of all this. He stabbed the end of the cane into a scattering of slate tiles that had fallen with the beam.

The bloody ankou would not consider the woman nothing.

Pitch stared down at the housekeeper. She'd come to plead for her son. To ask his help perhaps. Pitch closed his eyes, his exhaustion returning anew. Silas would despise him for this. How could he not?

The flames crackled and snapped their way along, gorging themselves on all the house could offer.

Let it fucking burn. Let this whole place burn.

The morose howl turned him about. The skriker stood at the ready, down by the bridge they had ridden across to return Mr Crane to his residence. Thought of the ankou made Pitch's belly clench. That bastard would pay, just as the Alp would. He walked towards the skriker, leaning heavily upon the cane as he went. Pitch crossed the bridge where Silas had paled and stared into the water with haunted eyes. The daemon moved as quickly as he could, his arm shaking with the spent energy, his spine tingling with forewarning. The ignition of the sabre had not overextended him, the amuletum had not been sorely tested, but he felt the distant niggle that told him that could so easily change. He must be cautious. So there was no fear that he'd be found wanting when the time came to free Silas.

The skriker moved off the road and down the embankment. A beaten path was clear there, a way to meander down closer to the running water. If this was the way Silas had come, or rather, been forced to travel, he would have despised every moment of it. It had been bad enough for him at Harvington Hall, where the whole infernal place was surrounded by water. He had seen how white Silas's knuckles went each time they crossed the small walkway to leave the hall, the way the ankou had spent too long at the window watching the night fall, staring down at the inky waters that lay flat and still.

Pitch quickened his pace, as much as fatigue would allow. He kept one eye upon the great length of bushy black tail that stood upright, leading him on as clearly as a beacon guiding a ship into port. The skriker crashed his bulk through the wild undergrowth, leading them into an area that seemed carefully tended, the arrangement of plants devoid of the randomness of nature, with neat pathways cleared through the soft, sandy soil. The overhanging trees made the air cool enough to draw gooseflesh. The evening was descending upon them, but Gidleigh Park House, well behind, made its own light. It was well ablaze, Pitch could hear the timbers protesting their demise. He spared a moment's thought for the horses. Lady Satine's nags were surely intelligent enough to flee the fire should it make its way to the stables. This intolerable day would collapse beyond repair if he managed to destroy the horses as well.

They walked. And walked. Through dense swathes of foliage that Silas would no doubt have bored them with naming, delighting over a gnarled tree the way Pitch delighted over a fresh teacake. The daemon used many a rough-barked tree to steady himself. His heels might as well be filled with lead, for they were a tonne to lift. By the gods, if this dog was not taking him to Silas, there would be all manner of hell to pay. Forneus kept up a cracking pace, and Pitch did not blame him for that. He was far more furious at himself for straggling so far behind.

What sort of bloody rescuer was he, that he could not break into a run for more than a few footfalls before it was too much? Gods, if Onoskolis lingered, she must be rubbing her vile hands with delight, trailing him like a wounded deer, waiting until all the life had left him. The stab wounds on his body fairly rang with pain, and he could taste the Gu that still swirled in his veins.

Pitch glanced back over his shoulder, as he'd done several times already. He could no longer see the house at all, not even the glow above the treetops. The river, not more than an overzealous stream really, moved over rocks alongside them. The bubbling was the only sound save for his own huffing and puffing and the hound cannon-balling through the shrubbery. Pitch clutched at his chest, damning himself for being so pathetic. His misdirected attention was costly. Pitch's toe met a lurking rock, and he toppled towards the stream.

'Shit.'

The water rose up to meet him, and he braced for a drenching, turning his head to avoid a mouthful of, no doubt, icy water. But the water truly *had* risen up to meet him. Great orbs of liquid, like translucent clouds gathered around him, settling in beneath his extended arms, lining up along his sides.

Righting him. Bracing him.

Lifting him off his godsdamned feet.

Pitch struggled, managing to swipe the cane at a bubble that pressed against his lower leg. The huge droplet burst, releasing a spray of water that soaked his trouser leg.

'Do not fear the asrai. We will not harm you.' The words warbled around him. Pitch was drawn forward out over the stream, which seemed to flow faster now, its gully fuller.

'Fine. Then set me down,' he demanded.

'We cannot. We must take you to the ankou.'

His pulse leapt unevenly beneath his skin. 'So you know where Silas – oh!'

The asrai swept him forward, whisking him above the surface of the river, which now swirled beneath his heels. He was but an inch above it, the heel of his boots catching at the surface every few feet. He was passed on from one gathering of orbs to another. They rose up out of the water ahead of him, drifting in to replace those that pulled away and returned to the stream. In a short time he was drenched through. His trousers clung to his nethers, his balls were tight and high with the chill. The shallow cuts of the Gu-infested knife and the deeper punctures of the Alp's fangs, stung mercilessly. But the caress of the water was a balm nonetheless, stripping away Onoskolis's touch and removing her stain from his body.

Pitch shivered. 'Why do you seek to help Silas?' He wiped at his reddened lips, relishing the dampness there, the cool cleansing of its touch.

'He is a creature of the water too. And he is good.'

They might have the latter part right. If ever a man could be described as good, Silas would be so, as well as oafish, and at times, infuriatingly proper. But a creature of the water? Enoch's tits, they were wrong in that.

'Are you sure you are not confusing my ankou with that other fiend? Silas fears the water above all else.'

'We know. But that does not mean he is not a part of it.' One of the orbs settled on his head, tugging him up so his heels no longer dragged. Thin trails of water found their way underneath his collar. No part of him was dry. He might as well have stripped naked and swam. 'You are wounded deeply.'

Pitch sucked at his teeth. 'It has not been my best day.' He pushed away thoughts of the lecherous Alp and the smouldering housekeeper.

'Are you strong enough? You don't seem so,' they bubbled, manoeuvring him deftly over the bulge of moss-laden rocks.

'I will make it so.'

'We shall see. Their magick is strong. Their anger makes good kindling.'

'Well, so does mine,' Pitch said. Allies or not, the asrai were irritating.

'Our cousins said so. It seems you make a habit of burning houses down.'

'Your cousins?' He shook his head, dislodging droplets that blurred his vision.

'The piskies.'

Pitch scowled. 'Those little stick bastards? So you are faekind?'

'None other.'

Was there no escape from the blasted fae? 'But we encountered those blighters miles from here. How could they...' He answered the question in his own mind. When last he'd seen the intolerable piskies they had been upon the back of the owl that had perched upon the branch of the nearest tree as Pitch had set the mansion alight. Not flying away until he was done and was striding to meet Silas, the ruins left behind. As though the bird desired to ensure that the daemon made his escape too.

'They did not care for you,' the babbling continued. 'But they said that the ankou does and is safest with you.'

Pitch stared ahead. 'How much further is it?'

'Far less than if you had walked. You were very slow.'

The asrai were testing his patience. 'As are you. You are being outpaced by a rabid dog. Can you go no faster?'

Apparently the asrai were no less susceptible to insult than any other race. The pace quickened. One of the orbs saw fit to burst all over his face, getting up his nostrils and making him cough. They overtook the skriker. The hound's tongue lolled from its dark mouth. It set one red eye upon Pitch as he was swept by and seemed utterly unfazed by the strange method of transportation. Pitch would take that as a good sign that these asrai did indeed mean no harm. He may think little of the skriker, but he had no doubt the beast had Silas's interests at heart.

Even with the asrai's damp help, the journey was lengthy. The sun was almost fully set, the day growing ever more dim, but there was a notable brightening ahead. The end of the forest approached....or at the very least a clearing. Pitch tensed, his skin covered now in gooseflesh, every scrap of fabric on him saturated.

'They are within the stones, using the ley lines to magnify their magick. Go there. This is as far as we can take you.'

That was all the warning he received.

Pitch was cast aside, hurled towards the bank. He uttered a short cry but managed to land himself quite well upon the ground, stumbling only once before he had the cane beneath him. The asrai that still clung to him collapsed in unison, going from rounded, bulging shapes to great gushes of water that drenched him anew. He muttered a hurried thanks and followed after Forneus, who had flattened himself low to the ground, skulking to where the shrubbery went from thick to nonexistent. Pitch pressed up against the wide girth of an oak that was covered in deep green moss. He peered ahead.

The landscape shifted from leafy and shadowed to bare and exposed. Unimpressive low hills, all hues of yellow and brown, rolled on for as far as Pitch could see. Their swells were such that he could see for miles out into a distance made up entirely of the same emptiness that was close by. There wasn't a stone in sight. He grimaced, edging his shoulder away from the tree where the bark pressed at a cut in his skin. The sooner Onoskolis's marks were gone, the sooner he might press the events of that room to the back of his mind.

'Where the blazes is he?' he whispered, sharp as the blade that had been used on him. His stomach was unsettled, as though the Gu were about to make a resurgence once more. 'There are no bloody stones. There is nothing.'

Forneus lay flat against the ground, even his jaw resting upon the litter of the forest floor. His growl was low, barely audible, his onyx lips parted slightly enough to show evidence of yellowed teeth. His brighter eye was set on the way ahead on the sparse landscape that could not have hidden a rabbit darting from burrow to burrow, let alone a considerable man such as Silas. A flash of brightness drew his eye. Pitch blinked and stepped forward, breaching the edge of the forest. He leaned against the cane, levering himself onto his tiptoes. Just off to the north there was a glint of green uncommonly lush ground cover compared to the straw yellows and dirt browns that hugged the landscape elsewhere.

And within that surge of colour rested a cluster of large, tilting stones.

*They are within the stones.* This was where the asrai had directed him. Pitch strode forward another few paces, taking himself up a slope that would afford him a better view. If he were not mistaken, the stones seemed arranged in a haphazard circle of sorts. As pleasing as it was to see the asrai had not lied about the stones at least, it did not lead him any closer to Silas. Clearly, there was no great oaf standing there on the carpet of startling green.

'Where are you, you dolt?' Pitch muttered, fingers tight about the cane.

The glint of greenery on the parched landscape was odd enough, but there was something strange too about the air surrounding it. A haze was evident, a dusting that shifted about like a swarm of flies about a corpse.

A pang struck beneath his skull. Pitch touched the side of his head, squinting. He worked a finger at his temple, seeking to shift the sudden discomfort.

'I do not like this place.'

The skriker huffed, scattering dirt with his hard breath.

A distant sound echoed across the land, far too familiar after so many days on the road. The rumble of carriage wheels, the rattle of tracers and buckles. He shaded his eyes. The carriage appeared as if from nowhere, emerging from behind one of the larger stones in the circle. But the brougham was far too large to have been properly hidden and was painted a fetching yellow that would have drawn his eye immediately. The carriage was just suddenly there, as though an artist had painted it onto the landscape.

It raced at speed away from him. Ludicrous considering the lack of discernible road and undulating terrain. The carriage lurched about madly as the driver urged his horses on.

Gods. Pitch was too late.

'Silas,' he cried. 'Silas.'

He broke into a clumsy, uneven run. The skriker snapped at his heels, snatching at his trouser leg. Pitch tore himself free. 'Leave off, you cretin. They have him.'

He didn't stop to ponder why the beast was reluctant to follow. Now was not the time for hesitation. His pulse thumped so hard that he felt it in his throat. He pushed one stumbling foot before the other. He was too slow. His rescue was a fucking farce. He could no sooner catch a racing carriage than he could a cold. They were too far away to even consider using the flame. He'd do no more than make a spectacle of himself. Silas would watch from the carriage and collapse into utter despair, realising then his guardian was a bringer of havoc and little else. If Pitch were not losing himself to his wild temper, abandoning Silas to the woods and the ash-men, then he was scurrying away with cock in hand, cream on his lips, and his mind soft with lust. Leaving the ankou alone and vulnerable.

Berserker Prince? Pitch was a fucking prince of stupidity, at best.

His breath scraped his ribs, his fatigue making his knees wobble.

The carriage drew away easily, headed east, back in the general direction of Gidleigh Park House. At least they'd not find that place as they remembered it. He held on to that thought with some grim delight, though only until he remembered the dead housekeeper on the doorstep. If they did have Silas, if he was still alive and they returned him to that house, he'd see the ruined body. The burns. And he'd know then his daemon was a terrible creature.

Pitch halted, shoving his hands into his hair.

'Fuck!' he shouted at the evening star overhead. The sole member of his audience, the witness to his pathetic attempt to come to the ankou's aid. Pitch coughed, doubling over to spit an unpleasant wad of black onto the ground. The Gu still plagued him, like an infection of the lungs the humans were so prone to. Leaning his hands on his knees, chest heaving, he contemplated the circle set at the heart of the too-bright greensward.

He frowned and drew upright. There was movement within the circle. His temples panged, and a weight seemed to shift behind his eyes. The skriker came to stand alongside him, and a cool wind moved with the hound, making every inch of Pitch's saturated body shake. The beast's lips peeled back to bare each of his enormous teeth, his intense red eye fixed on the stone circle, a rumble coming from his deep chest. With the descent of evening, the haze that floated around the stones seemed more pronounced, the silver tinge to the light enhancing it.

Pitch drew in a breath. 'Gods. He's here, isn't he?' he whispered.

Of course the hound didn't answer, nor did he need to. Pitch would have bet all the coin he'd earned in every dubious boxing ring he'd bled in that Silas was within that ring of stones.

And he was not alone.

Within the shadows at the circle's heart there appeared to be a dark mass low to the ground. Another stone perhaps. He could not make it out. Pitch narrowed his eyes. There was no doubt that something...or someone, moved about in the shadows. Small shapes, childlike perhaps. Dwarves or gnomes perhaps? One of them stretched its arms, the image fluttering like Pitch was viewing it through the clear flow of a waterfall.

The arms widened and wings appeared. Far too small for any angel.

'Fucking harpies.'

Forneus snapped his jaws, and Pitch could feel the beast's growl as though it came from his own chest. The hound set off, claws sending up sprays of grass behind him as he bolted at the circle.

Pitch drew on the flame, and it answered him quickly. It would dare do nothing else.

The heat flooded his palm, and at its touch the handle of the cane shifted back into its hilt-like form.

The daemon's rage flickered deep within, and the scratching came at his core. He could feel, faintly, the burn of Seraphiel's mark upon his back. The length of the cane shed its wooden appearance, glowing as the sabre of ember appeared.

*Their magick is strong,* the asrai had said. *Their anger makes for good kindling.*

Those magickal pricks knew nothing about anger. Oh how frightening it could make a man. Or a daemon. If Silas had been harmed, the angels would see the bonfire of Pitch's rage from the pristine windows of White Mountain.

# Chapter 23

Silas sank deeper, his body bucking and jerking with the strain of death upon it. He raised his hands to the dying light above and knew he would not see it again. Into the depths he drifted. Life was above him, far far above, flickering like shadows in the depths of a mist.

And sweet mercy, how he did not wish to let those shadows go.

He'd thought perhaps he'd find a saviour this time. He knew now he was wrong.

There was a reason he was here...a bitter reason...but his mind was twisting and contorting, and, like so many of his other thoughts, the reason slithered from him, winking silver before it melted into the watery chasm that surrounded him.

Silas sank deeper.

The weight of his past was crushing the recall of his present. A hundred stones tied to his ankles and dragging him ever down. One for each lifetime he had lived.

Little wonder the goddess had taken that weight from him. Kept him safe from the crush of too many last breaths and dying days. But now the past rattled free. Shaken loose by a nefarious force. The reason he was here.

Christ. Why was he here? With a misplaced coat and a head full of brutal memories.

Silas shrugged into himself. He'd not been graced with remembering any lives lived, only the anguish of losing them.

Always the same.

His brother killing him.

The young man and his bandalore.

The waters claiming him.

His mind was splintering with the thought of it all. With knowing now what he was. Or rather, what he had once been.

A ghost of horrors past.

A Nephilim.

The depths caressed him as though seeking to gentle away the pain of knowing.

The brother that had killed him, that first time as the world flooded, had spoken the truth. The man he held under the water, and offered to the gods in sacrifice, had been a monster. Perhaps not in deed or doing, but in existing at all.

What then was Silas now?

His true name was lost to the centuries and had been replaced so many times he wondered if there was a single moniker he'd not yet been given.

Silas. Silas Mercer. That was his name presently. In the here and now. A decent enough name and he'd not change it, for it was the name that the other man knew him by.

Silas clutched at his coat, burying himself in the folds as the waters buried him. The other man. Christ. Why did his name slip away so?

He must not allow it to vanish. Silas knew, like he knew to blink, that he must not give up searching for that name.

There was a reason he was here in the depths, and it was not simply to die. Not this time.

Silas saw the flash of emerald, the glint of sunshine in the darkness, and felt the heat of beauty and fire. The thought of the other man brought warmth into the cold tomb of his surrounds. A thump in his chest reminded Silas he had a heart, and that it still beat yet.

But the name was slippery as ice.

*Hold fast. He will come.*

With a start, Silas unburied himself from the folds of his coat. He blinked into the onyx sea, but the voice did not come from out there. It was inside, nestling with his chaotic thoughts. The gentle caress of earlier. Melodic in its soothing nature.

*Who is there?*

But she did not dignify him with an answer. For she knew as well as he that her name was known to him. A part of him. The goddess did not answer redundant questions.

*The sorceress is strong, but not so much as she thinks. She tests you, but she cannot take what she seeks. Hold fast.* The tune of Izanami's voice reminded him of something he had forgotten.

The scythe sang to him too. And he should not have let it slip from him.

Silas curled in on himself, pulling his knees to his chest. Shivering. Remembering where he was.

In the grasp of a sorceress. But she could not have what she sought. Nemain. The name stung him, but he braced and let the thought run on.

Nemain wanted his truth, his past, his loch. She intended to find a weakness in him and use it to guide her to the master she believed yet lived. The same angel that had made Silas. In a lifetime long ago.

*She cannot have what she seeks.*

The weight at Silas's ankles burned, tugging bone away from bone. Nemain could not have what she wanted, but she could torture him yet. Her scream reached him. Her rage at being undermined, of being reminded that it was *she* who was not enough, boiled the waters.

*Hold fast. He will come.* What was there to hold on to in this watery abyss?

Nothing but his coat. And the other man.

Sunshine and gems.

Light in the dark.

The waters shuddered. The depths drew at him. He heard the raven screech from where the shadows hinted at life above the surface.

'Silas.'

The cry pierced the waters like a fisherman's spear, cracking open the dark and sending a shaft of sunlight down into the abyss.

He had come.

# CHAPTER 24

The sabre flamed with all the brightness of Pitch's rage. A beacon that drew the harpies at once.

They burst from the shimmering circle, some only partly transformed from vagabond child to gangly, bald-headed bird. And there were so very few of them that it was laughable. A half dozen perhaps. Pitch might have pitied the creatures, if he were the pitying kind.

The harpies came screeching, flashing their wings and brandishing their claws as though they thought they were capable of making him afraid.

They were not.

The skriker was at the daemon's side, teeth clacking as it lunged, trying to latch on to a wing or claw, but the harpies were too quick for the beast. Nor were they interested in the hound as their quarry. They had their sights set on him. They came at Pitch en masse, like a great cloud shedding feathers as it went.

He slew the first with a lazy turn of his wrist, a directing of the flaming sabre that sliced the nearest harpy cleanly in two. Gods, this was pleasant, even with his stomach still rolling with the Gu, and his strength drained by the Alp. He chewed at his lip, the daemonic bitch distracting him. It caused his next strike towards a creature with a white scar that ran the length of its neck to flare wide of the mark. The harpy screeched its delight at a temporary avoidance of imminent death. The flock drew back, regathering. And Pitch marched forward through the shadows thrown by their ample wings.

He touched at his neck. The skin was still damp, his wet hair sticking to the place where Onoskolis had punctured him.

The flame leapt wildly, his baser nature snarled within and chomping at the bit for release.

He brought it under his control with a merciless hand. There could be no chaos here. No wild abandon.

Not with Silas nearby.

And he was here. If Pitch had not already felt it so certainly, he knew it from the skriker's actions. The hound was almost at the circle, moving so fast he appeared like a black blur against the landscape.

Pitch wrapped both hands over the sabre's hilt and incinerated the next harpy that dared draw close. The burst of oranges and reds was joined by the flutter of ash. Its brethren swept away from him with harsh, rasping cries resounding.

'Surely you aren't running away so soon?' he shouted, flourishing the sabre as though he were already the victor. Mr Ahari's provision was a remarkable conduit, he'd give the old man that. So far the cane, whatever it truly was, had held up well with channelling the flame's torrent. But Pitch was not ignoring the murmur at his back, the amuletum reminding him that it would not serve well to push too far.

Only so far as was needed. Into the circle.

Pitch dodged an attack from his right flank, the smallest of the infernal creatures making its move while screaming all kinds of horrors at him. Pitch pivoted away, feinting a retreat, only to cast himself around in a circle, slashing at the harpy's back, separating its tail from its head in one neat move. He flicked at a feather that rested on his coat sleeve, sticking to the wetness there. His drenched clothing tugged at him as he moved, unhappy with being peeled from his cold skin.

Pitch searched for the skriker. The hound was running at speed around the edge of the circle, working back and forth, throwing its shoulder against the haziness that Pitch had noted. The red-eyed beast rose onto hindquarters, great padded paws scratching at nothingness. Sparks flew from the creature's claws as though a flint stone had been struck.

A shiver ran through Pitch, one that had little to do with being soaked through on a day so near to winter.

The skriker could not enter the circle.

Pitch took off the next harpy's head with a dramatic sweep of his arm, which ended with him bowed down low like an actor appreciating his curtain call. The harpies were persistent. He'd give them that. And damned well everywhere. Their numbers had swelled, reinforcements appearing out of nowhere. One swept low, managing to land a glance against his trouser leg. The sharpness of its wing cut through the material and his skin. Pitch snarled and removed the creature's right wing first, a cauterising blow that had it spinning like a pinwheel for a brief moment before he lost sight of it as another of its kin attacked.

Their tenacity was irritating, and strange. They fought like creatures possessed, despite being clearly outclassed. Just as those in the cemetery had done. Encounters with the Berserker Prince, even at half the strength he'd held in Arcadia, would only end one way for them. With roasted birds strewn about in pieces. They were fighting a lost cause.

He cut at another harpy, this one large as a fattened turkey, but his strike went wide with his attention drifting to where he'd last seen the carriage. A lick of doubt struck him. What if he was wrong about Silas being here? And this paltry assault was merely a distraction? He spun about, catching one of the creatures by its eelishly long neck. The harpy squawked, as best as it was able, and flared its clawed feet, scratching at the air as he held it away from him. It was a weighty beast. His muscles strained with holding it aloft.

'You are pissing me off.' He squeezed. The creature's lustreless brown eyes bulged even more. 'Where is he?'

The harpy in its death throes morphed from winged beast to scrawny youth in sudden violent shudders.

'In a grave you cannot drag him from this time.' The words came like the hiss of heated iron in a blacksmith's well. 'And oh how he screamed to be saved when the Morrigan touched him. Screamed for you, daemon. And you did not come.'

A tongue of green-grey, foul as meat two days in the sun, whipped from the harpy's mouth and found his wrist. Fleshy barbs pierced him. Fucking hell, he was tired of being a pincushion. Pitch tightened his grip on the harpy's slender neck. The creature gurgled. Bone snapped, and blood ran between his fingers as his strength tore skin and his nails sank into flesh. He released the carcass and ground his heels into a bony chest, relishing the pop and snap and squelch of death.

The harpies roared, a manic cacophony of sound that would have annoyed him normally. Here, it only fuelled him. He drank it in, letting it feed down into where he was every bit as chaotic as the sounds the creatures made. The notes rattled at the cage within. Pitch was pushing dangerously close to the precipice here, he knew it. The markings at his back pulsed with the strain of keeping him together. Contained. The harpy's awful words were a taunt and likely untrue. If Silas were beyond help, the skriker would not be so desperate to breach the circle. Pitch would have...what? Felt it? Known it? Gods, now he imagined himself a fucking soothsayer. But surely Silas could not slip away from him silently. Pitch couldn't remember clearly the last thing they had said to one another, and that made his pulse quicken, his belly tighten. Those godsforsaken pastries had made a moron of him. Mute and stupefied.

He recalled the sound of Silas's voice outside the doorway. The ankou had searched for him and had been angered...and hurt...by what he'd found.

Fuck, that sorry moment could not be how things ended between them.

With Seraphiel, the parting moment had been enormous, so loud it still deafened him even now. But Pitch thought the silence that existed between him and the ankou just as dreadful.

He strode forward, his thoughts like a swarm of gnats. The harpies clamoured around him, renewing their attack with vigour, seemingly mindless in their intent to stop him.

Distract him? Delay him?

He was tired of it, whichever it was.

Pitch allowed the sabre to burn brighter, the flame to ignite more brilliantly. He grunted against the burden. Even in his true daemonic form, controlling his power had been a vicious task, one all of Arcadia knew he had failed in the end. Keeping his grip on it here, in a suit of bones and sinew, he was ever fearful he would fail again.

But he was done with the swarming of these ridiculous creatures.

Pitch danced the sabre like it were a calligrapher's pen, and he the author of a list of the dead. The world blazed, and the harpies fell. He felt a pinch at his spine, the warning tap of the amuletum, and shoved it aside. Another strike, another feint, one more uppercut. The carcasses rained down around him. He drove the tip of the sabre into a harpy's heart. The creature shifted into its human form at the very last, perhaps seeking to draw from him a shred of empathy. But they had confused the daemon with the ankou, for where Silas might have hesitated, Prince Vassago never would. Such things were not what he was made for. He was capable of devastating the highest of angels. He would hardly pause for the likes of this miserable cunt.

Pitch cut through the ribcage of the mealy-mouthed girl without pause, and her death stare held shards of surprise.

The ground around him was peppered with smouldering lumps, the reek of harpy skin burned crisp wrinkling his nose. A distant fluttering in the sky told him one of the creatures had fled. But that was not his concern.

Pitch set off towards the circle, where tiny particles of flimsy curtain floated before him. The inner circle was hard to make out, the haze blurring it so, but it appeared far emptier than he would have liked. And far quieter. A dark patch at the centre with a lighter hue to one side of it may have been someone lying upon the ground.

'What are you waiting for?' he growled at the hound.

Pitch strode towards the subtle veil of light. He stepped into it. White sparks flew, his nerves coming live with searing pain. He cussed and cried and threw himself back. He kept to his feet, but only just. Thin tendrils of smoke curled from the cuffs of his sleeve as though the material had been singed.

'Fuck.' He snarled and repeated his action. At a run this time.

A foolish move, it turned out. The result was the same, though certainly more painful. His bared torso was a mess of risen veins, as though the surge had thrown even the finest of them to the surface of his skin. He could make out their aquamarine patterns even through the damp fabric of his ruined shirt. The singeing on his coat was evident now too. Ash-black on the edge of his cuffs.

'My fucking coat. Gods damn this place.'

He lifted the sabre, drawing the flame forth despite the protest at his back.

Pitch faltered. He stared at the place where his body had collided with the dusty veil. The depth of the haziness there had lessened. He could see through into the circle far more clearly.

The flash of white he'd seen *was* a body, but not one that lay on the ground. This one floated facedown on a small pond. A pond with water the colour of rust.

The skriker's rumbling growl made him jump.

'It's not him,' Pitch said, a piece of his resolve chipping away. Gods. It was not Silas. This man was much slighter, ganglier. Far more fragile than the ankou. And this man was very much dead. 'He's not fucking here.' He turned about, glaring at the path the carriage had taken.

Forneus jumped in his path, blocking the way with every hairy inch. The beast's lips wobbled, caught between a snarl and something stranger. Like it sought to bring forth words.

'Out of the damn way, cretin.' Pitch swung the sabre close to the hound's snout. The flames were subdued. He might singe a wet nose, nothing more. But the fiery-eyed beast did not step out of the way. Instead Forneus lunged forward, ducking beneath the raised weapon, clamping his jaw down upon Pitch's coat-tails.

'Not my fucking coat you – ah!'

The skriker dragged him about, facing him towards the circle once more. Shoving his muzzle hard against Pitch's hip, he forced the daemon to retrace his steps back to the veil. The hound released his coat and launched into that horrid shriek he was so fond of.

Pitch's heart raced, his back ached. But now he saw.

A piece of material had caught on the dead man's boot. A fabric of royal blue.

# CHAPTER 25

Pitch slammed the cane against the barrier, setting off a flurry of brilliant sparks and sending molten heat tearing down his arms. Forlorn wails surrounded him.

They had put Silas in the water.

Drowning a man who was terrified of a rain puddle. They *knew* the ankou's fear. Those fucking arseholes knew it and were torturing him with it. Pitch was sick to the very pit of his stomach, his hands trembling.

He cast the sabre aside.

Conduit be damned.

He'd burn the whole bloody countryside to ash and care no two ways about it, so long as it got him to that pond. Pitch released the flame. It roared through him, spilling from his palms like waterfalls of molten lava. He lifted his hands, stepping up to the veil that kept him from that blue coat. He threw his hands against it and roared beneath the shower of sparks that exploded around him.

The cries were terrible. And they were not all his.

They dripped with anguish, with grief and loss. He knew these keening sounds. This was the woeful concerto Pitch had heard when he freed the spirit of the forest from its Blight-infested prison.

Pitch shuddered beneath the onslaught, and the truth.

Whatever nefarious magick had constructed this veil, the Blight had been used again to form it. And while there may be no prism of glass this time, the veil was a formidable hurdle to surmount.

He screamed through clenched teeth, eyes shut tight against the almighty glare of a battle fought between flame and maleficium.

Pitch's knees buckled, the frailty of his pathetic human body betraying him. In daemonic form he might well have been wading into the pond by now, dragging Silas coughing and spluttering from the water, laughing somewhat cruelly at how foolish the ankou was to abhor a simple pond.

But Pitch was not mighty and fierce and considerable. He was incomplete and full of fissures that threatened to crack wide open. The wildness that so often fuelled him had not yet recovered from his time in that sigil-covered room. It was dazed, confused, and slamming about inside him like a blind tiger.

This magick sought to douse his paltry strength, to make it wither and die entirely. Gods, the power between these stones was staggering. Pitch poured his intent into the struggle, sent the flame rushing forward, a tidal wave that had always served him well. But the veil returned it, bending the daemonic onslaught back upon itself. The potency of the maleficium had him flabbergasted. Azazel was powerful, certainly, but Pitch had not expected the humans to have learned so well from him. He understood now why it was that Sybilla used her blade so ruthlessly to cull divine magick from the world.

Pitch hunched forward, trying to keep his cracks from widening, casting the misery to a distant place. He drew deeper on the power the gods had granted him.

The Celestials had made a fucking mess when they'd forged him in the creation fire. When he was brought forth through Lucifer's seed, they had produced a daemon like no other. A weapon none could truly control, not even Pitch himself.

He was a travesty. But perhaps he could be a useful one for once. The Order needed their pale Horseman. This pitiable world with all its strawberry tarts and inane inhabitants had likely never needed Silas more.

Pitch staggered to his feet.

Gods, *he* needed Silas. The ankou could not leave him. Not yet. Not now. Not being so very godsdamned awful at billiards as he was. Pitch's laugh rose, manic and taut. He bunched his shoulders, heaving like that foolish king of myth Sisyphus against his boulder. The pacing tiger at his centre shook itself, one of its eyes at last opening. The barrier vibrated against him like a thundering heartbeat. Beneath Pitch's hands there was a strange softening, a weakening, a slow splitting of seams through the magick. His hopes and his desperation soared. The tiger's eyes opened wide. The wildness within found its feet at long last.

With one surge, he might break through.

With one surge, he may lose control entirely.

Heat ran from Pitch's nose, a stream of blood forced from a body under duress. And gods this body had endured more than its share of torments.

Let this be done.

He dug his fingers into the veil, sank them into the spitting maelstrom of force that pushed back at him. Felt the splintering of bones as he did so. Fingers breaking.

The place where Seraphiel's mark lay stung as though bladed fingernails danced upon it. There was an unpleasant twist, a wrench along his spine, an unmissable declaration that he'd gone too far.

But it was not far enough yet.

A great shudder ran through the veil, through him, and into the ground at his feet. The world shocked white for an instant, and Pitch's screams sank beneath the cacophony of mournful cries that tore from the barrier. He was overwhelmed, dragged to his knees by the weight of the anguish swelling around him.

A sob tore from Pitch's lips, as though the Blight hungered for his grief as intently as the bluecaps.

He toppled forward as the barrier vanished. He hunched on all fours, gasping and panting. Forneus raced past him, the flick of his paws sending up tiny green blades into Pitch's face. He coughed, spitting at one that clung to his lip, and his rage flared, reminding him how close to the surface his own beast was. The daemon struggled to gain the upper hand.

Just a little longer. He must keep the wild abandon in check a little longer. Eyes wide and clear.

Pitch pushed to his feet with a grunt, cradling one hand against his chest. Several of his fingers were dislocated, at least three of them were fractured as well, throbbing with the damage. But there were far more important things to consider.

The hound rushed into the pond, creating low waves with his bulk that caused the body to rock. The man's hair slithered about like seaweed caught in the current and snaked about the cluster of unhealthy lily pads that bobbed at the centre. The pond was deceptively deep. The skriker was no small animal, and yet he was forced into a paddle, his muzzle lifting to keep his head clear of the olid water. He dove under just as Pitch reached the edge of the pond.

'Silas? Can you hear me?' Ludicrous question but speaking helped distract Pitch from what stirred within.

The water was a rusty brown, with unpleasant yellow flecks of foam floating atop it. The highest concentration gathered around the dead man like piping on a vile cake. Pitch waded in, his boots sinking into muddy sediment. The sudden shock of icy cold went some way to granting him a greater hold over the beast that pressed at his ribs, demanding release. He knew the amuletum to be damaged. There was an unpleasantness at his back that told him the mysterious ink had been severely compromised. Pitch waded in deeper, up to his hips now. Sweet gods it was cold. The skriker was entirely beneath the surface, and there were no tell-tales signs to pinpoint the great animal's location.

Not at first.

Bubbles rose further out and teased at the side of a lily pad that was brittle with death-brown patches.

'Forneus?' Pitch sank deeper. 'Silas?'

It was unnaturally quiet. The forlorn wails had long since faded.

The bubbling grew stronger, breaking the surface with tiny, choppy waves of white. Pitch shrugged off his singed and torn coat, irritated at how it dragged about him. He wanted to move forward without being pulled back. The coat drifted behind him, a heavy shroud that turned from pristine white to macabre crimson in an instant. He spread his hands through the water, the lower half of his body numbing with the cold. Desperation rankled him. Flame licked from his fingertips. He would scorch the fucking pond dry if the hound didn't show sign of himself in the next instant. Pitch laid his hands flat to the surface of the water, his breath short. The flames danced in the liquid, unhindered by the wet.

The foetid water exploded in a massive upward spray, and the skriker broke the surface. The hound was not alone. Pitch saw a head crowned with dark lengths of hair. A strangled sound flew from him. He heaved himself through the water, slipping and sliding upon the slope of the pond's bottom until he could feel it no more. The hound somehow managed to push Silas towards him, the broad body of the man crashing into Pitch's open arms.

'Gods, Silas. Can you hear me?'

The ankou was an enormous rag doll, unmoving, unprotesting. The daemon's legs were kicking double time to keep the both of them from sinking.

Pitch's temper pressed warm against his aching spine. By the gods, he would take his sweet time dismembering whoever was responsible for this. He would make them suffer. The water glowed with the spreading of the flame. He grabbed fistfuls of Silas's coat and swam him towards the shore. Making his cumbersome way to shallow ground with his unhelpful passenger, Pitch found himself submerged more than once, his mouth beneath the waterline. The water tasted foul like it had been strained through a tosher's sifting pan.

'Silas?'

There was no answer, not even a groan to show the ankou had not died again. Is that how it even worked? Could death arrive a second time, to finish what was started? No. There was not a godsdamned chance these morons could fell Silas so easily. They could not take him away over a cup of tea and a fucking chocolate eclair.

Pitch held Silas tighter, cradling him against his side and fighting to keep them both marginally above water. The daemon nearly whimpered with relief when his boots touched the shifting sediment once more. But those boots were like bricks and sank him far too easily into the mud. Twice more he submerged himself and the ankou. But while Pitch spluttered and cursed and spat, Silas didn't make a sound.

A vicious snarl sounded from behind, followed by a violent splash that cut it short. Pitch did not stop to look back. He drove himself harder, clutching at the ankou, whose bulk was cumbersome and difficult to manoeuvre. Pitch swore the pond had grown in size since he'd set foot in it. He was gasping for breath by the time he had Silas's upper body upon the shore and clear of the water.

'Sickle, your assistance would be gratefully accepted.' He slapped the ankou's cheek. Silas's skin was cold as the heart of winter. 'Silas Mercer, open your bloody eyes.' Water from Pitch's hair dripped onto Silas's face and his closed lids. There was no fluttering, not a flinch. The thin skin over his eyes was washed out with blues and greys. His beard concealed a good portion of his face, but what Pitch could see of his skin, he did not like. It was far too close to that which belonged on a corpse. Silas's lips were smeared with grit from the pond's depths. Dread mingled with Pitch's restless ire. 'Damn you, man. Enough of playing about. If you think I'm carrying you back to those bloody horses, you are sorely mistaken.'

Silas lay very still. Pitch slapped him again, hard enough to shift the ankou's head sideways. 'Listen to me, damn you. I said wake up. I'll not stand for this. You do not get to leave me here. What am I supposed to do with that stinking hound of yours?'

The ankou's stillness made Pitch wince. The air was thin; his body ached. The beast within hungered, sensing his growing distress, licking at his pain. He cupped his shaking hands to Silas's face, the rough scrape of facial hair strangely comforting. He remembered its rasp upon his chin when they had kissed.

'Please, Silas,' he whispered. 'Not like this.'

Not this soon. Not now. Not when Pitch had discovered that the ankou bothered him the very least of all the people he knew. And he knew a vast amount of people.

'I know you can hear me.' Pitch was determined. He was so very afraid. 'You can hear me, and you are pissing me off now. Open your fucking eyes. Take a fucking breath.' He thumped a balled-up fist against the ankou's broad chest. 'I'll keep this up until you stop this foolishness. I told you to play their game and *win*. This is surrender. This is defeat.' His teeth chattered from the cold and the icy clutch of panic. 'What is a guardian without someone to guard? I thought we were companions in this wretched farce.' Two souls as lost as any of those Silas sought to save.

Pitch delivered another blow. A strike at the centre of the ankou's chest that was far too hard, but so be it. What was a broken rib if it made the man open his blasted, damned eyes?

The daemon could not look on that washed-out face another moment. Pitch laid his forehead against Silas's chest. If he were not holding so hard to the ankou's coat, he might have shaken apart. 'You are intolerable, do you know that? I hope you hear me and know it. Because it would be so very wrong if you were to die now and it had not been said.' Pitch rubbed at his face. He needed to keep speaking, even if every word was utter nonsense, or he was quite sure he would burn away. 'You have made everything so...so fucking confusing. And my circumstance already lent itself to unfathomable. I don't know why I am here, after all I have done. For all the use I am. I thought you another punishment, but...' He swallowed thickly. 'You asked once if I had loved him...the Seraphim. Gods, that is so like you to speak of such trivial things. But I didn't answer. So I'll tell you now, my answer is no. I have no bloody idea why I feel the need to speak such dribble...now, here...but there we are.' Pitch dragged in a hurried breath. 'It was not like that. It never could be. Infatuation, perhaps, on his part and mine. His taste for me always confused me. It bothered me at times. I felt like a strange trophy, a curious fetish, to be kept behind locked doors. But who was I to refuse such an angel? I did not love him. But I did a terrible thing to him nonetheless. I must tell you, Silas, I need you to know...' He faltered. 'I am truly the monster you insist I am not. For I killed him. I destroyed one of Arcadia's greatest. I am a traitor and a horror both. And now...now my failure will be unsurvivable if I have failed you too.' The silence hugged the air, misplaced and loud in its oddness. Pitch was vaguely conscious of the fact that the skriker had not emerged. But he was not yet done. 'Open your eyes. For if you do not, this prince will be lost, once and for all. Please, open your eyes, Sickle.'

The booming crash of pond water saturated his appalling confession. Pitch spun about.

'Shit.'

Forneus kicked and thrashed at the centre of the body of water. But the skriker was not alone. A serpentine creature wrapped its long length around the hound's middle. The aquatic beast's head was larger even than the skriker's, with eyes bulging from the top of the flattened triangular skull, set just in front of a pair of twig-like appendages that stuck up from its colourful scales like the horns on a stag. But Pitch knew this creature's horns to be far more resilient than the wood they resembled. He also knew panlong tasted a little like chicken. The river-dwelling dragon had given him terrible indigestion on a trip to the Orient with a baroness who had a penchant for the opium dens.

This panlong was a long way from its homeland.

The crackling embers of Pitch's rage ignited. His own beast hummed at his core.

This is how they had held Silas underwater. Using a water dweller that dragged its prey deep and slowly crushed it between massive, powerful coils.

'Fucking bastards.' Pitch dug his hands beneath Silas's shoulders, finding purchase and heaving back with all the might he could muster. The man weighed a small tonne, drenched as he was, and that infernal coat might as well have been made of marble. Pitch's entire body protested the weight. Gods, he was as exhausted as he was ready to set himself aflame and ignite every inch of this damned greensward.

One more heave saw him pull Silas clear of the frothing waters. Waves lapped at the edge of the pond as the skriker fought with ferocious tenacity against the dragon that held him. The hound's teeth were proving an issue for the panlong. Forneus had torn a considerable chunk out of the coil nearest to his mouth, and the panlong's blood, a viscous, oozing, pale pink, lightened the pond water to a less gruesome shade of rust red. The dragon's tongue slithered from between thick lips, darting at the skriker's ear and slicing the entire thin sheath of flesh away. The hound bayed, an unearthly sound that had Pitch's teeth chattering all the harder. The skriker and dragon went down again, disappearing under the water, their violent movements churning the pond, rocking the lily pads like tiny boats caught in a typhoon. The corpse was almost flipped onto his back, his pale face glancing at the light before being submerged once more.

Pitch glanced down at Silas. The ankou rested on his side. His lips were an off-putting hue of bruised green. Not even the skriker's terrorised howls were reaching him.

Silas was not waking.

Pitch had lost another.

Not by *his* hand this time, but through his failings nevertheless.

The flames spilled from Pitch's fingertips.

And he let himself burn.

Silas was gone.

The daemon's wail bruised his lungs, and he lay a curse upon every one of the Order who had put him and Silas here. Only a fucking dog had bothered to come to their aid. Satty's flea-bitten nags were missing in action, the Lady herself had abandoned her Horseman, not even the Valkyrie had bothered to show her face as their precious ankou suffered.

As both Silas *and* Pitch suffered.

Perhaps the daemon deserved what had come to him, but the ankou did not.

The cage within rattled. Pitch's innards bled into an inferno. The control he tried so very hard to hold on to was slipping from him. And why should he fight it?

When he failed to keep the wildness contained, someone died. But when he *did* fight his nature, the same was also true. There was death.

What was the fucking point? Of him? Of having this power that did more harm than good?

It had not saved his ankou.

Pitch turned his back on the body lying beneath the royal-blue coat. His anger made him steady, made him numb, with no sign of his limp, of his ineptitude. The daemon prince waded into the cold depths, taking his beast to the fray. He was resolute and empty. Blazing like a star fallen to Earth.

# CHAPTER 26

S ilas opened his eyes. And shut them again at once. Christ, it was
bright. And, by all that was holy, he felt awful. Like he'd been driven
over by a wagon, which had then turned around and repeated the act.

He lay against damp ground, in sodden clothes, utterly drained of
energy. There were points of great pain upon each shoulder, and he dared
not move too much lest it grow worse. All was silent about him, thanks
mostly to the water clogging his ears, but he knew that the sorceress was
gone. The weight of her upon him had lifted, the terrible ache behind
his eyes removed.

He was living. This could be nothing else but life. Living was a
bruising, damaging thing, and he had never been so glad to feel so
wretched. He'd been rescued. A voice had called for him. Come for him.

With a muffled grunt, Silas reached into his pocket. His laugh was
bitter and terribly sweet.

'They did not take it,' he whispered, caressing the bandalore where it
lay.

But of course they had not. They *could* not.

For without him the bandalore was merely the trinket it appeared.
Whatever secrets they searched for, they were his alone.

Silas rolled onto his back. His throat was raw, as though he'd
swallowed a blade, not the contents of a pond. His shoulders screamed
with pain, and his ribs ached so fiercely that he was sure a few were
broken.

Bloody hell, he could not tell Pitch the truth of what he'd remembered. Silas squeezed his eyes tighter. The daemon could not know he protected his mortal enemy. No matter how far removed Silas may feel himself to be from that poor wretched Nephilim who'd been sacrificed by his own brother.

Oh god, Pitch. He was here. Silas's eyes flew open, and he gasped. The world truly was ablaze. Silas pressed upright, blinking to keep the world from tilting clean off its axis. He shaded his eyes, searching desperately.

'No...no, Pitch.'

The daemon was half-naked and on his knees in the shallow cradle of what had been the pond. The waters were gone, burned up, Silas assumed, by the flames that slithered from Pitch's body. They shone much more golden than the flaming wings Silas had watched with awe at Goodrich Castle, and were far narrower and more numerous. Their movement was haphazard, the various streams at odds with one another, setting off sprays of light yellow sparks where they collided. It was as though all the ribbons on a maypole were caught in a whirlwind. Pitch sat slumped amongst them, his head down and face covered entirely by the fall of his hair, which did not glint despite the cast of the flames.

As though he were dulled.

Around him lay the scorched and torn remains of the monstrous creature that had dragged Silas to the bottom of the pond. Some of the chunks still smoked, curling wisps of white that cast a mist about Pitch's body.

The daemon had protected him, just as he had done at the castle. And, just like there, the price he paid was heavy.

Pitch held the head of the creature in his lap, the severed neck seeping a pinkish blood, drenching his trousers and covering the mud with a sticky topping. He had his fingers dug into the bulbous eyes, buried right up to the knuckles. A gruesome sight, but not Silas's greatest concern. The serpent had been no ally. Silas would not mourn its death. But Pitch was much too still.

'Pitch.' Damn it, his voice sounded so small against water-logged ears. Silas wasn't even sure how loudly he was speaking. It clearly was not loud enough, for Pitch did not move.

Silas opened his mouth to call again.

A faint whimper drew his reluctant attention elsewhere. The skriker lay on its side nearby, chest heaving and tail lifting as their gazes met.

'Forneus.' Silas moved on hands and knees to the hound's side, ignoring the angry punch of tired muscles and damaged ribs. 'What are you doing here?'

His heart was lightened by the sight of the hound. The skriker seemed to be uninjured, wriggling itself onto its belly, tail thumping, the brightest of its red eyes glowing like fresh embers, reflecting the glow of Pitch's flames. Silas had feared, for one guilty moment, that perhaps Pitch had harmed the skriker. Nothing intentional, the daemon knew the hound was no foe, but there were times, Silas knew, when the flame became Pitch's master and he its servant.

'I must get to him. He will see me, he will find his way back.'

Forneus licked at his hand and nudged him away with a wet, muddy nose, as though agreeing that Silas's idea was not a ridiculous one.

With an unsteady motion, Silas rose to his feet. The pain behind his eyes was gone, but he was not entirely free of headaches. He set one foot in front of the other, jaw tight. The ache of the wounds on his shoulders, where the harpies had gouged flesh with their claws, was making him terribly woozy. But he must keep his bearings.

'Pitch. You need to hear me now.' Silas sank into the mud, though it was not such a quagmire as it should have been. Some of the dirt was so dried out that it would not have been out of place on a desert plain. Parched of any moisture by a heat that radiated still. The air warmed tenfold as Silas moved closer to the daemon. The unpredictable switch and turn of the flame ribbons made for a nerve-racking journey. Silas faltered more than once as the distance shortened. At least the warmth seemed to be drying up the moisture in his ears. As he moved closer, sliding his boots through the silt, the crackle of the flames became more evident.

'Pitch. It's me. Silas.'

The ankou flinched, shifting his beleaguered shoulders in time to avoid the lash of a ribbon of flame. The scalding heat made the old mark on his cheek burn. Pitch had not intended to harm him that day in the graveyard. The daemon had pulled back the moment the fog of his anger cleared enough for him to see Silas clearly. The ankou sent up a silent prayer to whichever god bothered to listen that the fog would clear here just as easily.

'Pitch, it's Silas. I'm all right. You have done enough.' He had done too much. 'Pitch, you can let go now.'

Silas's face held a thin sheen of sweat in the shimmering air. There was no way the substance they had needled into Pitch's back had survived this onslaught. The daemon would be returned to that dreadful place Silas had found him in at Harvington Hall.

'Pitch,' Silas raised his voice. 'Tobias Astaroth. Please hear me.'

If the daemon had heard him, all there was to show for it was another strike of the flame, a whip of light that came awfully close to taking a piece of Silas's coat...and his leg. But he took only the merest step backwards. The skriker growled from somewhere behind, but Silas was not about to take his eyes off the daemon for a moment.

He must get closer. Just a few steps more. If he could touch Pitch...either he'd lose an arm or he would make this right. Silas gathered himself. The strips of fire curved and carved around him. They drew close, yes, but none so close that he was sent running. With their reach they could have cut him off at the knees three times over by now. They had not.

Silas held on to that knowledge like it were a shield. If his idea was right, that somewhere in this Pitch still maintained some control, then this should have a happy ending. If not...well, Silas's terribly long existence was at an end.

He needed haste, not hesitation. Pulling back his shoulders, deciding the pain there was not so great, Silas hurried along.

The dash to cross the few feet remaining to reach the daemon was not an elegant thing. Silas stumbled on a hidden rock, one slippery with years beneath the surface, then sank into wet mud that was striped pink with the serpent's blood. Clumsy a journey as it was, he made it.

He fell to his knees, wincing against the shocking heat that enveloped him. Good god, he'd melt before he could get a word out if he did not make it quick. He should have thought to cast off his coat before he considered this foolish idea. The flames fanned about Pitch's body, spraying out like a marvellous but viciously hot fountain, moving not unlike the creature that Pitch had slain. The one that had woven itself around Silas's body like a living straightjacket.

Silas bit at the inside of his cheek. His harrowing encounter was not important right now.

The daemon was.

Ignoring the gory prize in Pitch's lap, Silas reached for him. He pressed his hands to Pitch's smooth skin, finding his cheeks somehow beneath the ragged, dirty tangle of hair that covered his face. Silas took his desperate gamble.

'Your Highness. Look at me.'

The daemon raised his head. Silas's breath caught. Christ, there had never been anything so terribly beautiful.

'Silas.' Pitch's eyes were entirely made of golds and oranges and reds. Each iris glowed like a blacksmith's furnace.

'Yes. I'm here.'

'And you know.'

Now, yes. Not always. Silas had wondered for a long while, since the boggart had wrinkled its nose at the daemon's scent and told his tale of maddened princes. Since Pitch's secret had torn the bluecaps apart. But the idea that Silas rode alongside a fearsome daemon prince had seemed too fantastical, too wonderfully terrifying to imagine.

'I do. And it changes nothing.' Silas was earnest. But would the daemon think his *own* truth so unconcerning? He did not wish to find out.

The most peculiar look crossed the prince's face. For a brief second Silas wasn't sure if Pitch were about to burst into tears or into a rage.

'You know.' He was slack-mouthed. 'And you still came too close. You are here.'

'Of course I am.' Though for how much longer remained to be seen. The heat emanating from the daemon was beginning to resemble the surface of the sun. Silas ran with sweat, his broken ribs seemingly alight. 'But the flames...Pitch...do you think perhaps, you could set them away?'

The daemon recoiled, and his expression shifted from something vulnerable and hopeful to one of horror. He jerked his head free of Silas's grasp.

'Flames...what are you...gods, are you determined to die today?' Pitch jumped to his feet, and the serpent's head landed with a wet thunk upon the mud, the slick contents of the creature's eyeballs dripping from his fingers. The flames erupted into unpredictable movement once more.

Silas doubled over, covering his head, his nose too close to the reeking silt. 'Pitch, the flames, if you don't mind.'

'Gods, Mercer, you are an utter fool,' Pitch shouted. 'You should have stayed away like I damned well told you.'

Silas could hear the daemon's haphazard footfalls, mistimed, devoid of any rhythm. He was staggering about in the mud, but Silas dared not look up. The chance of having his head severed by a restless strike seemed far too great. From all about there came the crack and hiss of a devouring fire. Silas was drenched with sweat. The scent of his own armpits was ripe against his nostrils.

This was definitely a terrible idea.

All at once the oppressive heat lifted, sudden as a candle being doused. Silas raised his head, tentative at first, peering up over the eyeless remains of the beast's head. A pair of legs came into view, rushing up to him. Hands grasped his shoulders and pulled him up roughly.

'What is wrong with you?' Pitch glared down at him. The flames were gone, and his eyes were their usual brilliant verdant. He was sweating as profusely as Silas, beads dangling from his chin, his bare chest slick and muddied. 'Fuck, how many times must I tell you? Stay away.'

'And leave you here after you had saved me?' Silas shook his head. 'I knew you would not harm me.'

'You could know nothing of the bloody sort.' Pitch spoke through gritted teeth.

'Maybe I could not know it, but I could *believe* it. And as it turns out, I was right.' He offered up a weak smile. None was returned. The daemon held a haunted air, the shock of events still upon him.

'Gods, you are a madman. If you were wrong...'

'I wasn't.'

'Others greater than you have been.'

'Lucky for me, I am less.'

'Fuck, you are intolerable.'

'You are not the first to think so.' Silas was grave, his thoughts on his brother.

The grip on his collar lessened, and Pitch's lips quivered with words unspoken. More reprimands were coming, most likely. Silas raised himself a little higher on his knees, conscious of how close Pitch's bare skin was to his mouth. Though the daemon was covered in all manner of unpleasant things, Silas was still tempted by the notion of leaning forward and pressing his lips there. The last of the daylight was almost gone, but there was enough to see the fine cut near Pitch's left hip and another closer to his ribs. There was a more dastardly wound at his shoulder and another on his right forearm. Cuts from a blade that had struck deep. Silas held his breath, his fingers fluttering above the wound on Pitch's arm.

'They hurt you,' he said.

'Never mind that. Are you all right, Silas?'

'I am now, yes.' And he had much to tell, though wished in truth to tell none of it. 'And you?'

'I've had worse experiences.'

Silas sighed and lowered his hands. 'I suppose you have.' He took in the injuries done to Pitch. He counted at least seven shallow cuts upon his skin, bruising at his shoulders, and more alarmingly, at his hips.

'Your dog could likely say the same though.' He cast a careless hand towards where Forneus lay, head on his paws, regarding them through his fiery eye. 'He was moderately useful, I have to say.'

Forneus thumped his tail.

'I'm grateful for you both.' Silas gave the hound a nod and was rewarded with another flourish of black tail.

This had been the most awful of days. Their worst yet.

But they had, somehow, survived it.

Pitch sank to his knees, but he would not meet Silas's gaze. 'I thought you...I thought I was too late.' For all else the Berserker Prince might be, Silas had seen what he *could* be. Fragile. A delicately boned creature that remained alluring, despite being coated in muck. 'I thought I had failed you.'

'You did not. Your timing was quite wonderful, actually.' Silas smiled, wanting to ease the anguish he saw lining the daemon's face. 'Thank you.'

Pitch's shoulders hitched with a smothered laugh. 'You fool. But you-'re welcome.'

The daemon lurched forward, throwing his arms about the ankou with no warning. His haste nearly rocked Silas back onto his heels, and the jolt was unkind against Silas's wounds. But the ankou gathered the daemon in, wrapping his arms about him. Holding him tight.

Too tight. Pitch made a small sound against his chest.

'Oh god, I'm so sorry. Your back must bother you after everything that's happened.' Silas moved to let go, and Pitch's grasp tightened.

'Not yet...give me a moment more.'

Silas's pulse skittered. He slackened his grasp, just a little, fearful of the pain his touch might cause. In truth, it was the very opposite of what he really wanted. He wished to hold on until they were fused together, and no one, not a sorceress nor a dead king, a princedom nor a grievous injury from the past, could tear them asunder.

Silas pressed his cheek to the side of Pitch's head, not sure if he should speak. It might bring the daemon to his senses, see him pulling away and ending this strange and wonderful moment. He chose silence and instead watched the skriker as the hound paced around the edge of the vanished pond. Forneus stopped to stare down at them, red eyes aglow, head held high. And as Silas met his gaze, the bandalore released a gentle note that blossomed into a curious melody, brimming with far more detail than he'd been able to discern before.

Something approached. Silas should be cautious, the scythe told him, but do not run. Wait.

That suited him very well, for he was enjoying too much where he was now.

'Are you in any pain?' Silas asked the daemon in his arms.

'Not at all.' If Pitch had not said it so quickly, and were not trembling so hard, Silas might have believed him.

'We should go.' He spoke into Pitch's hair. The scent of it was really quite dreadful, but he wasn't ready to lose the feel of it against his skin. 'It is not wise to linger. They had harpies –'

'They are taken care of.' Pitch released him. The grime on his chest now stained Silas's shirt and coat. Marked him. 'This was a very unwise side trip, wouldn't you say?'

Silas flinched and did not answer. They both remained on their knees.

'Can you promise me that we shall take lodgings that have a tub on offer? I shall need to submerge myself for hours to recover from this.' Pitch stiffened, eyes widening. 'I'm sorry, that's thoughtless of me.'

How very odd it was to hear an apology cross the daemon's lips.

'Never mind that.' Silas shook his head. The bandalore's notes still flowed. *Soon she will be here.* Who exactly escaped him, but he knew he was meant to meet her. 'And you are quite right. You do really need to bathe, Pitch' He pinched his nose. 'You are quite pungent.'

'And you are a bastard.' Pitch grasped Silas's raised arm and pulled it away so he could lean in. His lips parted, and Silas saw exactly where this was headed. It was completely the wrong time for it, they would not be alone much longer, but then perhaps that made it exactly the right time for such things.

He met the daemon halfway, landing himself upon Pitch's mouth with a great hunger. They were rough with their embrace, the crush of lips indelicate and manic. The plough of mouths dismantled the time spent apart. Hands were everywhere, messy searches upon one another's bodies, scrambling to find a place that would satisfy: the curve of a neck, the jut of a chin, tangled in dank hair, upon the swell of an arse cheek. Pitch splayed his hand over Silas's chest, and the ankou covered it with his own. He frowned into their devouring kiss. One of Pitch's fingers seemed all wrong, bending where it should not.

'Don't fuss,' the daemon mumbled against his mouth. 'I'll fix it when we are done.' His tongue swept away Silas's protest, warm and coaxing. And the ankou needed no more persuading to return to where they inhaled the air from one another's lungs.

The skriker's bark, right at Silas's shoulder, made them both jump. Teeth clacked, and the ankou nipped Pitch's lip.

'Oh god! I'm sorry.'

'That bloody mutt.' Pitch dabbed a finger at the injury. His ring finger was undoubtedly dislocated. 'Send the damned thing away, will you?'

'I'm not sure I could. He's not the type for ordering about really.' Silas shifted his hips, where damp trousers and a rousing member made very uncomfortable companions. 'Besides, we are about to have company.'

Pitch scowled, withdrawing lips flushed bright pink with use. He stood, steadying himself with a hand to Silas's shoulder. 'I am entirely sick of company.'

The ankou settled his hand over the daemon's own. 'We are not in danger. The scythe has warned me of what comes.'

'Well it had best be a barber and a tailor.' Pitch gestured at his naked top half with his free hand. 'I have looked finer, I'll say.'

'You don't look so terrible as you imagine.' Silas smiled, face warm. He spoke with an honesty he would not have dared before this terrible day.

'That is because you have awful taste.' Pitch ran his hand through Silas's hair, letting his palm cup the side of the ankou's face. His expression was hard to pinpoint. *Wistful* might define it. Certainly far more demure than the look the daemon normally wore, as though he were abashed at his own gentle actions.

'I think I'm rather discerning.' Silas turned his head and pressed his lips to Pitch's wrist. One of the few places that mud did not cling. 'You look to me as though you have endured, and emerged the victor.'

The daemon seemed to shake a little harder at that. 'Who knew you were prone to such poetic fancies?' He laughed, truly amused, and brushed his thumb beneath Silas's chin. 'Shall we leave this rancid place?'

'Yes.'

Silas hadn't lied about Pitch not looking so terrible. The daemon somehow managed to be mesmerising despite being covered in mud and entrails and hues of that vile candy pink that ran from the serpent. Perhaps it was the royal blood giving him such presence, or Silas was simply so bloody glad to see him alive and relatively well. But with his mussed hair, nipples tight with the cold, and trousers clinging to all the right places, Pitch was splendid. And Silas's thoughts appallingly sordid.

God help the Order in their time of need. Their Horseman was too busy getting stiff in the drawers to mind the predicament he was in.

Silas got to his feet. Pitch was already moving up and out of the hollow of the empty pond. His limp was pronounced as he struggled up the mild incline. Discomforting cracks echoed as he snapped his fingers back into place.

'Do you have your cane?' Silas called.

'Stop mollycoddling.'

'Do you have it or not?'

Pitch heaved a put-upon sigh. 'Gods, it lies beyond the circle somewhere. I threw it away.'

'Why would you do that?'

'I didn't feel that it suited my outfit.'

Silas choked on laughter. 'That is utterly ridiculous.'

'So is going on a stroll with a dead man who is intent on delivering you to those who wish to do you harm.'

'I hardly knew that at the time.' Silas was grim. There was nothing amusing about Balthazar Crane's betrayal. 'Have you seen him?'

'No. And when I do, it will not be pretty.'

Silas had no doubt of that. 'I never imagined I could not trust someone who...well, someone of my own kind.'

Silas wondered just how like him Mr Crane might be. Was he too an old soul, moved from life to life? Did he take his first true breath with Samyaza's blood in his veins? Silas stared down at the head of the serpent. One of its branchlike horns had been torn off, a deep gouge in strangely colourful flesh left behind. The creature's eyes were twin hollows, their contents oozing along its snout. Pitch had popped them like they were translucent eggshells.

'Well, we know now they are not to be trusted,' Pitch said quietly. 'And I've learned a few lessons myself. I'd say it is safe to assume there are few we can trust and many who wish us ill. Evidently we have pissed off those who would rather the Blight run rampant. Did you learn anything of their motives? What is all this about?'

'They did speak of motive, yes. I dare say you will not like it much at all.'

'I dare say that is the safest bet you will ever make. Go on.'

Silas cleared his throat, filled with nerves. He feared the daemon prince's reaction every bit as much as the sorceress's words.

'The sorceress, she called herself Nemain, told me that they are searching...for someone...'

'Spit it out, Silas. I am the one with a knotted tongue, not you.'

'Samyaza,' he blurted. 'She said that the Blight is his voice. And that I am destroying his vessels when I strike down the teratisms.' Silas stared up at the daemon, who stood too quietly for his liking. 'Pitch, she said Samyaza still lives. Here in this world. And they intend to find him. Is such a thing possible?' He waited on a snide comment, a deprecating snort of laughter to tell him it was all nonsense.

Pitch did and said nothing at all for a good few moments. 'I've come to learn that nothing is impossible.' He was not nearly snide enough.

Silas's nerves jangled. 'That is not the answer I hoped for. Did you not say the Seraphim struck him down? That he bled so much his blood ran like a flood?' Silas stumbled on that. He'd been an unwilling witness to the Flood that came after Samyaza's fall. There had been no blood in the loch when Silas was held under until he died, but he could not forget the drum of the rain upon his head. It was the last touch of the world he felt.

'I told you the story, as it was told to me.' Pitch dug his fingers into his hair, scratching roughly. 'And did I not say that Enoch enjoyed weaving a good tale? Fuck. Surely such a lie is too much even for the likes of White Mountain. And the Order are hardly capable of guarding such a secret, surely?' He seemed to be musing out loud, so Silas waited. 'More likely it is your magicians being sent mad by divine magick. They've become delusional. What do you think?'

The question caught Silas off-guard. Pitch usually seemed to have the answers. 'Perhaps. She was certainly formidable. The sorceress had me trapped...' In more ways than one. 'And I was powerless. If you had not come...I don't know how far she might have gone. Azazel's magick has not just reappeared, it appears to be thriving. They are organised and purposeful. They managed to separate us, and they had us both at their mercy.' He noted the twitch of Pitch's shoulder at that. Silas's chest ached to think on what he'd endured. 'They certainly *believe* that Samyaza yet lives, and that he calls on them through the Blight to release him. Nemain wasn't alone. She had a raven...and two other men with her as well. She called one of them Iblis, though he did not seem to work any magick.'

Pitch turned, the silver-white of the last throes of daylight framing him. 'Iblis?'

'Yes, do you know him by any chance?'

'Why the blazes would I know him?'

Silas sighed. 'I don't know. I thought maybe you recognised the name from Arcadia. It would just be bloody nice to know something for certain. He seemed a caretaker of some kind, without any true power of his own. None that he showed anyway.' Thank all the saints for that. There had been enough show of power for his taste that day.

Pitch sniffed. 'Do you have any idea how many angels and daemons and all else there are in Arcadia? I'm barely four hundred years old. Far too young to know even half of them. '

Silas was struck by the mention of age. Christ almighty, he was a veritable geriatric in comparison to the daemon. What an unpleasant thought.

'Silas?'

'Yes?'

'Are you going to faint?'

'Of course not.'

'Good,' Pitch said, negotiating his way gingerly. 'I asked if we should be more concerned about the approaching carriage, or is this your mysterious company?'

Silas needed no song from the bandalore now to tell him a carriage was coming. The thunderous arrival was obvious. The rumble of the wheels was familiar enough, but there was an oddness to the drum of the horses' hooves. An unevenness that was strange for animals confined to the same riggings. But the bandalore's melody played resolutely. This was indeed the company he was expecting. Silas winced, lifting an aching shoulder.

'The scythe bids us wait. I don't think we need be concerned, no.'

'You don't think?' Pitch muttered. 'So it is not your magicians returning, then?'

'No. Definitely not.'

'You seem very sure.'

'I am.' Silas considered that a moment. 'The bandalore has always had a tune...a melody that it uses, but it seems that now I can read the music far more deeply. We are to meet this carriage.'

Silas made his cautious way up the slope of the pond. Though it was not a great incline, mud in this area had not been parched by Pitch's flame and was still damp and slippery. He was so busy keeping his feet that he very nearly tripped over a long-submerged log, and, in turn, the body of the young man wedged behind it.

'Oh god, the poor boy.' Silas grimaced. 'This was the housekeeper's son. They used his blood to...' He paused as the events of the past few hours rushed up to find him. 'It was truly awful. However shall we tell his mother?'

'We won't. We're not going anywhere near the fucking house. The purebreds are not our concern.' Pitch was brisk, sharp. 'Let the Order worry about cleaning up the mess here.'

He stood just beyond the reach of the pond, arms folded, his gaze set towards the oncoming carriage where evening was taking control of the landscape, dulling it, forming shadows. Forneus sat nearby, his attention focused in the same direction. The hound was calm, the flare of his considerable tail swaying back and forth like an elaborate fan. Silas edged around the dead man. The slit in his throat had turned a garish blue grey, and his eyes were already whitening with the touch of death. The ankou hastened his escape and made his way to the daemon's side.

'Oh my,' he gasped.

The greensward was no more. The grass within the confines of the stone circle had been bright and green and lush when he had set foot here. Now, it was scorched beyond recognition. Blackened by the firestorm that had consumed it. But it was the stones themselves that had Silas staring with mouth agape. Three of them appeared like charcoaled stumps, pieces broken loose by the intense heat. He had an idea that if he were to kick at them, they would crumble away to ash.

Silas stared, a little breathless on imaging the power of the flame it had taken to do such a thing. Of course he knew Pitch to be formidable, but here was stark reminder of it. Where magick had been burned away.

'You did this,' Silas said with no small hint of awe.

'I did.' In a smaller voice Pitch said, 'They had you under the water. I knew how frightened you must have been.' He scuffed his toe. 'I would never have heard the end of it from Satty if you had been lost. What else was there to do but save you?'

If all the Dominion were this devastating, how was it that the Severance War had not ended centuries ago? How did any Nephilim still live? He glanced at Pitch, who did not seem eager to catch his eye. He shoulders were tensed as though he braced for a rebuke.

'You are remarkable.' Silas refused to allow himself to think what word the daemon might use in return, if he learned Silas's truth.

Pitch shrugged into himself, looking away. 'You know who I am. You know that is not true.'

'I cannot speak for what happened in Arcadia, only for what I've seen here with my own two eyes, and I stand by what I say. You are remarkable.'

Pitch shook his head and seemed primed to return a comment when all at once his gaze locked upon something in the distance.

'Silas, tell me I am not going mad. Do you see what is coming?' He pointed across the rise and fall of the land to the north, where the racing blur of the carriage was evident.

'Oh dear,' Silas breathed. 'Well, that is unexpected.'

# CHAPTER 27

The carriage headed towards them at a mad gallop. But it was not the dangerous pace that left Silas wide-eyed.

'Bloody hell, is that Lalassu?' He rushed to the edge of the circle, passing just beyond the stones with no issue – as though he could have walked free at any time. How he wished that had been so. 'Do you see her, Pitch?'

Pitch answered with a grunt and pointed. 'There's my silly nag too.'

Sanu and Lalassu flanked the carriage, two great thundering escorts for the four black steeds strapped to the riggings. Silas shaded his eyes, as though that was some help with peering through the gloomy drift of evening. He had not even had time to wonder at the whereabouts of the horses before now, but there was no denying it was Lalassu and Sanu approaching, saddled and with stirrups bouncing about. Lalassu's pale coat shone in the dimness like a harvest moon. And as they drew closer, the truth of how involved they were with guiding the carriage grew more evident. Lalassu's mane stretched out from her neck, pulled taut like threads upon a loom, with the lengths tangled about the rigging. Sanu, on the opposite side, did the same with her roan mane. But they were not alone.

A man in a towering top hat sat upon the driver's seat that perched high at the front of the carriage, reins in hand. Silas was impressed at first that the man managed to keep the hat in place, considering their speed. But at a squint he noted that there was no luck involved in it at all.

For the driver was quite transparent, the passing landscape just glimpsed through his form.

'So now the bloody horses arrive, when we need them the least,' Pitch declared with airy disdain.

'At least they are here.' Silas watched the approach with some trepidation. He was cold and weary beyond measure but feared he knew more of this carriage than he liked to know. The scythe hummed, and he wished he could ignore its tune.

'I might forgive them, considering they have brought us a carriage, I suppose.'

Silas leaned against the stone, which still harboured some heat from Pitch's flame, and sighed. 'It's not for us.'

'Not for you maybe, but I for one will be choosing a seat over a saddle for the return journey, I can assure you.'

Silas darted his tongue against his lip. 'This is the Lady Howard's carriage. The one I was sent to deal with.' He took the bandalore from his pocket and rubbed his thumb over the cool, damp wood.

'Your teratism is right there?' Pitch sounded doubtful. 'Just trotting up to us?'

'Well, it is more of a gallop really.'

'You fool.' But Pitch grinned as he said so, and Silas could have happily stood there all night trying to make him smile again. Despite the work which lay ahead of him, and the calamity this day had made of things, Silas could not deny the sheer joy it was to have Pitch back at his side.

'We must ready ourselves,' Silas said. 'The horses seem to have the carriage contained, but who knows what state the lady is in.'

All trace of Pitch's amusement faded. 'Silas...I'm not certain that I can...' He muttered something beneath his breath, and Silas held back from reaching for him, trying to offer some comfort. Coddling, he knew, was not appreciated. 'What I mean to say is that it might not be wise for me to assist...'

Pitch had his arms wrapped tightly about him, which made the muscle in his arms rather fetchingly pronounced. But even in the shadow of evening, his exhaustion was evident. Silas threw off his attempt not to fuss. He laid a hand on Pitch's arm. The daemon's skin was clammy, as though the remnants of the pond water still clung to him, and he'd not stopped shivering in a long while. Little wonder considering it was a December evening and he wore barely any clothes.

'Of course,' Silas said. 'I understand. I will handle this without you.'

'No need to sound so sure of it.'

Silas fought a smile. 'I am certainly not that.' He tucked the bandalore into his trouser pocket and slipped his coat from his shoulders. Good god, it was a cool night. 'Here, put this on.' The scowl he received was impressive. 'This is not coddling, for goodness sake, it is mightily cold, and you are half-dressed –'

'Gods, Silas, I'm not a delicate damsel in a flimsy gown.'

Nor was Pitch steady. A good wind would topple him, but now was hardly the time to mention such things. Besides, Silas was too busy shepherding his thoughts away from the picture that had formed of the daemon in a satin gown with shoulders bared and corset tight. Christ almighty. Is this what trauma did to a man's mind? Set it all off-kilter and lurid.

'Take the bloody coat, Pitch.' Silas gave him no choice in the matter.

He stepped up quickly, before the daemon could protest again, and draped the coat about his shoulders. The hem rested on the ground, and the seam at the shoulders rested some way down Pitch's arms, but he did not shirk it off. He nodded and may have mumbled a thanks.

The night was falling, dark and steady, but the carriage, an impressive berline, was well equipped, with lit lanterns on its forward sides. The points of brightness drew ever closer. Now Silas could make out embellishments upon the roof, a brocade trim that perched around the rim like a square tiara. The rear wheels were large and brash, red paint on the spokes, their wide circumference seeing them reach halfway up the sides of the carriage, while the front wheels were half their size, creating a dramatic silhouette. This was no meagre vehicle. And no plain one either.

There seemed to be streaks of white against the darker panelling of the carriage door, a pattern he could not make out. A family crest perhaps.

Christ, Silas was no more prepared to take on a teratism than Pitch was. He still had the gritty taste of the pond in his mouth, and the calamity of his time in the clutches of the water serpent felt far too fresh. His death still played out in the back of his head, his origins haunting him. He was bitterly cold, covered in gooseflesh. His trousers were chafing his thighs, and he wanted nothing more than to be lounging on a comfortable settee in front of a roaring fire with a fine brandy in hand. Pitch would be there of course, perhaps less clothed than he was now, lips pursed and ready to steal Silas's breath away again.

The ankou pressed his fingers to his brow. Good lord. One fevered kiss had made him lecherous.

'Right.' Silas tugged at his vest and adjusted his shirt sleeves. 'Best we are done with this, then.'

Pitch nodded. The prince was, not surprisingly, splendid in the folds of royal blue, despite the tattered and dirty state of the coat. Silas bit at his lip. This was going to take some getting used to. Suspecting he knew who Pitch was, was very different to knowing for sure.

The daemon did not follow as Silas made his way towards the carriage. He glanced about for Forneus, and would have been quite glad to see the hound moving with him, but not only was the skriker not beside him, he was nowhere to be found. Disappearing as suddenly as he'd appeared. Silas hoped that was a sign they truly were in no danger.

The horses moved at a trot, a pace still too quick for the terrain which had no evident path marked. The clatter of the carriage leathers and bracings was loud, but not loud enough now to conceal another less banal sound.

From the depths of the cabin dragged a low moan, a sound of duress if ever Silas had heard one.

'Sickle, are you certain you can handle this?' Pitch called. 'It has been a day.'

He'd not deny that. Silas lifted his hand in an airy wave. 'Stay there. I have it in hand.' His confident declaration was marred by a stumble in a shallow rabbit hole.

'As well I can see.' At least Pitch seemed amused by it, which took the edge off Silas's humiliation. The less he saw of that haunted look in the daemon's eye, the better.

Lalassu whinnied as he walked nearer, her tail flicking out like a spray of seafoam. The driver was intent on his four, his shoulders hunched with his concentration, and he did not appear to have noticed Silas at all. Again came that dragging, wretched howl of duress from within the carriage. This was not the wild, mindless fury of Black Annis, but rather an abysmal sorrow. It tugged at the very edges of Silas's own enduring soul to hear it.

The six horses were in near perfect unison as the carriage halted. Silas took in the green-grey slivers of Lalassu's mane that extended back to the carriage proper and had woven themselves around the handles of the double doors, keeping that which was within from escaping. But Silas only had eyes for the collection of markings upon the door itself.

'Oh my god,' he breathed.

What he'd thought from a distance to be a family crest was actually bone. Thin, fragile pieces, from the fingers maybe. Or somewhere along the spine? The design was reminiscent of a mosaic tile, vaguely floral and set within a honeycomb-shaped frame.

The four black horses were restless, shaking their heads, noses skyward, eyes hidden behind blinkers. The driver stared down at him, his gaze darting between Silas and the pale mare. A thick scarf hid most of his face, reminding Silas of Holly Village's surly driver, Isaac. Of course, this driver didn't have Isaac's dark skin tone, being pale as the moon, nor did Isaac have any wounds so vicious as this driver carried. Death by shotgun blast, Silas would wager, with a jagged hole cut open to expose shattered ribs and decimated innards. In the right light, he suspected that the hole travelled all the way through.

The bandalore, in its new rich language, told him what was evident enough. A wraith drove the carriage. But the scythe, its notes rising higher, was not bothered by this soul. It was what was within the carriage that concerned it.

As though she knew how close she was now to the blade, the teratism howled like she was the very banshee herself. Lady Howard was unhappiness personified, her grief etching a place upon him. She was so very plainly sad.

'Good day, there.' Silas moved forward. 'Do you know who I am?'

The driver nodded. *I thought we had already met, ankou-of-the-pale-horse. But I see I was being led by a shadow.* The driver pulled the scarf down, revealing a more delicate visage than Silas had expected. The loose clothing had deceived him, for it was a woman who held the reins. Plump-cheeked, she had kind but worried dark eyes and a mole above her top lip, drawing the eye. *You were not upon your horse's back as I thought.*

Silas was mildly impressed that Lalassu could fool a ghost with her illusions.

'No. I was not. I was occupied here. But we would have come to find you eventually.' Silas kept his gaze lifted away from where the driver's ribs shifted like a macabre accordion as she nodded.

*I know. I only wish it had been sooner.* Her gaze narrowed and drifted beyond Silas, up to where Pitch stood silently. The prince was as much a ghost himself standing in the large drape of Silas's coat, the colour faded by the distance between them. *They say you have a fearful devil at your side. You'll not let him harm her, will you?*

'He is no threat to her.' Silas clipped the words smartly. 'He is my guardian, my protector, and he has placed himself in very great danger to set things right.'

It made him wonder, having heard so many times now the untrue things said about Pitch, whether all that was said about the Berserker Prince was entirely true.

Silas's reprimand gave the driver pause, and the Lady Howard's mournful sobs lifted louder.

*My apologies. I've upset you. But it seems harder each day to know who can be trusted.*

'I'll not disagree with you there.'

*You will help her, won't you?* The driver clenched the reins. *Now that the witches are done with her, they have left her in a terrible state. She does not want it. She fights as best she can, but it is too much. The gloaming is too much for us all these days.*

The carriage rocked on its axles as a heavy weight shifted within the cabin. The ground-out moan rose like the howl of wolves with gravel in their throats.

'Silas, at least have your trinket in hand.' Pitch's call was filled with exasperation.

'I am fine. It is all right.' Though Silas did reach for the bandalore. The scythe sang a hymn of caution, preparedness.

The doors rattled as a pressure hit them from behind, causing them to strain against the binding of Lalassu's mane. The bones tinkled as the whole carriage swayed. The trapped soul settled after a moment, and silence resumed.

The bandalore hummed. *Be ready. Be ready.*

*Mr Silas, sir, I beg you to help her. You are known to be merciful. The same cannot be said for those who used her so.*

'I will help her, of course. But tell me some of what has happened. What did the witches want from her?' He had the distinct idea that Nemain would be none too pleased to be called a witch. She'd gone to dramatic lengths to tell Silas she was a sorceress. 'I'm sorry, I don't know your name?'

*Phillipa. Phillipa Adamson.*

'Silas Mercer.'

*I know.*

'And that is Tobias Astaroth.' Pitch remained watching from afar, but no less intently. Silas could practically feel the burn of his gaze.

The driver shrugged into her ample scarf, which did distasteful things to the shape of her wound.

*I know his name too. There's much talk about him.* It seemed to take her some effort to pull her eyes away from Pitch. *The witches wanted Lady Howard for her carriage mostly. A couple of hundred years she's gone about her business and left well enough alone.* Phillipa leaned down towards him, and the flayed skin around the hole in her chest dangled in such a way that Silas found his stomach clenching. *She rides to the castle every day without fail, same route, so they had no trouble finding her. She has never stopped looking for him, you see. Searching for the Lord Howard, where he was last seen.* Phillipa shook her head, staring down at the reins. *He didn't deserve her, I'll tell you that much. Run off and left her, that's what the townsfolk have always said. Heard as much myself when I was still walking among them...when I was still right as rain, I mean...not shot through by some maniac who wanted my husband for herself.* Phillipa got lost in her memories there it seemed. Silas waited while she gathered herself. *Anyway, they knew where her weakness lay, sure enough. And it weren't me, no matter how long I've been at her side now, no matter how many times she tells me she loves me.* Phillipa was wistful. *The lady has herself fixated on her old man. Twenty years I've kept her company, and she cares for me, I know it, but not enough to stop her riding to that castle every day for sign of him.* Phillipa veered towards bereft in the way she spoke, her affection clear. It was not so strange as it might seem, Silas supposed, to find such intimacy between the dead. Was it not a reason lost souls became lost to begin with? Love gone wrong. Love lost. Love desperately sought. Why then would it not transfer to this realm between the living and the dead? He thought it quite lovely to find it.

'How did they use her carriage?' Silas said as gently as he could.

*I don't know the ins and outs of it, but I heard them call it a trap. One just for spirits. They set their fancy words and talismans upon it, had all manner of awful things hanging inside: dead toads, foot of a day-old cock, the skin of snakes. They'd have her ride to wherever the fresh dead were. I know she was at a hanging just a few days ago. The man was still jerking at the end of his rope when his spirit was taken. And a carriage crash up near Tavistock a few days before that, five spirits there, two of them children, snatched up before they'd even come to their senses long enough to know they were dead. These are foul times, Mr Silas, sir. Foul indeed.*

'They were trapping these souls?' Just the words were dreadful enough, causing a heaviness near his heart. Silas slumped with the weight of it and touched the carriage wheel to steady himself.

Barely had he touched the wood and the lady uttered a godawful scream, as bad as any sound the skriker was capable of. Silas stepped back quickly. Bloody hell. Where was the hound? He scanned about in a rush, but there was no sign of the animal that had helped Pitch rescue him. A shiver touched at Silas as he spotted the daemon. He was sitting down with the coat flared about him. His arms were wrapped about his knees and his head lowered. Despite the way the lady's scream tore up the evening, he did not look up. Silas would have called to him, but he doubted anything would be heard over the din.

Phillipa bounded down from her seat with such vigour that Silas feared her heart would slide out of the hole in her chest. All manner of other runny things did.

*There, there, my love. He is here, and he'll set you right.* She perched herself upon the pedestal step, caressing the door like it were the Lady Howard herself. *There, there. Easy now. Not much longer.*

If not for the way Phillipa's ruined flesh rubbed dark smears against the shaded window, it would have been a scene touching enough to bring tears to the eye.

*The bones.*

Silas rolled back on his heels.

This was not Phillipa's voice crashing its way into Silas's head. The Lady Howard, as unwell as she was, sounded like a fox with its foot caught in a trap.

'The bones? What of them?' He shook his head, trying to ease some of the weight of the lady's enormous grief. Good god, how had she lasted this long, carrying this?

*They told her those bones belong to the Lord Howard.* Phillipa ran her hand over the timbers, her voice down to the barest whisper. *Told her that unless she did as they bid and took her carriage where they ordered, they would keep a curse on these bones and see him stuck fast in eternal damnation. His soul would linger in hell, with all its torments, so long as these bones survive. It was the other ankou who told her that. Grim prick, he was. Told her he would burn the bones as soon as they were done with her. You see for yourself it was a lie. Or maybe you had them running too quick to bother. They set upon this carriage not a few hours ago like vultures on a carcass, grabbing the souls from the trap. Panicked they were, and it was nice to see.*

Silas fairly snarled at mention of Mr Crane. How was it that the goddess had not ended that awful ankou's servitude with a swift kick up the arse and a formidable piece of her mind? The sorceress had claimed to be blessed by the goddess Morrigan, the very same who had protected Samyaza. Might she also protect a wayward ankou?

He shrugged off the uncomfortable thought. 'And are these truly the Lord Howard's bones?'

Phillipa laughed, an abrupt, dismissive sound. *Neither hide nor hair has been seen of the man in these parts since he went for a stroll at Okehampton Castle in sixteen thirty-five. He's dead of course, and there's as much chance these are his bones as me living again.* She barked a laugh. *It is lies that held the lady hostage, and a lie they have left her with. But she believes it with all her heart. She was always fragile. Then that lot came along with their traps and forced her to serve them. Now I'm so terribly afraid that the gloaming will find her. Send her on her way, I beg you, Mr Silas, sir. Before I cannot recognise her at all, and she does not know herself.*

But Silas did not have the heart to tell Phillipa that the gloaming, what he knew as the Blight, was already at work upon the Lady Howard. He glanced down at the bandalore, where the scythe's tune spoke of readiness. There was no telling if the Blight had been purposely inflicted by the sorcerers, as it had been with the Verderer, though it seemed likely, considering Phillipa's talk of talismans and spirit traps.

'I will help her, of course.' Silas nodded, the touch of the lady's sadness pressing against the back of his eyes. 'Does she know what the sorceress wanted with those souls? Did she tell you?'

The carriage rocked, thumps coming from within.

*The bones. Save him.*

Silas shuddered at the new voice that glanced against the back of his mind. The words were like the scratch of diamond against glass.

Phillipa pressed her cheek to the window and closed her eyes. *We will save him, my dear. Calm yourself.* The din coming from within the carriage quietened into the restless shuffle of an unhappy passenger. Phillipa sighed and opened her eyes. *She said little to me. She feared for me, if I knew too much.*

Silas sucked at his bottom lip, considering. 'Forgive me, but it is important that I learn all I can of what was done to her. I cannot let her go just yet.'

If there were any evidence of Samyaza in all this, he must search for it.

Phillipa turned, revealing all too much of her garish injury. *Very well, but promise me you shall not push her if it is too much. You seem a man who keeps his promises, Mr Silas, sir. There is a comfort about you.*

Phillipa waited until he nodded and made his promise. She stepped off the pedestal, leaving the way clear to the door. In all likelihood, Silas could have moved through her, but he would not have done such a thing to the lass who was every bit as anguished as the woman she loved and protected. Silas touched his fingers to where Lalassu's mane still encased the doorknobs. The horse snorted, head turned, yellow eyes upon him. Silas inclined his head, and the strands released. He set his hands on the brass knobs and took a steadying breath.

'Madam, Lady Howard?' The groan from within was almost an acknowledgement. He pushed on. 'I will send you to your rest, and you will be at peace. But I need your help.' He gripped the handle and pressed down. The door came open with a click. He edged it open so that a thin gap existed between door and frame. The carriage shuddered as though a great weight had dropped upon the floor.

*The bones. Burn them. Save him.*

Not a scream, or even a raised voice. Just a tired whisper.

'You have my word that the bones will be dealt with, and your lord will know peace.' In some ways Silas felt himself no better than Mr Crane for making promises he had no clue whether he could keep. 'But I beg you, if you can find yourself still, tell me what you know of their purpose. What need do they have of those souls?'

There was a long hiss, like the escape of steam from a train funnel, and the carriage shifted so hard to one side that the black horses shied in their rigging. The wheels cut up the parched grass as the carriage slid sideways and the handle was tugged from Silas's grasp. The door flew open.

And in the blink of an eye, the Lady Howard was upon him.

# CHAPTER 28

S he flew through the doorway like a dark fog, her skirts billowing, making her appear larger than the carriage itself. Her scream was an unholy release of rage and anguish. Lady Howard came at him, her fine-featured face carved with lines of horror and unbridled loss. Silas had but a moment to take in her blue lips and hollow eyes, the white frill of lace at her neck and her shock of blonde hair gone every bit as mad as she, before he was tumbling backwards. The bandalore slipped from his grasp, dangling from his finger by the string.

The lady landed upon his chest, her black satin skirts spreading around him, her weight intolerable despite her slight size. The clench of panic descended upon him, as Silas found himself held down once more. He struggled beneath her, desperate not to be rendered powerless again so soon. The memory of the pond was still raw and cutting.

*My love, stop, I beg you.*

Phillipa's protests made no difference. Lady Howard swiped at Silas's face. Her fingernails burned as though she'd dipped them in acid, their tips raking across his right cheek.

'Shit.' Silas fended her off with one hand whilst he grasped at the bandalore's string, trying to find the wooden discs. God damn it. His fatigue had made him careless.

*The bones.* Lady Howard's mouth opened grotesquely wide. *You promised, ankou. Keep your promise.*

Her hissed words rained spittle on his face. Christ almighty, her breath was foetid, the scent of long-dead things.

Phillipa did a valiant job of trying to soothe her maddened lady. *This ankou is not our enemy, my dear one. Calm yourself.*

Lady Howard rewarded her companion with a blow to the chest that threw Phillipa towards the carriage and sent her sailing right through. The ghost vanished with a frightened shriek.

'Here are your precious bones.'

The booming voice held the lady still. Her head swivelled, though her shoulders did not. Silas tilted his chin, one eye stinging and almost closed by the vile coating the teratism held on its nails. But he saw well enough.

Pitch stood by the carriage. He held out one hand, palm raised. There was several pieces of bone sitting there, infant flames teasing at them.

'You want your bones burned?' he said. Sanu shifted behind the daemon, a looming, guarding presence. 'Then you will get off him, now.'

Lady Howard made a strange sound in the back of her throat. The glare she directed at the daemon might have unsettled anyone else, but Pitch returned the look in kind, with extra embellishments. Flecks of yellow light mingled with brilliant green.

'Perhaps you did not hear me,' Pitch said, low and dreadful. His flames extinguished.

The Lady Howard cried out. *No, no. Please.*

She dragged herself off Silas, and at once Pitch released the flames. They flared like a magnificent candelabra spluttering to life. Silas wasted no time in gathering up the bandalore. The scythe was forming before he had slipped it fully into his palm, shaping itself into a manageable dagger. He got to his feet with a grunt, his eyes never leaving Pitch, whose attention in turn had not left Lady Howard. Silas feared for what this show of strength was costing his guardian.

'Are you all right, Sickle?' The bones were engulfed in fire on the daemon's palm.

'I am. But Pitch, be careful –'

'Just do what you need to do.'

Lady Howard swayed along with the flames, mesmerised by their motion. Silas shifted the hilt in his hand, making his grip sure. 'Lady Howard, what did they want with the souls?'

*To heed his call.* She spoke in a dreamy, worryingly calm way. He did not trust it.

'Is she answering you?' Pitch's gaze shifted for the first time from the teratism to Silas. The daemon could not hear her.

'She is.'

'And?'

'They want the souls so they can heed his call, that's what she said.'

Pitch raised his free hand to press it against one of the large rear wheels, bracing himself. 'Hurry it along, Silas.'

'Are you all right?'

'Hurry it along.' He spoke through clenched teeth.

With worry furrowing his brow, Silas moved his attention back to the lady. 'How can they use the souls for that, Lady Howard?'

Her sway back and forth grew more pronounced, a little less controlled, and a tad more ragged. *They will find where he lies.*

'How? Whom do they seek?' The Lady Howard jerked her head like he'd slapped her. 'My lady? Whom do they seek?'

He needed to hear it again. To be certain that it was not he who had been delusional in that circle, hearing words that were not really spoken.

Lady Howard's fingers curled, and her arms twitched. *Burn all the bones.*

'Answer me,' Silas shouted.

*The Watcher King.* Lady Howard whispered the dreaded name, leaving Silas in no doubt of what he'd heard as the sorceress tormented him.

Sanu squealed and rose off her front hooves as though readying to strike out at the teratism herself. Her sudden violent movement drew Silas's attention back to the daemon.

'Silas,' Pitch grunted, his hold upon the carriage wheel rigid, and his outstretched arm shaking hard. His flames curled high above his palm, almost concealing his face from Silas's view. 'I don't think I –'

'Oh god, Pitch. Stop, no more.'

Without the carriage wheel to support him, there was no doubt Pitch would not be standing.

'Do you have what you need, Silas?' he coughed.

Not quite. But he'd not see the daemon pushed any harder.

'Yes. Yes. Let the flame go.' Damn it, this had been a mistake. Silas should have insisted he stop the moment Pitch worked his flames to life.

*You promised. The bones. Burn them.*

The unbridled rage sent Silas to his knees, and he barely contained a bellow of pain.

'He cannot do it,' he gasped, struggling to raise the scythe, despite its manageable dagger form. Why the hell did it seem to be made of lead all of sudden? The scythe began to sing. A melody that spoke of broken promises. 'Oh shit.'

'Silas!' Pitch's voice was muffled, distant. 'Talk to me, I cannot hold on much longer.'

'I promised her. I'm sorry.' Silas grabbed at the carriage to right himself. 'The scythe won't finish this until the bones are gone. But don't use your flame, we will find another way.'

A tidal wave of curses left the daemon, joining the horrendous keening that came from the Lady Howard. If Silas could still hear well after this, it would be a miracle.

'Unless you have a match on hand, and a wagon load of kindling,' Pitch shouted, 'this is the way.'

The flames snaked from his wrist now, creeping their way up his arm. He reached for the bones on the door.

*Don't burn the carriage!* Phillipa appeared in front of the door, waving her arms in the daemon's face, her limbs passing through his flames without repercussion. *You'll kill the horses. Use the dagger, ankou.*

Silas dashed forward. 'Pitch, hold on.'

'Then hurry up.'

With a single swipe of the blade, a good portion of the carriage paint and the bones came away. They scattered over the ground like hailstones, stark white against grass made yellower by the glow of firelight. The Lady Howard was inconsolable, and her grief was grinding Silas into dust.

*Now. Tell him to do it now.* Phillipa pressed her hands to her ears as her lover's anguish tore the air apart.

'Pitch, burn them. Let her see it done.'

Silas's teeth rattled, his insides were churning. Lady Howard slipped further and further from what humanity she had retained. She was being consumed by the Blight before his very eyes, and the scythe now hummed with the approach of an inevitable end.

Pitch went to his knees, and the flame ran from him like iron straight out of the forge. The daemon's face was cinched with pain, illuminated by the blaze he poured forth. He was suffering. Silas had never despised the Blight more. Nor the greater powers that had meddled in this world and made such a nefarious force possible. Pitch was suffering because of it all. If Lady Satine wished for Silas to spend a thousand more lifetimes fighting it, he'd do so gladly.

Phillipa swept in close to her ethereal lover. The lady quietened with her nearness. Together they watched the bones turn to ash. The scythe hummed the Lady Howard's plight. She was strong. Perhaps even more than she knew. Her obsession with seeing the bones set right had put steel in her backbone. She had fought the Blight until the end, but there was no returning now from the path that had taken Black Annis and the Verderer.

And Silas could no longer stand by as his daemon suffered.

'It is done, Pitch,' he whispered and touched his hand to his shoulder. The daemon pulled away. Silas was pleased to see the flames subdue quickly. The prince had not lost control. Not here. 'Are you all right?'

Silas dared hope.

In answer Pitch curled up against the carriage wheel, covering his face with his hands. They held a subtle but unmistakable glow. Silas's hopes wavered, his throat suddenly dry. Christ, let the daemon be well. The sooner this was done with now, the sooner Silas could ensure it was so.

He moved to Lady Howard. 'It is time to rest.'

The scythe's song enveloped them both, with hope in its tune. The lady looked up at him, and through her anguish, her torment, and her bereavement, she found the wherewithal to smile. She was quite lovely when she did so. Phillipa took her hand, but the Lady Howard pushed her away.

'You may be taken too, if you touch her,' Silas warned.

*That is fine by me,* Phillipa declared. *I don't wish to stay without her.*

Lady Howard shook her head. Words seemed beyond her now. Her face was darkening, the colour slipping from her eyes. Her battle was being lost. But still she refused to allow the one she cared for to touch her, keeping Phillipa from the fate that was hers. The coach driver's time would come, but it need not be now.

'It is time to go,' Silas said.

Phillipa remained close, her fluttering hands betraying her desire to touch her lover. But she did not. *Goodbye, my love.*

Lady Howard writhed, a spasm gripping her ethereal body, but she found her farewell. *If we had met in life, what a happy one I'd have known.*

Silas drove death's blade into the wraith's heart.

Lady Howard uttered not a sound.

Her smile was the very last of her to crumble. Phillipa whimpered and drifted into the carriage. The lady fell away, piece by piece, as the bones had done in Pitch's hand. But Silas did not wait for her to vanish. He was at Pitch's side in an instant. The daemon lay curled up in a ball, his eyes closed tight. A subtle golden sheen emanated from the collar of Silas's coat.

'Pitch, it will be all right. I have the amuletum –'

'Leave me alone.' Command of a prince or not, Silas ignored him. Though it was much harder to ignore the warmth radiating from the daemon.

'I will do no such thing.' He touched at Pitch's shoulder. 'Stop struggling, damn you.'

'Silas stop.' The words barely squeezed from the tight press of Pitch's mouth. 'Piss off, I said. Before I hurt you.'

'You will not hurt me. I'll say it until you believe it.' He sought out Lalassu, only to find the mare right at his side, her breath blowing in his face. 'Here, the amuletum is right here. I can help you.'

'Gods, go away.' Pitch curled up tighter, burying his head in his knees. 'I don't want you here.'

'Fine, be that as it may, I am here. And you may as well let me help you because I'm not leaving.' Silas's heart pounded hard, despite his cool reply. 'If we get that coat off, I can give you the amuletum.' He reached for the saddlebag upon Lalassu's back, unstrapping it as quickly as he could manage with his hands so unsteady. The search was short; he'd been sure to pack the satchel at the top, where he could grab it at a moment's notice.

*Will he live?* Phillipa reappeared, standing over the grey ashen pile that stained the grass. The remnants of her companion.

'Of course he will live,' Silas said, rather harshly. 'He will be fine. Perfectly fine.' Damn, with fingers shaking this way, how was he going to use a needle? 'I just need to administer some...medication...and then I must take him to some people who can...can help him...and he'll be fine.' Christ, they were so far from Harvington Hall, from London and Holly Lodge. From help. The amuletum was one thing, but it had not stopped Pitch from falling into a terrible slump the last time. At least the glow around the daemon had not grown any brighter, a good sign, surely? But he was making small noises of discomfort, subtle grunts and moans, with his eyes still shut fast. Silas fumbled with the knot in the ribbon tying the satchel. 'Bloody god-damned hell.' His fingers were far too thick for such fine work.

*Take a breath, Mr Silas, sir. How about you get him into the carriage rather than have him here on the ground? Tell me where to take you, and I'll get you to where you need to go. The very least I can do.* There was a pause. *The Lady Howard would want me to help you, I'm sure. You saved her, after all.*

'I don't know where to go, damn it.' Silas's voice cracked. 'We are so far from anywhere...' From anyone.

Lalassu and Sanu were wonderful companions in a pinch, but they were useless when it came to piecing a daemon back together again. Surely the Lady Satine knew of the predicament they were in?

*Well then, first things first. Let's get you both inside.* Phillipa was using the very same calming voice she'd done with the lady. It was little wonder that it had worked before the Blight became too much. *Come on now. In you go.*

Silas nodded. 'Yes. Yes, you're right.'

The carriage was a perfect idea. He could minister to Pitch's needs while the horses had them on their way. Shoving the satchel into his pocket, Silas crouched down beside Pitch. 'I'm going to get you into the carriage.'

'Piss off. Stay away from me.'

'I cannot do that.'

He bent beside the daemon, scooping his arms beneath him, careful as he could be not to touch where he knew the injuries were worst of all. Pitch called him all manner of things, and Silas let every word slide like the water off the proverbial duck's back. The daemon's vitriol was nasty, but his actions were not. He allowed Silas to scoop him up in his arms, draping an arm about the ankou's shoulders as he was lifted off the ground.

'Gods, Silas. You are a fool.' Pitch nestled into the crux of Silas's arm and chest.

'You are too, if you think I'll leave you here.'

How well the daemon prince fit into Silas's hold. As though he ought to be there.

'I'm trying to protect you.' Each word seemed an effort. 'You have no idea what I'm capable of.'

'I know that I have ridden alongside you, day in and day out for weeks now, and I am unscathed. Well, unscathed from anything you have done, at least. The rest has not been so easy.' He adjusted Pitch's meagre weight. 'I don't think you are so frightening as you imagine.'

'You are ridiculous,' Pitch said. 'Or perhaps just anxious to die again and be rid of me.'

'I can assure you, I want neither.' They settled well against one another, but Pitch was warm enough to cause a thin sheen of sweat to form upon Silas's brow.

Phillipa aided them by opening the carriage door. Silas muttered his thanks, ignoring the pinches at his back as he angled himself the way he thought least taxing on the daemon. He intended to settle Pitch on one of the seats, but the prince had other ideas. The daemon pulled from Silas's arms the moment he was inside the cabin. He shuffled on his knees across the carpeted ground between the seats until he was up against the door on the far side with nowhere else to go. He stayed on his knees, bracing his elbows against the bulging seat cushions, like a man in prayer. Silas let him be. If that was where he was most comfortable, then so be it. The interior of the carriage was luxurious, filled with lush materials and extravagant embroidery, tones of pale blue and shining silver. Tassels dangled from the window sashes, mirrored glass trimmed the roof edges, and two small but handsomely embellished silver sconces held brand-new lit candles.

Silas withdrew from the cabin, managing to bump his head on the doorframe as he went.

*Any more thoughts on where we should head, Mr Silas, sir?* Phillipa waited outside, her gaze still fixed on the ashen patch upon the ground.

'Head towards London, if you will.' He turned and jumped as he found Sanu right behind him. She nudged him aside so she could stretch her nose into the cabin. The horse flared her nostrils, making Silas's coat flutter about Pitch's heels. With the light spilling from the carriage lanterns, her coat was the rich hue of redwood.

'He'll be quite fine,' Silas said with a surety he didn't feel. 'You'll see. But I think it best you go ahead. Bring someone to meet us, if they are not already on their way.'

Sanu eyed him with pools of deep brown, warm as chocolate. She nickered and pressed the velvet of her nose to his arm. A moment later she turned about on her hindquarters. Silas stepped back, in danger of being trodden on otherwise. The red horse set off at a gallop, mane and tail fluttering like banners. Lalassu watched her go.

'Let us be on our way, Phillipa.'

Silas hunched over to step into the carriage. Barely had he gotten inside, the door just closed behind him, and his ghostly driver had them on their way.

# CHAPTER 29

The sudden lurch of the carriage threw Silas into his seat. For a terrible moment he feared he had landed upon the satchel. A hurried search in his pocket found the glass vial and the needle with its cradle perfectly intact. He heaved a sigh.

'You should be out there, on your nag.' Pitch clutched at the blue-grey velvet that cushioned the seat. He was still on his knees, but the coat had slid from one shoulder, revealing pale skin marred by dirt stains and a scattering of awful cuts.

'Then how would I give you the amuletum?' Silas withdrew the needle, which looked entirely more like an intricate pen of tortoiseshell. There was a curl of metal near the head that one could slide a finger into like a brace, enabling a greater accuracy and surety of hand.

'Do you have any idea what you are doing?' Pitch said.

'Of course I do. Bess showed me how to hold it and add the ink as needed. There is nothing to it, for me. All I need do is guide it, and the needle will do all the work.' That is what Old Bess had said at least. Silas could only pray it was so.

Pitch lowered his forehead against the seat. 'You are too close,' he muttered into the cushion. 'It is not wise.'

'There is nothing for it, I'm afraid. I cannot help you otherwise.'

Pitch mumbled something he did not catch.

'I will need to take the coat off you, is that all right?' Silas didn't know what had happened to the daemon behind that closed door at Gidleigh

257

Park House, but he could make dreadful guesses. And each one of them made his gut roil and his anger flare. There were distinct marks upon Pitch's exposed shoulder, the crescent shape a fingernail would make if pressed too hard into the skin. Through the grime, the blotting of bruises was evident upon his shoulder and arm both. The daemon had been held down, and with no small amount of force either. Silas looked away. He had to work hard to ask his question again when no answer came.

'Pitch? May I take the coat from you?'

'Get on with it.' The daemon was holding on to the seat like a man dangling over a cliff's edge. His knuckles were whitened lumps.

Silas pulled with gentle purpose, and Pitch shrugged his shoulders, slipping his arms free of the sleeves, grasping hold of the seat again the moment he was able. The coat fell away, catching at Pitch's trousers and gathering about his hips. Silas caught himself before he cried out at the sight of Pitch's back.

The daemon's skin gleamed with the flame's presence just below the surface, and there was still much of the pond's grime clinging to him, but it was the awful spread of a burn upon the right side of Pitch's back that left Silas dry-mouthed. The skin appeared melted, the usual flawless, marble white of his skin utterly ruined. It was twisted and swirled into raised welts that were a mixture of different hues. Some was the reddish glare of a fresh burn, other sections tinged the same shade as the many bruises he had upon the rest of his body. The destruction was extensive, covering him from hip up to near his shoulder blade.

'Oh god, Pitch...they burned you?'

The daemon released one hand from its death grip upon the seat and touched at the wound. 'You see it?'

Silas touched his wrist, urging his hand away. 'Of course. Christ, I'm so sorry.'

'For what?' Pitch held on to his seat once more.

'That I did not realise at once that something was wrong. I was too busy being angry, assuming you had left to indulge. If I had known...the truth...they tortured you.' The lump in his throat stopped him from saying any more.

'Yes, but *they* didn't burn me.' Pitch made a discomforted sound, shifting on his knees.

Silas could not take his eyes from the sickening damage. 'Was it the serpent, then?'

'No.'

'Then who did this?' Silas demanded. He'd see them punished.

'The Seraphim.' The words were slurred, through difficulty with his tongue or the pain, it was hard to say. Likely both.

Bloody hell, the wound was not new at all, then. This was the old injury that Sybilla had spoken about, had lied about if she knew Pitch's truth as Silas suspected she did. Here were the remnants of a daemon prince's battle with a high angel. A battle only one of them survived.

'But...how is that...I could not see it –'

'Amuletum.' The word was growled. 'Hurry.'

The carriage lurched hard to one side. Pitch snarled against the violent motion. Silas threw his hands wide to brace and prevent himself from falling onto the daemon. The vial slipped from his grasp, landing on the seat behind Pitch.

'Shit,' Silas hissed.

He slid to his knees in the small space that remained beside the daemon. It was a pinch. His feet were pressed up against the door, which he hoped was locked fast, and his knees were brushing against the bunching of his own coat as it lay pooled about Pitch. But the ankou was near enough now to reach the vial. Silas snatched up the amuletum and sat back on his heels, as much as he was able. His injured ribs struck the side of the seat, but already the bones were beginning to heal, and with so much filling in the cushions the blow barely made him grimace.

This felt the right place to be for what he must do.

He could have sat on the seat behind Pitch, perhaps, and coaxed him to edge away from the door a little so Silas could sit straddled, but he did not like the idea of looming over the daemon, like a painter over a blank canvas. Pitch was not a lifeless piece of material.

Silas would stay where he was. As close as he could be.

He took the needle point, which was thick like something a seamstress would use on coarser fabrics, and plunged it through the sheath of pig skin that stoppered the vial. The metal plunged into midnight-black fluid. He drew back on the thin stalk of metal at the top of the pen-shaped needle, and the suction pulled the amuletum from the vial and up into the body of the device.

He swallowed, all at once terribly nervous. 'All right. I'm ready. You must tell me the moment this hurts and I'll stop.'

'You are carving into my skin. It will hurt.' Pitch shifted his left hand, the one nearest to Silas, adjusting his grip upon the seat. 'If I tell you to get out, promise me you will do so. If I feel I am losing control –'

'You won't –'

'Silas.' Pitch fairly snarled his name. 'You may recall that I was chained the last time this was done. That was not merely to pander to Satty's fetish for bondage. It was so I would not tear off the limbs of the human she wore.'

Silas considered protesting again and set it aside. 'Fine. Yes. I will leave if you say so.'

A grunt came from the daemon, and nothing more.

Silas stared down at the long length of black upon Pitch's back. He had no idea where to start. He blew out a short breath, holding the needle like it was the pen it resembled. He placed his free hand just below Pitch's shoulder blade, grateful that he'd ended up on the daemon's left, away from the scorched scars. Pitch was rigid with tension. If Silas could see his face, he was sure he'd see teeth gritted and jaw muscles taut, but the daemon's hair hung lank and concealing. His skin was still unreasonably warm, heating the entire cabin too well.

'Here we go,' Silas whispered.

He set the needle point where the tattoo separated into three distinct prongs. Two ran over Pitch's shoulder blades, the one on the right barely high enough to escape being contorted by the wretched burn, and the third running up his spine and into the dampened wavy strands of hair at the nape of his neck. Barely had Silas placed the tip of metal over the skin and he felt the device tug at his grasp.

The needle dove into Pitch's skin.

The daemon gasped, and the gold sheen about him flared like a fire that had found new fuel to burn.

'Are you all right?'

'Just get it done.'

There was no difficulty in that. The needle worked as though Silas were not there at all. He was in danger of having it whipped from his grasp, such was the speed with which it moved. The needle hammered tiny punctures into sweat-drenched skin, staining it a deeper black as it went, creating those same intricate etchings within the body of the tattoo that he noticed when he found Pitch near to senseless in a lightless and hidden room at Harvington Hall.

Pitch did not bleed, for which Silas was exceptionally grateful, but the daemon was desperately unhappy. He growled curses, condemning gods Silas had never heard of, shouting into the cushion with threats of such violence that Silas wondered if he would escape this unscathed. But it was when Pitch whimpered and cried that Silas truly considered abandoning the task. The needle was relentless in its monotony, caring little where it landed, not slowing over delicate places were there nothing between skin and bone. When it struck its way through the vulnerable place at the base of his neck, where the spine was a visible lump beneath the skin, Pitch sobbed, a wretched, exhaustive sound that made Silas's heart thump. He tried to take Pitch's hand, to entwine their fingers and offer paltry comfort, but the daemon kept his hold on the cushion, clamping his fingers together to keep Silas out. The ankou refused to be deterred. He rubbed his fingers against the back of Pitch's hand and murmured encouragement.

'Almost done, now.'

'You are doing so very well.'

'It is nearly over.'

The moment Pitch's shoulders relaxed and his hold slackened, Silas had their fingers interlaced. The amuletum, painful as it was to administer, was beginning to take effect. The daemon was not so terribly warm as before, nor was the glow about him so evident. Silas did not often look away from the harsh burns that scarred the daemon's back, so he knew at once when they too began to fade.

The needle continued its dreadful path, and the ink bled along Pitch's back into thin veins of liquid. The cabin was warm with the windows shut and the drapes closed, and the air was ripe with the sweaty heat of their bodies. Silas watched the needle as it made its way down the length of Pitch's spine. He hoped it would not need to be refilled, for he had no wish to let go of Pitch's hand, not when the daemon clung to him so.

They were so very close.

The burns were all but hidden now, the smooth white skin returning, as though the amuletum had made it possible to wipe the marks away as easily as the traces of mud from the pond.

Silas guided the needle along the small of Pitch's back. There were just a few inches to go, but he winced at every dart of the needle into the thin layer of skin. Phillipa had the carriage moving at a rapid clip, and no sooner was he wondering if he should call out for her to slow down when they struck a deep pothole. Silas was thrown forward, and he could not stop his weight bearing down upon the needle.

'Fuck!' Pitch's squeeze would have broken a lesser man's hand.

'Oh god, I'm sorry,' Silas cried. He wrenched the needle tip from where it had embedded itself deep and threw it onto the seat with a grimace. 'Damn it. Are you badly hurt?'

'No.' Pitch's glow had all but vanished, and his skin was the clammy, cool temperature of someone who'd been wandering about in the cool of evening. His eyes were fluttering as though he sought to open them but couldn't quite find the energy to do so. 'But I am done.'

He still had his fingers woven through Silas's, and neither of them sought to untangle themselves.

'Yes, yes.' Silas was firm. 'We are done. That is enough...for now. If need be we can do more –'

'It is enough.' Pitch was sharp.

'Let me help you onto the seat. You can rest more comfortably there.'

Silas had thought to settle the daemon across one and take his place upon the other opposite. But it was not to be. Pitch did not release his grasp on Silas's hand when the ankou sought to pull away. Silas changed tactic and ran his free hand around the daemon's waist. He hugged the daemon against his chest, careful to keep Pitch's back free from pressure. It was a good thing that the prince was so featherlight and limp as a marionette on loose strings, for it made him very easy to manoeuvre.

Silas's considerable height meant his arse was already lined up with the seat quite well, so it took only the slightest of heaves to haul both himself and the barely conscious daemon up onto it. One of Silas's knees cricked loudly, and his back twinged at the hips as he turned at an odd angle. Pitch's elbow dug into his belly.

Silas grunted and grimaced and, with very little dignity, dragged them both back onto the thankfully wide seat. He found himself pressed into a corner, half against the wall panelling and a window with its blind drawn. Silas had landed with one leg up on the seat and Pitch resting on his side between his thighs. Both the daemon's feet were still on the floor, one foot hooked over Silas's other ankle, all three limbs caught up in the royal-blue coat. Somehow Pitch had ended up with Silas's arm around his waist, their hands still clasped. Their interlocked fingers rested against Pitch's bare belly.

Silas's breath came much too fast for so small an effort.

He could not discern where one of them began and the other ended. He lay there with the softness of the seat beneath him, the cabin rocking gently on smoother road, and the weight of Pitch against him. He listened to the other man's breath slide between parted lips. It was, at once, the most uncomfortable and yet perfectly positioned Silas had ever been.

'Do you feel any better?' He lowered his chin, but Silas could glimpse only flaxen hair.

Pitch's cheek shifted against his chest as the daemon nodded. 'Hmph. You did quite well.'

'I'm not sure I can take the credit.'

'Well, I'm giving it to you. Take it or leave it.' Pitch yawned. He flexed his fingers where their hands were entwined, and Silas thought he would let go, but the daemon was merely resettling. 'I'm just going to rest a while.'

'Very good.' Silas cleared his throat roughly. 'There is enough space for you to lie upon the other –'

'This is fine.' He adjusted himself a little, nestling into the space between Silas's legs, adding pressure to a delicate area that the ankou tried to ignore. Pitch drew their clasped hands to his chest.

He said something else, it might have been a thank-you, and shortly after, the tempo of his breath fell into that floaty rhythm of one who is fast asleep.

'Pitch?'

The daemon prince did not stir.

Silas stared at the drapes, watching them sway side to side, their tassels bobbing.

'Right then.'

He settled his free arm over Pitch's hip and rested his head back against the velvet cushioning that encased every inch of the interior. At some point the puncture holes in his shoulders had ceased to ache. He suspected if he were to check, he'd find the wounds inflicted by the harpies healed. Silas gazed about the cabin with a small, oddly contented smile.

There were certainly more unpleasant places to be. No expense had been spared in the decorating of the cabin. Thick sky-blue drapes kept the world at bay, their tasselled sashes hanging from silver hooks that highlighted the matching silver thread shot through the fabric. He peered about, trying very poorly to keep his mind off the daemon in his arms, and spied the elaborate brackets of the twin sconces, silver fittings beaten to resemble the spread of a peacock's tail. Specks of gold danced behind the glass on the tip of candles of ivory white.

In an hour or so he may not find the seating so comfortable when his body was tingling with pins and needles after too long without moving, but for now Silas would relish the peace of it. He tucked his chin down against the top of Pitch's head and closed his eyes.

Silas drifted in and out of sleep for some time. He could not say how long a time had passed, but he woke at one point to find the carriage had stopped, and Phillipa was poking her head through the wall opposite. There was no need for a ghost to leave her seat, after all.

*You've been very quiet a long while. I'm just resting the horses and making sure I wasn't moving a couple of corpses.*

Silas mumbled something to affirm he was still in the land of the living. Pitch snored quietly against him. The sound made him feel quite peculiar. The daemon was not prone to sleeping well, or deeply. He complained of it all the time. Yet the way he lay so heavily against Silas and did not stir despite the changed pace of the carriage said perhaps he rested well here in the ankou's arms.

The idea had Silas smiling like a silly fop.

That was until he recalled what he'd learned from his time in that pond. His smile faded. If Pitch knew Silas's roots, that he had taken his first breath as a Nephilim, the daemon would not lie so easily. Silas closed his eyes. Bloody hell. Why had the goddess claimed him to begin with? Why had she bothered to save one born of Samyaza's treachery?

Silas ran his teeth over his bottom lip.

When Pitch had told him about Samyaza and the Nephilim in the quiet of Ottelie's cottage, he'd thought it a story more fit for myth. Certainly he would never have dreamed, in the wildest one he could imagine, that he himself was a part of that myth. A monster born of a rebellious angel.

Silas closed his eyes. Had he been monstrous, when he lived? What terrible things had he done?

Was his brother right to have wished him dead?

Silas winced, his fingers tightening about Pitch's hand. What if he were capable of turning monstrous again? He rocked his head side to side. All of this was difficult to comprehend. A story he could barely fathom. A story he did not feel himself truly a part of, for he remembered mere snippets of it, tiny fragments. The whole notion that he might have lived life after life, and recall nothing of it, seemed every bit a dream. That his death had come, over and over, at the hands of his own brother seemed a frightening tale to be told around a fire on a cold, dark winter's night.

Nothing but *here* held any real substance.

Here, where two men nursed their wounds. Both sullied and harrowed and in desperate need of a wash, their scents crowding the cabin.

Here, where Pitch's elbow burrowed into his ribs, and Silas made no move to shift, lest he wake him.

Here, where the faint clink of glass hinted at the presence of a decanter in the carriage's storage somewhere.

Christ, let it be brandy that was stored. Who was he kidding? Silas would drink moonshine right now if it was offered. Anything to dull the edges. The rasp in his throat and the dampness of his clothes would not let him forget his unremembered past. A past so foreign it might as well not be his. A past that meant nothing to him.

But would it mean so little to a prince of the Hellfield?

Silas brushed his chin against Pitch's sodden hair.

Let the truth be long in coming. Let it stay known only to him for now. And someday later, much later, when death was returning him to his grave once more, would Silas risk driving Pitch away with the truth.

# CHAPTER 30

Silas was pulled from sleep' threshold by the brush of something soft against his neck, a caress that sent gooseflesh rising along his shoulders. He tensed, uncertain of where he was.

And of who was touching him.

'You're safe,' came the whisper, a warm breath against his skin, and he relaxed at once to hear Pitch's voice. 'Keep your eyes closed.'

Silas's smile was lopsided, curious. 'Why would I do that?'

'Because I asked you to.'

Silas exhaled and sank back. In truth he was keen to stretch, for his shoulders were aching, but he was still groggy beneath sleep's blanket, and the daemon *had* asked very nicely.

'All right.' He smiled. 'Did you discover some clothes beneath one of these seats? If you are worried about me seeing you undress, I shan't remind you that I've already seen rather a lot of you.' And rather longed to again, though Silas kept hold of his senses enough not to say it out loud.

'But I' – Pitch kept whispering – 'have not seen nearly enough of you.'

Silas's eyes flew open, and at once Pitch laid a hand across the ankou's face, keeping him in the dark.

'What are you doing?' Silas said, amused, but with an odd fluttering in his belly now. 'Is there something wrong?'

'No. Right at this moment, all is very well.'

Pitch no longer lay against him. He must have been upon his knees on the floor, for there was no space on the seat to settle with Silas spread across it so. Odd that one could miss having an elbow jabbed into one's belly and a dead weight slumped between their legs. Silas shifted, his face warming. There still *was* a weight between his thighs, it just did not belong to the daemon.

'What is going on, Pitch?' For a fleeting, ridiculous moment, he wondered if he should have said *Your Highness*.

'I want you to sit up, make yourself comfortable.' The prince grabbed at Silas's shirtfront with his free hand and tugged. 'Come on. You'll have a dreadful crick in your neck if you lie like that for much longer.'

The crick had already taken hold. Silas winced as he followed orders and sat up. He rubbed at the back of his neck. Pitch still covered his eyes, but Silas caught glimpses of flickering light through the tiny creases between slim fingers. The candles illuminated sea-green eyes and damp pink lips.

A hand touched at Silas's knee.

'Spread your legs for me.'

Oh, Christ. 'What? Pitch...'

'Please.' Pitch ran his fingertips along Silas's thigh, and the ankou quivered. The fluttering in Silas's belly became a veritable restless flock. He parted his knees, and the daemon settled himself between them.

Silas flushed, tongue thick in his mouth. 'So, you have your appetite back, then.' It was a good thing, for sure, that Pitch hungered as an incubus did, for it meant that he was well. Vibrant. Seeking succour. But it did steal some of Silas's own vigour to know this was simple necessity at play.

He felt the daemon edge back. 'You think I am using you to feed.'

'Are you not?' Silas forced brevity into his tone. 'But that is fine, I understand the needs you have –'

'No, you don't. I'm not sure anyone does, least of all me.' A long pause, and his hand grew warmer against Silas's eyes. 'Today was...well, it was not our best. And I think perhaps I had been too arrogant before now. I was so very sure that I could deal with any pissy troubles that were sent our way – until I found you in that damned pond.' Pitch paused again. Phillipa had the team of four at a brisk walk, their tack jingling faintly.

'Your hound was terrified that I would not reach you in time, so were the asrai that guided me to you. And I think their fear was contagious.' Pitch shifted his weight. The cabin was stifling, though not, thankfully, due to the daemon's flame. 'I'm going to take my hand from your eyes, but I want you to keep them shut. Understand?'

Silas nodded, and Pitch withdrew his makeshift blindfold.

The shift in brightness was evident even behind closed lids. Tempting as it was, Silas did not open his eyes, and after a time Pitch continued.

'I thought I had lost you today. And that my pathetic cravings were the reason for it. You said you were too busy being angry to realise I had not left of my own volition, well...I was too busy imagining...wondering...' His voice was the unsteadiest Silas had heard it. 'What it might be like...to know you...to have you inside me.'

Silas stopped breathing. Oh god. Had he heard that right? The rhythm of his heartbeat made no sense.

'I had been caught in a weakness. They were able to toy with me so readily that it is shameful. And it was equally reprehensible how slow I was to realise I was being manipulated. That is how swept away I had become.' It was entirely possible that Phillipa could hear Silas's clanging heartbeat from outside the carriage. 'I do not like how today went, at all. It was far too close to being our last. And we would have gone to our respective graves, you for a second time, without me having the chance to repay you for all that you have done for me since we met. So, that is a long-winded way of saying that no, this is not about my need, my pleasure, not entirely. It is about yours, Sickle.' He drew in a rushed breath. 'Tilt your head forward for me.'

Silas did as he was asked. A soft, though thick, material was pressed against his eyes. He bit his lip to stop from gasping.

The daemon was blindfolding him.

'Bloody hell,' Silas croaked. His prick was intolerably tight. He was likely to lose himself with just a few more words if the daemon kept up such talk. 'You don't need to...'

A finger pressed to his lips. 'Hush. And relax.'

Laughter hiccoughed from Silas. 'Relax? Good god, you are making it —'

His words were stolen by the touch of lips to his. He sighed against Pitch's mouth, opening for him. Drinking in the welcome return of familiar swells of flesh and tongue. There was no hesitancy, no ambivalence. Both of them found their position with ease, slipping into their rightful places. Silas made his way in the dark, tilting his head to work himself deeper. Finding the daemon there, and ready. Willing and very much wanting. He raised his hands, eager to do with his touch what he did with his tongue. To explore and tease and caress.

Pitch pulled back. 'No touching.' He grabbed hold of Silas's hands and pulled them back down to the seat. 'If you don't mind, I will do the work here.'

'I cannot touch you?' Silas kissed the prince's chin, darting his tongue against the curves. 'I thought you said this would be pleasurable? That is torture.'

A delightful, airy laugh fell from the daemon. 'But it's pleasant torture. There is a difference, believe me.' He worked his mouth down the side of Silas's neck, teeth nipping, tongue following the line of muscle all the way to his collarbone. Silas groaned. Now it was *his* turn to have knuckles white against the cushions.

Pitch released Silas's hands, muttering a warning to keep them there. No touching?

If there were a hell, then surely this scenario would be favoured by Beelzebub himself. Having a body as wondrous as that which belonged to Tobias Astaroth so close and yet out of reach was sure to send a man mad. Silas was smiling into his thoughts when hands found the waist of his trousers. Pitch was deft with the buttons there, and before Silas could gather up a moan, the daemon had him released, wrapping firm fingers around a much firmer prick.

'Oh sweet Jesus.' Silas pressed back into the seat, fighting the urge to tear the damned blindfold free. If he did so, and Pitch stopped his play, the torture would be complete. Silas would lose his bloody mind.

'No, just me, I'm afraid.'

Silas's laughter took the brunt of some of the pressure. 'You will do, then.' He sounded like a man being strangled. Which he was, in many delightful ways.

Pitch worked at him with a sure hand. Actually, two were involved. One upon Silas's balls, kneading at the twin weights, while the other mastered his shaft. Moving with a twisting motion that joined a rhythmic up and down, a flick of that delicate, deceptively manoeuvrable wrist that had Silas's eyes bulging. The prince was working all kinds of guttural sounds out of him, some of them not altogether pleasant to hear. If Silas were not so enraptured and intent on ensuring he did not spill too early, he might have been mortified at the farmyard grunts he was making.

Christ, he wanted to hold Pitch, though.

Just a hand to the shoulder perhaps, a connection in the darkness. They had been kept apart too long already this day.

He was raising his hand when Pitch's mouth sank down over his cock.

The world filled with starbursts, and Silas's cry flew high and startled and astonished.

'Shit.' He ground the word through clenched teeth, spreading his legs wider. 'Oh, shit.'

It was not the right word at all. Not for something this sublime, but it was the only one Silas could wrangle. And he uttered it over and over, while Pitch sank him deep to the back of his throat. He held Silas there a second, in the warm, divinely soft pressure, before sliding his lips and the very gentlest edges of his teeth back over taut, throbbing skin.

The burn at the base of Silas's spine, the shudders that were keeping time with his own heavy pulse, grew ever more intense. Pitch quickened the pace, using his fingers to squeeze at the base of Silas's rigid member, while his tongue slid over the beading wetness at its top. With Silas wriggling and rocking his hips so, he did remarkably well to keep his mouth in place. The daemon prince did an even finer job of causing the man he sucked upon to pant like a dog in summer heat.

He was relentless, and Silas was beginning to crumble beneath the onslaught. Crying out to any god that was listening.

Before long, the calamity of approaching climax had Silas's hips jerking, driving upwards.

'Pitch,' he gasped. 'I'm close.'

The daemon spoke through his mouthful. 'I know.'

Pitch withdrew his mouth with the smack of wet lips. Silas whimpered a protest. When next the daemon found him, he was not so kind. Pitch went low and sank his teeth into the delicate skin that covered the hard nubs of Silas's balls.

The ankou squealed.

There was no other word for the humiliating sound that left him, but in that moment Silas could not have cared less if the Queen of England herself had heard him. He defied Pitch's command to keep his hands to himself and thrust them forward, into the darkness. He found the daemon, the unholy prince of mouth and tongue, and ran his hands over his shoulders. Fingertips brushed the crescent marks that had been cut into alabaster skin, and Pitch tensed. Silas withdrew his hand at once.

'I'm sorry.'

'You have nothing to be sorry about. She on the other hand...' Pitch stumbled. 'She will be very sorry.'

The burn of the moment's passion ebbed. Silas considered taking ahold of Pitch and drawing him in. He discarded the notion at once. The daemon had created a space between them for a reason.

'I have no doubt of it.' He took a breath, searching for the right thing to say. 'We can stop this...I don't want –'

'But I do. I want this. Surely what *I want* counts for something...with you at least?'

Silas blinked against the fabric covering his eyes. 'Of course it does.'

'And you want this?'

A wry smile tilted Silas's mouth. 'I think the answer evident.' His mind worried over what had happened to Pitch behind that closed door, but his body was still remembering the heat of the daemon's mouth.

'I cannot give you everything...not today.'

The ache in Silas's chest was blinding. 'You need never do so, if that is what is best for you.' The silence drew out. 'Pitch?' He raised his hands to take away the blindfold. At once he was held, a gentle but resolute grasp around his wrist.

'I'm here.'

'I would like to see you,' Silas said. And touch him. Good god, how he wanted that.

'I don't like the way I look...not today. And I'm tired of you seeing me at my worst.'

He pressed his hands to Silas's thighs and moved himself closer. Silas felt the brush of firm body against his arousal, and he clenched his teeth so as not to shudder. A touch to his shirt released one button, then another. He could hear Pitch's breathing, feel the flutter of it against his skin. And it took all of Silas's wherewithal not to reach for him. The material clung to his chest, not yet dried, and Pitch drew it away slowly.

'Now, where were we? Here I think.' The touch of lips against clammy skin drew out the shudders Silas had worked hard to control. Pitch placed his lips over a nipple, and a wet, searching tongue explored the cold rise of skin. Silas arched his back, pressing himself against Pitch's mouth.

'Oh...bloody hell. Yes. That's where we were.'

# Chapter 31

The daemon worked his way from one nipple to the other, teasing at the hairs on Silas's chest, sending tiny thrills through him as he played them between his teeth. He slipped his hand down between Silas's legs and found his want, as rigid and upright as it had ever been. Silas exhaled, a languorous release of breath, his hips moving in time with Pitch's caresses.

The motion of the carriage worked in their favour. Either Phillipa was keen to reach their destination and throw out her bawdy passengers, or they had simply reached a place in the road where it was safe to run at a gallop, but she had the horses bundling along. The carriage rocked back and forth on its rails in brief, urgent motions, matching those Pitch bestowed on Silas's prick. Christ almighty, the daemon knew how to work his hand, the slick rub of his palm pushing Silas ever closer to unreserved completion. He was spilling already. Though he could not see it, he felt it ease from him, felt Pitch use it to his advantage as his fingers caught at the fluid and slicked it down over a cock that was swollen to bursting. Silas pushed himself into Pitch's hands, giving himself over.

Slowly, but ever surely, Cupid's bow lips worked their way down the length of Silas's body, pressing soft kisses against a heaving chest, onto a trembling belly, and then lower still to where rigid tension awaited. Pitch kissed the very tip of Silas's cock, a flickering contact that had the ankou's shoulders wrenching back. He quivered like a lunatic.

Pitch took Silas into his mouth once more, picking up where they had left off. He drove down, going deep.

And all of Silas's sensibilities fled.

'Christ.' He thrust his hips forward, too savagely perhaps, but his grip upon any control was fast slipping.

The blood thundered in Silas's ears. He could barely hear the clatter of the carriage over his own ragged gasps.

He could not help himself. He unfastened one hand from where it was near to tearing a hole in the cushion and searched for the daemon. His fingers slid into tangled strands and curved against the back of Pitch's head.

'Please, let me,' Silas whispered.

There was no pause in Pitch's rhythm and no protest at being touched. He moved with Pitch, his hand anchored in gold-flecked curls, as close to him as the daemon would allow.

Silas closed his eyes beneath the blindfold and felt the rushing, undeniable approach of his climax.

The prince worked recklessly up and down the length of Silas's cock, the unpredictable tilts and rolls of the carriage adding to the frenzied air. He coaxed the heat from Silas's body, drawing out that tingling, stunning crescendo that lurked somewhere between belly and spine. The approaching release had his balls tight and lifted, his shaft a swollen turret of delicious, agonising pressure.

Whimpers came from them both.

The carriage struck a hollow in the road.

Pitch was driven down, hard, and he gagged on the sudden weight against the back of his throat. Silas shifted his hand, thinking to allow him freedom to come up for air. But Pitch grabbed at his wrist, making it clear Silas should not retreat. The ankou slipped his fingers back into the strands, and the daemon prince found his pace again.

Silas's body went taut, every inch of him rigid, clinging to the precipice of release. He brought his other hand to the back of Pitch's head, needing to feel more of the daemon before he was swept beyond reach of reason.

Pitch groaned against his skin, each noise matching the rise and fall of his mouth over Silas's cock. The vibration that came with the sound was a lit match to a powder keg.

Silas arched, and his body roared. His hands slid from Pitch's hair. He shouted at the darkness, and his ecstasy flowed, hot and thick into Pitch's ready mouth. The daemon did not shy away, free as he was to do so. He took what was given. He held on while Silas writhed and shook and cursed, his arse jerking from the seat, his heels sliding against the carriage floor.

He only pulled away when Silas slumped, spent and gasping, against the seat. Silas lifted a trembling hand towards his blindfold.

'Just a moment more before you take that off,' Pitch said in a breathless whisper. 'There is something I need to take care of.'

Silas nodded, too drained to do much more. He relished floating in the bliss that came after all was said and done. Truthfully, he would have been more comfortable if he adjusted his position, hunched as he was at an odd angle, but that would mean disturbing this tranquil nirvana and urging Pitch to shift away. Silas was not ready for that yet.

He was vaguely conscious that the carriage had slowed again to a walking pace. He should tuck himself away, he supposed. It would be a sight that Phillipa could do without if she were to poke her head into the cabin now. Silas narrowed his eyes beneath the fabric. Bloody hell, how loud had he shouted as he came? If he recalled rightly, it was damned bloody loud.

Pitch uttered a strangled, light moan.

And all thoughts of decency, and indecency, vanished. Silas caught his breath, all his senses now fixed on the prince. With his eyes bound, his ears led him to the whispered hush of skin against skin. And again there came that subtle moan. A sound trapped between pleasure and discomfort. Christ. This is what Pitch had needed to take care of. Pleasuring himself.

Silas tilted his head back, seeking to peer beneath the folds. His just-sated cock twitched. Stirring anew.

'I know you like...to peek...' Pitch was strained. 'But stop, or I shall...never...suck you off...again.'

Silas dropped his chin and squeezed his eyes shut. 'You are not being fair.'

'I made...no...promises...'

Pitch placed a hand on Silas's thigh and dug his fingers in, his breath coming in the same stuttered fashion as Silas's had not so long ago. The slap of palm against pillared length filled the cabin. The urge to reach out and place his hands on the man who knelt between his legs was wretchedly strong, but Silas resisted. He chewed a hole in the side of his cheek with the effort it took to hold back.

Pitch worked himself, his hip bumping Silas's knee as he began to lose himself to the mindlessness of his ardour. Silas edged his widened legs closer together and hissed as Pitch leaned into his side, his body sliding back and forth against Silas's thigh. The cries of the daemon rose, the approach of the end so very near, and his fingers were like pincers where they held on to Silas's leg. But the ankou did not wince; he did not think on how painful it was, for if this was as close as Pitch would allow him, he would take the discomfort gladly.

The end struck, the calamitous moment that threw all sense to the wind, and Pitch's releasing cry soared from him. He clutched at Silas, shuddering against him. Silas tensed his legs, weathering the hard slam of the daemon's body as he spent himself with high-wrung gasps of relief. Silas relished every minute sound, every scent that drifted. He held Pitch upright, kept him secure, where the daemon's climax made him vulnerable and unsteady. The ankou remained there until the tight clench of nails on his thigh released, and Pitch sat back on his heels, shifting out of the shelter Silas had made for him.

Silas gave them both a moment to catch their breath. But he'd give the blindfold no more time. He tugged it free and blinked madly in the sudden light. The two subtle candles might as well be entire chandeliers. He could just make out vague shapes about him, but the only one he truly cared to look at was moving from between his legs. About to distance himself.

He could not allow that. Not yet.

Silas reached through blurred space and found Pitch's face, placing his hands lightly around the prince's cheeks. He leaned in and kissed him, a subtle brushing of lips, seeking to speak all the words he could not find in that instant. He met no resistance, and they lingered against one another for a long while.

'Quite the day,' Pitch mumbled.

'Quite. I'm rather happy with the ending though.'

The daemon laughed and bit at Silas's lip. 'Idiot.'

'So some say.' Silas pressed his forehead to Pitch's. 'We should get you off your knees. You must be awfully uncomfortable.'

'I hadn't noticed till now,' Pitch said, not without a hint of breathlessness. 'I've made a mess of your trousers, I'm afraid.'

Silas shrugged. 'It's not as though they were in good shape to begin with, and it was a better choice than the seat. I'd not like to explain that stain to Phillipa.'

Pitch's smile broke their kiss apart. 'I'm fairly sure she expects to find a cabin in need of a clean as it is.'

'Christ, do you think she heard us?'

'You dolt. I'm fairly sure Mr Ahari's family in the Orient heard us.-' Pitch swept a fine-fingered hand over his belly. 'Gods, I'm hungry though. You taste delightful, my dear Sickle, truly, and I dare say I could make another meal of you.' He blinked prettily at the semisleeping weight between Silas's legs. 'But I'm rather craving a decent pie right now.'

Reddening, Silas turned his attention to where he needed tidying up. The blindfold was draped in his lap, and he saw that it was one of the sashes that was supposed to hold back the drapes. Pitch had improvised well. Silas set hurried fingers to his trouser buttons, tucking himself away. Pitch did the same for himself, but he was every bit as unsteady as Silas and having a hard time with the final brass button.

'Damn it.'

There was every chance he'd receive a slap, but Silas decided on the risk. He moved in and gently pushed Pitch's hand away, taking no time at all to slide the button, sized like a halfpenny, into place. 'There we are.'

'Could you sew me a shirt while you are at it?' He spread his bare arms, drawing attention to his lack of attire. He was a glorious picture of disarray, with lips swollen, the delicate skin around his mouth scraped pink by the touch of Silas's beard, and his tangled hair framing his face in haphazard waves.

'No. I see no need for you to wear a shirt at all. In fact, it should be declared forbidden,' Silas replied, feeling silly, and rather happy, despite the day it had indeed been.

The creature who knelt before him was the reason for that, he knew. For all that Pitch had to say of himself, in Silas's mind the Berserker Prince was utterly splendid. Terrifying only because of the way he turned Silas inside out.

Pitch widened his eyes, and candlelight met emerald in a spectacular collision. 'You are grinning like some kind of madman.'

'I'm feeling rather good.' Silas fastened his shirt buttons. 'You seem quite bright yourself. And not in any pain. The amuletum seems to have done its job?'

The daemon was slow to answer.

'Pitch? Are you well?'

He was met with a delicate roll of eyes. 'Yes. You did wonderfully with your needle. Is that what you wish to hear? Gods, are you back to coddling so soon?' Pitch turned about and pushed at the base of the seat opposite. 'Let's see if your Lady Howard's carriage is as well equipped as it appears.' The seat lifted, swinging up on hinges at its backside and exposing a hollowed-out section beneath. 'Ah, thank the gods.' He bent to withdraw something from within, the movement setting off the ripple of muscle at his back. Silas was pleased, though astonished, to see that the hideous, cruel burn scars had completely vanished. The skin had returned to resembling smooth marble. Hints of the fresh markings within the tattoo were evident, the scrolled etchings that had appeared despite Silas's ineptitude with the needle. The ink had smeared in places, causing the skin to appear as though bruised there, but it was nothing that a sponge and hot water would not repair.

Now there was a rousing thought, and it was far too early for more of that.

Silas fiddled with the sash as Pitch rummaged through the compartment.

'I asked Phillipa to take us towards London,' Silas said. 'But I feel we must stop soon, for we are both in need of a change of clothes.' He glanced down at the fresh dampness on his trouser leg. Some stains were far less irksome than others. He sighed at the thought of a return to London.

To the Order.

Silas dallied with the idea of calling out to Phillipa and having her turn Lady Howard's magnificent coach around and run them somewhere sorcerers and vengeful harpies would not find them.

Wistful fantasy, of course. Lalassu was here, for one. Clandestine carriage rides were unlikely. Silas's thoughts of vanishing were ludicrous but so sweet to imagine.

'Aha! Wonderful.' Pitch lifted a fur into the air, a rich brown that might have been a bear once. 'Wherever we stop, I insist it is somewhere I can bathe. A very hot tub is a must for me.' He dangled the fur in the air between them, smiling around its edge. 'A washbasin and rough cloth for you, of course.'

'Of course.' But Silas could not find any enthusiasm for the idea of being near water. Even the idea of the washbasin left him oddly cold. He shuffled upon the seat, his back stiff where he'd been angled strangely.

'You do not like that idea?' Pitch placed the fur on Silas's lap, his hands lingering on the ankou's knees.

'Thank you. Is there one there for you?'

'There is.' He hauled out a much less lush blanket, a thick wool weave of plain black. 'But you did not answer my question.' He kept one hand upon Silas's knee. 'I'd not be surprised if even the washbasin was too much for you, after what you endured.' It was a surprisingly astute assessment. Silas covered Pitch's hand with his own, drawing some comfort from the touch.

'There is much we need to speak of.'

And so much else they did not. Silas caressed Pitch's fingers. His stomach turned at the thought of driving a distance between them. He'd hungered for this closeness, more than he'd imagined. To ruin it now by speaking of a past he barely recalled was unthinkable. The Watcher King was already too close to the Berserker Prince as it was. The sorceress had spoken of the fall of Seraphiel as a catalyst for what was happening now. Pitch, that very same prince, would not take the news well. He would need Silas nearby. Now was not the time to complicate things with long-distant matters of origin.

Silas said, 'The Lady Howard was forced to collect souls, and she said it was to find where the Watcher King lies. The sorceress claimed that the

Blight is connected to Samyaza somehow. She said it was his voice. But none of this makes sense, for the Seraphim killed him, isn't that right?'

Pitch's hand tightened on his knee. 'That is without dispute. I've seen evidence of it myself.' He wrinkled his nose at whatever it was he saw in his mind's eye. 'Raph had rather strange ideas when it came to decorating a home. There was a Sanctuary he would...he would bring me to.' Silas tried to keep his expression smooth, nonchalant at the thought of Pitch's forays with the Seraphim. 'He kept a trophy there. A relic, really. A leg bone, I think it was. A piece of Samyaza's human form. I came across it once when I was wandering about in endless halls. I got bored often. He was either all over me or leaving me alone for hours...I think he would have been happy had I stayed on my back the entire time, at his beck and call. I slept far too much whenever I was there. So much so, I often wondered if he were not drugging me to keep me from whining about how bored I was. And if I was not asleep, we were...' Pitch glanced up at Silas. 'Never mind all that. Suffice to say, I had much time to myself.'

The daemon did not seem to be relishing the memories. And it was not that Silas was happy about that, but he couldn't deny the relief that came with knowing it had not been utter bliss to lie with the angel. Silas splayed his fingers so he covered Pitch's hand entirely. He forced back the images that came of the daemon prince beneath his angel and focused instead on talk of the garish trophy.

'Is that Sanctuary here, then?' Silas said. 'In this world?'

'It is. Though I haven't a clue where. We could have been in Timbuktu for all I knew. He didn't allow me to leave. It wouldn't have done for anyone to know he had me bending for him. I'm not even sure the lieutenant would know where it was he kept disappearing too.' The daemon shrugged as though shirking the weight of his thoughts, his nostrils flaring with obvious displeasure.

Christ, Pitch sounded more a prisoner than a lover. Any jealousy that Silas had harboured...and he'd not deny it had bloomed...was fast fading.

'Bloody hell.' He steamed. 'This Seraphim chap sounds like a damn –' He pressed his lips, realising his inner thoughts had escaped him. 'I mean to say –'

'You almost said exactly what you mean, and you would not be wrong.' Pitch had his head lowered, moving his fingers to meet Silas's caress. 'But I was hardly going to say no to the likes of him. If only to delight in imagining how much it would piss off White Mountain, should any discover Raph's taste for daemonkind.' Silas could hear the grin which must have graced Pitch's face. 'I tell you though, a fucking ugly thing it was. The relic, I mean, not the angel or his Sanctuary. Both of those were quite beautiful. My dear Sickle, you would have lost your pretty mind over all the flowerbeds and rose arches in the gardens. It was exquisite. I don't care much for such things, but even I could not deny it. The interior, however, ugh, now there was a different story. Most of the furniture was still sheeted. There were rooms that had never been used because he was always fussing about in the east wing. In his study he had this damned bone, framed and set on folds of blood-red velvet, hanging over the mantle. The fucking thing looked like it was moving about when the firelight caught it –'

'He hung the bone on his wall?'

'That is where wall hangings hang, yes.' Silas let the snide remark pass, and Pitch continued. 'But it was just a single piece. I don't know what he did with the rest, for I understood that each of the Seraphim took a piece of Samyaza's corpse when he fell.'

Silas recalled him saying such a thing when they had spoken in Ottelie-'s cabin. Admittedly, he'd thought Pitch had said so just to ruffle him.

'They saw it as their trophy, a reward for a job well done. Fine reward it was too. The bones of an angel make for powerful weapons for those who can wield them. And after the Day of Ruination, there were quite a few lying about. All the Dominion's weapons are formed from those unfortunates that fell that day.'

Silas drew in a breath. 'Formed from angel bone?'

'Do you still have water in your ears?' Pitch snapped, then shook his head. 'Gods, sorry...yes. Our vestiges...that's what the Dominion's weapons are called...are in some part angel bone. Of course none of ours came from any angel as strong as Samyaza. The gods only know what strength a weapon formed from the Watcher's bones would possess. It could well rival a halo, and the angels would not want that in the hands of any daemon.' He laughed derisively, as though the very notion was beyond contemplation.

'A halo?'

A shadow flitted across Pitch's face, but perhaps that came from the shift of the drapes as the cabin swayed. 'Mmmmm. Only the Seraphim and Archangels possess them. They are conduits, more so than weapons themselves, to channel the higher angels' flames.'

'Like your cane was supposed to be for you?' Which reminded Silas that they had given no thought to Mr Ahari's offering. The fox-head cane had been left on the ruined greensward.

'A pale comparison, but I suppose so, yes.'

The daemon pulled away, sliding his hand from beneath Silas's touch. The ankou resisted the temptation to gather him back. Pitch turned and lowered the upraised seat so he could settle onto it. His blanket was long and wide. He wrapped it about his lithe form entirely, so it covered him from chin to toes. Much to Silas's regret. Pitch lifted his feet onto one end of the seat and leaned his back against the padding at the other. Silas watched him, disappointed that he had moved away but pleased that the daemon could do so readily. He obviously had no lingering discomfort in his back to lean as he did.

'So, Sybilla told you nothing of the halos?' Pitch asked.

'No, not that I recall.' And Silas would surely remember such a word being bandied about.

'She told you of my old injury though.'

'Yes.'

'And now you have seen it.'

Silas stared across the space that divided them, seeing at once where all the pieces fit. 'The burns. Yes, I did.' He swallowed, dry with anguish. 'It was a halo then...Seraphiel's halo, that did such terrible damage?'

'You are well hung and clever. An admirable combination, my dear Sickle.' Pitch laughed, a flimsy attempt at disregard. But Silas knew more of him now. Knew him better.

Silas leaned across the dividing space. The daemon did not shift or growl any warning to keep away, but he did not look at Silas either. He kept his gaze fixed on his lap. Silas perched on the edge of the seat so he could reach him. He touched a hand to a slight, firm shoulder. 'Pitch, I'm so terribly sorry.'

'Aren't we all. But what is done is done.' The daemon rearranged the blanket bunched around his neck, shaping its folds into a hood. He vanished into the makeshift cave, hiding himself.

'How long have you suffered this way?'

'Not long. I suppose a little more than a year.'

That sounded more than long enough. 'And how long until it heals?' Silas wanted to pull him back into the light, out of the shadows he had submerged into.

'Lord Enoch would prefer it did not.'

Silas settled back into his seat, frowning. 'What does that mean?'

'That he wishes me to remember what I've done.'

Now Silas's temper flared, like a match striking the flint. 'Well he sounds like a mean-spirited arsehole.'

Pitch's laughter held notes of surprise. 'Gods, Mr Mercer, such passion, such language. You've insulted the Lord of Arcadia and his Seraphim so far this day. You shall have me all riled up again if you keep on with it.'

The thought of such things was not so terrible. Silas gave him a crooked smile, despite the lingering sting of temper. 'Well that is far better than making you incensed, which I also seem talented at.'

'To have just one talent would be so dull really, wouldn't it?'

That Pitch jested at all lifted Silas's mood. 'Absolutely.' Grinning, Silas folded his arms and rested his eyes behind closed lids. It was possible he would sleep for a week if he drifted off.

'Now, we have chatted of my pleasant life for too long.' Pitch ruined the restful moment. 'You have not told me what it was exactly that those cretins sought to achieve by placing you in that pond. Was there a motive behind their madness?'

Silas kept his eyes closed. Maybe the daemon would think him asleep.

'I know you are not asleep,' Pitch said. 'Your mouth goes all slack at one side when you are.'

Silas gave up the ruse and opened his eyes. 'And you know that how?'

'I'd have thought that rather obvious. I don't sleep well, as you know...so I watch you instead.'

That revelation was not nearly as discomforting as it should be. 'God, I don't dribble, do I?'

'On occasion. You snore too.'

'So do you,' Silas grumbled. 'And you scratch at your chin a lot.'

The jibe succeeded in bringing Pitch out from the folds of his makeshift hood. Lashes fluttered over viridian eyes. 'Mr Mercer, I would never have picked you for a voyeur, but you really do enjoy a peek, don't you?'

It was no small feat to remain indignant whilst being fluttered at so. 'That is not true at all. I did not once try to remove the blindfold you had on me.'

'Not entirely true, but I'll let you have it. Bravo, sir. What remarkable discipline.'

'How gracious.' Silas laughed, caught up in the dippy conversation. 'I thank you, Your Highness.'

Pitch stiffened. The carriage rumbled on, and Silas cursed his loose tongue. He'd been far too presumptive.

But then the daemon laughed. A high, blithe sound.

'I thought I should never, ever wish to hear that said of me again.' A note of whimsy clung to Pitch's words. 'But I think I shall make an exception with you, Sickle, for you have an effecting way of saying it. A foolish way, but also, I must say, rather rousing.'

Silas's poor heart had had a day of it today. It would run out of beats before long if this kept up. His tongue had certainly run out of words to say.

'Still,' Pitch carried on. 'Someone has gone to a lot of trouble to hold my tongue and obscure my presence here. I'm sure someone will bother to inform me exactly why at some point. Satty might find it in herself to tell us, if she ever bothers to enquire as to our well-being. Until then, shall we save the name-calling for the next time we lay our hands upon one another?'

Silas was warm in all the best of places. 'If that is your wish.'

'It is. So long as it is also yours.' The daemon's gaze drifted over him. 'I'd not have you offer yourself simply out of some fucked-up sense of duty.'

They really should open a window. The cabin was a furnace.

'That is not it at all.' He was having trouble speaking, his throat dry as the damned pond they had left behind. 'And you know it, Your Highness.'

Pitch darted his tongue across his lips. 'A good try, Sickle my dear, to distract me. But I've not forgotten that you have not yet answered my question. Were those bastards hoping to get rid of you by placing you in the pond? Or was it some sick way to force you to their side perhaps?'

Silas edged open the drapes. The night was dark and empty, with no flutter of light to mark the presence of a house. The only brightness evident was the moonlight glow of Lalassu's coat as she ran along with the carriage. 'Where do you suppose Forneus has run off too? How did he find us to begin with?'

Pitch poked his muddy boot from beneath the blanket, aiming to swipe the drape from Silas's grasp, but his reach was not enough. 'Come now, my dear. I know it must be difficult to speak of. You believe your death came through drowning, and here they are, sinking you to the bottom of a pond. That cannot be just a fortuitous coincidence I'm sure. And must have been a nightmare for you. We shall make them pay, I assure you of that.'

The promise nearly brought Silas undone. He blinked, looking down at clenched hands in his lap. 'For what they did to you and I both, Pitch.'

The daemon remained quiet, and Silas's throat tightened. He'd not push Pitch to speak of what had happened, of course, but the ankou grew more and more concerned. Anything that could render Pitch so silent must have been vile indeed.

Silas spoke so the silence could not gather strength. 'They sought to imitate my death...for they believe that is when I am weakest.'

'And is it?'

'It is hardly when I am strongest, as you know, but whatever they searched for, they were left wanting.' Or had simply been interrupted before they could retrieve it. He knew that their departure had been rushed and sudden. Their panic had reached him, even at the bottom of the loch. Silas suspected Pitch was responsible for that harried conclusion to his torment.

'And how did they know the means to your end?'

'You won't like the answer,' Silas said. 'You did not like the creature much.'

Pitch was quick to find it. 'The fucking boggart,' he growled.

'But to be fair, I would say the information was taken from him under duress. They said he would not speak readily of his encounter with us, and the words he spoke would be his last. We were betrayed in other ways too, though not with any true ill-intent. I think maybe Mabel...at The Moon Inn...told them something about me having refused to bathe in a tub. I know she thought me quite daft at the time for not doing so. But I'm sure she did not betray us knowingly.'

'Why not? Everyone is capable of betrayal of some kind, Silas.' Pitch had shrunk back beneath his blanketing hood. 'You know me now to be the master of it.'

Silas didn't speak for a while. Choosing the right words was difficult. 'Harming Seraphiel was not your intent.' It was something he believed to his very core. He'd heard the daemon mumbling through his grief enough times as he slept.

'You know nothing of it.'

'Perhaps not, but I believe I know you. And I've seen how you protect me.'

'I could just as easily harm you. And will, if you don't stop talking of such things.'

'That is rubbish. You won't betray me that way. And I don't believe you ever intended to harm Seraphiel –'

'Stop saying his fucking name.'

Silas paused, conscious of the treacherous ground he stood upon. 'I apologise. But I cannot help but think it must have been a terrible accident.'

'Accident?' Pitch's laugh spat from him. 'That would suggest there were circumstances involved that were beyond my control. That I would have stopped it, if given the chance. But this is what you do not understand – I did not *wish* to stop myself, Silas. The bloodlust was intoxicating, the rapture was unlike any I'd experienced before. And when I saw...when I saw him there...it only grew stronger.' He breathed through his nose, noisy intakes that spoke of his duress. 'I knew I was losing control of my flame long before that day. The wildness within me had become a beast that was slipping from grasp. And that is where the betrayal lies. I should have absented myself from the Hellfield before it seemed a perfectly fine idea to strike down a Seraphim simply because he wanted me to stop.' He dug his fingers into the darkness beneath the hood. 'Fuck, even that bitch Onoskolis could taste how wretched I am.'

'Onoskolis?'

Pitch seemed to shrink deeper into his corner of the cabin. 'The daemonic bitch who fed me poisoned eclairs and worked me into a stupor until I was out of my mind enough for her to violate me as she willed.'

There it was laid bare. The most vile truth.

Silas went cold. 'Oh, Pitch. Christ, I –'

'She knew it...knew that I was foul,' Pitch rushed on. 'She couldn't get the taste of me out of her mouth fast enough when she took a bite.' His breath dragged through his mouth now in staggered inhales. 'She said I was no daemon at all. Perhaps she is right. I didn't need to be poisoned, for I was poisoned already. She ran from me screaming. As they all did that day I had the *accident* you are so certain of. And she'll not be the last.' He pressed his fingertips to his eyes. 'So you see, Mr Mercer, if you think yourself some damned priest who can absolve me from my mistake, I'm afraid there is very little holy about you. We will not speak on this again, do you understand?'

Silas nodded, cursing himself. 'I understand. I'm –'

'Apologise and I swear I'll throw you in the next river we see.'

But Silas refused to allow the chasm he'd so stupidly formed between them to open wider. 'You don't taste wretched at all,' he blurted. '- Perhaps I am wrong...about that day on the Hellfield, perhaps I'm wrong about all else, but I am not wrong about how intoxicating you are. Christ, you are finer than any brandy could hope to be.' He winced. Too much perhaps, but he was on a roll. 'I'd get drunk on you every day if there weren't so many arseholes trying to kill us. You even have me able to forget those arseholes when you are near. And you can hurl me into as many rivers as you like. I'll not take anything I've said back.' He flicked his hand at his trousers. 'What sort of priest has this done to him and enjoys it so thoroughly?'

'You'd be surprised,' Pitch mumbled. But it was just a mumble, not a growl or a snarl that came with a warning to shut the hell up.

'Well whatever the case, I am certainly not holy. Nor am I trying to absolve you. But I'm not going to run from you screaming either, Pitch. So get bloody used to it.'

The prince tilted his head so that one green eye peered from beneath the makeshift hood. Silas couldn't see his mouth to know if he'd managed to lure a smile there.

'Good gods, Silas. You've finally gone and done it. You've gone completely mad.' But he sounded bemused, did he not? God, Silas prayed it were so.

'Quite likely. But perhaps it's the only way to survive this.'

The huff that came from the daemon was not quite laughter, but it was close enough.

Now as the silence fell between them, it seemed, to Silas at least, not to be so bursting at the seams with anguish and long-simmering regret. He'd made a right tit of himself, really, with all the painful sweet talk, but he did not regret it. He'd managed not to have to speak of what he'd learned of himself while the sorceress dragged him into his past. And he would not say a word to Pitch of her talk of the fall of the Seraphim aiding the Blight in strengthening. For it did not matter a damn what had happened in the past. Only the here and now was important.

And in that here and now, Silas had but one wish.

That when the time came for Onoskolis to breathe her last breath, Silas would be her messenger of death.

'Silas?'

'Hmm?'

'When you were in that pond, what did you see? Do you know who you are?'

# CHAPTER 32

The carriage made its rocking, cumbersome way across the darkened landscape, with Lalassu at its side. Phillipa had so far kept to her driver's seat. He considered tapping upon the roof to signal a request to stop.

'Do not even consider ignoring my question by having the driver stop right now,' Pitch demanded.

Silas stared at him. 'I wasn't going to do that.'

'Liar. Now go on. You keep going a strange shade of pale every time I speak of the pond. What is it, Sickle?' He was gentle about it, prying, but doing so with a softness that chipped at Silas's reticence to say too much.

Silas decided this was the moment to gather up his coat from where it lay bunched on the floor. It was still damp. He would have to placate the daemon with something at least. 'Well...it would seem...that I have not drowned just the once.'

'You recalled another life?'

He took his time to fold his sodden coat, then nodded. 'I recalled many other lives. Well, deaths actually. I didn't see much living at all, only the end of it. But it appears that I...I am rather old.' A lump in his throat was difficult to navigate.

'How old?'

Christ. 'I am older than you. By quite some years, I would say.'

Pitch snorted. 'Truly? And you are still so terrible at billiards?'

'Perhaps I have never played billiards before now.'

'Mmmm, your lack of talent would suggest it. So with all those lives, you recall nothing?' The advanced years between them did not seem to bother Pitch in the least. Perhaps it was irrelevant in a world where four hundred was considered young. There was every chance Seraphiel had been of an age beyond comprehension.

Silas ran his hand over his folded coat. 'Smudges, I suppose. I think I lived in Scotland, and I've seen a woman in lavender who seemed to know me. But it seems only death is there for remembering. I drown every time.' He could recall too well a throat rubbed raw. 'And each time it is at the hands of a man I believe is...was...my brother...' He placed his hand over his pocket, where the bandalore was now an unexpected relic from all the lives he'd lived. 'It is always the same.'

He did not speak of the boy with the cornflower-blue eyes.

Pitch let the blanket slip from his head and stared at Silas. 'Your brother kills you? That's unfortunate.'

'Indeed.'

Even hearing it said out loud gave Silas no sense of it being his reality. The deaths he'd suffered, the man who had killed him, held that faint sense of the dreamlike. A fortunate thing really, for it would be awful to grieve so many losses.

'What did you do to piss him off so?'

'Pardon?'

'Your long-lost brother, why was he angry enough to kill you? I mean, you are annoying at times, but that seems excessive.'

Silas dropped his gaze, pretending the coat needed extra attention. 'Must you jest about something so serious?'

'Those are the very best things to jest about.'

Why would Pitch not look away? Damn it. The daemon would pounce if he thought Silas lying, and he was so adept at spotting it.

'I didn't learn why...why he killed me,' Silas said.

'Perhaps it was simply because you existed to begin with.' Pitch stretched his legs, setting the heels of his boots on the narrow length of sill beneath the window. 'Jealousy can make monsters just as well as any rebel angel. The other Dominion abhor me, for I am greater than them. That's just the way of it. Orobas must be beside himself with relief that

I am gone. The little prick has long had his eye on our sire's crown.' He winced and touched his lips.

'Are you having trouble speaking?'

'Well that's just it – I am not. There is resistance, but now it feels as it did after I had you in my mouth. My tongue is a little swollen, and my cheeks a bit sore, but it's not awful.'

Silas covered his face with his hands. 'Promise me you won't say such things when we are not alone?'

'Are you ashamed of what we have done?'

He needed no time to consider. 'No. Not in the least.'

'Well, then I'd say we have far greater things to concern us than worrying if people will learn we like to do more than ride horses together. Were we not just discussing maleficium and murderous brothers?'

'We were.' Pitch gave Silas cause to smile, even when the situation did not. 'I wasn't sure that you wished to do any more...than ride. Ride the horses, or course...I mean...not me. Oh god. I mean to say, after the hall, you seemed to withdraw. I thought I had done something wrong.' Silas rubbed at his cheeks, which he was sure were reddened. His unshaven chin was in dire need of a trim. Pitch had done very well not to complain of it.

'And I thought you were repulsed by what you had done for me,' the prince replied. 'I was certainly repulsed by what I had become by the time you got to me. How could I expect you to enjoy bedding such a wretched creature? And with the way you looked at me in the parlour, afterwards...I wouldn't have been surprised if you'd ridden off without me.'

Silas raised his brows. 'Repulsed? Have you ever looked in a mirror?'

'I never go a day without it.'

'Well then you know I was not repulsed.'

'But I was.' Pitch pulled at the blanket as though he were annoyed with how it had settled. 'Do you know what it is to go from being the leader of a forceful legion, a menace on the battlefield, to a quivering, pathetic wreck who is desperate to be held, because he cannot hold on to himself any longer?' He lifted his knees, making the blanket billow. 'I am not used to being fucked out of pity. I am certainly not used to someone coming to my rescue.'

'Oh my god,' Silas huffed. 'I did not lie with you out of pity. Will you stop saying such things? God knows you have come to my rescue too many times to count, and you don't see me throwing a tantrum about it.'

'This is not a tantrum.' Pitch drew his hand from beneath the blanket, pointing at Silas. 'You would know full well if I were throwing an actual tantrum.'

Silas blew out a breath. 'Yes, you are right there.'

'Well then, back to you. You say you have been reincarnated, many a time. I thought an ankou had his blade for a year only. And only the once.'

'That was my understanding too.'

'But you are different.'

'It would seem so.' He bothered at his lip with his teeth. 'I think, that maybe...I am the first of my kind. The original ankou.'

'The original?' The doubt was ripe upon Pitch's reply. 'I suppose it might account for why you were singled out to be a Horseman.' Pitch edged open one of the drapes. 'One house in sight and not a candle in any window. Perhaps we could stop anyway and rob their kitchen. I'll consider eating my own hand soon.' He sighed and let the curtain fall closed. 'But if you have been living and dying for so long, presumably becoming an ankou each time you pass, you are remarkably inept at your job.'

Blunt as it was, Silas could hardly deny it. 'Jane said once that Mr Ahari and Lady Satine were waiting for my true nature to reveal itself. And they seemed...uncertain around me, worried. Maybe I was supposed to have been reborn with more knowledge?'

'Seems likely, for you couldn't have been born with *less*. Perhaps all those years of existence is too much for a mortal soul, and your mind could not hold all the memories. Instead of an able ankou, they found themselves with a blundering oaf.' He softened the words by reaching to touch Silas's knee. 'A very fine-looking oaf, mind.'

The carriage slowed to a pace that would not challenge a snail. Phillipa seemed to be bringing the four to a stop.

Pitch's and Silas's fingers lay a whisper apart. 'I am worried, Pitch.' He edged his fingers forward so their tips met.

'That I might not wish to bed an elderly gentleman again?'

The carriage halted, and they were rocked briefly before all went still. One of the horses snorted.

Silas brushed at Pitch's hand. 'Perhaps I do not wish to bed a daemon prince again.' A deaf man could have heard the lie. Pitch inclined his head and held his tongue. 'But does it not worry you? All this about the Watcher King. I know you say Samyaza is long gone.' And how Silas wished to believe it. 'But the Blight, its strength, is undeniable, and we know that it comes from the Day of Ruination. Mr Ahari told me as much. Lady Satine too. A chaos at the heart of the world, they said, that was born the day Samyaza was brought down. Is there any chance those bones you saw at the angel's Sanctuary were not his? That perhaps he is alive still and truly calling to those with Azazel's magick in their veins? The sorceress implied the Order was keeping something hidden. What if it truly is the Watcher?'

Silas's voice rose with a twitch of desperation. What did it mean for him if the angel who had created him yet lived?

Pitch was staring down at their fingers. They had become entwined without Silas even noticing.

'They said they sought to find where he lies, did they not? That doesn't sound like he's bounding about at the centre of the Earth to me.'

'Oh god, yes, yes you're right.' Silas's relief bubbled up, leaving him light-headed.

He was dead. Samyaza must be dead. All at once Silas's mood fell again. *He* himself was dead, that did not make him powerless. It made him greater. 'Shit. But what if he is not here in body, but in spirit?'

It would make some small semblance of sense, in a world with so little.

Pitch insisted Samyaza had died at the hands of the Seraphim. He'd seen a piece of the Watcher King's body on Seraphiel's wall.

'Might the soul of an angel who is strong enough to defy the Lord of Arcadia defy death as well?' Silas was grateful for the reassuring clasp of Pitch's fingers in his. 'Those ghosts and wraiths and spectres I've met along the way are capable of doing so. Why not one of Arcadia's mightiest angels?'

Samyaza might be the greatest of all the lost souls. A Blight upon the world.

Pitch ran his thumb over the back of Silas's hand. 'My dear Sickle, I wish I could tell you you are being a fool. But I fear you are making more sense than I would like.' He glanced up from beneath thick lashes. 'I have always wondered at Seraphiel's fascination with this world, for it seemed to have nothing at all to do with the pleasures he could find here. Not even those he led me to believe he sought from me. He was so easily distracted. Even when he was buried in me, I had the sense he was not truly there.'

Silas had to look away at that. He pulled back the drapes. 'There is a residence out there, a manor house.' He squinted into the evening. A figure approached from around the side of a two-storey house of tawny brick. 'Pitch, there is someone coming.'

The daemon released his hold on Silas's hand and tugged at the drapes nearest to him. He would have a clear view of what Silas saw: a woman dressed in a gown of white, a night-shift if Silas assumed correctly. She made her way towards the carriage at a haphazard lope as though she'd drunk too much evening sherry. Most of her features were indistinguishable in the darkness, with the glow of her gown all that the night could cling to.

Silas knocked at the roof. 'Phillipa, perhaps we should drive on,' he called.

The soul pushed her head through the wall over Pitch's shoulder. He startled and hissed a curse at her.

*Best we don't, Mr Mercer, sir. Your horse made it quite clear we were to stop just now. Got her mane all tangled about us again.*

Silas eased the window down and poked his head out through the gap. The shock of the cool night air was bracing compared to the stale air of the cabin. Sure enough Lalassu was up near the first of the four black horses, the strands of her mane stretching out to wrap about the rigging like the ropes that tied a boat to the dock.

Fine. So this is where they were to stop, then. Perhaps this was a housekeeper, roused at a late hour by the clatter of the approaching carriage.

Silas pulled back into the cabin, closing the window. 'It seems we are to stop here. Perhaps they'll have some bread for us, or a stew if we are lucky. It will be cold at this hour, though I suspect –'

Pitch was half-hidden behind the drape. 'Will you stop nattering.'
'Why? I'm hungry now you've mentioned it.'
'Because the last thing Satty will do is cook us a damned meal.'
Silas frowned, quite lost. 'This is Her Ladyship's house?'
'No, but that, my dear, is Her Ladyship.'

# CHAPTER 33

The carriage door swung open, and the woman standing there was backlit by the lanterns that blazed on the outside of the berline. Her hair was a blue grey, caught up with pins and curlers usually reserved for the privacy of the bedchamber.

'Gentlemen, it is a pleasure to see you again.' She was a lady of some years, but that did not make her cautious in her movement. She was nimble as she clambered aboard. 'Oh dear mercy, what on Earth have you two been doing in here?' She touched a finger beneath her nostrils. 'Actually, do not answer that. It is evident enough. I had hoped you two would not despise each other at the very least. But I didn't imagine you might go the opposite way.'

Silas nearly swallowed his tongue. Wielder of death's blade or not, he was in that moment simply a man struck dumb by intense mortification.

'Are you all right, Silas?' She frowned from beneath thin, sharply plucked brows.

'I'm...' He coughed. 'Lady Satine?'

'Of course. Yes.' She peered down at herself, tugging at the night-shift, an intricate embroidered linen with lace at the cuffs of the long sleeves. Not a housekeeper at all, Silas suspected. Rather, a lady of the manor. 'I suppose I look a little different to the last time you saw me. Rather more breasts.'

With there seeming no adequate reply, Silas nodded.

Lady Satine had possessed the body of Clarence when last he'd seen her. A spindly young chap, with definitely less breasts, whose mouth had formed the words that had begun to shape Silas's world. It was when Lady Satine embodied Clarence that he had met Lalassu and been named a Horseman.

'How very sweet of you to bother to remember us.' Pitch was caustic.

He stretched his legs along the seat when Lady Satine sought to settle next to him. She narrowed the brown eyes of the woman she inhabited, but said nothing and found a place alongside Silas. There was just enough of a gap between them so that their legs were not forced to touch, for which he was most grateful. He was also very grateful for the fur draped over his lap, covering unsightly stains.

'Tobias, I have never forgotten you, not for a single moment. You are far too important for forgetting.'

Had the lady given Pitch that name when she took his true one from him?

Sybilla had told Silas that it was the Lady Satine's work...an enchantment, a curse...whichever it was, that kept Pitch from speaking of who he truly was. But then, the Valkyrie had also told him Pitch was just a deserter from the prince's legion.

How vast a lie that was.

'Then why the fuck have you abandoned us?' Pitch demanded. 'You nearly lost your precious ankou because you were idiotic enough to place me at his side.'

'If it was idiotic, then I would have no reason to be here in this, admittedly, very fine, carriage.' She glanced between them. 'You both seem very much alive to me, or close enough to, as is your case, Silas. And from what Lalassu relayed to me, I'd say you each survived your ordeal well. Certainly your lungs are well enough for crying out to the gods.'

'Oh shit.' Silas was grateful for the still-open door. He took deep breaths of the damp night air, willing his stomach to stop turning.

The lady waved her hand. 'Mr Mercer, don't look so mortified. It's a fortuitous thing that you find comfort in one another. Especially if it is of your own free will and not Mr Astaroth meddling –'

'I'm not bloody meddling.'

'He's not meddling.'

Silas and Pitch spoke in indignant unison.

'Even better, then. We had no idea how this union would run. I'd hoped at the very least you would not kill each other, or wish to, so the fact that you enjoy pleasuring one another is really –'

'Satty,' Pitch cut in, brash and unaffected, whilst Silas died a little more inside. 'Aside from knowing what sounds we make when we come, what else did your nag hear? Or must we fill you in on every miserable detail of this ill-fated fucking excursion, seeing as they dozed in their stables whilst we were in peril.'

Lalassu stamped her feet, her neigh rough with insult. Her sudden restlessness disturbed the black horses, and their shifting made the carriage rock.

'I know that our enemy has shown their hand, and their play was altogether stronger than we might have liked.' The Lady Satine's words chilled Silas every bit as much as the breeze.

'The sorceress I met called herself Nemain,' he said. 'And she claimed to be working with the blessing of the goddess Morrigan.'

'Well, I call her a damned pain in the arse.' Lady Satine leaned her head out the open door and peered up at the sky. 'But not one that can be ignored.'

'How is it that Sybilla's blade has not found this merry bunch of magick arseholes before now?' Pitch said from the folds of his blanket.

'Clearly someone has concealed them from us.' Irritation laced the woman's words. 'I'd have thought that fairly obvious.'

Noting the glint of annoyance in Pitch's eye, Silas sought to divert the conversation. 'The sorceress thanked the man who was with her for protecting her and her brethren,' he said, wincing at recall of his time in that infernal circle. 'His name was Iblis.'

That caught the lady's attention. She scowled as she regarded him. 'Iblis?'

'Do you know him?'

'Oh, I really hope not. The Iblis I know of was a Watcher angel.'

That was more than enough to raise the gooseflesh on Silas's arms. 'Is there a chance the man I saw was a Watcher? Have they returned?'

She shook her head with vigour. 'Returned, no. The only way in or out of here is via White Mountain, has been since the Ruination. But if one of them never left to begin with…' She tugged at a strand of hair, gazing at a spot on the floor. 'And if they had sat biding their time, finding the magick we had missed…cultivating it. Shit. Damn it. Patient little bastard.'

'Gods, I'd love to be at White Mountain when they hear that news,' Pitch said. 'Seraphiel was always so pompous about how good a job the Flood had done in weeding out all the riff-raff. Like I actually gave a damn about that bloody Day of Ruination.'

Lady Satine's head snapped up, and her gaze flitted first to Silas, then to Pitch, where it remained. 'Your tongue doesn't bother you to speak of such things?'

'Not anymore. No thanks to you.' He brushed a fingertip to his lips. 'And at least not so far as Silas is concerned. The truth has been coming easier to me for some time, when I speak with him.'

'Hmm, so I see I was right to think you could not keep your mouth shut without some encouragement.'

Silas broke in. 'He was not exactly spouting it about that he was the prince.' He stumbled over his words as Lady Satine's glare came his way. 'And to be fair, I guessed it of him. He didn't tell me.'

'Guessed it?' The woman scoffed. 'Good gods. How does that make it any better?' She seemed inordinately interested in the outside world, sending cursory glances through the open door as though she were fearful the household might wake. 'You were simply able to guess he was the daemon prince who is supposed to be wallowing in the depths of an abaddon? Wonderful.'

'Goodness, Satty, you are losing your marbles, aren't you?' Pitch was as patronising as only he could be. 'My punishment was changed at the eleventh hour. I was banished, if you recall. I've never understood why you needed to shackle my tongue to begin with. All of Arcadia knows I was exiled.'

'No, Tobias. They bloody don't.'

'I beg your pardon.' The temperature in the cabin seemed to plummet.

'They don't know you were exiled, because you were not,' Lady Satine said. 'All of Arcadia thinks you are rotting slowly at the bottom of an abaddon.'

'Enoch did not alter the punishment?' Pitch said, slow and precise.

'No.'

'Then how am I here?'

'I know you were mindless in the early days, but surely you recall? Your sire delivered you to me.'

'I recall. But you are saying that Lucifer defied Enoch's command to have me imprisoned, and brought me here instead.' The uncertainty wrinkled Pitch's smooth expression. 'Why would he do that?'

Lady Satine stared hard, as though trying to peer beneath Pitch's layers. 'Because it is what Seraphiel would have wanted.'

The daemon, for all his years, seemed so very young in that moment. 'What did you say?'

'You heard me.' She was gentle, cautious. 'But do not ask me to say more here, for it is not the place.' Silas jumped when her eyes switched to fix on him. 'You were able to administer the amuletum yourself?'

He frowned, confused at the switch in questions. 'Yes. With no trouble at all. He was very good about it.'

'Or you were,' she said, thoughtful again. 'No chains?'

'No!' Silas exclaimed. 'Certainly not. There was no need.'

'Not with you evidently.' She returned her sights to Pitch, who had emerged from the depths of the blanket. It fell about his shoulders like a cloak. 'And you were able to use your flame without being reduced to a raving lunatic. This is good, gentlemen. Very good. Considering what a turn things have taken for the worse.'

'Satine.' The growl was low, a hint of warning. 'If you don't make some sense in the next breath, I'll –'

A tapping came at the roof. Silas raised his eyes to the black wood, thinking for a moment that someone was there, knocking out a misplayed tune. The tapping grew more rapid, and his gaze shifted to the open door. It was not a someone at all. A deluge hit. A torrent of rain that fell hard and heavy, blurring the landscape.

'Aha, at last.' Lady Satine swung the door closed but did not latch it. 'You'll be on your way shortly.'

The carriage rocked side to side, and Silas planted his hand against the softness of the wall. 'What is going on?'

'I've arranged for you to be returned to Holly Village quickly.'

'How quickly, exactly?' Pitch too braced to steady himself.

Silas peered through his window out into the pouring rain. Lalassu was obvious with her gleaming pale coat. Her mane wove away from her like moon-coloured tentacles, reaching in towards the front of the carriage where the horses stood in their riggings. A moment later two of the black geldings trotted away from the carriage, tossing their heads at the rain. Free of their strappings.

'The horses...they have come free,' Silas said. 'Should we be worried?'

Phillipa appeared then, poking her head in through the roof. *Mr Mercer, sir. We seem to have lost our horses. Are you all right with that?* The coach driver's eyes fell on Lady Satine, and Phillipa shrank back. *Oh my, you are ever so bright.*

'I've heard it said.' The lady gave the ghost a terse nod. Evidently, Lady Satine could hear the souls, which made Silas only wonder more on his mysterious benefactor. 'No need to worry, Mr Mercer. I directed Lalassu to release them. No need to look so bothered.'

'That is his concerned face.' Lightning flashed along with Pitch'-s words. 'He gets a dimple in his cheek when he is bothered. Rather fetching, but I am very much less so when I am pissed off. Shall I show you my irritated face, Satty? Or will you deign to tell us what you are up to? We've not had the best of days you see, and I'm in no mood for surprises.'

'I'm afraid you may find the coming days rather taxing, if that is the case.'

The cabin shuddered as a great weight landed upon it.

'Something is on the roof,' Silas cried.

'Nothing gets past you, Mr Mercer.' Lady Satine raised the woman's lips in a bemused smile.

A pattern of heavy thuds had the carriage rocking so vigorously that the decanter tinkled in its hidden place. A squawk, not terribly dissimilar to anything the skriker might manage, cut through the drumming beat of the rain. Pitch cursed and moved as though to reach for the door.

'Settle back, now.' The woman waved her hand, lace fluttering. 'I assure you, you are safe. Far safer than you have been the rest of this day. Those are sirin out there, and they are here at my behest. They will see you back to Holly Village...and Matilda's rainclouds will keep you hidden. She's overdoing it with the lightning, I'll say, but there we are.'

Silas recognised Matilda's name. She was the water elemental from the Village. The one who had guided Pitch to Silas's side when the harpies attacked him in the cemetery, and placed a rain cloud over the carnage that followed, sending the humans running for cover and out of harm's way. Silas glanced out the window and caught sight of the most astonishing creature settling on the ground outside. He unlatched the window, pulling it open, caring very little about the damp.

'Gods, close the bloody window,' Pitch huffed. 'I've had enough of being wet today.'

But Silas ignored him, for he could not move an inch. He stared down at the creature, uncertain if he could trust his own eyes. There before him was a bewildering chimera of beast and woman. The head was that of a young lady, quite beautiful in many ways, with long dark hair, a plump freshness to her skin and a good strong brow, but the beauty was marred. Not least of all by a nose that resembled the beak of a bird of prey, and eyes set just a tad too wide, making them unsettling. But that was not all that was disconcerting about her. Below her shoulders all semblance of womanhood vanished entirely. Her body was that of a bird, with some semblance of arms and hands evident, though nearly lost beneath a swathe of feathers coloured in all manner of shades, as though she had flown through a rainbow. Her legs were folded back at the knees, and her talons would have made a hawk envious. The creature rivalled the childlike harpies in size, but the sirin was a hundred times more graceful and far more pleasant to look upon than those creatures.

*Mr Mercer, sir? I'm not sure I like this.* Phillipa's alarm made her voice tremble. She had stuck her head and most of her torso into the carriage, hanging over a scowling Pitch like a hunter's trophy mounted on the wall.

'It's all right, Phillipa,' Silas called, not sure he believed a word of it. 'You are quite safe.'

'Indeed, Mr Mercer.' The woman Lady Satine possessed placed a hand on his arm. 'Everything is fine, but there is no need for your lost soul to stay with us. In fact it may be a good time for Phillipa to be on her way. Did she come with the carriage?'

*I did, madam. And if you don't mind, I'll stay with the ankou if I might. I've nowhere else to go.*

'Of course you can stay,' Silas said absently.

He watched the sirin stretch her wings and rise off the ground. He lost sight of most of the creature as she settled somewhere up front of the carriage, on the empty riggings, he suspected. All Silas could see now was the flowing length of the creature's tail, feathers of sky blue which swept along the ground like narrow streams.

'Do you like what you see, Mr Mercer?'

'I...well, yes...she is remarkable.'

'Gods, don't let her hear you say so.' Pitch sighed. 'The sirin are vain enough as it is. That's a djinn trait though isn't, Satty? You're all quite fond of a look in the mirror.'

'You are one to talk of a fondness for mirrors, Tobias,' she said. 'Your vanity far exceeds that of any djinn.'

'I suppose you might be right,' he said with another careless sigh. 'But when one is as beautiful as this, it is difficult not to be vain.' He sent Silas a sly wink. 'Wouldn't you agree, my dear?'

Bloody hell, the daemon could make Silas's pulse trip with the silliest of gestures. He shook his head, doing his best to appear annoyed, and turned to the woman at his side.

'You are a djinn?' Silas asked, though truly the word meant little. His gaze moved past her through the open door. He caught a glimpse of another sirin, this one with feathers the colour of browned butter, and with the swell of breasts evident through the downy covering upon her chest.

'I am.' The woman shifted so that she was in his line of sight. 'You do not recall any of this...still?'

'He's no longer totally oblivious.' Pitch was tight, acrid. 'I'm sure you'll be delighted to know that as they held him down in a foetid pond and tried to kill him, he recalled he was a man of many lives.'

Lady Satine laughed as though attempts at murder were so amusing. 'They would need to do a lot more than that to finish you off, Mr Mercer.'

'It did not feel like that at the time.'

'Of course.' She wiped the smile from the woman's face. 'But you did recall your past? I am pleased to hear it.'

Silas curled his hands into fists. 'I was not so pleased to do so. There was a lot of time spent dying. There was nothing of my life.'

'No. And there never will be.' Lady Satine was matter-of-fact. 'It is too much of a burden upon your soul to carry it all with you. Your life memory dies each time you do, I'm afraid. But this is good news indeed that your death days have returned. I was worried for you this time. I thought perhaps...well, perhaps you had gone as far as a soul could go in this world. You were quite the blank slate when you were summoned.'

'Not quite so blank now.' Silas was grim. 'But we can speak on that another time.' He turned his gaze Pitch's way, hoping she understood this to mean he wished to say no more in the daemon's presence.

Lady Satine studied him, peering deep, right into his soul, it felt to Silas. She nodded. 'I understand. We shall speak on things once you are back at Holly Village. It will be safer there. But you see now you are unique, do you not?' Silas nodded. 'And that difference is what makes you stronger than the other ankou.'

He understood. Though he wasn't sure it made him feel altogether better. Silas wasn't sure he liked being unique. Especially not by way of having Samyaza's blood in his ethereal veins. Christ almighty, he had been hoping his theory about Samyaza's soul was utterly wrong, but the more time went on and the more he heard, the more he held a sinking suspicion there might be some truth to it.

The rain continued to pelt down, the lightning to flash, but the carriage had been still for a while now.

Pitch spoke up. 'Evidently we are both wonders. According to the Alp whore who devoured me, I am unlike any other daemon she has come upon.' He perched on the edge of his seat. The blanket slipped from his shoulders, and he caught it as it bunched at his middle. His nipples were pert with the chill, and the bruising on his body was tinged yellow now as the wounds healed.

'An Alp? Interesting. I thought they had become quite rare.' Lady Satine edged towards the door, reaching to set one hand on the handle.

'They have. And will become more so once I find her again. She was strong and made quite the fool out of me.' He attempted laughter, but it snagged, sounding stale.

Silas edged forward and put his hand on Pitch's thigh. The daemon was trembling. Silas was sure he'd be called on to stop his damned mollycoddling, but Pitch stayed silent, and after a few moments, the trembling eased. He flashed Silas a look that might have been gratitude or warning he was about to lose his hand if he didn't shift it. Reading the daemon could be difficult at times. Silas rubbed Pitch's leg briefly, caring very little that the Lady Satine watched it all with the intensity of a hawk. Then the ankou erred on the side of caution and pulled away.

'Tell me, why did she think you were like no other daemon?' Lady Satine asked. 'Did she say anything else of you?'

Silas noted the clench of her knuckles upon the brass latch.

'She was too busy running away,' Pitch said, stronger this time. '- Quite terrified, along with the bluecap who had stabbed me with a Gu-drenched knife. They were very put out that I did not die immediately.'

The woman turned her head to stare at him, and her expression was one of clear wonderment. 'You were poisoned with Gu and were unaffected?'

'I wouldn't say that. It was exquisitely painful, and there was a moment when I wished I would die.'

'But you did not.' Her lips twisted.

Pitch cocked his head. 'Are you disappointed, Satty?'

'Don't be so intolerable. It is quite the opposite. I am very pleased that you both managed so well today. You have no idea yet of just how much so. For the very first time, I'm wondering if this entirely ludicrous idea might have substance.' She threw open the door and stepped out into the downpour.

'Are we to be enlightened or kept in the dark as per usual?' Pitch's smile was devoid of much warmth.

'You'll be enlightened, but it must wait till we are in the safety of the Lodge. He'll be waiting for you there.' The nightgown clung to the woman's figure, revealing all too much of the body beneath. 'Now best you make sure this door is locked fast. I'd rather I don't lose you somewhere over the Thames, never to be seen again.' She closed the door with a thunk. 'We need the both of you.'

'Who will be waiting?' Pitch slid along the seat, discarding his blanket and reaching for the door.

'No, Pitch.' Silas grabbed at his hands. 'She said we should stay in here.'

'Satty says a lot of fucking things, and yet very little at all.' He pulled down the window over the door. 'Damn it, Satty, who will be waiting?'

The sirin squawked from their places about the carriage, and the berline rocked hard back and forth.

*Mr Mercer, sir. I'm not sure if I should stay in my seat.*

'Stay where you are, Phillipa.' Silas shrugged off the soul's worries. He was too busy watching Pitch, who had grown mightily agitated by Lady Satine's parting words.

'Who is waiting, Satty?' The daemon's nostrils flared, and his eyes widened. 'Wait, why would we fall into the Thames?'

'Because you'll be flying above it,' Lady Satine called.

'No, no, no.' Pitch slapped at Silas's attempts to stop him from opening the door. 'Let me go. I'll not fly. Saddle Silas's nag, I'll ride her. Very quickly. Let me go.' He wriggled like a caught eel.

'Pitch, settle down. We'll be there before you know it.' Silas knew no such thing, and he wasn't sure he was so enamoured with the idea of gliding through the clouds in a horseless carriage either, but he was intrigued rather than scared out of his wits, as Pitch appeared. His face was blanched white.

'I'm not going. I'll not fly. I'll not fall. Let me go, Silas.'

The ankou dodged a slap. 'You fear flying?'

'Yes. And you can mock me all you like, I don't give a fuck. Just let me out.'

'Oh gods.' Lady Satine threw the door open once more. Pitch rushed at her, but she raised an unhurried hand. Silas thought he saw a tiny flash of colour at her fingertips, a hint of blue. Her fingers met the daemon's neck. Pitch grunted.

'Damn you,' he mumbled and slumped forward.

Silas was there, gathering him up before he could knock his head against the frame of the door. 'Pitch?' The daemon hung like a coat draped in his arms. 'What have you done to him?'

'He's fine. And quiet. You can thank me later. Would you like to sleep too?'

'No, I would not. Thank you.'

The door snapped shut again. Lady Satine waved at him. 'I will see you at Holly Lodge, Mr Mercer.'

The carriage rocked, dipping at the tail end hard enough that Silas was sent tumbling back onto the seat. Pitch landed across his knees. Silas moved quickly to set him more comfortably, rolling him onto his back and cradling him against his own chest. Phillipa peered through one of the mirror panels set about the eaves.

*Ah, Mr Mercer...what is happening?*

'We are being taken somewhere safe, Phillipa. Stay with us, please.' The world beyond these meagre walls seemed terribly dangerous all at once. 'I'll see that you are kept safe at the Village.' He might be making a promise he could not keep, but he'd not leave the soul here alone in a world where the Blight grew vaster and more dangerous with each passing day.

Phillipa's face bunched. It looked an awful lot like she was going to cry. *Thank you, Mr Mercer, sir. You are a good man.* She glanced down at Pitch, whose lips had parted as he slept. *The both of you are.*

The carriage lifted from the ground. The timbers creaked and groaned their surprise. Silas gasped, clutching Pitch a little tighter. Phillipa's eyes fairly bugged from her translucent head.

*Oh my! This shall be a sight.*

The lost soul withdrew through the wall, leaving Silas with the unconscious daemon. He gathered up the blanket and did his best to ensure Pitch was warm and comfortable. It was actually rather lovely to be able to fuss over him without fear of being scolded. He tidied up gold-touched curls and wiped away a smudge of grime from the daemon's ear. Silas shifted about until he cradled Pitch like he were an oversized newborn. He ran a finger over his cheek, and toyed with the idea of laying a kiss there.

'You have every right to be so vain,' Silas whispered. He grinned like a smitten fool and didn't give a damn. There was no one here to see it, least of all the prince. He was safe to do so.

Silas settled back and pulled the drapes aside. Beyond the glass, where the rain continued to pummel the carriage, he glimpsed the sweeping expanse of a rose-pink wing as the sirin worked to lift them high above the countryside. Silas stared down at the gradually miniaturising landscape for as long as he could, watching until the clouds swept in and enveloped them in a dense bath of grey.

# CHAPTER 34

On horseback it would have taken a couple of days, even with the speed and endurance Lalassu and Sanu were capable of, but Silas estimated the sirin had them airborne only a few hours before he felt the descent begin. Their cloudy cover descended with them, wrapping them in a shroud he hoped had not been spotted on the busy streets of London.

Silas had dozed for much of the journey – there was something terribly soothing in the subtle rocking motion that moved through the carriage with each sweep of a set of wings – but he woke now feeling not much refreshed. He shifted Pitch upon his lap, easing the daemon's weight onto the seat. Lithe as he was, any weight at all began to take a toll after being settled upon one's body for so long. Silas shook his arm, wincing at the tingling and flexing his fingers to shake off the numbness that had settled in places.

The landing was even gentler than the lift-off. And the timbers and leather sighed and groaned as they resettled with the touchdown. Pitch stirred, mumbling incoherently and scratching at his chin, a familiar habit that did something quite odd to Silas's chest. He looked away and busied himself with checking on his own appearance. His shirt had certainly seen better days. One of his buttons was missing, which left the fabric gaping open at the centre of his chest. There was no way anything but a wash and change would make him halfway decent. But he had still fared better than the prince. Silas fixed the blanket about Pitch, wrapping it tight and tucking it in where he could, in the hope it might stay in place long enough to move him indoors.

They had landed upon the green that took up the centre of the Village layout. Silas had once thought the carefully manicured turf to be quite wonderful to look at from his window. Not so now.

He closed his eyes a moment. Taking in the quiet.

*Right, what should I do now, Mr Silas, sir?*

Silas's eyes flew open. Phillipa was entirely in the cabin and seated opposite him, with her garish shotgun wound on full display. Silas's empty stomach turned. 'Perhaps stay with the carriage for now.'

*Very well.* She nodded, folding her hands in her lap and gazing down at them with such a forlorn expression he could barely stand it.

'Wait,' he said. 'There is a rather grand cemetery, just next door. Perhaps there might be a grim there who would –'

*Wonderful idea! This way?* She pointed out the window on the right.

Silas peered out into what might be early morning or early afternoon. The light was fragile and dim. His vine-covered cottage was there, and a pang of relief struck him, quite unexpectedly. This was as close to a home as he had.

'No, that way.' He gestured to the left. 'But do be careful, and come back in a few...'

The wraith had already gone.

Silas opened the door and stepped out, grimacing as his muscles protested the steps down to the ground. He turned about and leaned back into the carriage to gather up Pitch. The exit was not easy, nor elegant, but after a bit of grunting and twisting, he extricated the sleeping daemon from the cabin. Silas settled him in his arms. Pitch made a positively adorable sound, like an infant cooing in their sleep, and slipped his hand into the buttonless gap in Silas's shirt.

'Are you awake?' Silas said, amused.

'No,' came the mumbled reply. 'Sleeping.'

With a grin, Silas turned about.

And nearly collided with a bespectacled man standing there. He was wiry and impressively tall. They nearly saw eye to eye. And apparently what the man saw, through thin glass and narrowed eyes, he was not pleased about. He scowled down at Pitch in a way that made the hairs on the back of Silas's neck stand up.

'I beg your pardon.' The ankou stepped around the stranger. 'Do you mind, sir? It's been a long journey.'

'And will only get longer.' The man planted his hands behind his back and peered down his nose at the sleeping daemon. He wore an extravagant coat of cobalt with silver trim, the collar so high it touched at the lobes of his ears. His moustache was a slick, oiled line of black upon his top lip, and his eyes were a grey so pale they neared white. Silas took a step back.

'Do I know you, sir?' he asked.

An arched brow arched higher. 'It hardly matters.' He jerked his chin at Pitch. 'Get him on his feet. There's no time for pissing about.'

Silas stared. 'Excuse me?'

'You heard me. Bring him to the Lodge as soon as he is presentable.'

'You are being exceedingly rude, sir. And I am not his valet.' Silas stepped around the prickly fellow, taking a wide berth. The man gave off an air of being much wider than he appeared. 'Mr Astaroth needs rest, as do I.'

Apparently Pitch had indeed returned to sleeping, for he showed no sign of hearing the exchange.

The stranger sniffed. He was studying the daemon with a disdain that was stirring Silas's ire. 'There is no time for that, and far more important things to do than twiddle each other's cocks –'

'That is quite enough.' Silas was curt. 'Now, piss off, out of my way, sir. For *I* have far more important things to do than listen to your drivel.'

Silas stormed past the stranger, not unhappy when Pitch's boots swung close to the pristine coat, causing the man to step back in a hurry. 'The Lodge, ankou,' the man called. 'Don't dally about.'

By the time Silas reached the front steps of the cottage and paused to look back, the man was gone. 'What an utter arsehole,' he muttered.

The door was unlocked, and the latch sprung open with only the slightest twist of the handle. They were inside in a moment, where the faint hint of jasmine clung to the air. The interior was cosy and warm. Someone had lit the fire, and it snapped merrily in its hearth, glistening against the polished copper of the grand tub that had been set before it.

Steam rose from the water within. The tub was set right where it had been that first fateful time Silas attempted to bathe. He wrinkled his nose and looked away. A washbasin would suffice.

Even though it was still light outside, candles flickered in all the available sconces, with more placed upon any flat surface available. The entire cottage was aglow, and it was so beautiful and welcoming that a lump formed in Silas's throat. He had Jane to thank for this. He had no doubts. But if the tub was meant for him, her optimism was grandly misplaced. He would offer it to Pitch, for the daemon was sure to enjoy a soak. Perhaps he would like some company whilst he bathed. Silas's thoughts were impure as he laid Pitch on the couch.

Christ, what a change it was from the last time the daemon had been in his cottage. Drunk as a sailor or three, Pitch had strewn himself, bare-arsed naked and intolerably lewd upon the bed upstairs. Silas had desired nothing more than to send him far away.

How those desires had shifted, and that time seemed so very distant.

'Pitch, we have arrived at the Village.' He shook him gently. 'Come now, it's time to wake up.'

The prince tried to burrow into the couch. 'Not if we are still flying.'

'We are not, I promise you. We are back in my cottage.'

Pitch stretched, his arms coming from beneath the blanket and casting it away. He was bruised and marked in ways that Silas despised, but his rough treatment did not steal his beauty. With his body taut and arched as he stretched, every curve of muscle was evident. Especially the V-shaped ridge that struck down alongside his hips, with its tip hidden beneath the fabric of his trousers.

Silas bit his lip. Pitch blinked open his eyes. The candles seemed to flare brighter as they struck emerald beneath heavy onyx lashes.

'Gods. Do I look that much of a disaster?' His words were muffled by a half-stifled yawn. 'I certainly feel it.'

'You look wonderful.' Silas's blush tried to burst its way out of his skin.

The bashful words saw the daemon grow still. He watched Silas from beneath lowered lids. 'You are not so terrible yourself.'

With a laugh weighed down by a rising ardour, Silas forced himself to his feet. 'Here, take a look at this. It is wet and warm and ready for the taking.' Silas pressed his lips. That had not come out as he intended at all.

The daemon sat up, eyes amusingly wide, pink lips parting as he saw the bath. 'Oh, thank all the fucking gods and their taints.' He jumped to his feet, turned towards the bath, and pushed his trousers down, exposing pert, pale buttocks.

'Christ.' Silas choked on his own spittle.

Pitch padded, naked and eager, to the tub. 'Sweet, sweet fucking mercy.' He stepped over the high sides and lowered himself, far too slowly, into the depths. Silas did his level best not to stare at the length of lazily aroused flesh between Pitch's legs, but by god, the daemon did not make it easy.

'Will you just get in the tub, for goodness' sake?' Silas was curt. He pulled at his shirt front, warm beneath. 'I met a rude fellow who said we were to be at the Lodge as soon as possible.'

'Who was he?'

'I have no idea, but I had the sense we had best do as he says.'

'Are you not tired of doing as you are told after the day we've had?' Pitch lay submerged up to his neck in the clouded water. Jasmine petals floated on the surface. He weaved his finger through them. 'This tub is pure heaven, Sickle. I don't suppose I could persuade you to join me? Just for a soak, to soothe the muscles.'

Dear god, Silas might not survive this day yet. He stifled a groan. If ever there were an incentive to overcome his fear of water, it was lying in front of him. The thought of joining Pitch made him tight beneath his trousers, but his heartbeat ran a calamitous race. He trembled, and not because of desire alone. He recalled how small that tub had seemed, how much like his coffin it was.

Silas clenched his fist. Bloody hell, he didn't want to say no. Especially not when Pitch was evidently feeling more sure of himself. There were no blindfolds here. But still, Silas could not bring himself to say yes.

'Sickle.' Pitch's voice shook him from his panicked thoughts. 'I'm sorry. I shouldn't have asked that of you.'

Frustrated, Silas shook his head. 'I want to...you have no idea how much I want to.'

'Oh, I have some idea.' Pitch's gaze swept low on Silas's body. 'But it was a fucking awful thing for me to ask.' Silas waited, sensing that was right. After a long pause, Pitch continued. 'I only said it because I knew you would have to say no, and I'd be saved from disappointing you.'

'Disappointing me?' Silas struggled to follow.

'The way you look at me, damn you. The way you touched me in the carriage when you thought I was asleep...gods...I see your desire. And she saw mine, Silas, and used it against me. She took my longings and made them vile. Threatened to try to make me hurt you with them. I was so fucking weak, and *you* paid for it.' Silas wanted to protest that, but now was not the time. 'Being so powerless, if only in that moment, did not suit me. I did not like it. And now I don't know what to do with how it has left me.' Pitch lifted a hand from the water and rubbed at his shoulder, pressing his fingers upon the place where only the faintest trace of Onoskolis's marks remained. It was, without doubt, the most honest the daemon had been with him, but Silas despised the need for that sort of honesty. He ached to move closer, but they were back in the carriage again. Where the daemon needed him blindfolded, nearby, but not too close.

'The only thing that will disappoint me is if you do not give yourself time, Pitch,' Silas said. 'All that you need. I am here, as close by as suits you.'

Pitch lifted a handful of water and let it run through his fingers. There was a distance to his gaze that Silas worried over. At last, the prince nodded. 'There is one thing I need.'

'And that is?'

'For you to go and wash up. You truly are a state. I can barely look at you.'

Silas smiled. Onoskolis was chased from the room for now. 'I'll not deny that there is a rather unpleasant smell coming from me.' He was stepping up to the bath before he realised it. He bent and pressed his lips into the wet curls atop Pitch's head. The daemon did not pull away. Did not flinch. 'Take your time,' Silas said it again, hoping the prince heard him. 'Enjoy the bath for as long as you like.'

'Well I would if the giant, stinking oaf who is bothering me would leave.' Pitch flicked his fingers, spraying Silas's face with warm droplets.

'Fine, fine. I'm gone. See. I'm leaving.'

But the daemon did not see, for he had already slid beneath the water, hiding himself away.

There was indeed a washbasin, with warm water, ready for Silas in his small room. Cold water would likely have been more useful, with the image of Pitch lying in the jasmine-scented water refusing to leave his head. Silas cleaned himself up as best he was able, tying his hair back with a crimson ribbon that had been set on the dresser. He selected a fresh set of clothes from the wardrobe. A pair of black trousers, rather more snug than he preferred, a linen shirt, and a simple cotton waistcoat whose colour matched the rainclouds Matilda had used to conceal them on the journey into London. He hoped to thank the elemental one day. She'd done so much for him, and he'd never set eyes on her.

Silas bowed his head to do up his laces, pushing back a damp strand that evaded his hair tie.

'Silas! Are you here?' His name was shouted from downstairs, and he knew the speaker at once.

'Jane.'

Silas ran down the stairs, still shrugging on his coat, a bland fabric of a slightly darker grey than his waistcoat. He did not reach the bottom, for Jane raced up to meet him. The air elemental breezed up the steps, leaping and wrapping her arms and her legs about him, her scent heady with jasmine.

'Jane, my goodness. It is wonderful to see you.' Silas laughed, clutching at her with one hand, using the other to steady himself on the banister.

'Oh gods, it is so good to see you too.' She kissed his cheek. Her hair, a rich cocoa brown, was free flowing, satin beneath his hands. 'We heard you have had a terrible time of it.'

Silas navigated the final two steps blindly, for Jane showed no sign of letting go.

'It certainly could have been better, this is true.' His delight shifted to grim appraisal. 'I never thought I'd miss doing seances in front of a bunch of drunken rich folk, I assure you.'

'You poor love.' Jane patted his back and released him. He held her steady as she set her feet to the floor. 'I'll admit it has been quite a circus of late. The Order is run off its feet with appointments. Talk of the walking dead has spread amongst the naturals and the purebreds, and both are scaring themselves silly. The naturals especially are in quite the panic, what with the Blight turning the bluecaps and the spirit of the forest near mad, the harpies just as deranged, and now a boggart found murdered.' Silas felt a tug at that. The boggart had been no friend, but he dreaded to imagine what the sorcerers had done to the creature to make him speak of an ankou's fear. 'The purebreds are whispering of witches and sorcery. And the reports of hauntings are at an all-time high. Your ghosts are restless, Silas.' Her sun-touched skin darkened at her cheeks. 'I do not like the whispers the wind brings me.' She squeezed his hand. 'Mr Ahari says the Blight is stronger than he's ever known it.'

Silas nodded.

'And no one's gonna fix that by pissin' around 'avin' bloody baths and doing our 'air.' Tyvain stood, hands on hips in the open front doorway, her hair a spray of wild auburn about her head. She wore the garb of a stablehand, baggy trousers and a loose shirt with a kerchief tied at her neck. 'Where's ya daemon?'

Apparently a 'hello' or a 'good to see you' was to be dispensed with.

'What do you want with him?' Silas positioned himself at the door to the parlour, wary of the soothsayer's uptight manner.

'My arse,' Pitch sang out. 'She's always wanted it.' Water splashed in time with his laughter. Outwardly at least, he was much more himself.

But Tyvain was in no mood for a jest. 'Get out of the feckin' bath, you stupid –'

'Tyvain.' Silas was sharp. 'Enough. Leave him be. He is entitled to a moment's peace.' He turned to Jane, who was regarding the scene with the marked calm he so admired. 'Speaking of which, I met a man earlier, in a blue coat, thin black moustache. He was quite rude in his demands. Do you know who he is?'

Jane's mask of calm slipped ever so slightly. 'Oh...him. Yes, he is rather...imperious, isn't he? He arrived a short while before you did. He's a guest of the Lady Satine.'

Which told Silas nothing whatsoever. 'He demanded we make our way at once to the Lodge.'

'Not till I've 'ad a word with the prissy prick in there.' Tyvain strode the short distance from the front door to the parlour door. She planted herself in front of Silas, arms folded. 'Gonna move that enormous body a' yours?'

'No, I'm not. Is Charlie with you? The last I heard, you had him out and about, tending to some business of yours. Is he here or back at the hall safely?' Charlie hadn't divulged what task the soothsayer had set for him, but he'd been far too excited by it for it to have been anything so menial as a trip to the village for supplies. It had bothered Silas often since he and Pitch had journeyed out. And now, knowing there was some kind of connection between himself, the bandalore, and Charlie's bloodline, he was even more concerned with learning the lad was safe.

'Well, about that.' Tyvain dropped her gaze, her bullish manner losing its lustre.

'Tyvain?' Cold fingers played along Silas's spine. 'Where is Charlie? Is he all right?'

The soothsayer heaved a great sigh. 'Now before ya get yourself all puffed up, 'ear me out.' Tyvain slipped around him, more nimble than he'd accounted for, and weaselled her way into the parlour, where Pitch still lay in the tub, head back, eyes closed.

'Hag, have you broken Silas's little boy toy?' The daemon draped his hands over the copper edges, letting water drip onto the floorboards.

'It's your toy that's broken,' Tyvain snapped.

Pitch opened one eye, rolling his head to find her. 'I didn't fuck Charlie.'

Silas made his way into the room and sank into one of the armchairs. Talk of the lad was dragging him back to that dreadful pond and his endless drownings.

'Course ya didn't. The lad has better taste. But I don't mean 'im.' Tyvain scowled. 'I'm talkin' about the lieutenant. I sent Charlie to find 'im.'

'What?' Silas cried.

Pitch sat up, sending water sloshing over the sides. 'Why the fuck would you do that?'

'Because 'e's important. The lieutenant is. I know it, feel it in me gut. I kept dreamin' of 'im –'

'Are you out of your damn mind?' Pitch gripped the edge of the bath as though preparing to hurl himself at the soothsayer. Tyvain must have sensed it too, for she took a step back.

'All right,' Jane said, finding her way between the tub and Tyvain. 'Everyone just calm down now. Ty, why do you think you need to locate one of Mr Astaroth's lovers?' Silas tried not to baulk at that. 'Are you sure your gut isn't just protesting too much garlic in your stews again?'

The soothsayer plonked herself into the free armchair. 'It ain't bloody garlic,' she huffed. 'Don't ask me 'ow it works, 'cause I can't tell ya. Ain't never 'ad the signs this strong before. I'm just gettin' feelins', really gassy ones, like me bowels are pullin' me along. Ya know?'

'Not really,' Jane declared. 'And it sounds disgusting.'

'Stay away from him, you silly bitch.' Pitch was a slender length of tension. 'Edward has been meddled with enough...' He darted a glance at Silas. There was no small amount of desperation in the look. 'Tell her, will you?'

Silas nodded. 'Tyvain, Edward Charters is not a well man –'

'I bloody know that.' Tyvain was unhappy. She dug at her hair. 'That was the last I 'eard from Charlie about 'im. Lad said 'e spotted Charters comin' and goin' from the family 'ome, 'ere in London, and 'e didn't look none too well. But now...' She took a breath. 'Well, it's gone kinda quiet for a few days now.'

Pitch's face darkened, but Silas leapt in first. 'What do you mean by a few days now, Tyvain? Where is Charlie?'

He was sick to the stomach with dread.

'That's the thing...ya see...' Tyvain would not meet Silas's gaze. 'I ain't too sure.'

Silas winced. 'You have lost him?'

'Maybe...or 'e's just slow gettin' a message to me.' She rubbed at her belly. 'But it ain't sittin' right. Got down 'ere quick as I could. Tried callin' on Charters' 'ome, thought maybe the lad got in there somehow, but they weren't keen on seein' me...bit of an arsehole that butler...'e said the lieutenant ain't well and ain't takin' callers. And that I shouldn't bother comin' back.'

'You've lost Charlie.' Silas was a little numb.

'I ain't lost 'im.' Tyvain shrugged, looking sheepish. 'Just mighta' misplaced 'is whereabouts temporarily. But 'e's a tough lad that one. Knows 'ow to keep 'imself safe.'

'That is what you and Old Bess were supposed to be doing,' Silas bit back.

'Old Bess don't know about all this. It was my idea.'

'To harass a sick man because you think you have an ounce of actual purpose in this world? You stupid meddling cow.' Pitch's words were more a growl than anything, and Tyvain regarded the daemon with rightful wariness. 'Stay away from Charters.'

Silas glanced down at the daemon's fingers where they curled over the edge of the tub. The copper was in danger of being dented.

'I ain't 'arassin' 'im. Can't even bloody find 'im.' Tyvain clucked her tongue. 'Why you so stirred up about this anyway? Not like you ain't got ya pick of London to fuck around with.' She glanced at Silas with a glint in her eye he did not like. 'Or ya pick of all manner of other places for that matter. Why ya gettin' so pissed off about Charters? Maybe I ain't just sufferin' from' a gut ache like you all think, ay?'

'Get out. Now. Just fuck off.' Pitch stood up, dripping wet, his skin dotted with petals. He was very, very naked.

'Bloody hell.' Silas shot to his feet, grabbing at the satin bathrobe he spied hanging over the fire screen, set well back from the hearth. The robe was a flamboyant affair, a stunning salmon-pink with elaborate Oriental dragons stitched into the length of the material. It was far too narrow a fit for Silas. The tub and the robe had never been meant for him. 'Take this.'

Pitch accepted the fine fabric but made no move to pull it on before he clamoured out of the bath, drenching the wood beneath his feet. Jane was admiring the view with barely concealed amusement, but Tyvain covered her face with her hands.

'Put that feckin' thing away, will ya.'

'Sound advice.'

The new voice had them turning towards the door. To Silas's dismay, he saw it was the arrogant man in the blue satin coat standing there. That air he held about him, one of being larger than the skin he was in, was no less evident now. The light caught his spectacles in such a way that his piercing amber eyes were hidden behind the glare.

'Who are you, then?' Tyvain said.

'That is none of your business,' came the tart reply. 'Leave us, all of you. I wish to speak with Mr Astaroth alone.' He sank his teeth into Pitch's name.

The daemon prince stood with the robe clutched to his chest, his privates only just concealed. Wisps of steam floated from his warmed skin. He stared at the man, a look upon his face that made Silas shift with unease.

'I said get out, now.' The gentleman's voice made the water in the tub shudder. Tyvain was on her feet in an instant, dragging Jane with her as they hurried out. Silas, though, held his ground.

'Pitch?' he said. 'Do you know this man?'

He did not answer. Nor blink. If Pitch was breathing, Silas could not tell.

'Mr Mercer, I told you to leave.'

It was said so coldly, with such absolute resolve that it set Silas's teeth on edge. And he knew then what he would say in reply. 'I will not. Mr Astaroth and I ride for the Lady Satine together. He is –'

The man held up a hand, fingers dressed with gold rings, and Silas fell silent. The stranger had not so much as set eyes on him since he'd walked into the room.

'What are you doing here?' Pitch's voice grated from him as though his throat was too tight for the words to escape.

'Is that any way to greet your sire?'

The floor seemed uneven all at once, the blood draining from Silas's face.

'Oh shit.' He snapped his mouth closed, horrified his thoughts had escaped him. But neither Pitch nor the man seemed to notice.

Pitch stepped one leg behind the other and knelt into a deep bow. He bent forward, so low his head almost touched the edge of the bath. It looked mildly comical. Silas suspected that was intentional. 'Your Majesty.'

Silas might have whimpered; he wasn't quite sure what his mouth was doing. He was too busy fighting the urge to turn tail and run.

Christ almighty. Holy shit...or unholy, as the case may be.

Not half an hour ago he had told Lucifer, King of Daemonkind, to piss off and stop talking drivel.

# CHAPTER 35

Pitch glanced at Silas. The ankou appeared ready to pass out. He was quite a picture with his wide-eyed stare and gaping mouth.

'Silas, if you are still capable of hearing me,' Pitch said. 'I'd like to introduce you to –'

'Lucifer. King. Daemons. Yes. Yes. We've, ah, we've met.' He dropped into a strange, wobbly curtsy. Fucking gods, the ankou had lost his mind. 'My Highness...I mean, Your Highness. Shit.'

'By Enoch's balls, are you having an attack of some kind?' Pitch shrugged on the robe with an extravagant flick that sent the fine material flaring dangerously close to the fire. For a moment he was fully exposed, a deliberate move on his part, for it would irritate Lucifer no end. It didn't help Silas's descent into oafishness any though. The poor man didn't seem to know where to look.

'I am not having an attack, no,' Silas said tightly. 'But I fear I did not make a good first impression.'

'Nor a second. But never mind. He's notoriously difficult to please.'

Gods, how Pitch would reward the ankou and his considerable balls the moment he was able. It had taken guts for Silas to refuse to leave. Pitch was more grateful than a dozen expert blow jobs could convey.

He turned his attention back to the daemon king. Between the soothsayer's nonsense and Lucifer's unexpected arrival, the relaxation of the hot bath was utterly ruined.

'So, Your Great and Noble Majesty, what is this all about?' Pitch, or rather, Vassago was borne of a piece of Lucifer's flesh. One that had been thrown into the creation flame and forged into a Dominion prince. He'd always wondered which piece of the king he'd come from. 'Have you decided your idea to secret me out of Arcadia was idiotic and are here to drag me back?'

He said it with all the flippancy expected of him, but Pitch's ribs were crushed by the weight of the idea.

Lucifer sat himself upon the seat that Tyvain had so hurriedly vacated. 'If I'd had my way, you'd be rotting away in the abaddon.'

'Charming. If not your way, then whose?' Pitch paused, tasting the name on his tongue first, ensuring it would slide free. 'Seraphiel's I take it?' Lady Satine had said as much, earlier in the carriage. He'd not been able to stop thinking on it. The Seraphim was dead by *his* hand. Why did they assume the angel would have wanted his murderer rescued and brought to this world? 'Well? Was it?'

Lucifer templed his fingers. 'Sit.'

There were suitable times to defy his sire. This was not one of them.

Pitch padded over to the other armchair, leaving a trail of wet footprints behind. Silas stood like a large but handsome fish out of water, still carrying his bamboozled expression. He wanted to run from all this, no doubt. What level-headed soul wouldn't? Pitch didn't blame him, but nor would he ever admit how terrified he was that the ankou might do so. Silas was steadfast, foolishly gentle, and Pitch had become far too reliant on his presence.

'Leave us, ankou,' Lucifer commanded in a voice that moved legions.

Pitch clung to his attempts to appear unperturbed. Bracing for the ankou to follow orders.

'No. I will stay.' Silas locked eyes with Pitch. 'If that is what you wish?'

Pitch's heartbeat did a quickstep. Gods, what delights were coming this oaf's way as soon as Pitch was able to give his all.

He nodded. 'If you have nothing better to do, then certainly, stay.'

'Sit, and hurry up with it.' The king's voice was like distant thunder. The ruler of daemonkind did so love theatrics.

'Me? Oh, yes, sir.' Silas scrambled, an amusing sight when one was built like a bruiser. He perched his delightful arse on the edge of the couch, seating himself at the far end, well away from the armchair where Lucifer sat.

Clever, silly ankou.

'Before you begin your no doubt fascinating story,' Pitch drawled, 'tell me, what are you calling yourself while here, dear Father?' Pitch enjoyed the glower sent his way. By human standards, Lucifer was no more a father than Vassago a son. The relationship between sire and spawn was not one the purebreds would recognise. All the Dominion were manufactured, made for a purpose. They were weaponry in Arcadia's arsenal. Vassago was a product. Not someone's child.

'Reginald.'

Pitch chewed on a smile. 'And you are quite set on that?'

'Shut your mouth. There are far more important things to speak of.'

'I suppose. The name is just a tad...underwhelming, is it not?'

Poor Silas was clutching at the cushions as though the couch were a life raft and he were cast adrift on a stormy sea.

'You will shut up and listen.' Lucifer's eyes matched the candlelight. 'For I do not have the time nor patience for your stupidity.'

'Right then. I'm all ears.'

Pitch crossed his legs, being sure to let the smooth fabric slip from his knee and expose his thigh. Lucifer would be despising the need to take human form. He had no love for the gangly lines and fragile bones of man. Seraphiel had mentioned that more times than Pitch cared to hear. Citing how disappointed he was that Lucifer refused to enjoy the pleasures of the human world. There had long been rumours in White Mountain about the Seraphim and the daemon king. Pitch suspected they were spread by the Archangels in an attempt to denigrate Lucifer's kingship and paint the high daemon as an angelic whipping boy. He doubted Lucifer had ever fucked another living soul in his long life. If the king had any appetite, Pitch had never seen it. But a lack of desire was not at all uncommon amongst daemons. The incubus blood so abundant in Pitch did not run rampant through all daemonic bloodlines. His voracious appetite was the exception rather than the rule.

So much about him tended this way.

'There are some things you have not been told before now, Tobias.' Lucifer mangled the name Satty had given him. 'But seeing as your strengths have been on such display of late, and it seems unlikely that our foes have failed to notice, Lady Satine believes it is time you are informed.'

'How dreadfully exciting.' Pitch kept his tone bland. Nothing betrayed the tension that held him. 'Come now, entertain us, but try to keep it brief. It has been a day.'

Lucifer's glare darkened behind his glinting lenses. 'Don't push me.'

'Then hurry up and speak,' Pitch growled. 'For I am very tired, and especially tired of half-truths and lies. What is this? What do you want of me? For you are hardly passing by to see how I am faring. If you care to know, I've had pleasanter days. Helping Mr Mercer keep his ghosts in check has been more irksome than it should.' He leaned forward. 'Now go on and tell me. If Seraphiel...' Damn it, would that irritating ache that came with speaking of the Seraphim never fade? 'If he is the reason I am here, then pray tell me why. What did he want from me? I thought it just my cock, but now –'

'Stop it, you damn fool.' The words would have halted a charging elephant. 'It is not enough that you murdered him. You must denigrate his name as well?'

Every drop of Pitch's blood cooled. 'It was not I who asked to be spared from the abaddon. I would have suffered it gladly.' For in there he might escape the relentless, ceaseless turmoil within. Pitch was constantly weathering a storm. Always at risk of breaking apart on the rocks. Just as he'd done that day when Seraphiel sought to take his vestige from him. But that storm had been building for a long while. Everyone, Lucifer included, had turned a blind eye as the Berserker Prince raged. 'I did not bring myself to this place. You put me here.'

'Believe me, I had no wish to do so.'

Pitch let the wildness strain against its tether. His eyes burned. 'Then why the fuck did you?'

'Are you going to strike at me too, then?' Lucifer snarled.

'Harder than I have struck any other.' Pitch rattled with rage, coming undone too quickly. The wildness bayed for blood.

'Go on then.' Lucifer flung his arms wide. 'Give me the excuse to destroy you, as it should have been done that day.'

'Why wait for an excuse? Take your aim.'

The arm of the chair snapped beneath Pitch's grasp. His body shook, and the scratching in his depths made him wince. His temper had raced away from him, faster than he could fathom. But so too had Lucifer's. The daemon king was incandescent with spite, and hatred, and something more. Stronger. Pitch blinked through the stinging heat.

'He made you a monster.' Lucifer's growl almost destroyed the strange words. 'Damn him for not seeing it.'

The wildness sank its claws into Pitch's gut, mingling there with the sourness of confusion. Made him a monster? Lucifer's fury was making him insensible.

A shadow fell between Vassago and his sire.

'Pitch. Please.' Silas crouched beside the daemon's chair. Too damned close.

Pitch shrank back, staring at the ankou through a fiery haze. 'What are you doing? Get back.'

'I am stopping this before it is irredeemable.' Silas, fearless or insane, cupped his hand over Pitch's wrist. He was the touch of autumn against the summer. 'I won't pretend to understand everything being said here, but I can tell you what I see, for it is something I know much about.' His smile was crooked, grim, and more of a life raft than the wretched chair could ever be. 'I can feel it, like the snow or rain upon me. This is grief that has its teeth in you both. Lucifer...Reginald...grieves, just as you do. And there is a path of mourning that all must travel, king and pauper alike. Beyond the sadness there is anger. I know you have a ferocity inside you, one that makes your life difficult, but it is not entirely to blame here.' He leaned in closer, his touch an anchor. 'Breathe, Pitch. Breathe. Come back to me.'

Pitch stared down at Silas's hand, letting the air find its way into his lungs. The calamity slunk away, retreating back into its cage. Pitch counted each of Silas's fingers. Studied every mark upon his skin, each wrinkle, each fine hair.

'Are you with me?' Silas asked.

Pitch nodded.

'Good.' Silas sat back on his heels. The daemon king was watching the ankou with the ghost of a frown, but Lucifer too was resettled, his eyes no longer twin beacons of ember. 'Now, perhaps we can return to the issue at hand.' Silas's balls grew bigger by the moment. He turned to the king. 'Reginald, would you care to tell us what urgent matter you wish to discuss?'

Pitch did not take his eyes off the oaf as he made his way back to the couch. Silas seated himself and caught the daemon watching. He offered up a fledgling smile, but Pitch was too busy with other thoughts of what he'd like to do with the ankou's mouth to return it.

'Perhaps,' Lucifer rumbled. 'The Lady Satine was not wrong in her appraisal of things between you.' He brushed at his trouser leg as though it were not perfectly lint free.

'Which was?' Pitch said.

'She told me that her Horsemen rode very well together. That the ankou withstood you in a way no other could.'

Pitch stole a glance at Silas. His cheeks were flushed.

'He tolerates me well enough.' Pitch shrugged a shoulder. 'And I him. Everyone makes it sound as though I'm the burden, but he is really very irritating at times.'

Silas's cheek twitched, but he said nothing. He looked terribly upright and uncomfortable upon the seat.

'I don't care for the trivial details of your partnership. Satine has bored me enough with all that.' Lucifer recrossed his legs. One of the laces on his shiny boots was undone, and he bent to fix it. It was oddly amusing to see the king of daemonkind perform such a menial task.

'Then what the fuck do you care for?' Pitch said. 'Because I am beyond hungry, and not really in the mood for a tête-à-tête, if you don't mind –'

Lucifer struck quickly. 'Seraphiel was obsessed with finding a way to end what he had begun. He blamed himself for the Blight, right or wrong. And he believed that in you, he had created a way to destroy its source.'

Pitch's mouth hung open awhile before he could work any words free. 'Excuse me?' was all he managed.

'You heard me.'

Pitch got to his feet, very much done with sitting still. He paced over to the window, barely noticing anything beyond it. 'That doesn't mean I understood a word. I don't even know what the fucking Blight is, let alone how to destroy it.' He flung a hand towards Silas, whose face was wrinkled with confusion. 'It is the human souls who are affected by it. Shouldn't you be talking to the ankou?' Gods, his pathetic heart was going to slam its way out of his chest. What had Seraphiel done?

'The Blight is a consequence, it is not the source.' Lucifer peered through glasses Pitch knew he did not need. 'Sit down. The pacing is distracting. And I'm about to tell you something that barely a handful of people in Arcadia know. It is rather important you listen carefully.'

'I can walk and listen at the same time. I'm talented that way. Go on.'

'Is it Samyaza?' Silas blurted, seeming to surprise himself with his sudden outburst. 'Sir, I mean, is the source the Watcher King himself? The sorceress I encountered spoke of such things.'

Lucifer nailed the ankou down with his stare. 'What did she say of it?'

'That the Watcher King was calling to them, that the Blight was his voice, and that I had to stop trying to stifle his voice. They are searching for him.'

Something dark and dangerous threw its shadow across Lucifer's face.

'I told you already, he is no more,' Pitch said. Dread needled him. 'Samyaza is dead.'

Lucifer nodded, sullen. 'He is dead –'

'And his corpse torn into three pieces and given to the Seraphim. See? I told you, Silas, did I not?' Pitch raised his arms, as though he were victorious in some way.

Silas looked aghast, and rightly so. 'You did,' the ankou said. 'But I was not speaking about his body. I am wondering if it is Samyaza's soul behind the Blight?'

Now Lucifer leaned forward, elbows on knees, regarding the ankou like he were considering dissecting him. 'They told me you had come back a shell this time. Practically mindless.'

Silas bristled, sitting up straighter. 'You didn't answer my question...Your Majesty.'

Lucifer's lips did the most curious thing. They curled with a smile. One that was almost pleasant. 'By the gods, this may not be a lost cause yet. You are brave if nothing else.'

'Will you speak your mind, damn it?' Pitch was far too sober, and by Gabriel's arsehole, he was tired. He'd like nothing more than to curl up in Silas's bed with the ankou's ludicrously solid arms about him, holding back his nightmares. 'Is the Blight to do with Samyaza or not?' And how the fuck was he supposed to destroy any of it?

'Very much so. But the ankou is not quite right. The Watcher King's halo is what haunts us, not the angel himself.'

Pitch spun about and felt the breeze between his legs as the robe parted. 'His fucking halo? Is here?'

'That is what I just said.'

Silas swore, in that entirely inoffensive way he had, and got to his feet. 'And this halo is responsible for the Blight how?'

'The halo is cursed.' Lucifer folded his hands in his lap as though this were a discussion of the weather, or a sojourn to the countryside. Nothing more important. 'On the Day of Ruination, Samyaza knew he was defeated, but he was a master cultivator of divine magick. He used his talents to ensure White Mountain would be haunted by him for a long time to come. The Flood sent by our Lord did as was intended. It wiped out the Nephilim and Watchers who remained, but it was a force borne of rage and by its nature became a vessel for all the death and destruction it wrought. What it created was a graveyard the likes of which no world had seen before. Samyaza used that blood and torment and fear to cultivate a curse of profound power, and he used his last breath to speak it. He could not save himself, but he could save his legacy. And he did so when he made the halo untouchable by all but Azazel. If the Exarch were ever to lay his hands upon it...' Lucifer paused, tracing the pattern of the armchair's fabric. 'There is every chance the Severance War would sway in Elyssiam's favour.'

There were not enough foul words in all the worlds for Pitch to spew forth. 'How did he have a chance to do this? To master such a cultivation, when he was facing three other Seraphim?' Pitch glared at Lucifer like it was he who had failed.

Lucifer cleared his throat, a guttural, unpleasant sound. 'Seraphiel hesitated. He held Samyaza a moment too long, and it was all the Watcher needed to cultivate his curse. There is great power in the moment between life and death, the place where divine magick is born. Seraphiel...' Lucifer was not one for being lost for words, but they seemed to slip from him now. '...faltered. It was he who was to deliver the final killing strike. His halo should have ended the Watcher who was dying from the wounds inflicted by Michael and Ariel. But he faltered. If not for that hesitation...there would be no cursed halo...nor the Blight that grew from its resentful energy.' The daemon king contemplated his knees as though all the answers lay in his lap.

'Seraphiel did not wish to kill the Watcher?' Silas's question came from a low, quiet place. The ankou kept shifting his gaze to Pitch. His concern was evident. Even in the presence of a king, Silas could still coddle.

Pitch wrapped his arms about himself. Strange how the fire couldn't seem to lift the chill from his skin.

'Samyaza was the first of the Seraphim, Seraphiel next. They were but a few decades apart in creation.' Lucifer stood and adjusted the lie of his coat. 'They had seen civilisations rise and fall and served Enoch together over thousands of lifetimes. When it came to ending his brother's life, he hesitated too long.' The lines seemed more evident on the king's face. 'And I know he never forgave himself for it.'

Pitch dug his fingers into the satin robe until he felt the pinch on his skin. The Seraphim had been a curious creature, aloof and distant much of the time, at others, playful as a child. But above all, he had been powerful. 'But this doesn't make sense. How is it that in all this time, no one has been able to destroy the halo? Seraphiel must have tried. Michael and Ariel as well, surely.'

He'd never say as much to their faces, of course, but the remaining Seraphims' flames were astonishing to behold.

'It is blood that gives Samyaza's magick its strength,' Lucifer said. 'The blood of all the Seraphim ran that day. His curse makes it impossible for those angels to step foot in Blood Lake.'

'Blood Lake?' Silas was pale. The grey of his coat did him no favours.

'The place where the remnants of the Flood have gathered. Where the Blight flows from. The halo's tomb.' Lucifer moved to the fire, stepping over the pools of water Pitch had left behind like they were spills of poison.

'Gods.' Pitch ran rough hands over his face. 'Then that is the place that those pissant purebred magicians are looking for.'

'Could she have been right then, the sorceress, when she said the Blight called on them?' Silas was grim. 'She said it was Samyaza's voice, that the teratisms it creates were his call. She was very pissed off at me for destroying them.' He was the only one still seated, weak-kneed perhaps. But the ankou was remarkably contained. Pitch was not sure that he could describe himself the same way.

'And Seraphiel thinks me capable of doing what the might of angels could not?' Pitch said, tongue thick and clumsy.

'He *did*...yes.' Lucifer was cruel with his reminder. 'I suppose his point was proved when you tore his wings from his back and killed him.'

Silas made an anguished sound. His fists were balled as though he were considering striking the daemon king.

Pitch dug his hands into his hair, pulling hard at the strands. '-That was...' What? An accident as Silas so fervently chose to believe. Hardly. But Seraphiel's death *was* a terrible fluke. A perfect storm of circumstance. An unready angel, a well-positioned and maddened daemon.

'Reginald, the past is not where this discussion needs to go.' Lady Satine entered the room in a sweep of dark russet satin. 'And I thought we agreed to tell the boys together, over supper?'

This was the Satty Pitch recognised, the form that London society would recognise too; violet eyes, her skin just a shade darker than Jane's olive tones. Her hair was a masterwork of varying shades of grey and white, set in tight spirals about her flat-cheeked face.

'They were taking too long,' Lucifer replied, indignant. 'I've been summoned back to Arcadia. Gabriel wishes to know how the seals on Blood Lake are faring, and he's not fond of waiting.'

She inclined her head. 'And what is your decision? Will you tell the Archangel there is nothing to be concerned with at this stage?'

'No concerns?' Pitch was incredulous. 'I'd say you have a damn wagonload of them. Or does it not matter a whit what Silas and I have been through?'

'Oh we have a wagonload all right. And of course it matters, for it helped us see our enemy more clearly. But there are those who would not agree with the way I wish to handle the issue, so we cannot dally about.' Lady Satine turned her head to find Lucifer, ringlets bobbing. 'Have you given it to him?'

The king scowled so hard his eyebrows pinched together. 'I was near to doing so.'

'Then hurry up and do so,' Lady Satine said primly.

The pair of them were intolerable. 'Give me what?' Pitch cried.

Lucifer worked his jaw. 'Gods this is madness. A fool's errand.'

'Perhaps. But is it not what Seraphiel asked of you at the last? This was what he wanted, did he not?'

'You already know the answer.' Lucifer scowled. 'But he was hardly in his right mind at the end.'

'I cannot speak on that, but I can tell you to look at what is before you.' Lady Satine gestured at Pitch. 'Tobias is on his feet. And more importantly, in control. He has endured, and there has never been any doubt he is powerful. I share your concerns, Reginald, it is perhaps a desperate act on our part, but I cannot help but think that the rise of maleficium is no coincidence here. Perhaps the cursed halo senses a threat. If ever there were a time to take a leap of faith, I believe it is now.'

Pitch threw up his hands. 'Stop. Just stop. What are you bloody talking about...what did he ask of you, Lucifer?'

'Let's try to keep to our false names, shall we?' Lady Satine said. 'We can speak freely in the Sanctuary of course, but practice makes perfect –'

'Tell me what he asked of you, Lucifer!' Pitch shouted.

The room quietened at once. All eyes were upon him. Silas was a muddle of handsome worry. Lucifer was an ugly scowl. Silent, with no sign he would speak any damned truths.

Lady Satine adjusted the folds of her gown. 'Before he died, Seraphiel had Lucifer swear that he would protect you and give you opportunity to find the halo and destroy it.'

Pitch stared at his sire. 'He lived? I did not...I didn't...'

'The angel had a few moments, before the end. It was brief.' Lady Satine was painfully gentle.

Lucifer stared at the fire, his expression stony, unreadable.

'And his last words were of me...and this fucking halo?' Pitch found himself close to Silas but did not recall moving there. Gods, his head was throbbing. 'He wasted his last breath, the fool. I could barely drag Silas from the clutches of a panlong without...' *Losing his mind* is what he wished to say, but he'd not admit that here, in front of Lucifer. 'I have no vestige...I am weakened in this form. Whatever delusions Seraphiel had about me...they are madness.'

His panic was rising, drawing up through his veins at a rate of knots. But he wasn't sure why. If he'd been dragged here to play at destroying an angelic weapon, what did it fucking matter? He was a doomed soul anyway, better to die quickly in this world than waste away for centuries in the abaddon.

He struggled to steady his breath, thoughts latching onto anything that might stop them spiralling. This idiotic mission was a good thing, for him, for Silas. Pitch could pay some penance for what he'd done, and the ankou could find himself a guardian who was not likely to turn on him at the slightest provocation. Silas would be safe, when Prince Vassago was gone.

'Tobias, what Seraphiel had were not delusions,' Lady Satine said. 'They were designs.'

The fire was roaring, and Silas had unbuttoned his coat with the warmth, but Pitch shivered. 'What are you saying?'

'Did you think he brought you here just because he wanted private time with his lover?' Lucifer's words curled with disdain. 'You are the strongest Dominion ever created. He had uses for you beyond the bedchamber. Keeping you on your back was his way of keeping you where he needed.'

'To do what?' Pitch hissed. *He made you a monster.* Lucifer's words. 'You truly remember nothing?'

'Is that not obvious enough to you? What the fuck did he do to me?'

'Perhaps nothing, perhaps all he could. He told no one, not even me, what his designs for you were.' Lucifer seemed at once bitter and sad, as though being uninformed was not what bothered him, rather that the angel had not deemed him worthy of the confidence. 'It began with him seeking to enhance the Dominion and make even greater warriors of you. Lord Enoch agreed to it, you were chosen, but I don't believe Seraphiel ever truly intended you for that purpose alone.' Lucifer strode across the room, and Pitch despised himself for edging back. Silas moved too, but only to ensure he stood slightly in the daemon king's way. 'You cost him everything. You had best make it worth it, at least in some small part.' Lucifer thrust out his hand. Pitch felt Silas tense. 'I do this only because he asked it of me. Take it. I have to go.'

Pitch stared at the king's clenched hand like it were a stick of dynamite. Silas watched on, the ankou braced as though ready to lash out at Lucifer if Pitch gave him a sideways glance.

'Oh for the gods' sake. I don't have time for this. Take it.' Lucifer opened his hand. Pitch caught his breath. On his palm rested a small gold pendant watch suspended from a gunmetal watch pin. The pin's swirling design had always reminded him of tiny bows, all interwoven. At the top sat a seven-point coronet accented with gold. A stunning design, utterly to Pitch's taste. He knew it well. Edward had gifted it to him some years ago, when they were new lovers and Tobias Astaroth wore another name and another skin. 'Seraphiel wished you to have it. He asked me to retrieve it from his rooms at White Mountain. Talk of this bloody watch were among the last words he spoke. Even as he lay dying his thoughts were with this infernal world...' Lucifer's cheek twitched. 'Just take it.'

Pitch stared down at the elegant and seemingly innocuous piece. He'd thought the gift lost for years. In fact, he'd not thought of it at all for a very long time, frivolous with all the presents he received from suitors and bedfellows. And Pitch did not care to have it returned now. He touched his fingers to his back, his skin crawled where the halo's mark lay. The beast at his core made soft, restless, murmurings.

'What did he intend I do with it?' Pitch already felt the weight of Seraphiel's offering. Silas seemed to sense it, the ankou had his arms slightly raised, as though readying to catch him if he fell.

Lucifer's fingers flexed about the watch and its pin. 'You will learn. That is all he said. Give me your hand.'

Pitch did as he was bid. The daemon king dropped the delicate trinket onto his open palm. The moment it touched his skin the figure of a man bloomed in his mind's eye.

Lieutenant Edward Charters.

The man the brattish soothsayer had come hollering about. The man who had chosen this watch long ago in the hope of impressing his careless lover.

*He was the key.*

'Oh fuck,' Pitch gasped.

'Are you all right?' Silas, of course, with his infernal worry. He stood right up close, and his hands were restless, as though debating the merit of reaching for him. Pitch would not have protested.

'Yes...yes, I'm fine.' His smile was a flimsy thing.

Silas set his broad hand on Pitch's shoulder, squeezing gently. The daemon almost swooned into him. 'Are you sure?'

It was pathetic how hungry Pitch was for this tenderness. 'Of course I'm sure.' He tried to shrug him off, but the ankou held fast. Damn him. 'Will you let go of me?'

'I'm not letting you do this alone. I want you to understand that.' Silas's hand slid free. 'You can brush me off as much as you like, but it still stands. Besides, did you not hear what they said? Blood Lake is a graveyard, Pitch.' His eyes were a delicate brown in the candlelight. 'You will need me.'

'Don't be stupid. You are not going anywhere near that place.' Wherever it might be.

'Yes, he is going with you,' Lady Satine declared.

She and Lucifer had made their way to the door. The king was already turning his back, his unhappy duty done.

'No, he is not coming.' Pitch was steely. He slipped the watch into one of the deep pockets on his robe.

'Actually, I am.' Silas matched his steel. 'There's little point debating this. But where are we going exactly? Where is this Blood Lake?'

'Never mind that for now. I suspect you are not yet ready for that place.' Lady Satine said, and Pitch suspected she was right. First, they must find Edward. 'That is a discussion for another time.'

'I must go, before I regret this any further,' Lucifer said. 'Satine, keep me informed. I can't keep Gabriel from here forever. He'll want to see for himself how the seals are faring before long.'

Lady Satine patted the daemon king's cheek. 'I know, Luc. I know. Be well. We will talk again soon. I know this has been a hard day for you, but you have done the right thing.'

With a grunt, the king walked through the door and disappeared. Not even sparing a glance at the prince he'd left behind.

Lady Satine watched after him a moment, then turned about. 'I think that is all quite enough conversation for tonight, don't you? You both look exhausted. Tobias, shall I walk you back to the Lodge?' she asked, rather too sweetly.

Silas gave him no chance to answer. 'No. He'll stay here. I mean, that is, Pitch, if you wish to of course.' He was blushing madly but leaned in closer. 'I expect nothing whatsoever.' He grew redder and redder. It was delightful. 'You shall have the bed, I'll have the couch.'

'You could barely fit a thigh on that couch.'

'That is not true at all. I've slept there many a time.' Silas was wringing his hands.

'Well, I'll leave you to this very serious decision-making, then.' Lady Satine waved a hand. 'Sleep well, and for as long as you wish, for I fear the road ahead will offer little rest. I will have Gilmour bring you some supper. He'll leave it on the front step so as not to bother you.' The glint in her eye was appalling. 'Good night, gentlemen.'

She moved in a whisper of fabric out into the hall. The front door swung shut with a gentle but definitive snap.

Silas and Pitch were alone.

'I shouldn't have been so forceful.' Silas stepped back. 'If you prefer to go to the Lodge, and have some time on your own, after all that…I would not be offended.'

Pitch ran his teeth against his bottom lip. 'I do not want that.'

Silas's shoulders slumped. 'Oh, I'm glad. The Lodge just seemed so very…this sounds silly, but it seemed so very –'

'Far away.'

The ankou stared at him. Gods. The look upon Silas's face. It could fool a daemon into thinking he was something more than a wretched, broken prince.

'Yes, that's it exactly.' Silas sounded choked. He held out his hand. 'Come, let us just sit and catch our breath.'

Pitch took the ankou's hand. It was like holding on to a boulder. Sturdy and unmovable. He tightened his hold.

'Could we sit, catch our breath, *and* get very drunk perhaps?'

Silas looked like the sort of man you'd loathe to meet in a dark alley, but he had the most delicate laugh at times.

'Absolutely.' The ankou grinned. 'I don't think I'll be able to sleep otherwise. This day has grown more momentous by the hour.'

He led Pitch to the couch. The ankou fussed about with the pillows, taking so long to rearrange them into a layout he was satisfied with that Pitch grabbed one in each hand and threw them onto the floor.

'There, that will be fine.' He collapsed onto the couch, legs splayed and the robe in danger of failing to protect his modesty in the slightest.

'I'm sorry,' Silas sighed. 'I'm fussing, I know, but I saw you touch your back earlier. I worry I did not do a good enough job with the amuletum, and you're simply not telling me that you are in pain.'

It was this sort of unbearable thoughtfulness that was going to see Silas earn a swift slap to the face. For Pitch didn't know how else to deal with a kindness like that.

'You know me now. Do you truly think I would not tell you?'

A wry grin came with the ankou's reply. 'You would make it very clear indeed.'

How far this man was from the one Pitch had encountered at the baron's seance. Then, a bumbling, painfully reticent chap with a damned fine head of hair.

Silas made his way to the cabinet that held the precious liquor and poured them the largest serves of brandy and whisky the glasses would take. He managed to get back to the couch without spilling too much and handed Pitch the whisky. He set down his own glass, shrugged off his coat, and plonked himself on the couch, his weight making the cushions puff. He exhaled in a long, exaggerated sigh.

Pitch curled his legs up beneath him, not bothering to adjust his robe when it slid open at the knees. Mostly because he was too damned tired to lift a hand to do so, and also because he was perfectly comfortable. Well, almost perfectly comfortable. He took a large gulp of whisky, but it did not go down well and he set the glass aside

'Gods, Silas...I don't know what to make of all that.' Pitch dispensed with anything but sheer honesty. 'It is...'

'Too much to think on just now. You are exhausted.' Silas reached and brushed his fingers across Pitch's cheek. When had such a touch come to feel so natural? Pitch managed not to sigh. 'We can speak on all this later, and you can tell me what you saw when Lucifer gave you that watch. But not now. Perhaps you should go to bed? The room upstairs is all yours.'

Laying alone between cold sheets and listening to his thoughts churn was not an attractive idea. Pitch feared that even if he were to fall asleep, the nightmares would come thick and fast tonight, after all that had been said. What if Silas were too far away to hear him cry out and did not come, as he so often did, to wrestle Pitch free of terrible dreams.

He toyed with the edge of his robe, licking his lips with indecision. He knew what he wished to do, but all at once he was inordinately reticent. This neediness was entirely new, and rather appalling. But by the gods he was too damned tired to fight it. Pitch stretched out, his head resting in Silas's lap, his legs dangling over the end of the couch. The ankou's face was a delight of pure surprise and, silly oaf he was, bald happiness.

'Don't get too excited,' Pitch said. 'I'm not here to suck, just to doze. If that is all right with you?'

'Of course it is. The sucking was splendid, make no mistake.' The ankou coughed. 'But I told you. I have no expectations. I just want you to be comfortable.' Silas's smile was quite ridiculous. As was the way it made a daemon's throat so dry.

'You are such a strange specimen, Sickle.'

'But perhaps not terrible company?'

'Perhaps not.'

The dark shadows beneath Silas's eyes seemed to vanish at that.

Pitch turned his head and watched one of the candles on the mantle burn its way down the wick, the flame standing bolt upright in the stillness. The warmth of the room pressed at his eyelids, forcing them down. He shifted his hip, moving so the press of the watch could not be felt, and the sting of the halo's mark not so evident.

'The Hag is right,' Pitch mumbled. 'We do need to find the lieutenant.'

'Hush,' Silas said. 'We can speak of that later.' He caressed Pitch's hair with long, soothing strokes. 'For now, just try to rest. I shall be here if you need waking from your dreams.'

Pitch closed his eyes, knowing it was true.

And sleep came slow but surely, there in the arms of the ankou.

"*Ancient Aliens*" meets "*Resident Evil*" with a
pinch of "*Predator*" - Goodreads Review

'*Brilliant start, Kick-Ass heroine more plot twists
and turns than you can take in. An absolute
pleasure to read, a real page turner more please.*' -
Goodreads Review

# About the Author

Danielle K Girl is an Aussie who lives in stunning Tasmania with her three furkids, cats Luffy, Sweetie (@sweetiebyname) and Ren.
Her idea of heaven is a farm full of rescue animals, with a vegie garden that sprouts peanut M&M's and chocolate wheaten biscuits.

Join the newsletter - Get a **FREE** D K Girl novella!

If you'd like to receive DK's monthly newsletter, and be first to know when a new book is ready, then you are in the right place.
Head to, https://daniellekgirl.com/subscribe/ and score yourself a
**FREE** Dystopian novella
in the deal.

Find D K Girl online:
**https://daniellekgirl.com/**
https://www.instagram.com/daniellekgirl/

Lightning Source UK Ltd.
Milton Keynes UK
UKHW011645031022
409847UK00004B/1120